# Praise for *Sofia's Song*

At a moment in our nation's history when heresy hunters seem to lurk just over the horizon, Petton's novel seems especially timely. Placed at the height of the Inquisition in Italy in the late sixteenth and early seventeenth centuries, one is brought face to face with the encounter—indeed, the confrontation!—between ecclesiastical power and authority and life lived in true concert with the Gospel of Love. *Sofia's Song* puts the sheer and unnecessary cruelty of the Inquisition on full display. As Blaise Pascal put it, "Men never do evil so completely and cheerfully as when they do it from religious conviction." Yet, even in the face of such brutality, and utterly in keeping with that Gospel of Love, the power of forgiveness is demonstrated throughout the novel—indeed, forgiveness of the most horrific and ruthless betrayals! One cannot but be reminded of Jesus' plea on the cross, "Father, forgive them for they know not what they do." Love shows through in the novel in other ways, especially in the profound affection of two women for each other in what in their time would certainly have been seen as an illicit relationship. Finally, the anonymous *Cloud of Unknowing* and the works of the Discalced Carmelite Teresa of Avila figure prominently in the formation of several of the later characters of the novel, demonstrating the power of a personal encounter with the divine in transforming the human soul.

A profound and moving read. I found myself in tears as the novel concluded.

—The Very Rev. Douglas Travis,
Dean and President Emeritus
The Episcopal Theological Seminary
of the Southwest

From Reviews of
*The Queen's Companion*
[the prequel to *Sofia's Song*]

The *Queen's Companion* is an enticing blend of historical fiction and romance, highly recommended.

—Micah Andrew, *The Midwest Book Review*

Once I started reading *The Queen's Companion*, I found it difficult to put down. I immediately became totally wrapped up in the lives of the characters. Interweaving actual historical events about the Inquisition into the story really brought the reality of what was happening at that time to life. Readers who enjoy historical fiction will really enjoy reading this novel. The author's chapter at the end of the book will also cause goose bumps! I highly recommend *The Queen's Companion*, and especially recommend it to reader's groups.

—Paige Lovitt, *Reader Views*

... as the narrative races toward a rather surprising conclusion, the enlightening words of Catherine's friend, Father Tim, seem to resonate as much today as they might have in the sixteenth century. So, the lessons of over 600 years of religious wrongdoing will not be lost, Petton personally helps to uncover the Inquisition's ultimate ... hypocrisy and holocaust.

An exciting, entertaining new literary voice, Petton has a unique talent for detailed, inspiring and humorous characterization. She has pulled a fascinating, transcendental tale out of this period—forgotten of late in our mundane age of communications technology.

—Brandon M. Stickney, *Foreword Reviews*

# Other works by Maggi A. Petton

## Historical Fiction

*The Queen's Companion*
*Heaven's Daughter*
*When Rain Remembers*
*Capturing Freedom*
(A revised, new edition combining *Heaven's Daughter* and
*When Rain Remembers* will soon be released)

Coming Soon:
*Searching for Home*

## Poetry

*Psalms of the Broken Hearted*
*Be: Psalms of a Contemplative Heart*
*Embracing the Sacred Wound*
Coming Soon:
*Only This*

www.maggiapetton.com

# SOFIA'S SONG

# SOFIA'S SONG
## A NOVEL OF HISTORICAL FICTION IN THREE PARTS

## MAGGI A. PETTON

Mercury HeartLink
www.heartlink.com

*Sofia's Song*
A Novel of Historical Fiction in Three Parts
Copyright ©2024 Maggi A. Petton
2nd Edition
ISBN 978-1-949652-38-3
Publisher: Mercury HeartLink
Silver City, New Mexico
Printed in the United States of America

Front Cover design: Stewart S. Warren
Author photo: Peggy Counelis
Layout: Pamela Warren Williams

Web presence at: www.maggiapetton.com


Mercury HeartLink: consult@heartlink.com

Mercury HeartLink
www.heartlink.com

*This work is dedicated to my spouse,*
*Peggy, and our daughter, Emma Lee, and in memory of my*
*parents, Ernest (Buddy) Anderson and Lucille Petton.*

# Contents

# Preface

Who can say how the past will be remembered? History may be written and re-written dependent upon those in positions of power. Will it be objective? Can those who remember, write, and document be trusted to honestly and fully remove the filters of their biases? Where is the truth? What are the lies? How much of what we know—or think we know—is part fabrication and part truth? Whose stories do we tell and how do each of us color the stories according to our individual frames of reference? Who are the heroes? The villains? The innocent? The guilty?

Perhaps the more pressing questions today are the ones that examine and accept the fact of our shadows. For all their goodness and godliness, even saints have their struggles and sins. But perhaps saints, like all good heroes and heroines, are generally more cognizant of their flaws—or perhaps they just become more compassionate as they make their way through the inevitable pain inherent in this journey of life. It is no easy thing to search ourselves for our demons. It is even harder to allow our fragile egos and psyches to hold them up to the soul's scrutiny.

The bloodied bodies of all our ancestors litter world history in known and unknown graves. And for all we know, the dust we breathe may be the bones of our own past. We may try to ignore the lessons by pretending that we would never have engaged in history's atrocities.

We tell ourselves that it was a different time and those were different people. But they were not. They were us. Until we understand that we—each of us—are capable of participating in or inciting violence against another, we have learned nothing.

Most of the characters in these pages are fictitious. They are, however, based upon different parts of ourselves. I will go as far as to say that each one of them is based on a frightening examination of myself. But I believe each of us has the capacity to transform—to become the humble helper, or the one who rushes into danger at the sight of an injustice. Who among us wants to admit that, however abhorrent it seems, we easily could have been convinced to join the Nazis in Germany or don a white robe in the Jim Crow south. In the years spent struggling with my own demons of doubt, anger, fear and pain—during which this book gestated, grew and changed— the comparisons between the medieval world of the Inquisition and the world in its current and disturbing state, have left me questioning if we have learned anything from our past. The rise in world religious violence, the slaughter of innocents, the intolerance of entire groups of people who are different from us, the untold number of rapes of small children considered "throw aways," and sexual trafficking and slavery have all grown in the years since I completed *The Queen's Companion*.

My mistakes have been many. I cannot predict the future, but I hope that my life and work offers readers the ability to go deep and to examine themselves and the world from a different perspective—one of tolerance, acceptance and an understanding of our own individual demons. For until we see and accept the truth in and about ourselves, we cannot accept the faults and flaws in each other. Our ability to love and forgive one another is compromised and we are destined to repeat the worst of the past. Until we see with our hearts, we remain blind.

Maggi A. Petton
Albuquerque, New Mexico
2024

PART ONE

_____A MEMOIR

## For My Daughter, Catherine Isabella

I am utterly alone. This fact is—and is not—by choice. My Church has seen fit to condemn me as a heretic. The authorities search for me so that I might be burned at the stake. I could not keep you with me. Your life is too precious, too valuable to risk. I say this not because you are the only heir to the throne of Montalcino, but because the moment you were conceived, I felt a joining to your spirit that was, and remains, my only connection to life and to hope.

My sweet love, you were only a few days old when I surrendered you to what I pray is a safe and happy life. That I will never hear your laughter ringing in the castle courtyard or be there to soothe you the first time you fall is sheer agony for me. Know that if there were another way, I would find it so that I could hold you in my arms once more. Until then, I hide in a small cottage on the outskirts of Aquapendente.

Will I ever see you again? Even as I ask the question, I feel the shuddering tremble in my bones and a tearing in my breast that tell me the answer. In all likelihood, I will be gone before you even know I existed. For that reason, I am compelled to write down what I can about the reasons I had to give you up for safe keeping. I will tell you everything so that you might know your mother, your grandmother, your history. Here, I will share what I can so that you might know what has transpired to force me into hiding. I hope you will judge your mother kindly. Someday, I hope you will find it in your heart to forgive me.

Forgiveness . . . that is something I know a little about.

## JUNE 14, 1585

My first memory is not of my mother or my father. It is not of my caretaker, Mary, or the man who nearly destroyed me through a life-long betrayal so hideous that it nearly destroyed an entire kingdom. No. My first memory is of the blond-haired, blue-eyed boy with whom I shared my life. His name was James.

Who knows why or how our first memory survives the way it does? I certainly cannot say, but I can still see his sweet face staring into mine. I must have been around a year in age, which means that James was about two.

*"Are you awake?" A voice called her from her dreams. "Sofe?" the whisper came louder. "Sofe, are you awake?"*

I remember opening my eyes and seeing his face looming over me as I lay in my crib. His smile illuminated everything. That bright, beautiful face beamed down on me. Soft, blond curls framed his smooth, creamy skin. That face is one that I remember. It is the face I long for and cry for and pray to in the darkest, most difficult days I endure. James's face is the one upon which I rely to forgive me every day. He must forgive me. For in truth, I will never be able to forgive myself.

But today is a good day. Spring has come to the woods outside Aquapendente. This morning I woke from a dream about James. Days are always better when I have dreamt of him in the night. It is as if his spirit has visited me in my sleep and decided to stay with me for a while.

There is a small meadow just on the other side of the tree line encircling my cottage. I exist in a small cabin. The tiny refuge, built of brick, is nearly invisible in this forest. Secluded within a grove of scrub oak and pine trees, you would only find it if you were looking for it. Sometimes as I sit in the sun on the small porch, I can just make out deer grazing in a small open space through the trees. Crocus and hyacinth fill the meadow. As I walk toward the meadow, the grasses whisper low and soft. I found a blanket in a cedar trunk in the corner of the cottage. Someone surely used it as I use it now. I float it out and allow it to drift down onto the carpet of grass. When I lay back on it, staring up into the sky, the smells of spring fill me with longing.

I can almost feel James lying beside me as I look up at the clouds.

*"Look, there!" James pointed upward. "That one is a crown."*

*"Where?" Sofia asked, trying to identify which of the myriad of clouds he meant.*

*He took her hand and pointed it to a fluff of white against a turquoise sky. The wind played with the band of white, creating feather-like peaks. "There, see it now?"*

*"Yes."*

*"I think it must be your crown," he said almost solemnly. "You are going to be queen someday."*

*Sofia did not want to talk about being queen. She was not happy about the idea. Although she was only eight years of age, she was happy less and less.*

*"Then it is a crown of thorns," she replied.*

*"Sofe," he propped himself up on his elbow and looked into her eyes, "Why would you say such a thing?"*

*"If I am queen that means my mother is not here anymore, does it not?"*

*"Oh," he said, "I guess I never thought about that."*

*He lay his curly, blonde head back down next to hers. Their bodies rested firmly against one another as they lay hidden in the flower fields near the castle just watching the clouds. Periodically, one of them would point and say, "Dragon."*

*"Swan."*

*"Snail."*

*After some time he said, "Still, I think you will be a great queen."*

*"And I still think it will be a crown of thorns."*

When I think back on that day, that time, is it any wonder that I was already beginning to feel the loss of my childhood? I was secretly tutored by the resident bishop, Thomas Capshaw. How I worshipped that man. I did not even think of him as a man but more a demi-god. To me he was the most holy and reverent person in the world. I felt his connection to God, and I was utterly convinced that his ability to communicate directly with the divine was honest and true. It humbled me to be in his presence.

The bishop made me feel so special. He always hid gifts or special confections in his robes for me. He never forgot to bring me a treat. Once he brought me a rosary blessed by a pope, although I do not remember which pope.

I knew the bishop was important. I watched how people always greeted him. They knelt and kissed his ring. Sometimes I could tell that people were afraid of him, and that made me feel proud to be so special to him. I was not afraid of him. He loved me, and I believed his love was true, infallible, and holy. Now, as I think back, I am struck by how aloof and distant he seemed to the people of Montalcino who revered him. His bearded face and narrow eyes appeared designed to keep people at a distance. That, I suppose, is part of what made my relationship with him so exciting to me. He did not let many close, but I was different.

Sadly, that was all to my detriment in the end.

The bishop convinced me that I was especially sent by God to the kingdom of Montalcino. He knew this because God told him. God made him promise that he would teach me the ways of the Church. When I was about five, or maybe six, the bishop arranged for my caretaker, Mary, to bring me to him in the church. Every week he would be waiting for me, and he was always deep in prayer when I arrived. God always spoke to Bishop Capshaw about me before my visit or so he told me.

*"Ah, my little Princess," Bishop Capshaw said as he pushed himself up from the altar. "I was just speaking with God about you."*

*He dismissed Mary and called Sofia over to him.*

*"Come here, my angel." He opened his arms and pulled her on to his lap. With his arms wrapped firmly around the child he said, "Sofia, you are very special to God. That makes you special to Montalcino. And that makes you very special to me."*

*Her chest was bursting with pride. "What did God say, Your Grace?"*

*He sat her on the pew next to him. "Well, God sent you here to protect the kingdom from heretics."*

*"What are heretics?" she asked.*

*"Oh," he said, furrowing his brow, "I would have thought that your mother had instructed you on this by now."*

*She shook her head, her face full of concern that she did not yet know about heretics.*

*"Well, heretics are those people who think or act against the Church. Anyone who does not follow, exactly, what the Church and the pope tell us, those people are heretics."*

*"Why would anyone do such a thing?"*

The bishop rubbed his neatly trimmed beard. "There are many who think they know better, and more, than God. They believe they can make their own rules and laws. Those men and women are dangerous to the Church and to their neighbors and friends."

The young princess nodded, not knowing what to say to such a thing. She could not imagine that anyone thought they were better than God.

The bishop continued. "It is our duty to try to help those unfortunate people to understand that they are in danger of losing their souls."

Sofia moved closer to him, resting her head in the crook of his arm. He stiffened slightly, but the child was oblivious to his discomfort. He forced himself to respond to Sofia's affections. In truth, he disliked small children.

"That is why," he continued gently, "you and I have been sent to Montalcino. You have been given a great gift by God, Sofia."

"I have?"

"Yes," he smiled, "and God has asked me to help you develop your gift and your understanding of all that is important. Will you do what God has asked of you?" The child nodded solemnly.

"Good. I told God that I had no doubts about you. I knew I was correct."

He stood and took her by the hand to the altar where they knelt to pray.

"God wants us to pray for your mother," he said softly. "She is in danger of losing her soul to the devil, and it is up to us to prevent that from happening."

Sofia fought the urge to cry. Her small body felt utter panic at the thought of her mother going to hell. Up until that moment the child thought her mother the most devout Catholic, the best queen and the *best mother anyone could have.*

*"We must pray for your mother diligently, Sofia," the bishop said sternly, noting the fear on the girl's face. "Especially you. God has told me that your prayers are important to the well-being of the entire kingdom."*

## JUNE, 15, 1585

It was years before I learned what an unholy creature Bishop Capshaw really was. As I think back, I am appalled that anyone would place the destiny of an entire kingdom on the shoulders of an eight-year-old. Is it any wonder that I was becoming less and less content?

I remember choking down my fear, holding back the sob threatening to escape my throat. It is funny what we remember. The ache in my throat returns to me now as I think back to that time and the beginning of all that pain.

By the time I was eight the bishop had already spent years tending the subtle garden of doubt he had planted in me about my mother. He had me absolutely convinced that he cared about her. He had me convinced of so much, my love, and I believed his every word.

As I think back on those days, I am aware now when it is too late, that I was surrounded by the true love of my family, but I was fooled into believing the malevolent lies of a man who was bent on destroying my mother. If you can take anything from my life, take my admonitions to be cautious. Do not trust someone just because they tell you they are trustworthy. Do not fall in love with someone because they make you feel good, important, or special. Beware the souls and intentions of men—especially men who paint God as theirs alone. God is yours. He is in you. You do not need anyone else to intercede for you. Be still and listen, for there is where you may hear God's own voice within your soul. Do not let the noise and destruction of others drown out the purity of the divine voice within you.

**JUNE 16, 1585**

It is the middle of the night, and I write by candlelight. There is noise in the forest. Some I do not recognize. Animals prowl the area around the cottage. There are times when I fear that the animals may be human ones, come to fetch me for the pyre. Tonight, it was the sound of my own sobbing that awakened me.

There are dreams in which I am holding you, cradling your tiny body. I feel the weight of you in my arms, the suck of your warm mouth on my breast. Your sweet smell fills my nostrils. I bend to kiss you, but you disappear. In desperation I search for you, but you are nowhere to be found. I know I have lost you forever. I wake to the sounds of my cries, "Catherine . . . Catherine!"

The grief of my dreams is more than my sleep can bear.

**JUNE 17, 1585**

I know you are safe. That, at least, gives me comfort. Gio has seen to your safety. I hope you will grow to know him. Gio and James were my family as I grew. Gio is your cousin.

James and Gio were very close. James was the son of your grandmother's lady-in-waiting, Isabella. Although James and I were raised like siblings, he became so much more to me, but I squandered and rejected what could have been because of my foolish belief in Thomas Capshaw and my childish notions of God.

Gio's father, Robert, and your grandmother, Queen Catherine, were first cousins. Robert was the Captain of her Guard and ferociously protective of her. They were very close. Gio, James and I were close, as well, in age and friendship and we were inseparable as youngsters.

Gio is a good man. It is he who came to our rescue just before I was to be arrested. I still carried you in my womb as he led me to safety. It was to Gio that I entrusted your new life, even as it broke my heart.

Periodically, Gio comes to the cottage to check in on me. I will not let him stay to watch over me like a mother hen. I would rather he not leave you at all, but he insists on seeing to my safety. Although you are being raised by his sister and brother-in-law as their own, I made him swear to guard you as if you were already queen.

I have been hiding for nearly two months now. Surprisingly, except for my longing for you, my daughter, I am not lonely. I have a small collection of books from your grandmother's library. I have this journal where I spend time with you. And I have my thoughts; thoughts that continue to torture me with regret, with memories that I cannot erase, with the knowledge of my past. In many ways, I suppose I accept my isolation as punishment for my past.

Gio came last week for a couple of days, but I sent him back to you, too anxious to enjoy his company for very long. It takes him three days of riding to get here.

Three days here and three days back is too long away from you for my comfort. Adding to the time he spends with me it is over a week. Too much can happen in a week. It only takes a moment for an accident or a tragedy to strike.

I do have one regular visitor. Umberto comes every week.

The first few times he came he frightened me beyond belief. He comes once a week to bring me supplies. Gio made the arrangements with him and insisted that he change not only his time but his day every week in case someone might follow him.

I was still sleeping soundly the first time Umberto arrived. I awakened to a rustling outside the window and was certain that I had been discovered. My mother's sword rested against the wall next to my bed. I was determined that I would not go down without a fight.

*The light was faint, just barely filtering through the tall trees, so the cottage was still dim. Sofia slipped as silently as she could from the bedding. Without looking, she grabbed the hilt of her mother's sword. Her heart was pounding, and she found herself wishing Gio was with her. Holding the sword firmly, she made her way barefooted to the door. She stood for what seemed an eternity, waiting for the door to burst open. Instead, there was a faint knock.*

*"Who is it?" she demanded.*

*There was no reply. She said louder, "Who is there?"*

*The only answer was, again, a knock. Her hands began to shake. She thought her legs would give out under her. Even as her heart slammed in fear against her breast, she determined not to die —not yet.*

*"I am armed, and well trained in the use of my weapon." When, again, there was no answer, she opened the door slowly to find Umberto standing sheepishly on the other side.*

*"Umberto!" she cried as she swung the door open wide to let him enter. "I am sorry. Please come in."*

*Umberto entered but did not take more than a few steps inside the cottage. He handed her a burlap sack that held supplies for another week. The sack held cheese, bread, wine, dried meats, eggs and flour. Sofia went to the table to retrieve an empty sack and handed it to him.*

*He took the sack in his calloused hand, then knelt and kissed her hand.*

  *"Thank you, Umberto. I am in your debt."*

  *Without a word he disappeared into the trees.*

I would love to tell you that I felt brave, but it would be a lie. I thought I might faint from panic. Umberto does not speak. His tongue was cut out of his mouth when he refused to name the names of heretics to the Grand Inquisitor. That was a year ago. He lives with his sister whose husband abandoned her out of fear after Umberto's torture. He left her with one small child and one in the womb. Umberto and Lucia care for each other and for victims of the Church whenever they can. Umberto is a small, thin man with a large heart. He is as brave as any soldier in all Montalcino. His chestnut brown hair hangs to his shoulders, and his bearded face is highlighted by big, dark eyes; eyes so full of sadness that it is alarming.

### JUNE 18, 1585

I used to feel that I could do anything, but the two things I have wanted to do most have found failure in me. The first was to find a way to stop this Inquisition. The other was to hold on to my family. It seems that this Inquisition will never end. Despite the hopes, prayers, and struggles of so many, the abuses of our Church have continued for several hundred years. How much longer can we endure such horrors? Why does God not hear the prayers of so many? There are times when I despair and begin to believe that the prayers of the popes, the bishops, and the archbishops of the Church simply carry more weight. Else how can we make sense of what continues so senselessly?

  I have no family left save you and Gio, and I have lost you

because of my fight and failure to end the Inquisition. At times I feel myself longing for death so that I can escape this disaster of a life I have created. Truly, truly, my intentions were noble. But alone here with only my thoughts, I am forced to examine my motives with intense scrutiny. Through the magnification of my tears, I find my motives empty now. Bereft of any merit, my intentions sift as crumbs through my fingers to be consumed by the intentions of those whose ambitions must be more compatible with God's plan.

I am left questioning my lofty desire to rid the world of Grand Inquisitors. Perhaps my actions have angered God. That the Inquisition has endured and grown stronger is perhaps God's answer to our prayers. If we have failed, what if our failure is because we are wrong? What if our perceptions are so inherently flawed that we do not realize that the Inquisition is the path of righteousness? Can it be that we fight God in our fervent desire to be faithful? How can we know? How can we be sure?

I was so certain when I was young. When Bishop Capshaw held my small hand in his, led me in prayer and took the time to teach me the way of the Lord, I knew. I knew. I knew...

*"Pray with me, Sofia," the bishop whispered hoarsely, choking back his tears. "Kneel here next to me and pray."*

*Sofia knelt next to Bishop Capshaw. He took her folded hands between his and pleaded with God to help her mother, Queen Catherine, to cease her visits to the heretical priest of Castiglione d' Orcia.*

*"Heavenly Father," he prayed in earnest, "help our queen to see the error of her ways. Help her to know that she is in danger of losing her soul. Give our queen the desire for your truth, the only truth of the Catholic Church. Help us to know how to help her. Do not allow her to drag our precious Princess Sofia down this dangerous path. Keep Sofia safe from the snares of the devil." The bishop*

*feigned wiping his eyes with the sleeves of his robe.*

*Sofia's prayers echoed the bishop's. She found herself crying, too. How could her mother not see how much damage she was causing by disobeying the bishop and the Church?*

*"Lord," he continued, "give us the strength and courage to go into battle for You. You have blessed our princess with such wisdom and faith. Help her to know how to use them to Your glory."*

And so it went for years. I prayed so hard for my mother. I prayed even harder for James. Perhaps I thought that my mother, as queen, needed less intervention than James. I always thought of James as an innocent. He seemed as honest and pure to me as the petals of the white rose. I worried more about him. He was being dragged down this path of destruction by my mother and his own. I was the only one who saw that he was in danger.

When we journeyed to Castiglione d' Orcia to attend Mass with Father Timothy, I armed myself with prayer to protect my soul from allowing heretical thoughts to enter me. While Father Tim preached, my prayers created a shield, deflecting his dangerous words and ideas. Everything within me stood guard against that man. By the time we began our long ride home to Montalcino I was nearly always exhausted from my efforts.

I did not want to lose my mother to the fires of hell, but more, I feared for James's soul. Even though we were young, I knew that we were destined to spend our lives together. Once, when we were quite young, we talked about our future together.

*"I am going to marry you, you know." James announced as they sat playing a game of stones.*

*"I know," Sofia said. Her smile brightened.*

*"Will I be a king if I marry a queen?"*

*"I am not really certain. Probably."*

*James looked into Sofia's eyes. "It does not matter if I get to be king or not, I am still going to marry you."*

And still, I wonder, if I had not shut out my own love for James as I waited for him to denounce his affiliation with Father Tim, might he still be alive? Am I responsible for his death, too?

### JUNE 19, 1585

What can I tell you about James? He was beautiful. But it was not just his outward beauty that captured nearly everyone. James walked into a room, and you would swear that the sun itself had just entered. His smile, warm and playful, never failed to melt me.

I have been trying to remember when I realized that my feelings for James had grown into more than friendship. There is no one particular moment that stands out in my mind. I only remember that until we were about nine or ten, I assumed that we would always be together. The feelings I had for him were so strong that when he left to accompany his mother on royal visits to various parts of the kingdom, my whole chest ached with missing him.

When he returned from one of those trips, I thought I might faint from relief.

*Sofia heard the horses and the announcement that the queen had returned from Voghera. Her heart was racing. That meant James was back. She ran to the courtyard in time to stroll, nonchalantly, toward the returning party.*

*James dismounted and she went to greet him.*

*"Princess," he said rather stiffly. "How are you?"*

*She felt her heart skip, wondering if his feelings had*

*changed while they were gone. Cautiously, Sofia responded with what she hoped was an equal amount of formality, "I am quite well, thank you."*

*She watched his face for any sign from him that he might be toying with her.*

*"How have your studies fared in my absence?" he asked. His face revealed nothing indicating that he was at all pleased to see her. Her heart fluttered with the beginnings of a fear she had never known.*

*Holding back her true feelings, she responded, "My studies proceeded well."*

*"Hmmph!" he snorted. "I would have thought you would be bored to tears without me to explain everything to you!"*

*At that a large, beautiful grin burst across his face and she threw herself into his arms. He whispered in her ear, "I have missed you so. It was agony without you."*

*"Every day here without you was drudgery," she whispered back.*

*He reached into the bag hanging from the pommel of his horse and said, "Come. I have brought you something."*

*They left the others in the courtyard and followed a narrow path around past the church. There was a small bench in a tiny garden alcove. They sat hidden by the grapevine covered trellises arching over the bench.*

*"Here." He handed her a package wrapped in a linen cloth.*

*Turning the bundle over and over, she allowed the cloth to unwrap itself. Finally, there it was, a hand carved cross with the most intricate designs interwoven around all sides.*

*"Oh, James!" she exclaimed. "It is so beautiful! Where did you find it?"*

*"I made it." His broad smile told her that he was very pleased with her response. "Working on it while we were gone helped me to feel close to you. I am glad you like it."*

*Before Sofia even realized she was crying, one of her teardrops fell onto the cross. James lifted her chin with his finger and kissed her so tenderly on the mouth that her breath stopped. Her heart stopped. In fact, she thought the world may have stopped. It was her first kiss.*

That kiss remains in my memory, and on my lips, as the single most sacred moment of my life. I hope, my darling, that your first kiss is with the love of your life.

It was not long after that kiss that I began to realize that I might be losing the battle to turn James and my mother from their zealous, heretical religious beliefs. In vain, I pleaded with my mother to cease her weekly outings to Castiglione d' Orca. The bishop had convinced me that my mother was damning her soul to hell because of those visits with Father Timothy. I begged James to join me for Mass in the castle church.

I saw his refusal as a weakness. I did not realize at the time that it was my own weakness, my own naiveté that grew its crooked and curled fingers around those I loved, strangling forever the joy that might have been.

I pulled away from James. I hoped that my distance might persuade him that I was deadly serious about the matter of our religious future. I knew that I needed to do something desperate to convince him to denounce his heretical views. James's soul and salvation became my reason for living. I vowed that I would not rest until he came to understand the importance of staying away from Father Tim and turning to Bishop Capshaw for his religious training.

He was so stubborn. His responses angered and frightened me.

*"Why will you not just come to Mass with me?"*

*Sofia insisted, believing that if she could just get him to listen to the bishop, he might begin to understand.*

*"Sofe," he smiled at her, "ask me anything but that."*

"Stop going to Castiglione d' Orcia, then," she raised her eyebrows at him.

He stopped smiling, and his shoulders dropped and slumped a little. He lowered his head, and she thought he was considering the suggestion. Then his head began slowly to shake back and forth. "I cannot," he said so softly that she had to strain to hear him.

"You must." Sofia decided to make her move. "There is no way we can be together if you continue along this path of sin. We are doomed unless you stop." He looked at her with horror.

"You cannot mean that."

"I am deadly serious," she said with more forcefulness than she intended. Nevertheless, she continued her tack. "You know that my faith and my kingdom must come first. I cannot have a heretic ruling by my side!" They had not openly talked of marriage since childhood. It was an unspoken pact, and she knew that she was using it as her trump card. She hoped the ploy would work. Even though they had years to consider the possibility of marriage, she was determined to win this one, most important soul, for the Church.

They were walking in one of the many gardens surrounding the castle. Grapevines hung over and around them, sunlight streaming through their leaves. He stopped and turned toward the castle, pursing his mouth as if he were considering her words. When he turned back, she saw that his eyes were red-rimmed. He did not try to hide his tears.

"You act," he said quietly, "as if there is no shred of doubt in you. It frightens me. I cannot explain it, but it does." He took a breath, exhaling it slowly while lowering his head. "I cannot do what you ask of me." When he looked up his face was filled with sadness.

Sofia was furious with him. Her eyes returned his look with a coldness intended to force him to change his mind. She was used to getting her way.

*He turned and walked away. As she watched she heard her insides scream, "Come back! You do not understand the risk you are taking!"*

*She pushed down the pain in her chest as he disappeared. He never turned back. How could she make him understand? She knew James loved her, why could he not do this one thing for her?*

We resumed our daily lives. There was no way for James and me to avoid one another. At first it was awkward, but eventually we fell into a cool comfort. I realize now that we simply avoided dealing with the issue of religion. But things were never the same between us. We never spoke again about marriage. We never kissed again. On only one other occasion did I try to convince him of the heresies that plagued our mothers.   I thought he was such an innocent. I was so wrong.

I prayed night and day that James might see the error of his ways.  If not for his own soul, then because he wanted me in the way I wanted him. I could not lose James forever. It just was not part of my plan.

## JUNE 20, 1585

Quite abruptly, in my fourteenth year, my secret sessions with the bishop stopped. Although I did not know it at the time, my mother had discovered that the bishop and I had been meeting in secret. I was devastated.

I already knew enough about my mother and her life of sin to have her imprisoned for heresy. The queen and her "lady-in-waiting." Their lives of sin disgusted me.

I missed my bishop. I knew he must be heartbroken, too. I worried about him and wondered what punishment my mother might inflict on him.

If not for my enduring hope of saving James, I would have reported my mother and Isabella to the authorities when I was forbidden to see the bishop, but I decided to bide my time. I was afraid. I did not understand why, but I simply did not have the courage to act. At times I just thought I needed to pray harder. Bishop Capshaw always encouraged me to act thoughtfully with Christ's guidance. I felt he was so spiritual that at times it nearly broke my heart. I wondered if I could ever be that close to God. I tried so hard to be like Bishop Capshaw.

Once James had pulled away from me, I depended on the bishop even more. I knew that I would be a great queen with him by my side. When my visits with him stopped, I found that his sermons became our secret language. His lessons were filled with the dangers of heresy and the importance of stopping the evil menace of sin.

One day I realized my foolishness. I was quite old enough and needed no permission to seek out Bishop Capshaw on my own. My mother might be able to control an entire kingdom, but she would not damn my soul to hell. She would not keep me from my religion or my beliefs. I would not allow that to happen.

Confession. That is how I did it.

*"Bless me Father, for I have sinned," Sofia said. She was kneeling in the small wooden confessional, a purple cloth the only thing separating her from the bishop. She felt sin was rampant in her. She saw her failure to convert the souls of James and her mother to the true work of the holy Roman Catholic Church as her biggest sin. And her failure to act on the known heretics in her midst tormented her in unimaginable ways. So, she confessed. Day after day, week after week she confessed her sins, pouring out her heart to God, to her bishop. And she knew that she was failing them both.*

*"I miss you so, my Princess," the bishop whispered from the*

*other side of confessional curtain. "Are you well?"*

*"How can I be well when I am kept from you?" she whimpered. "It is so unfair. I must see you," she cried. "I must."*

*"God will help us find a way, Sofia.  Be patient.  Guard your soul well.  Pray unceasingly."*

*"I will.  I do," she answered. "But I do not understand why no one sees what is so important!"*

*"God reveals Himself only to those worthy of the revelations, child.  You know this. You know that you are special. Do not give up."*

*"I will not," she vowed. "You know I will not."*

*"Pray for wisdom in knowing what to do in the case of your mother and her paramour. God will show you the way when the time is right."*

*She saw his hand in blessing and heard the soft Latin. The blessing washed her, filled her. She was cleansed once again by the love of God.*

*"Tomorrow, Bishop."*

*"Tomorrow, Sofia.  Go with God."*

So it went for some time.  I found ways to continue to meet with the bishop. He found ways to speak to me in sermons. I did not let my mother stop me from fulfilling my religious training. I was fourteen years old, and no one could keep me from my spiritual guidance.

Still, my heart was broken about James. No one knew how I had felt about him, so no one knew the depths of my despair. Although we seemed fine in the presence of those who mattered, I remained cool, aloof, from him. I knew it hurt him, but no more than his refusal to stop going to Castiglione d' Orca hurt me. And it did hurt me.

For the first time in my life, it occurred to me that James and

I might not be together forever. It was not just this life, but the afterlife that worried me. How could heaven be heaven without James? As I look back from here, from where my life has led me, only now do I cringe in shame for my foolish thoughts and actions. Interesting, is it not, my daughter, that the things of which we are most certain are the very things about which we can be the most wrong?

James, my mother, Bella—these were always the heaven-bound souls.

I remember one morning in particular. It was the morning that I announced to my mother that she had not, in fact, stopped my religious instruction with the bishop. I had been feeling as though James might be close to coming around to seeing my way. Although for the life of me I cannot remember why I felt that way.

I had just come from seeing the bishop and felt bold enough to make no attempt to hide my visit. I saw the panic in my mother's eyes and knew that the fear was from knowing that she was leading a life of sin. I thought she was so transparent.

Lady Isabella, whom I had come to detest, tried to deflect the argument into which my mother and I were headed. If it were not for the fact that she was James's mother, I would have turned her over to the authorities without hesitation.

I had joined my mother, Bella, and James in my mother's quarters. They were having a light breakfast.

I found myself wishing that I had not come. James saved me.

*"Want to go riding, Sofe?" James asked.*

*"When?" Sofia asked, trying to look bored.*

*"Now might be good," he smiled.*

*As they rode toward the flower fields Sofia felt her heart soar, but she feigned indifference. She decided to try another tack with him* and was about to explain about their mothers and their real relationship. She stopped herself, suddenly realizing that he might hate her forever if she were the one to expose their sin.

Her cowardice infuriated and frightened her. She realized that she was more afraid of losing James forever than she was about losing his soul. It confused her that it was so easy to allow feelings of excitement and anticipation that James might still love her, keep her from doing everything possible to save his soul. She longed for him to take her in his arms and kiss her, but instead, she heard her voice chiding him for his innocence.

"Deep in your soul you know you are on the wrong side," Sofia said. "You must know what a heretic my mother is! Why do you insist on defending her?" she asked after James had suggested that she was a little too hard on her mother.

James did not answer but let her rant on until she finally ended the diatribe about Father Tim and her mother. Then she started in on James and his inability to think for himself.

They had reached the flower fields and dismounted. A guard took their horses to graze.

Sofia was quiet and James finally said, "So, you think me a heretic, as well."

The sadness in his voice nearly broke her heart. She loved him so but did not know how to love him and save him at the same time.

"I think no such thing!" Sofia nearly shouted. Then with every ounce of love and hope she had for him, added more softly, "You are an innocent. You cannot help but do what your mother tells you to."

She hoped he heard the love and understanding in her voice. She desperately wanted him to feel it and to feel for her the way he once did. But, instead of sounding loving, she heard the superior tone of her own voice. She hoped he had not. They found some large rocks and were sitting at the edge of an open meadow. Sofia waited, hoping he would take her in his arms. She could almost feel his breath on her, *his lips kissing her, thanking her for helping him to see everything so clearly.*

*Sofia closed her eyes and waited with eager anticipation.*

*"You are wrong, Sofe."*

*She opened her eyes. He was standing over her, and his eyes were filled with things she had never seen before. Suddenly, she was afraid.*

*"I choose to go with our mothers," he said softly, "because I believe the Church is making a grave mistake. I believe in what Father Timothy stands for and what our mothers fight for."*

*She could not believe her ears. She had always thought that he just went along with them because he was unable to stand on his own two feet. She thought he was caught in an unholy trap. Her disbelief and disappointment were evident on her face. She felt exposed, vulnerable.*

*"I wish you" he emphasized, "would join us."*

*She knew he was waiting for something from her, anything. She was speechless. This was a side of James she did not know. All her beliefs about James began spinning, then whirled, circled her head and finally shattered, crashing around her like broken glass. She was heartsick and reeling from the sting of his words.*

*She did not know how long she sat, mute and stricken, but finally he spoke again.*

*"I am suddenly very cold." With that he mounted his horse, instructed the guard to stay with her and rode off.*

Sometime after that—months perhaps—I really cannot remember; I learned that James was courting a young woman named Teresa from Montalcino. Gio told me. I remember keeping my face unreadable even though it felt as if a sword had been thrust through my center. I forced a smile as Gio made jokes about James and Teresa. I kept my pain to myself. No one ever knew how I felt about James. I wanted it to be kept that way.

## JUNE 21. 1585

I worry that the sins of me, as mother, might visit you. What dreadful punishment might be exacted upon you for my sins. Oh, Catherine, I pray that this life I endure is sacrifice enough to save you.

I console myself with the thought that perhaps not knowing me will keep you from serving any part of my sentence. My sentence. Perhaps my existence is my sentence. The hours I spend reviewing all that my life has been, eats away at me like so many rats gnawing at my memories. If the rodents were not of my imagination, there would be nothing left. Only crumbs of me would remain.

I turned from the love and loves of my life with such arrogance. They loved me all the same. I did not deserve their love, but it bathed me in its inherent eternity. I never expected it not to be there when I was ready to accept it, to embrace it, to return it. I gave my love to a man who did not deserve it, who stole it from me little by little like an invisible pickpocket. I was not aware of what he had done until it was too late. He only pretended to love me, and I, in my ignorance, believed the lies of Bishop Thomas Capshaw.

Then, in an instant, James was gone. Murdered. He went to the flower field alone. Why he went alone I do not understand. There, a man attempted to steal his horse. James caught him, and a fight ensued. I know James would have won that fight if not for the pistol. The man shot him. And in one of the most unbelievable mysteries to shake loose from that dreadful day, the thief who shot James turned out to be the very person who had impregnated Lady Isabella all those years prior. The thief was James's own father.

James was gone forever, and I had failed to save him. I was beside myself with grief. What would happen to his soul? Where would he spend eternity?

My feelings vacillated between torment for having failed him, being angry with him for refusing my love and God's promise, and sheer terror at his being gone from my life. What would I do without him? He was my hope. I had been waiting for him to realize that he did not really love Teresa. He could not be dead. I was not ready for his death.

I flew to the bishop. I needed his reassurance that James was in heaven. I could not bear living with the thought that James might suffer eternity in hell. I needed to know that he would be waiting for me in heaven.

The bishop pulled me into his arms but was unable to console me. I so desperately wanted consolation. He offered none. My heart sank. I felt physically ill. My legs quaked beneath me. My sorrow bled out of my eyes, nose, and mouth.

I remember pacing so anxiously in the bishop's quarters, that I thought I might leap from my own skin. My guilt and grief regarding James were intolerable to me. I had to rid myself of it. I could not stand the feelings that filled me. Unbidden, I found a place to lay those unwanted feelings. Blame. This was all my mother's fault. She was to blame for James's eternal damnation.

New emotions began to take over. They mobilized me. They energized me. They filled me with strength. As I paced, I steeped my anger, my pride and my grief in the bubbling, unholy water provided by the bishop. A thought emerged and quickly transformed itself into a plan. I knew that I was to fulfill God's promise in my kingdom. Without James there was no reason to wait, or to hope for the change I had failed to bring about in him or our mothers. I would be the queen God wanted. It was time to do what I should have done long ago.

What I did at that moment shattered the kingdom. It shattered me, but I did not yet know that. Here is the sorry truth of the matter. I set in motion a series of events that shame and humiliate me. Your mother was a foolish coward. I was foolish because I believed that the bishop loved me, and I relished in his lies because they made me feel good, powerful, and special. I was a coward because I could not face the anguish I felt over losing James. The pain was too great. Instead of abiding the pain, I chose to abort it.

I went to the authorities and denounced the queen, my own mother, as a heretic. I would make her, and her sinful lover pay for everything. I gave Captain Bello, someone to whom the bishop had introduced me, the information he needed to arrest my mother and Isabella as they traveled to bury James the next day.

Here is what you must believe, lest you think that your mother was a heartless creature set on destroying for destruction's sake. I honestly believed that I was doing God's will. I was utterly convinced that God would reward me for my actions.

Once the plan was set in motion, however, my grief returned. It did not leave me. I could not rid myself of it. I went to the church to beg God to alleviate the agony of it. I was doing what the bishop had taught me was the right thing to do with heretics. I thought I was fulfilling God's will. I pleaded for relief from the hideous pain that overwhelmed me. It did not come.

As I left the church, I ran into Lord Giovanni, Gio's grandfather. I wanted to get away from him, but he pulled me to him when he saw that I was crying. I still do not know how it happened, but in his efforts to console me, he began to tell me things about James, my mother and Lady Isabella that made no sense . . . and yet resounded with truth, even in my grief-stricken soul. The conflict started a raging war within me.

The more he talked, the more I railed against the madness growing in my breast. I wanted to run from him, from his words, but it was as if I was nailed to the spot, unable to move. The more he told me, so lovingly, about my mother and Lady Isabella; the more he filled me with information about the bishop's hate for my mother and all women; the more he tenderly comforted me, the more my madness increased. I thought I might shatter on the spot from the hysteria exploding in me.

If what he was saying was true, then where was the truth? How was I to justify all I believed, all I had known, and all that I was, with this new information? There was no way to do so. It was simply not possible.

Then suddenly Lord Giovanni was leaving.

He walked away and left me alone with my madness.

God above, what had I done? What could I do to stop it? I ran after him and told him everything.

Within a fleeting time, I and a small army raced to save the queen. Our horses threw clumps of dirt into our faces as they ran full speed toward what I hoped would be a rescue. I begged God that we might be in time. The look on Lord Giovanni's face told me that my mother faced not arrest but an execution. I had to get to her in time.

I was not in time. My mother died in my arms. Next to her was Robert, Gio's father, also dead. What had I done? What had I done?

But for a few moments, we might have saved them. Oh, how those moments torture me. If only we had left five minutes sooner. If only our horses had been swifter. If only I had not been so stubborn and stupid. If only . . .

I was queen, but I no longer even wished to be alive. I knew

I was broken beyond repair and would never be whole again.

### JUNE 22, 1585

Perhaps there are single mistakes for which we can never be forgiven. No matter the penance, no matter the faith, no matter the effort to right what we have done wrong, that one error follows us for the rest of our days. It haunts our waking and our dreaming. No matter whether we ignore or acknowledge it, it persists in reminding us that for but one brief lapse in judgment our lives would be very different.

I wonder whether my own forgiveness eludes me because the others—Bella, Gio, Father Tim, and Lord Giovanni—did find ways to forgive me. Perhaps if they had not, I might have, in defiance of their anger, forgiven myself. I suppose it is of no matter. They did find forgiveness in their hearts. It is only my own heart that holds the reminder of what I caused and how it changed the course of so many lives . . . even, sweet child, those that did not exist at that moment in time.

So here I am, struggling to learn how to cook for myself; such a small, simple thing, but one that I never before had to consider. It would be comical if it were not so frustrating. I have burned more food than I have eaten. It is probably just as well, because the food that I do manage to create is not so edible.

I only cook at night after the sun has set to avoid attracting notice from the smoke. For now, that is fine, but I worry about keeping warm if I am still here in winter.

So, my sweet, I have come to the part of my story that holds the secrets, and the treasures, of your grandmother. How different our lives would be, yours and mine, if I had not been seduced away from my own mother by Bishop Thomas Capshaw. (A note here about what happened to that vile personage: the coward killed himself before I could get to him. If there is any religious justice, he rots in hell for what he did!)

If there is anything I can truly offer you in these pages it is that I might bring your grandmother alive for you, that you might know from whom you are descended, and what strength and courage and love has passed to you. I fear that those magnanimous traits have passed by your mother, but I offer them to you as a testament to her who bore me and loved me regardless of my failings.

It is only after the fact of her death that I began to know, really know, my mother. I could not allow myself to know her before then, for the picture painted of her by the bishop made that too risky to my soul. The irony is too much to bear.

Lady Isabella, Bella, survived the attack on the funeral party . . . at least part of her survived. She, whom I detested and whose presence I railed against when my mother was alive, became my only connection to all I had lost. After all that happened, she was my family, and I came to love her with all my heart.

From Bella I learned so much about my mother. Bella. Perhaps the place to begin knowing your grandmother is to know how Bella came to be in her life.

From both Lord Giovanni and Bella, I learned that your grandmother, in her role as queen, was enroute from Rome back to Montalcino Castle. Robert and a handful of other soldiers accompanied her to petition the Pope to assist in patrolling the kingdom. There had been many rogue attacks by fanatical religious groups claiming to be acting on behalf of the Holy See. These zealots were targeting innocent citizens and killing them in the name of God.

The Pope offered no help, and so the party was returning

home when they happened upon a woman tied down and being brutally tortured and raped. They rescued the woman, who was not expected to live. That woman was Lady Isabella.

My mother took the nearly dead woman to her quarters, where eventually Bella started the long road to her recovery. Kidnap, torture and rape were only a part of what Bella endured. Her kidnap occurred during an attack on her family. One of the rogue groups so elusive to the queen had been in the process of torturing and murdering Bella's family. She watched as her husband and her parents were executed after they had been dragged from their beds as they slept.

What I tell you next is for God to judge. I hope you will not make the same mistake that I did for so many years. I not only judged but tried and convicted my mother and Bella. To my unending shame, I brought about their ruin. The Queen and Bella fell in love.

Around the same time, it was discovered that Bella was pregnant as the result of her rape, and it was clear that there were rumors being circulated by the bishop that the women were living in sin. Bella devised a plan whereby they might be safe from the rumors.

It was risky for the queen and Bella to remain together without arousing suspicions. As queen, everything you do will be under the intense scrutiny of thousands of eyes. There are few you will be able to trust. Be forewarned, my love, there will be many who will watch your every move for the slightest crack in your armor so that they may enter to destroy you in a heartbeat.

The plan was simple. Your grandmother had no ladies to attend to her. She preferred servants to the thought of surrounding herself with incessantly chatting women. Your grandmother was intelligent and independent, admirable qualities for a queen, but those very qualities also made her a threat to the men who wished to control the kingdom. Bella arranged for the queen to marry. The marriage created a convenient reason for the queen's change of heart regarding accepting a lady-in-waiting. So, Bella became my mother's constant companion.

Your grandfather was Ambrose of Perugia. He was a good man, a good father. He would be so proud to have a granddaughter. I loved him very much. Were he still alive, he would adore you. Your grandfather died more than a year ago, struck down by the sweating sickness. I miss him so. His was a sweet, gentle heart with the soul of an artist. He created beautiful oil paintings. They fill Montalcino Castle. I hope someday when you gaze upon them, you will feel his love surrounding you. His love was a great comfort to me—even after my childish act nearly felled the kingdom. From your grandfather I learned playfulness, patience, and creativity. Without him . . .

### JUNE 23, 1585

Forgive my weakness. Sometimes my emotions overtake me. As I reflected on my father, my tears blurred the words I tried to write, forcing me to stop.

Both of your grandparents were models of steadfast faith. Would that I could have seen that faith instead of being blinded by the lies of the bishop. I used to have so much faith. After James and the others were murdered my faith was shattered. It was only in retrospect that I realized how horribly my faith was misplaced. It took my father and Bella years to convince me that God was good. My self-hatred consumed me in the months following all that happened. I suppose, as I sit here in my solitude, there is a goodness that prevails—that provides us with hope and light.

It was not really until your conception that I felt my faith return. The dark cloud under which I had lived for so long fled from me. From the moment I first held you in my arms and looked upon your sweet face, it was as if your birth had rebirthed me.

Is that it? Is life itself the miracle, the thread that weaves faith from one generation to the next? That is the only thing that makes sense to me anymore.

As I read what I have just written, I realize once again that thoughts of you, memories of you, distract me from my task.

Before your birth my faith altered from the childish thing that it was to a subtle, steady acceptance that was the result of Bella's influence. I still marvel at her strength, her resilience and courage. There was no other explanation for her ability to continue living life the way she did without some sort of faith.

She had lost everyone she ever loved—her parents, husband, son and her true love—and yet she found it in her heart to love and forgive me. That seemed impossible without a miracle.

So, regardless of my faith, or perhaps because of it, I came to understand that without the series of betrayals (mine by the bishop and my mother's by me), I would never have had my eyes opened to the realities of this Inquisition. It was only after my mother's death that I began to understand that the Inquisition was created by the greed and lust for power of men. In many ways, following my realization of those facts, I clung to my belief that my transformation was much like Paul's on the road to Damascus. It was only after years of persecuting Christian believers that Paul awakened to his truth and became a disciple of Christ's.

But I am not Paul. In fact, after years of fighting against the Inquisition, I find again that I struggle with my beliefs, sometimes wondering if I have any faith at all. Finally, perhaps I am a heretic, but my heresy is the result of years of blind faith followed by years of unraveling faith. Finding no answers to my prayers sometimes brings me to an utter lack of faith. My heresy is that I no longer believe in anything beyond what I can see, feel, or know. Then suddenly, I feel the presence of God in the warmth of the sun on my face or smell of the forest in the morning. This life we live can be baffling!

I know that the Inquisition lives. It thrives. It seems indestructible. I so wanted to see its end and create a world of hope for you. My failure saps me of my strength and causes me to weep for the loss of a world none of us has ever known. As the Inquisition grows stronger, I wonder whether this earthly plane is hell. Perhaps Satan has already won, and his minions rule the earth with despicable cruelty.

For years following my mother's death, I cradled the pain in the eyes of victims of the Church with my own love and hope. Now, I know that I did not hold their pain. I absorbed it. The despair of the kingdom rots within me, eating away at what is left of me, spewing putrid tears from my eyes, and smothering my spirit with its stench. Oh, that I could have made a difference. Knowing that I did not torments me.

Even as I write, I try to find something to give you that might help you hold onto your own faith, your own hope. If I can offer you anything, my daughter, it is this: question everything. Do not believe just because someone tells you to believe. Question. My own mother tried to teach me that one most important lesson. I ignored her, and an entire kingdom paid the price for my ignorance.

I have just returned from a walk through the meadow. It was so peaceful. I was reminded of the flower fields near Montalcino Castle. Someday you may walk those fields. When you do, I hope you walk with hope and lightness of foot. Cherish the field and the memories you make there. That field holds some of my fondest memories of life. How bittersweet that it is also the sight of James's murder.

James was buried in the family plot. After the funerals for James, Robert and your grandmother, Bella took to her bed for some weeks. When it seemed that she was beginning to come back to herself, we took a summer outing to the flower field to honor the memory of James. It was there, as we sat near some rocks at the edge of the field, that Bella began to tell me about some of her history with the queen.

"Your grandfather," Bella began, "was instrumental in instilling in your mother a sense of the injustice regarding the Inquisition."

"How so?"

"He and the bishop grew up together and were adamantly opposed to the ways the Church was dealing with heresy."

"The bishop? Capshaw?"

Bella smiled and looked at Sofia. "The very same. But, following an extended trip to Rome and returning elevated to the position of bishop, he had changed dramatically.   According to your mother the change broke your grandfather's heart."

"Did you know my grandfather?"

"He died before your mother and I met."

A pair of swallowtail butterflies fluttered nearby, lighting on flower petals. Sofia and Bella waited in silence until they went off in search of other nectar.

"Bella," Sofia said hesitantly, "tell me about meeting my mother."

Bella's eyes drifted out across the flower field. Eventually, her gaze rested on the clear blue of the lake in the distance. She drew her knees up, wrapping them with her arms.

"I have no memory of Catherine finding me.  What I do remember is waking in her quarters after what, I am told, was a period of three days following my rescue by her and Robert."

Sofia stretched out on the blanket, resting her head on her hand, as she listened to Bella.

"She insisted on caring for me in her quarters. My recovery was

*long and painful, but she made me feel so welcome, not at all an intru-*
*sion on her life. I did not know she was queen, you know."*

"What? Why?" *Sofia sat up again and faced Bella.*

*Bella smiled and shook her head as she recalled discovering that*
*Catherine was queen.*

*"I was nearly completely recovered and had fallen hopelessly in*
*love with her. In fact, we had come to this very spot for my first out-*
*ing. She knew how I felt, and I knew she felt the same, but she fought*
*her feelings for me so hard." Bella released her legs and leaned back*
*against the rock just behind her.*

*"One of Robert's soldiers came racing over that ridge," she pointed*
*to the rise they had just crossed. "He leapt from his horse and knelt*
*addressing her as 'Majesty.' I had not known. She had done a very*
*good job of keeping the information from me."*

*"Why did she not tell you?"*

*"She claimed that the physician feared that the knowledge might*
*compromise my recovery."*

*Two birds swooped past as they sat, startling them a bit.*

*"What did you do when you found out?" Sofia asked.*

*"Oh, I was furious with her. But I could not remain so for long."*
*Bella closed her eyes as she settled softly into her memories of her first*
*night with Catherine. She continued after a bit, "We worked it out, but*
*not without some difficulty. It was shortly after that I discovered I was*
*pregnant with James."*

*Neither of them spoke, slipping silently into the sadness they still*
*held for James.*

*"We were very happy, your mother and I," Bella finally offered.*

*"Even after she married my father?" Sofia asked.*

*Bella raised her eyebrows and shook her head. "I suppose you*
*should know everything." She adjusted herself on the quilt, reaching*
*for a grape. Thoughtfully, she chewed on the fruit then said, "I pushed*
*your mother to marry Ambrose. I knew the bishop was relentlessly*

*pursuing his aim of accusing us of heresy. I thought it was the only way to keep us safe from him and Lord Carfaggi, who both suspected us of being lovers."*

*Sofia leaned forward, listening intently. "He really was a despicable man."*

*Bella reached her hand to Sofia's cheek. "You need to stop torturing yourself over your relationship with him, Sofia. You were so young."*

*A tear fell from Sofia's cheek. "Go on," she said.*

*"Your mother never intended to do anything but conceive a child from your father, then allow him his honorary title of king and nothing more." Bella leaned back against the rock, her mouth turning up slightly at the corners. "She, neither of us really, expected to like him as much as we did. In many ways, he had such a sweet heart."*

*"Walk with me, Sofia. My legs are aching." Bella got up and Sofia joined her on the path to the lake.*

*"The arrangement between your parents was agony for your mother and me. Once she was pregnant with you, she dispensed with the marriage bed. Initially your father was hurt, but eventually they came to mutual admiration and respect for one another. They became very good friends."*

*"I know you and my father were friendly, but how was it for both of you back then?"*

*"I suppose that is one of the reasons that I always liked Ambrose. Despite his knowledge of our relationship, he never treated me with anything but respect. And he never gave us over to the Church. He could have, you know."*

*"I miss him."*

*"I miss him, too."*

*As she slipped her arm through Sofia's, Bella said, "We have many to miss, you and I. I am glad we have each other."*

## JUNE 24, 1585

I am a queen without a kingdom, a mother without a child, a lover without my beloved, and a Catholic without a church. Why do I even continue to exist? I have lost the ability to hope, and some days I pray for the end to come quickly.

Oh, my sweet daughter, I will continue with my story. Perhaps in the telling of it I will not feel quite as maudlin.

It was with great difficulty that I assumed my role as queen. I do not know what I would have done without the support of my father and Lady Isabella. It was at Bella's suggestion that I ordered the bishop's quarters searched. What we found was so appalling, so unbelievable, that despite my despondency, an anger rose in me that forged a rage so intense that it changed the course of my life.

As if it were not bad enough to have discovered his vile betrayal of me, the bishop kept a journal of his intent and actions. Along with his personal writings, were volumes of detailed accounts of the many interrogations he led over the years. Finally, there were several manuals, *Inquisitor Manuals*, written by men of the Church. These manuals instructed those charged with ferreting out heretics as to how to elicit confessions. The brutal tortures endured by so many were not only condoned but taught by the Church. The Church, in its arrogance, was so confident, that every word, every single torture, and trial, and every scream and cry of its victims, were transcribed. He even added the income from confiscating items of worth and imposing fines. The monies spent on ropes, straw, and wood to burn those from whom the treasure had been taken, were recorded, as well. It appears that Capshaw, like all the enforcers of the Inquisition, was utterly convinced that he was doing God's work. He collected and preserved the evidence of his own hatred and cruelty with relish and pride. We even discovered correspondence with Rome about his manipulation of the "the malleable princess."

Bella and I read, even when it sickened us, the accounts of every interrogation. My darling, if it were in my power to save you from the world created by this monstrous Inquisition, I would do so. God knows I have tried, as did your grandmother before me and your great-grandfather before her. I pray that you will live to see its end.

*Sofia and Bella were sitting in Bella's quarters, near the balcony windows. Sofia had been engrossed in reading the Inquisitor Manual written by Bernard Gui. She looked up to see tears streaming down Bella's face,*

*"What is it?" Sofia asked.*

*Bella sniffed and reached for her handkerchief. After dabbing her eyes, she looked out the window toward the valley. Sofia waited.*

*"I knew that he hated your mother—I always knew that," Bella said of Capshaw. She was reading his personal journals. "I did not realize that his hatred of women, all women, was so strong."*

*Sofia stood and walked over to where Bella was sitting on the pallet under the window. Sitting beside her, she took the older woman's hand in hers, "What have you found?" she asked softly.*

*Bella looked up, shook her head and lowered her eyes to the pages in her lap and read.*

*"The woman brought to me was ugly as sin itself. She was thin, her eyes sunken and dark. She had the look of a wraith. But what appalled me the most was the mole. A hideous, large thing, it drew the focus away from her eyes to the side of her nose where it loomed enormously between her cheek and nostril. Several dark hairs sprouted*

*from the thing. The mole itself screamed her guilt. I knew before I even began the interrogation that she was guilty. To save themselves from any suspicion, her neighbors have already given her up. All that was left was for me to pronounce her guilt. Like most women, she fell apart before my eyes, a disgusting display of weakness and pleading. But I knew it for what it was, a woman's ruse of helplessness to play upon man's mercy and compassion. Mary DeMarco was a witch, but she would find no mercy, no comfort from me. She would burn."*

*"I remember that day," Bella finally looked up, and back out the window.*

*"What day?"*

*"The day Mary DeMarco was burned at the stake," she said. "Your mother was convinced that the poor woman was being executed simply so the bishop might prove that he held the power to do so. She believed he was sending her a message. It tortured her, both of us really, that we were unable to save Mary DeMarco from the pyre. She had small children. God knows what happened to them."*

*Bella inhaled deeply and looked down at the book again, then smiled a strange smile. "There is another reason I remember that day, in particular," she continued.*

*She looked into Sofia's eyes, and for the first time in a long while, her smile bloomed in her eyes, not just her mouth. "That was the day we discovered that your mother was pregnant with you."*

I knew that whomever the Church sent to replace Bishop Capshaw, he would expect to find the detailed records of interrogations, trials and executions. It was with that knowledge that Bella and I transcribed the information in them so that we might attempt to clear the names of the wrongly accused by cross-referencing what we could with the accounts in the personal journals. I was more hopeful than Bella that we might be able to convince the Church leaders that abuses were rampant in their processes. However, Bella, whom I had come to realize was an incredibly wise woman, pointed out that the Church was well aware of its own actions and intentions. She had only to point me back to the Inquisitor Manual, where instructions on how to force confessions were brutal and filled with sexual depravity. There was no doubt that even the most sainted and devout Catholic could be tortured into a false confession.

"Sofia," Bella often warned me, "you must learn to hide your knowledge, disguise your revulsion of all that you know and see. If you cannot convince the Church that you believe in what they do, you may as well ride to Rome and declare yourself a heretic. You will help no one," she admonished me one day as I ranted about the injustice, "by openly warring with the Church. They will put an end to you very quickly."

I wonder how many times she had uttered the same words to my mother.

### JUNE 26, 1585

Within a few months of the death of Bishop Capshaw, Archbishop Pietro Biondi arrived at Montalcino castle. Rome was taking no chances in leaving us without an overseer for our mortal souls. The archbishop moved into Bishop Capshaw's old quarters. He appeared a very reverent and holy man. I must say that his faith in God and the Church seemed very sincere, but I was guarded and cautious by then. I had been too easily fooled once. I would not let that happen again.

The archbishop seemed intent on convincing us, me especially, that the Church was inherently good and had only the benefit of souls at heart. Truly, I think he believed that. I do not know how he convinced himself— strike that. I do know how he convinced himself. It is too easy for some of us to believe what we hear *because* it is easy—because we want and need so desperately to believe. I am the guiltiest of all in that regard.

The archbishop approached his duties with as much objectivity as a man of the cloth can, I suppose. For all intents and purposes, he appeared to try those brought before him for heresy with fairness. He did not seem to hate women or feel the need to persecute them based upon any particular bias. His sermons, although long-winded, were filled with passion for God and Church. He was likeable and kind. His kindness was present in his face. Archbishop Pietro was older, in his forties, with a slender build. The salt in his salt and pepper hair was pure white, giving him the sage look of a goodly man. His face was earnest, lined with creases reflecting years of a life lived in constant thought and prayer. He had a habit of looking up when he was deep in thought, as if he were always communicating with the heavens.

It was evident that the archbishop's role in Montalcino was to keep a very close eye on her queen. To that end, his presence in the court and on the Privy Council was impossible to avoid. While I resented his ubiquitous shadow, I learned how to conceal my distaste for being constantly watched. Bella was adamant that I learn to abide his comments and suggestions with grace. Fortunately, the man did seem to have the best interests of Montalcino at heart, else I would have not been able to carry off my appreciation for his remarks and his prayers for the kingdom.

While I begrudgingly accepted his presence, toward the end of his first year in Montalcino his behavior underwent a change. I was unable to determine the reason for his increasing support of me on the council, but one evening following dinner in the great hall Bella came to visit me in my quarters.

*"Lady Isabella to see you, Majesty," the servant announced.*

*Sofia was reading near the fire and rose to greet Bella with a hug and kiss on each cheek.*

*"Sit, Bella.  Some wine?"*

*"Yes, thank you."*

*When both women were settled with cups of wine Sofia said, "There is something on your mind, what is it?"*

*Bella sipped.  When she lowered her cup, she looked directly into Sofia's eyes and smiled an odd smile.  "You have no idea, do you?"*

*Sofia placed her cup on the table beside her.  "No idea about what?"*

*Bella chuckled and shook her head.  "You have been wracking your brain about the change in the archbishop as of late, have you not?"*

*"Yes," Sofia answered, puzzled by Bella's line of questioning.*

*"I suppose I should come dine in the great hall more often.  Perhaps taking meals in my room, while a peaceful enjoyment for me, is detrimental to the wellbeing of the kingdom."*

*Sofia leaned forward.  "Are you going to tell me what this is about, or are you going to make me guess?"*

*"Sofia," Bella's eyebrows raised even as her voice lowered, "he is in love with you."*

*"What?" Sofia stood abruptly.  "Nonsense!"*

*"Not nonsense, my love, but pure observation," Bella continued.*

*Sofia stared at Bella, then collapsed back into her chair.  "Oh, dear Lord."*

*"Dear Lord, indeed," Bella's face turned serious.  "If his belief in himself as a holy man of God is as fervent as I think it is, he can only come to one conclusion."*

*Sofia's mind raced, her thoughts already forming the same conclusion.  "He will believe that his feelings for me are of the devil," she said sadly.  "Damn," she whispered under her breath.*

*"Damn, indeed," Bella intoned softly.*

Bella saw plain as day that the archbishop had fallen in love with me. I was oblivious until she pointed it out. Of course, as soon as she said it, I knew she was right. How could I have been so blind?

I had begun to relax a bit, especially in council meetings, nearly relying on the archbishop's support. After I understood the underlying reason for his support, I knew that I would need to exercise great caution in my dealings with him.

I wore blander colors on meeting days and to Mass. Bella assisted me with my hair, pulling it back in a severe looking style. She even helped me apply powder to my face that gave my skin an almost sickly pallor.

The archbishop's concern for my well-being and his attentions toward me only increased.

Bella abandoned dining privately in her quarters and made it a point to join me for the evening meal in the great hall. I do not know what I would have done without her. It was clear that the effort exhausted her, but she sat by my side every evening attempting to distract the archbishop's attentions.

I took to traveling the kingdom more often. Actually, I enjoyed my sojourns about the kingdom. Your great grandfather, King Edward, and your grandmother made it a point to visit the various towns under their rule. While I enjoyed the travel itself, for Montalcino is a beautiful place, I must confess that the relentless stories of pain and oppression endured by the people of our kingdom wore me down more than I care to admit.

I wish I could tell you that my efforts to get the archbishop to fall out of love with me succeeded. They did not. Increasingly, he wore the look of a pained man. It was evident that his feelings for me tortured him beyond words. I fear that his desire shook him to the very core of his faith.

I have just returned from a walk to the meadow. As I neared the edge I heard the unmistakable snort of a horse. I moved quickly and quietly toward a small grove of trees where the grass grew higher on the meadow side. Squatting down, hidden in the grass, I listened to determine from which direction the rider approached.

As the sounds approached, I lay flat in the grass and did not move. He was riding slowly through the forest but did not seem to be searching for anything, just passing through. I waited until he was well out of sight and sound before I ventured out of my hiding place. He did not appear to notice the cabin. I returned and poured a glass of wine to calm my nerves. I have never been alone this long.

Solitude wears thin on a soul.

The thought of anyone being so close to the cottage unnerves me. This is a very isolated spot. Unless someone knew about it and was looking for it, there is truly little likelihood that it would be happened upon by accident. The closest road is miles from here and there is no discernible path. Some nights as I lie waiting for sleep I wonder if I will make it through the night without being dragged from my bed as so many in our kingdom have been. I do not know how one ever recovers from such an ordeal. Bella once shared with me that after the night her family was dragged from their beds and executed, there were very few nights that she ever fell asleep without wondering what the night might bring.

Bella was not alone. As my royal travels connected me to the families of Montalcino, I met many, so many, whose peace-filled slumber was shattered, never to return. Of all the victims with whom I met, the one that had the greatest effect upon me was a little girl I met in Castiglione d' Orcia.


*"Queen Sofia, I would like to present Daria Intaglio." Father Tim held a young girl by the hand during one of Sofia's visits to Castiglione d' Orcia.*

*Sofia squatted down in front of the child, who could not have been more than five years of age. "Hello, Daria," she said softly The child only stared at the queen with the oddest expression. Sofia searched for words to describe the look in the child's eyes. She never saw such a look in a child, nor even an adult. It was bereft of joy or life. Momentarily, Sofia felt dizzy, as if she were spiraling into the depths of darkness. The ragged edges of raw fear floated in the child's large brown eyes. Sofia hoped never to see such a look again.*

*Father Tim knelt next to the child. "She no longer speaks, Majesty," he said as he encircled the child and drew her close to him. "She was brought to me in hopes that I might find a home for her." Father Tim waved over a young woman who helped tend to his little chapel. She had been sweeping the floor near the altar.*

*When the woman and the child left, Sofia stood and watched them make their way across the courtyard. The child turned once and looked back at Queen Sofia.*

*"What happened to her?" Sofia asked, already dreading the answer.*

*Father Tim suddenly seemed older, sadder than Sofia ever remembered. She thought that it might be simply age. He is nearing fifty, after all. I must make it a point to visit him more often, she decided. "The same that has happened to so many, I fear." Father Tim walked over to the where the young woman had left a little pile of dirt. He picked up the dustpan and broom and swept up the pile. When he had dumped the dustpan outside the door and returned, he said, "Daria was the youngest in her family. She had three older brothers and four older sisters. The family was not from Montalcino, but just outside of Firenze.*

*They sat in one of the center pews. "It was a nighttime raid, I fear. The family was not well off, so all the children slept in one large room. The family was taken in the night.*

*"One of the neighbors watched from her window as the house was swarmed by men on horseback in the early hours before dawn," Father Tim explained. "The men were dressed in hooded, dark robes. One of*

*them wore a huge crucifix and seemed to be the leader."*

*Pictures from the past pushed their way into Sofia's mind. Images of Captain Bello, who also wore a giant crucifix, and was the man in charge of the party that killed her mother. She pushed the memory and feelings of guilt back down to their hidden place.*

*"Another rogue group?" she asked.*

*"It certainly has all the signs," Father Tim answered. "Once the family had been bound and gagged, they were dragged on foot behind the horses. Townspeople discovered them early the next morning hanging from tall spikes just outside the town. We have no idea what the child saw or heard. She was wandering the town streets that morning, much as you just saw her." The grief in the priest's voice frightened Sofia. In all the time he had worked along- side her mother and so many others in his effort to stop the violent murders perpetrated by the Church, or those pretending to be of the Church, she had never heard such quiet desperation in his voice. He stopped speaking, as if the despair he felt was confirmed by the sound of his own words echoing in his ears. He shook his head as if he could banish his thoughts from mind.*

*"The neighbor who found the child knew she would be in danger if anyone discovered that she had survived the attack," he said as he walked away from me. "The risk in caring for an abandoned orphan in such times is too great. The neighbor suspected a local businessman of being sympathetic to our cause and brought the child to him."*

*"That is how she came to you?"*

*He nodded. But as he did, Sofia saw how tired and infinitely sad his lined face looked. She thought she understood what he was feeling, but Father Tim was more than just an ordinary, disillu- sioned person. He was an extraordinary man of deep convictions. Watching him bend under the weight of his feelings was like watch- ing an angel lose faith.*

## JUNE 27, 1585

Father Tim was an angel to many. What I did not know at the time he introduced me to Daria was that his brother, Thomas, who had been instrumental in aiding the cause against the Inquisition, had been crucified after a lengthy torture. Father Tim had received word through the underground weeks after Thomas's death. He did not tell me. I never had the relationship with him that he shared with my mother or Bella. He did eventually confide in Bella, who later told me that she feared that his brother's death may have broken Father Tim. He never stopped fighting or trying to help. The good priest continued in his role of organizing and thwarting the Inquisition tortures, but the heart was gone from him. The sadness he carried after his brother's death wove itself into his garments It was as if the weight of his unshed tears transferred to his cowl. It pressed down on him, and he bent under the burden.

We all carried on, however, and I felt my own burden driving me to do more, to be more, to save more. Bella cautioned me at every opportunity. She tried to convince me that I was only responding to my guilt and that was why I drove myself so. I know she was right, but only in part. As I travelled and met more and more victims, witnessed more and more pain and anguish, my need to right all the terrible wrongs, not only mine, compelled me onward. I was not able to stop or even slow down. There were simply too many broken souls.

At one point, I was returning from a visit to Lord Giovanni in Voghera before my pregnancy. The visit exhausted me. Gio had, at that time, refused to see me. Other of Lord Giovanni's relatives were cordial and kind, but I felt the distance from them.

They adored my mother, and I knew it was difficult for them to be gracious to me. Nevertheless, they treated me well and seemingly without judgment. Still, I left there feeling weary. Bella had instructed the guard to take me to visit a waterfall just outside of Voghera. She had often told me of the spirituality of the place and how it soothed my mother when she travelled. It was magical. How is it that a mere place can heal? You will undoubtedly discover the waterfall, too. When you do I hope you feel the energy and love of your mother and your grandmother in that place. Feel us both loving you as the water sprinkles lightly onto you face . . . and know how much I love you.

After my visit to the waterfall, on my return to Montalcino, I was struck by an idea that I could not shake from myself. Although I knew that it was in my best interests to be cautious regarding the archbishop, it occurred to me that I might put his feelings for me to work for the underground. What if I were able to convince him of the injustices that were being perpetrated around the kingdom and he were able to significantly decrease the tortures and deaths of innocents? He had been willing, recently, to allow the clearing of several names of the convicted after arguments from me. Why not more? Why not use my knowledge of his feelings for me to save families from the pyre? Perhaps I could even convince him to join us. It was conceivable. After all, there were many religious men who already worked opposing the Inquisition. I knew it was horribly manipulative, but I decided to try.

By the time I reached Montalcino, I had a plan. There was no question but that I would keep my plan from Bella. The mere thought of what I was thinking would frighten her too much. I decided to tell no one of my intention. That way I was the only one in danger. And really, could I be in any more danger than I already was? The archbishop was already in turmoil regarding me. It was only a matter of time before he would conclude that I was intentionally eliciting sexual feelings in him. Such stories were common. If I were going to be blamed for such a sin anyway, I might as well gain something for my trouble. My mind was made up.

I initiated the beginning of my plan when I returned to Montalcino. Upon my arrival, I requested a Privy Council meeting for the next day. Although I knew that all the members were not present in the castle, I had the prerogative to call impromptu meetings at my whim. At the conclusion of the meeting, I requested to speak with the archbishop.

*"A word in private, please, Archbishop Pietro," Queen Sofia said as all the council members were gathering their papers and notes.*

*The archbishop flushed bright red and looked furtively around the table. No one paid any attention to the request.*

*"Of course, Your Majesty," he finally replied as his color faded slowly.*

*When the rest of the council had left, the queen indicated for the archbishop to sit.*

*"It has not gone unnoticed by me that you have been generously supportive of many of the issues that are of greatest concern to me and the kingdom of Montalcino," she began. "I wish to thank you for that support."*

*She watched as the man squirmed slightly in his seat.*

*"I am not aware that I have gone out of my way to give my blessing to anything that I do not believe to be in the best interests of serving God and the Church," he said as he readjusted his papers.*

*"That may be," she smiled warmly, "in which case I am even more grateful to have you on the Privy Council. After all that has happened, it is good to know that God and government are on the same side."*

*He said nothing, but Sofia noted that perspiration had begun to bead on his nose.*

*"Also," the queen continued, "I wish to personally extend the gratitude of the Guilia children. Your intercession on their behalf to clear the name of their father, who was murdered by the Carfaggi brothers, gave them the security of knowing that they will not lose their land."*

*"They were done a grave injustice by a greedy family. It needed to be done," the archbishop waved off her gratitude.*

*"Many grave injustices have never been righted. And it takes a courageous man to stand up and say so. You are a courageous man."*

*He looked up and directly into her eyes for the first time. His look was confused, questioning. For the second time his face flushed bright red. Sofia saw the telltale trickle of sweat roll down from his temple and disappear into his beard.*

*"Perhaps we might discuss some of the other injustices that have come to my attention, Archbishop?"*

*He stood awkwardly and fumbled with his papers. His chair accidentally toppled over backward.*

*"I am late for another meeting, Majesty. Perhaps another time, if that suits you?"*

*"Of course. I did not mean right now. By all means, take your leave."*

*As the archbishop rushed from the room, Sofia could not help but smile. Why had she not thought of this earlier?*

### JUNE 28, 1585

A dmittedly, I used the archbishop. I really could not see the harm. Yes, I knew the struggle put him in conflict with his vows, but when I weighed the lives of so many against one man's feelings . . . well, I felt justified in what I did. It is not that I am proud of taking advantage of him, but it seemed a small price to pay for even one life.

I suppose this journal is my confession, sweet Catherine. Hopefully, you will bless me for it someday. That being said, I will tell you that I exploited the archbishop's feelings for some time. I knew how it tortured him to be in my presence. He was so transparent. While I never made any attempt to seduce him, that was not part of the plan, I do think he might have felt seduced. A few times, when we met in my office I could almost sense that if I had accidentally brushed up against him or even just reached a hand out to make a point, he would have succumbed to all the desire that smoldered within him. There were times that I felt enormously sorry for him. But lives were being saved. Names were cleared. Justice was winning some long-fought battles.

There was one time that I went into the church to speak with him. I knew he would be there. He had just finished hearing confessions and was locking up when I arrived. His discomfort at my arrival always surprised me. There always seemed to be the tiniest interval of adjustment when we came together. I could almost feel his surprise at the sight of me. It was as if he had talked himself into not feeling what he was feeling and struggled to hold onto it. But then I would arrive, or call for him, or he would see me sitting in the front pew during Mass, and I watched his resolve crumble.

So, when I found him in the church, we had been meeting and working together for over a year. I had not yet convinced him to intercede on behalf of a woman named Rosa, a long-time friend of Lord Giovanni's family. Rosa had been in prison for years for engaging in a sexual relationship with the local priest. The same priest had been fornicating with multiple women for some time and was executed for his crime.

Rosa shared a cell with another of his paramours, a woman named Bettina. Bettina died in prison of injuries from her torture, which was particularly harsh.

Lord Giovanni's youngest son, Benito, grew up having strong feelings for Rosa. Those feelings were lost along the way. But after your grandmother spent time in Voghera, and even went to the prison to visit with Rosa, Benito was emboldened to visit her as well. It was not easy to get in to see her, but he was persistent, and having a father on the Queen's Privy Council and the queen for a friend did not hurt his cause.

As Benito and Rosa visited, his feelings returned. Benito was the only visitor Rosa ever had. She was, at first, ashamed for him to see her and told him so. Prisons are not conducive to romance. They are rife with filth, rats, lice and the smells of human suffering and waste. Nevertheless, against all odds, Rosa and Benito found love.

I desperately wanted to secure Rosa's release. To hear Bella tell the story, the reason my mother stepped up her fight against the Inquisition was because of Rosa and Bettina. My mother was incensed that a holy man of God was responsible for the fate of the two young girls who thought he loved them alone.

*Sofia pleaded for Rosa. "Her crime," she said to the archbishop, "was to fall in love with a man of the cloth!"*

*She followed him as he walked around the church extinguishing candles. "He encouraged it. He used her for his own sexual depravity! He made her feel that it was God's will!" Sofia argued.*

*"And," he stopped and turned to her, "he was punished for his sin accordingly."*

*"And she has been, as well," Sofia said softly. "She has been tortured with* la pera. *She will never have children. She is in pain nearly continually. As if she was not already pained beyond belief to discover that the man she loved was using her even as he used dozens of others, she rots in that hell hole with no hope of anything but death. Enough is enough, I beg you!"*

*And then she did the unforgiveable. She knelt before him and reached for his hand. Clasping his hand in both of hers, she kissed it and held it to her cheek. She did so without forethought, without intent to deceive or disarm or seduce. The expression was honest and heartfelt.*

I truly wanted him to grant the request. I was near tears. When I realized I was holding his hand and he had said nothing, I looked up, dropping my hands quickly.

The archbishop had a pained look. He did not drop his hand but allowed it to turn against my face. His palm caressed my cheek. I heard his breath quicken and recognized the hunger in his eyes. I sank onto my heels, away from his touch, and lowered my head. "Forgive me," I said. "I know I ask too much."

The spell was broken. I stood. "I just thought that since a man of God ruined the girl, a man of God might save the woman."

As I turned to leave, the archbishop told me he would pray about it. I left him on his knees.

I avoided Archbishop Pietro for some time after that. Until that moment I had convinced myself that he was always in control of his feelings. His reaction frightened me. I knew I had tread on shaky ground. It was careless of me, and I would not let it happen again.

Much of the next year was spent with my traveling. I went often to visit Father Tim. He always seemed glad to see me, but I knew he missed my mother and I feared that my visits only reminded him that she was gone. He did once tell me that they had longs talks about God and life and that she challenged him in ways no one else could.

It was around that time that I was returning from Firenze, having met with other royals from surrounding areas. A pair of soldiers from Montalcino found us camped along a dry riverbed and told me that Lady Isabella had taken quite ill. I rushed home to be with her.

Although we rode hard and rested infrequently, it took us nearly two days to get back to Montalcino. Bella had a raging fever and was having difficulty breathing. The castle physician was a barber-surgeon who had recently come to us from Venice. He diagnosed her with sweating sickness and wrapped her in rose cloth to sweat the fever from her. She was delirious when I arrived.

Against the physician's advice, but not until he left the room, I had a tub filled part way with cool water. With the aid of two servants, we lowered Bella into the tub and washed her in the cooling water. She opened her eyes. When she saw me, she smiled weakly and said, "I am glad you are home."

For several days Bella moved in and out of consciousness. Her fever rose and fell depending upon the time of day. I did not leave her.

The physician was frustrated that she was not getting better and tasted her urine to confirm his diagnosis and treatment. Finally, he announced that the combination of her melancholy humors and the sweating sickness made it likely that she would succumb to death soon. He gave her small amounts of hemlock to ease her pain.

Her breathing became increasingly more labored as she developed pneumonia. I sent word to Father Tim, who came as soon as he could. As he was administering Last Rights, Bella opened her eyes and her face filled with light when she saw him. I thought she was coming back to us, but then she turned her gaze on me. I wish I could describe how lovingly she looked at me. I never knew how she was able to forgive me. Had our roles been reversed, I am certain I would have hated her until my last breath. I never deserved her love, but she blessed me with it anyway.

As she looked at me, I held her hand in mine and could not help but smile thinking that she was going to live. Then she looked beyond me. I remember turning to see who she looked at behind me, because I did not hear anyone else enter. Her face beamed so bright, for just an instant, as she pulled her hand from mine and reached out to the air and whispered, "Catherine." That was her last breath. She was gone.

I do believe that my mother did come for her. Perhaps that is just another aspect of my heresy. So be it. I cannot be executed more than once no matter how numerous my heretical beliefs. But despite my joy that Bella was out of pain and with her true love, I was grief-stricken. I sat with her body through most of the night and left to sit in the church a little before dawn.

I remember kneeling for some time on the cold stone floor. I did not have the words to pray, but my mind began to recall the losses of all my life, and it was not long before my heart broke open and the sobs spilled from me. Surprisingly, although it was my grief over losing Bella that brought me to my knees, it was James for whom I ached. I found myself longing for everyone I had lost— Bella, my mother, and my father, but it was James whose loss in my life I felt most acutely at that moment. Perhaps that is one of the harder life trials . . . every loss rebirths the most important ones; each new grief compounds the ones before it; every good-bye reminds us of past good-byes and serves to prepare us for future farewells. It is too much. This life of loss can be unbearable.

There was no holding in my agony. I begged James to come and take me. I no longer wanted to remain on this earthly plane without the love of everyone I held dear. I sensed James's presence. It was so powerful that I swear I smelled his sweet scent. I felt his love surround me, fill me, comfort me. I was crying so hard that I did not hear the chapel door . . .

*Sofia felt the touch of a hand on her shoulder. She had been sobbing uncontrollably, but at the gentle touch she looked up to find the archbishop standing behind her with a look of such concern that she collapsed against him and continued to wail. He knelt next to her.*

"*There is no one . . . no one,*" *she sobbed into his chest.*

*He wrapped his arms around her and held her, giving her a place to vent her anger and grief. She gave herself to the safety of his embrace. He was a man of God; it was natural that he should offer her solace. She opened herself to the one person left in her immediate world who might care about how she felt.*

"*Why?*" *she sobbed into him.* "*Why?*"

*He held on to her as she wept, and as his own tears began to fall, he buried his face in her hair. Together they wept.*

*When Sofia's cries began to subside, she again felt James's presence—his touch, his smell. When the hands lifted her face, she opened her eyes and saw the soft blue eyes of the man she had loved her whole life. He lifted her face in both of his hands and looked deeply into her eyes. Softly, tenderly, James wiped the remaining tears from her cheeks with his thumbs, then lowered his lips to her eyes, kissing away the last of the salty droplets from her eyelashes.*

*With a barely audible moan he lowered his lips and kissed her, gently at first, then deeply, passionately, and hungrily. She did not resist, but responded with like desperation, not understanding her own need.*

*When his arms encircled her waist, she felt James pulling her to him. She responded by wrapping her own arms around him as their bodies moved into each other. His breathing became shallow as hers quickened. His mouth found the hollow of her neck, and she lifted her head, opening herself to her hunger for the only love she desired. James.*

*When his hands found her breasts, she felt the press of his hardness against her abdomen and she pressed herself against him, moving slowly at first, then more rhythmically.*

*Wordlessly, they stood, never removing their hands and mouths from each other. He reached down, grasped the skirts of her gown and lifted them. She pulled at his robes until his erect member was exposed, then she moved back down to her knees kissing him, stroking him. James, her mind whirled,* my James, you have come back to me.

*She was delirious with passion. Her entire life had been spent loving a man who had only ever kissed her once. Her need was huge.*

*It was James who joined her on his knees, frantic with desire, and lay her on her back. She was oblivious to the cold stone floor. All she wanted was to satisfy her desire. She guided him into her. There was pain as he broke through her virginity, but it passed quickly as she moved with him, arching to meet his thrust, needing to be filled with him . . . to be filled with life.*

*Life.*

*When she finally cried out, he exploded within her. He shuddered long, hard, and momentarily collapsed on top of her. As he shrank within her she felt his tears hot in her neck. Then the archbishop rolled off her and pushed himself up to a kneeling position.*

*Slowly, Sofia's breathing returned to normal, and her body cooled on the stone floor. James's presence hummed within her, then shot away, like an arrow flying upward through the chapel ceiling, up and out to the freedom of sky. She opened her eyes to find the archbishop hunched beside her, his head bowed and shoulders sagging. She sat up and covered herself. So convinced was she that she had just been with James that she shook her head, trying to eliminate her confusion at finding the archbishop on the floor next to her. She swallowed hard.*

*The archbishop had spent his life in service to God, celibate, and recently denying his urge for this woman with whom he had fallen madly in love. Now he had succumbed to the greatest temptation he had ever known.*

*"Archbishop," Sofia said, but her voice came out strangled and weak.*

*His head raised slightly, then turned toward her. She saw the look of horror on his face. In an instant she knew he would never forgive himself for allowing this weakness. He buried his head in his hands, then lifted his face to the heavens and let out a long, sorrowful howl before standing and rushing from the church.*

*Sofia remained where she was until her body began to shiver. She was too weak to stand at first, so she lay there trembling and worrying about what might be in store as the consequence of her own weakness.*

*That is when it happened, a burst of warmth in her loins. At first, she was startled. It was different from what she had just experienced in the throes of passion. It warmed her. It comforted her. It gave her hope. Again, that sense of life.*

*Life. From the depths of her despair came a reason to live. She knew in that moment that she had conceived a child.*

### JUNE 29, 1585

I do not know how to describe the instantaneous feeling of knowing that I was pregnant with you.

The best way I can think of is to say that I no longer felt alone in the world. There was a shift, like the movement of the earth during a quake, or the jolt you feel when you wake from a nightmare and nearly cry with relief as you realize it was only a dream.

Here is the strangeness about it. I never felt the presence of Archbishop Pietro that morning in the church—only James. I felt like I had been with James. It was as if I had been given a double gift, and I relished the gifts of James and you. My desire for death left me as I basked in the warmth of two vastly different kinds of love.

We buried Bella next to your grandmother. They were together again. Ambrose, your grandfather, was next to Catherine on her opposite side. Bella's grave was between my mother and James. There was never any question but that Bella would be buried next to Catherine. The place had been saved for her. Perhaps someday you will visit the little cemetery. It is out beyond the grove of chestnut trees, surrounded by an ornate iron fence. I have often spent time there talking to my mother, my father and James. Strange how one can be comforted in a place of death, but I was often comforted just knowing I was near their bodies.

I did not know what to expect regarding the archbishop. How would he respond in the aftermath of our encounter? I was anxious to put the first interaction behind us in the hope that we could move on. That did not happen for some weeks.

Word had reached me that the archbishop had taken ill. While I did not believe that he had succumbed to any illness that modern medicine could alleviate, I worried that his absence from everyday life in Montalcino might make his eventual return all the more difficult. After nearly three weeks of seclusion in his quarters, I sent word to him that I was concerned about his health and requested permission to visit him. He refused.

It was not until the following Sunday that he finally appeared to say Mass for congregants of Montalcino. He looked awful. His face was drawn and pale. Usually, he looked resplendent in his robes, but now they just hung on his emaciated form.

I was horrified and tried to catch his eye as he looked out over the assembly. He never once looked in my direction. He disappeared immediately following the Mass, not even milling with his flock as he usually did.

It was not until the next Privy Council meeting that he was forced to deal with me. Even then, he avoided eye contact, greeting the group at large and offering me the most cursory of nods. When members of the council asked about his absence, he said only that he was suffering from a mild case of sweating sickness, and he hoped that his absence did not inconvenience the council. He offered little else during the meeting and left hurriedly afterward.

The next Sunday, however, he returned to the pulpit. He seemed stronger, for which I was grateful, until it came time to deliver his sermon.

Although the archbishop's sermons had always varied greatly, from the dangers of greed and heresy to God's love, his sermon that day centered upon the wages of sin being death. The sin he focused on that morning was lust.

It was difficult to tell whether his admonishments were directed at me or himself. Perhaps he was speaking to both of us. Regardless, I was frightened, truly frightened, for the first time. I could not tell if he was blaming me for leading him into sin or chastising himself for his own weakness in giving in to his earthly desires. I suppose that in the end it did not really matter. What I knew without a doubt following that sermon was this: even though the archbishop was blaming himself for what had happened that night in the church, he could not tolerate the feelings he had for me any longer. Eventually, he would find, as all men seem to find, that I was to blame for his own weakness.

Bella had foretold this would happen. She was right.

I kept my distance from the archbishop as much as possible. It was fortunate that I experienced little of the morning sickness during my pregnancy with you, and I gained very little weight. Then about three months into my pregnancy, Lord Giovanni, Gio's grandfather, came to visit me from Voghera.

I had not seen my cousin, Gio, since the death of our parents. At the time of their deaths and funerals, he would not speak to me or look at me. I knew that Gio was unable to forgive me for causing his father's death. While I did not blame him for his anger, I did miss him. We had been as close as siblings.

Shortly after the funerals of our parents, Lord Giovanni and his entire family, what remained of it, left Montalcino

and returned to Voghera.  Only Lord Giovanni came periodically to visit me. He would sit in on Privy Council meetings
at my request and advise me privately if he suspected secret agen-
das on the parts of other council members. Despite his advancing
years, he remained aware of the goings on around the kingdom
and always guided me with Montalcino's interests at heart.

I do not know how he managed to balance his family's anger
at me with his continued support and love for me. I was grateful for it, though, and always glad beyond words when he visited.
His was the only affection available to me. When he entered my
private office, he always greeted me appropriately, then held out
his arms.  I never failed to fall into them, allowing his soft, round
flesh to surround me with love. Truly, if he were to fail to hug me,
I think I would wither.  His arms held the healing love I craved.
There were times, as I cried myself to sleep at night, that I could
only comfort myself with the memory and anticipation of that
man's hugs.

If it were not for the traces of sadness I saw in his eyes, I could
almost believe that I had not been responsible for devastating his
daughter and grandson. When at last he returned for a visit, I was
desperate for his company.

*Queen Sofia lingered in the arms of the man whose truthfulness
awakened her to the horrible events she had unleashed upon her mother
and his son-in-law. Lord Giovanni's love and forgiveness never failed
to amaze her. His were the only arms left in the world into which she
placed her whole self. He seemed to know that and fully embraced her,
reaching his pudgy hand up to stroke her head.*

*When, finally, she stepped back from him and invited him to sit,
she inquired about his family.*

*"How is Gio?" she asked with a touch of sadness. While she did
not blame Gio, she had hoped that time might soften the depth of his
anger. She had written to him, begging his forgiveness, but her letters*

*went unanswered.*

*"He is fine. They are all fine, Sofia. They send their regards."*

*Sofia had insisted that he call her by her given name when they were in private. She needed him, of all people, to drop the formality of her title. He agreed, but the transition was awkward for him at first. His family always sent their regards, she noticed, never their love. It pained her, but she accepted the slight as punishment rightfully deserved.*

*"Do you think," she asked, "that he will ever find it within him to forgive me?"*

*Lord Giovanni inhaled deeply and rubbed his face with both hands. When he looked at her again, he smiled a sad smile. "I believe he will, Sofia. Give him time. He is becoming restless in Voghera. I can see it."*

*"What causes his restlessness?" She leaned forward in her chair, concerned and curious about Gio.*

*"He does not yet realize it, but he inherited his father's heart for soldiering. I can see that he struggles with boredom."*

*Sofia got up and poured them both goblets of Montalcino's best wine. She handed him one and sat back down.*

*He took a long swallow and kissed his free fingertips, "Perfecto," he announced. "I have missed Montalcino's wines."*

*"Then you shall have to take some home with you," she smiled. "We cannot have my favorite relative lacking such an important need."*

*He was quiet for a few moments, then said, "Gio is angry about more than his father's death, Sofia."*

*She waited, dreading what might be coming next but needing to know.*

*Finally, Lord Giovanni spoke. "When his grief over his father's death subsided and he found himself with time on his hands in Voghera, he became anxious and irritable. He lashed out at everyone within his circle. It took him time, but I believe he finally realized that his future was gone, as well."*

*Lord Giovanni waited for Sofia to grasp the meaning behind his words.*

*Sofia's head dropped into her hands. She moaned, "Oh, God. We always talked about his being the Captain of the Queen's Guard." She looked up at him, her eyes full of regret and pain. "It is all he talked about when we were young. He always had such dreams of protecting me when I came into rule."*

*"He is," Giovanni offered, "his father's son."*

*"I took that from him, as well," Sofia choked back a sob.*

*Giovanni reached over and patted her hand. She noticed it was cold. Sofia got up and tucked a lap throw around Giovanni. The room was drafty, and it gave her a reason to be close to him again. She leaned and kissed him on the cheek. When she sat back down opposite him there were tears in her eyes. Her emotions seemed less and less under her control these days.*

*When she regained control again, they talked about Montalcino in general. She told him of her travels, issues of the Privy Council and her attempts to free Rosa for Benito. As she finished talking about her failure to free Rosa, her eyes reddened and welled up again.*

*Lord Giovanni noticed and reached his hand to her. She took it gratefully, lowering her head.*

*"What is it, Sofia?" he asked.*

*Her throat constricted and teardrops fell onto their hands. When she did not answer, he asked, "Who is he?"*

*She looked up, startled. "How do you know?"*

*Smiling gently and patting her hand he responded, "I knew the moment I saw you yesterday. A woman with child has a certain glow about her that is unmistakable to those of us who have learned to pay attention," he chuckled. "And your tears are another sign."*

*"I do not seem to be able to control them lately," she lamented.*

*"Fortunately, a woman's mood is expected to be fickle," he said.*

*"That is a good thing, for I expect you need to keep this pregnancy secret."*

*She took a huge breath and stood. He watched her walk over to the window behind her desk and gaze out at the garden.*

*"Your mother always went to the same window and always looked out in the same way whenever she was contemplating difficult situations," he offered.*

*Sofia turned back to him. "I need my mother now."*

*"Tell me everything."*

I left nothing out, telling Lord Giovanni all of it. His concern was evident. He still had many friends in Montalcino. Next morning he announced that he had decided to stay the winter, for which I am eternally grateful. His connections probably saved my life . . . and yours.

### JUNE 30, 1585

As winter settled in around us I was more grateful than you can imagine that Lord Giovanni was near. There was no longer anyone in Montalcino castle to whom I felt close. Having him there made the castle feel like home again. Just knowing he was nearby comforted me. We made a habit of taking the midday meal together in my private quarters. The fireplace there was huge and kept the room warm. He was getting on in years. He never complained, but I could tell that the harsh winter was taking a toll on him.

One afternoon during our meal, he seemed distracted. I finally asked him what was bothering him. He picked up his wine goblet and walked over to the blazing fire. After staring into it for a bit, he turned to me and told me that he was concerned for my safety.

"Are you certain no one knows of your condition?" he asked.

"I have told no one but you. The dresses I have worn are from my mother's wardrobe room. They are slightly larger, and I believe conceal me fairly well." She stood and turned in front of him. "Am I deceiving myself? Be honest."

"If I did not know you, I would not suspect, no." He walked back over and sat at the table. "Nevertheless, a noble friend of mine stopped to visit me yesterday."

Sofia leaned back in her chair and waited for him to deliver his news.

"He asked if the rumors of your pregnancy were true." Lord Giovanni looked at me, shaking his head. "Of course, I denied it, saying that if anyone would know it would be me."

Sofia attempted to stand, but her legs were shakier than she thought, so she sat back down. "If someone passing through has heard this rumor, then everyone knows." Her mind raced with trying to figure out how, and who, had started the rumor.

"Let us not panic just yet," Giovanni reassured her. "Allow me to see if I can determine whether or not the archbishop has heard this rumor." He moved close to the fire again, thinking. When he turned back to her, he said, "We have a Privy Council meeting scheduled for tomorrow, do we not?"

"Yes," she affirmed.

"Good," he said. "Do not come." He was rubbing his beard, his brows furrowed in thought. "I will tell the council that I suggested that you were looking tired. I will tell them that I insisted that you rest, that since there was nothing of huge importance requiring your presence, you finally agreed just to keep me from worrying."

She smiled, knowing where he was headed. "At which time you will put forth a direct inquiry to the entire Privy Council regarding the rumors of my condition."

"Precisely."

Her knees had stopped shaking. She got up and went over to wrap her arms around his great girth. "What would I do without you?"

Lord Giovanni closed the doors to the Privy Council room as he entered.

"Gentlemen, Archbishop Pietro," he nodded as he strode over to the table, "I have insisted that the queen rest this afternoon."

"Is she ill?" asked the archbishop quickly.

"No, not at all," Lord Giovanni reassured them. "However, I convinced her that she was looking tired. To keep me from worrying, she gave in to my wishes. I am old I can insist on some things."

"And why would you want the queen to be absent from the meeting?" Lord Navona asked suspiciously.

Lord Navona was one of the three leftovers from Queen Catherine's court. Both Giovanni and Sofia remembered that Catherine had always complained about his endless support for anything Bishop Capshaw introduced. Even though he was a distant cousin of King Edward, Catherine's father, neither Sofia nor Lord Giovanni trusted the man. He was only interested in keeping his own interests safe, without regard to who held the reins of power.

"Because I have heard a rumor about the queen that disturbs me greatly. I wonder if any of you are aware of talk that our queen is with child?" Lord Giovanni remained standing. He looked around the table at the men seated there. None of them spoke or looked at him. One or two squirmed.

"I see." Giovanni made his anger evident. "I suppose I need not ask what the queen's council has done to dispel this rumor?"

"How do we know it is a rumor?" asked Lord Navona.

Lord Giovanni was furious. His face turned bright red and the veins on his forehead protruded as he pounded his fist on the table. He pounced. "Ah, so we should just assume that our queen is pregnant *without any question? Has she been seen with any suitors at all? Have any requested her hand in marriage? Is she close to or even interested in any men that we know of? Have you spoken to any of the guards to determine whether she has had visitors? Has anyone asked the queen if she is pregnant?" He paused. When no one answered he continued, still shouting. "Why not just build a pyre right here and now and burn her because, after all, we heard a rumor!"*

*"Lord Giovanni," the archbishop interrupted his tirade, "rumor or not, lascivious conduct does run in the queen's family."*

*Lord Giovanni glared at the archbishop. Through gritted teeth he asked, "Are you implying, Archbishop, that our queen is promiscuous?"*

*"It would follow suit, would it not?" His tone implied that he not only believed that the queen was, in fact promiscuous, but that her suspected pregnancy should come as no surprise.*

*"I sincerely doubt, Archbishop, that a man of the cloth, who has taken a vow of celibacy, can truly understand the desires of mere mortals," Lord Giovanni said pointedly.*

*The point hit home. The archbishop reddened under Giovanni's glare and said no more.*

*"Gentlemen," he looked around the table once more, "I fully expect this council to do all in its power to dispel the rumors about the queen. Queen Sofia has the right to expect her Privy Council to do no less than protect her reputation and her life."*

*With that, Lord Giovanni stormed out of the room.*

## JULY 1, 1585

The rumors did not dispel. In fact, they became more widespread. I wish I could tell you that I was unconcerned, but the danger that licked on the heels of the rumor grew, as well. It appeared the archbishop had convinced himself that I was promiscuous. Whether he simply could not accept the possibility that his weakness had become the very real possibility of a lifelong reminder in the form of a child, or he was really that naïve, I know not. All I do know is that Lord Giovanni's friend who was close to the archbishop maintained that the archbishop was saddened by the reports of my loose dealings with men. He was apparently "deep in prayer" about how to proceed. I was an unmarried woman. If it came to light that I had been an adulterer, there would have to be consequences.

Lord Giovanni was beside himself with worry. His worry worried me. I was less concerned about myself than I was about the toll his anxiety had on him. I could tell that he was not sleeping well. At one of our daily meetings, I told him that I would be fine and encouraged him to return to Voghera as soon as the pass was clear of snow. He agreed to plan the trip but wanted a few more days to see if he could come up with any alternatives to leaving me on my own.

As to the council, no one ever asked me about the rumors. No one came to me about the dangers. Meetings became awkward and uncomfortable. When I requested to meet with the archbishop in front of the other council members, he always made some excuse and promised to call on me later in the day. He never did. He stopped supporting my initiatives and suggestions. The rest of the council followed suit.

It was you, my sweet one, who kept me sane and hopeful. I had been thinking that I would need to leave Montalcino, alone and in disguise, to save you. The thought frightened me, but less so than staying and risking both our lives, yours more than mine. I had planned to tell Lord Giovanni about my plan the next day when we met in my office.

*"Lord Giovanni to see you, Majesty," Queen Sofia's secretary announced.*

"*Please send him in,*" *she said without looking up. She stood and was making her way around the desk to greet him. A total stranger entered. She stopped dead and forced herself to remain standing. What deception was this? Her mind raced with fear. Had the council baited her? Was she about to be brought up on charges of heresy so soon?*

*Her heart pounded in her chest as she and the stranger locked eyes. Sofia leaned heavily on the side of her desk for support. He was large, well built, fully bearded. She struggled to figure out who he reminded her of. Just as her mind connected to the memory, he knelt on one knee, placing his right fist over his heart.*

"*Majesty,*" *he said softly.*

"*Oh, dear God,*" *her hand flew to her mouth,* "*Gio!*" *She started to rush to him but held back, not certain he would be open to her rush of affection and delight at seeing him. He remained kneeling.*

*She walked over to him, not even trying to hide her tears of joy and hope. Perhaps he had not forgiven her. Perhaps he would never forgive her. Nevertheless, he was here, and she was grateful.*

*When she stood in front of him, she held out her hands. He placed both of his hands in hers and stood. Her tears filled the rims of her eyes and spilled down her cheeks, and filled and spilled some more. She so desperately wanted to hug him. Finally, he shook his head and his crooked smile formed slowly. He pulled her into his arms.*

"*I have missed you so,*" *she sobbed into his chest.*

"*I have missed you, as well.*"

*They sat. She found a handkerchief and mopped her face. When she could speak again, she asked,* "*How did you come to be here?*"

*You cannot guess?*" *He raised his eyebrows and looked at her.*

"*Your grandfather!*" *she said.* "*I do not know what I would have done without him this winter. He was my only friend.*"

"*He wrote to me several weeks ago and told me to get here as soon as possible. His letter only said it was imperative that I* come quickly. I arrived yesterday, late afternoon. It was the soon-est I could get through. There was a spring blizzard in the pass, or I would have been here last week."

"I am worried about him," Sofia said, tucking her handkerchief in her sleeve. "I think the winter has been more difficult for him than he admits."

"I agree. He will return to Voghera but only once he is convinced that you are safe." He looked at her and clucked his tongue. "It appears you have gotten yourself into a bit of a dilemma."

"He told you?"

"Everything."

"I thought to disguise myself and see if Father Tim could help me find refuge until such time as the baby is born. It is no longer safe for me to stay here."

"Agreed." Gio stood and walked over to an oil painting on the wall. "Your father painted this. I remember when he did it. He was really quite good. I was sorry to hear that he died."

"Gio," she started, then hesitated, "I never got the chance to tell you how sorry I was about . . . everything. I . . . it . . . please for-give me."

"It is the past," he waved his hand nonchalantly, but she noticed that it fisted slightly at the end of the wave.

"You look like him, you know," she stated. "You are every bit as handsome."

He blushed and moved quickly to change the subject. "Tell me about your Captain of the Guard."

"He is no Robert. He is not you," she added, "but he is adequate."

"Do you trust him?" Gio asked, turning to read her face as she answered.

"Presently, there are only two people in the world I trust, your grandfather and you," she said. "Does that answer your question?"

"From what my grandfather tells me, we really do not have much *time. We need to get you to safety."*

*"What are you thinking?"*

*"Your idea of a disguise is a good one. But you will not travel alone. To be safe, you need to be with a man. We will need to pretend to be husband and wife, especially in your condition."*

*"Gio, the last thing I want is to put you in danger." She was shaking her head back and forth as if the thought of causing more death to the family who had already given her so much was intolerable. "No, I can travel alone. I could not bear to risk any more lives."*

*"With all due respect, Majesty, you have no choice."*

*"What do you mean?"*

*"It is the only way my grandfather will concede to return to Voghera." He smiled. "He anticipated your refusal. Knowing how much you love him, he is willing to use your feelings for him to get his way."*

*Sofia's hands flew to her hips. "But he needs to be there. He cannot make that a condition. He needs to go home!" she nearly shouted.*

*"Hah! You are no match for my grandfather!" Gio laughed. "He always gets his way!"*

*"Gio, I cannot. I could not live with myself if anything happened to you."*

*"You have no choice, Sofe," he moved toward her and his emphasis on the childhood endearment of her name brought tears to her eyes again. "I never should have left. I am your new Captain of the Guard. It is where I was always meant to be. I will not let you take it away from me. I was born to protect you."*

*She sat, accepting her defeat, closing her eyes momentarily. "How soon do we leave?"*

*He knelt in front of her. "Prepare yourself to leave this very evening. My grandfather will come to your quarters after the evening meal. Say goodbye to him. When you are ready, I will meet*

*you in the garden at the back of the hermitage. I will have two
horses and all the supplies we can carry."*

*"But what about . . . "*

*"The plans are made. You need worry about nothing. I will apprise
you as we travel."*

*"Gio?" she searched his face, "You are certain you wish to do
this?"*

*"Sofia, I have never been more certain of anything in my life."
He stood, bowed and fisted his hand over his heart. "I will be waiting for you shortly after the meal. Eat well."*

*He left Sofia sitting in her chair. She reached down and placed her
hand on her swelling belly. "It is going to be alright now," she whispered. And with the kind of sigh that only comes with finally feeling
like a great burden has been lifted, Sofia nodded off in the chair.*

Gio's arrival at Montalcino meant everything to me. The fact
that he would be the one to see me to safety relieved me of the
uncertainty of my own guards. If the Privy Council did not have
the ability or desire to defend me, how could I think that anyone
else would? But Gio I knew I could trust.

When I went up to my quarters after the midday meal I sat
for some time. I had moved into Bella's and my mother's quarters
after Bella died. It was a way to feel surrounded by the love of
those I had lost. How long had my mother and Bella shared their
lives and their love in those rooms? I loved the looming bookcases
with the volumes lining their shelves like sentries guarding over
me. On cool winter nights I could feel them cradling me in the
warmth of their lap throws as I sat by the fire. I remembered the
meals we shared at the great, round table. I would miss this room
more than any in the castle.

I got up and pulled several volumes of my favorite books. I
stacked them on the table and then opened the drawer to the
dressing table. There, where I had placed it, was a bound book

of blank pages given to me by my father before he had died. It was made of Montalcino's finest paper. My father had bound the journal in soft leather and had painted my name in gold gilt on the cover. Finally, I knew what to use it for. It is the book in which I write these words, that I might find a way to connect to you if the worst comes to pass.

In addition to the few books and journal, there was only one other thing I knew I must take, my mother's sword. I lifted it down from the mantle over the fireplace, where it has lived since my mother's death. Holding it in my hand brought back a flood of memories from that day. I pushed them aside. There would be time and reason enough for tears once I left Montalcino behind.

The evening meal seemed to arrive so suddenly. As far as I knew, it would be my last meal in my own home. The great hall was a bustling hive of activity, as usual. Everyone gathered for the evening meal.

I knew it was important for me to eat well. The task was made more difficult by the lump that arrived in my throat as Lord Giovanni sat down beside me. Gio was not present. He had tried to keep his arrival quiet, as he intended to spirit me away. Lord Giovanni ate little, then excused himself to help Gio prepare for my departure.

My departure. As I looked around the hall, I found myself consumed by a combination of fear and overwhelming sadness. The faces I had become accustomed to seeing daily since my birth would no longer greet me after today. I did not know what would happen to me when I was no longer queen. What might life become for me?

I found myself desperately trying to etch each face into my memory. As I did, I said silent goodbyes to each person who had touched my life in some way. It is strange to be saying goodbye when no one knows you are leaving. The feelings evoked felt stronger and more powerful than sharing the farewell. Perhaps the difference lay in the fact that when both parties know the parting is imminent, both can share in the emotion. Only I knew I was leaving, therefore, only I held the power of the moment. The weight of the imbalance made me dizzy with grief. I tried to eat but found all I could swallow were my tears.

I stared at my food to hide the tears in my eyes as I tried to gain control of my emotions. When I looked up, I saw the archbishop. He was moving toward the table of Lord Navona. As he settled into his seat, I watched as he leaned close to Lord Navona and whispered something in his ear. Navona then looked up at me. When he saw that I was looking at him, he forced a smile. The archbishop turned to look at me and nodded without smiling. I read the disgust in his eyes. I felt his disdain for me and knew, beyond a doubt, that he had managed to obliterate his part in what happened between us. His blame shot arrows through me. For the first time, I finally saw that he could not live with himself if I were alive. And I knew that he had managed to garner the support of the council. If I did not leave, I would not live. Finally, I understood.

I left the great hall, looking back only once at the noisy tables, painting one last picture of that room. As I looked at the head table and the empty chair that I had just left, I saw a vision of my mother, my father and Bella. They nodded to me. My mother smiled sadly and mouthed, "Go." I turned and made my way to my quarters.

A short time later, Lord Giovanni came to say goodbye.


*"Sofia," he held out his arms and she fell into their loving comfort. "You must be brave, my child."*

*"I wish there were another way!" she sobbed, knowing there was not.*

*He said nothing but let her cry herself out as he gently patted her. When she finished, she stood straight in front of him and took his hands. "I am so grateful for you."*

*"We are family," he responded, "I shall miss you and I will worry until I know you are safely settled and have given birth to another member of our family."*

*She smiled. "I have Gio, thanks to you. All shall be well."*

*"There is not much time," he said. "I have left you a change of clothing with Gio. Do not change until you are certain that you are not seen. Gio is waiting behind the hermitage. We must say goodbye now."*

*He took her face in his hands and kissed her on both cheeks, then on the forehead. In a move that startled and moved him to tears, she knelt in front of him and kissed both of his hands.*

*He left her quarters. The sound of the door closing slammed the finality of farewell into her chest. She tied her mother's sword to her waist and hid it beneath a wrap. She went to the library where she and James studied as children. No one was there. She found the latch to the secret passageway and quietly opened the door. The stairway was dark, but she knew the way. The passageway curved down worn steps to a hallway near the kitchens. There was another corridor that led in a different direction. She knew that way intimately. It was the same way that Mary, her caretaker, used to secret her away to clandestine visits with Bishop Capshaw.*

*She felt her way down the stairs in the dark. When she could see the faint light from the kitchen hallway she paused, listening for sounds of anyone who might be close. Hearing nothing, she made her way quickly down the last of the stairs, turning toward the church.*

*Because she knew the archbishop was at dinner, she was not worried about anyone being in the church at this hour. The secret passageway led to a closet in the vesting room. Again, hearing nothing, she* opened the door of the closet and found her way to the back door of the church. From there she was close to the hermitage, which mostly sat empty. After letting herself through the gate, she quickly rounded the back of the hermitage and found Gio waiting near the garden.

"Here," he said, "no one is in the garden house. Go in and change into these clothes."

She took the peasant dress and shoes into the garden house and changed quickly. When she emerged from the garden house, she was holding the clothes she had just changed out of. Gio took them and stuffed them into a burlap sack. He went back into the garden house where he had already dug a hole. He dropped the sack into the hole and covered it with dirt. Then he pulled a chest of tools over the small mound. When he was convinced that he had concealed the clothing well enough he turned to her.

"Ready?"

She nodded solemnly.

He led her to the horses just outside the garden gate. After helping her mount, they nudged the horses down the well-worn path into the valley behind Montalcino castle. As they descended into the valley, Sofia turned back to see that the moon, slightly less than full, was rising over the church. Her eye was drawn beyond the church to the castle, to the window of her quarters. She had left a candle burning in the window. It glowed softly, flickering a farewell in the night.

She and Gio did not speak for nearly an hour. By then, they had crossed the valley and were ascending the ridge on the far side of valley.

"Your name is Maria. We have been married a year." Gio spoke softly as his horse was able to pull alongside hers where the path widened.

"What is your name?" she asked.

"Roberto."

Sofia stopped her horse. They were about to head over the top of *the ridge. She turned to look back at the castle one more time. It was awash in moonlight. She thought she saw the sputter of her candle as it went out but decided it was just her imagination.*

*"Roberto," she said, "a noble name."*

*"We should arrive at Father Tim's in Castiglione d' Orcia sometime between midnight and one. Night travel is much slower."*

*"How long do you think we will be there?"*

*"Not long. We should leave quickly. That will most likely be the first place they look for you," he said. "Father Tim will, hopefully, be able to direct us to a good hiding place."*

*"Does he know we are coming?"*

*"I did not think it wise to try to send him a message."*

*"Our dear priest is in for a little surprise."*

*"I wonder if he will remember me?" Gio said.*

*Sofia chuckled softly. "He may not recognize you, but I know he remembers you. I have often talked to him about you. I think he will see your father in you. He was very close to both your father and my mother, you know."*

*"I knew that my father accompanied your mother and Lady Isabella on visits to Castiglione d' Orcia, but I was not allowed to come."*

*She hesitated, then said, "Gio . . . "*

*"Roberto."*

*"Sorry, Roberto. You may ask me anything," she said as she pushed up to shift her riding position a bit.*

*They rode in silence for some time. When she finally decided that he was not going to ask her anything, he stopped his horse and rubbed his bearded chin. "How can you still believe in God?"*

*Of all the questions he could have asked, of all the questions she had expected, that was one she never even considered that he might wonder about.*

*"What makes you ask?"*

He spurred his horse again, and she joined him. "After what the bishop did to you, after what happened, and you realized the truth . . . I just do not understand how you can still believe in anything."

"Do you not believe in God?" she asked.

He paused long and kept riding. "I do not think I have believed in much of anything since . . . for a very long time."

"I see," she said sadly, believing herself to be the cause of his struggle. "Well, I am not sure I would have been able to continue to believe if it had not been for Bella and Father Tim."

"Tell me," he said.

An owl hooted somewhere overhead. The horses snorted, their hooves padding softly on the undergrowth of the forest. After a while she shared with him what she had never shared with anyone.

"Following the funeral of our parents I was thrust into the issues that come with being queen much too quickly. I hated myself. I hated everything I had done, everything that happened. On top of all that transpired as the result of my stupidity, I also had to come to terms with the loss of James and you.

She paused, waiting to see if he might offer anything about his leaving and not saying goodbye. He said nothing.

"It was more difficult than you can imagine living with myself. I found that I looked forward more and more to evening when I could retire and sleep. Even then, I was haunted by my dreams, frantically looking for James or desperately racing to rescue my mother."

The horses moved into an open meadow and moonlight showed down on them, creating shadows as they rode.

"Eventually, I requested a sleeping draught from the physician. It helped me to sleep through the night without dreaming. But relentlessly, morning came, and I was forced to face it." She shook her head from side to side as she remembered those days. "I had come to dread life and living.

"The days were endless. Bitter. Exhausting. I did not feel that I could go on," she continued. She wondered if she should tell him the next and considered keeping it to herself but realized how much she had missed talking to anyone her own age, at least anyone she could trust. "I hoarded several nights of the sleeping draught."

Gio pulled up his horse. "No! Sofia, no."

She reined her horse and looked at him. His face so like his father's, looked at her in horror. Tears began to well up in his eyes.

"I was a coward, cousin. What can I say?"

"You drank it all?" he asked.

"Every last drop. I did not want to wake up again . . . ever."

"What happened?" Gio asked as he clicked his tongue to move the horses ahead.

"I fell asleep quickly enough," she said, "but I woke up deathly ill and vomited my way through the night. The servants found me in the morning covered in my own vomit and excrement. The physician was called. He recognized the smell of the sleeping draught, even with the stench of the other horrid smells in the room. He was furious with me."

"I imagine he could have been executed for providing you with the means to do in the queen," Gio stated with considerable judgment in his tone.

"Once I was cleaned up and put back to bed, I slept for some time. The sounds of muffled crying woke me. I found my father sitting next to my bedside weeping uncontrollably into his hands."

A crackle in the underbrush startled them. Gio held up his hand and scanned the bushes near where they heard the sound. It was not long before a raccoon waddled out and crossed in front of them, oblivious to their presence.

"What happened?" Gio pressed as they resumed their ride.

"My father was beside himself with worry. He made me promise I would never attempt anything so foolish again."

*"Will you keep that promise?"*

*"Yes, I will."*

*"You have now promised two people the same thing," he said, making it clear that he expected her to keep the vow.*

*"Three, actually," she said. And when he looked at her quizzically, she patted her belly, looked down and smiled.*

*"Three, then," he said, "but you have yet to explain your steady belief in God."*

*"Perhaps 'steady' is not the word," she continued. "Before I regained my strength, I spent several days in bed. I was not left alone. If my father were not sitting nearby, looking worried and fretting, Bella or Father Tim would be constantly vigilant. Bella and I had started to grow closer, but it was more difficult than I could bear to be with her. Sometimes I would notice her drifting off as we sat together in her quarters. She would be looking at the chair that my mother always sat in. I would see the pain in her face, feel the emptiness I had caused her."*

*"Every time I looked at her my remorse filled every fiber of my being. And when I thought of you, the same thing happened. It did not matter whether I was . . . or would be . . . forgiven or not, I could not forgive myself."*

*They were moving back down the rise and were about five miles from Castiglione d' Orcia. The moon was nearly directly overhead, and the path well illuminated when they arrived at the crossroads to Father Tim's village.*

*"It was Father Tim and Bella who helped me to realize that it was not myself with whom I should be angry, or even God, but the bishop. I knew, of course in some way, that he was to blame, but I had covered so many of my feelings with my guilt and shame that I never really felt my anger and loss regarding Capshaw.*

*"They helped me to understand that, as a child, I was vulnerable to his particular kind of evil. By the time I finally realized*

*how hateful and cruel he was, by the time I realized that I was so blinded by the lies and hate he had planted and cultivated in me for so long, I exploded. If that man had still been alive, I believe I would have torn him apart with my bear hands."*

*"I would have helped you," Gio offered.*

*When she looked at him, she could see the sparkle of his tears in the moonlight.*

*"It took some time. I was still mad at God for allowing it all. But eventually, I realized that my faith should never have been in a man, no matter that he was supposed to be a man of God." She reached back to pull up the hood of her cloak. The night air was becoming chill.*

*"I spent many nights alone in the church, just sitting. One night, shortly after Bella and I had finished transcribing the journals and reports from Capshaw's quarters, I felt this peace come over me." She stopped her horse and looked over at Gio. "You will think me mad, but as I pondered all of the victims of this bloody Inquisition; as I considered how scores of innocent children, women and men continued to believe in God after they had been tortured, lost everything, and faced execution because of those men of God, well, I guess I decided that I needed to continue to believe for them."*

*"I do not understand," Gio looked puzzled.*

*"Someone needed to believe in the God of their beliefs and stand up against the monstrous god created by people like Capshaw, Pope Paul, the Carfaggi brothers. If Bella could suffer the kind of losses that she endured and continue to believe . . . forgive . . . and love, who was I to abandon the God of my childhood? Bella and your grandfather loved me, forgave me the unforgiveable. That, I realized, reflected the true love of God, the kind of love I always believed in. It was as I came to that conclusion a wave of warmth and peace flood my soul."*

*Gio nodded but said nothing. They rode the remainder of the way* to Castiglione d' Orcia in silence.

Father Tim opened the door to his residence looking both frightened and resigned, as if he had been expecting to be arrested and wondered what had taken the authorities so long.

When he recognized Queen Sofia, his eyes opened wide. He ushered her and her companion inside quickly. Before he closed the door, he looked outside to see if anyone had seen the two.

"What has happened?" Father Tim asked as he led them to his dining table. As they sat, Father Tim pulled a bottle of wine from the cupboard. He brought three glasses to the table. As he poured, he stole glances at Gio. With the wine poured and handed to his guests he said, "You look remarkably like your father, Gio."

Gio smiled at the priest. "You were a good friend to him. And to Queen Catherine." He paused. "That is why we have come here."

"What is it, what has happened that you left Montalcino under the cover of night," he looked at Sofia, "and in disguise."

"Queen Sofia is in danger," Gio stated. "We need to find a place for her to hide indefinitely. My grandfather and I have reason to believe that she is in imminent danger of being arrested on charges of heresy."

Father Tim looked at Sofia and asked, "Does this have anything to do with the rumors of your carrying a child?"

Sofia nodded. "Yes. And they are not rumors."

"I see. When are you due to deliver?"

"Most likely within the next two weeks. I have not consulted a physician or a midwife, so I am guessing, but my guess is based on fact," she said.

"What fact?" Father Tim asked.

Sofia reddened and lowered her head. When she did not answer immediately, Gio came to her rescue.

"The fact is that there is only one possible time that her pregnancy could have happened. The rest is just mathematics."

"I see," Father Tim rubbed his face. "Who is leading the charge *of heresy?"*

*"Archbishop Pietro," Gio said with anger.*

*"Queen Sofia," he paused, "who is the father of your child?"*

*Sofia looked up directly into Father Tim's eyes. "Archbishop Pietro."*

*The priest would have collapsed into his chair had he not already been sitting. At the news, he closed his eyes and brought his hands, fingers intertwined as in prayer, to his forehead. He sighed deeply, sadly, almost moaning.*

*"There is no time to waste," Father Tim said as he looked up.*

*Gio spoke again. "We need a place for her to hide, to deliver this child . . . "*

*"And some assistance to keep her hidden," Father Tim finished. He got up and walked over to his fireplace. The fireplace was not in use, but he reached his arms up and leaned into the mantel, thinking.*

*"Many years ago, when your mother, Lady Isabella, your father," he stopped and looked at Gio, "and I were desperately fighting to find ways to hide travelers sent here by my brother, Lady Isabella referred to a place. It was near the home where she grew up."*

*"Aquapendente?" Sofia asked.*

*"Yes, that is it. She said her father had built a small cottage hidden in the woods a few kilometers from the main house. She remembered him taking her there once and telling her that if there was ever any trouble as the result of his beliefs, that was where she should go."*

*"What else can you remember?" asked Gio.*

*"Let me think." He paced slowly back and forth in front of the fireplace. "I remember. She said he had built it so that the main house was between the town and the cottage. That way he felt that no one wandering to or from the village would be likely to find it. The cottage was on their land, but on the far northern edge and well hidden. It is likely to be in shambles."*

*"It is worth trying to find," Gio stood and walked over to Father*

Tim. "*Is there anyone you know in that area, someone who might assist us? There is a baby to be delivered and I . . . *" *he hesitated.*

*Father Tim went to the far side of the fireplace and moved a basket containing firewood. He knelt. As Sofia and Gio watched, he slid a large stone out from the base of the fireplace and reached in. His hand emerged with a rectangular, wooden box, which he brought over to the table where Sofia had remained sitting.*

"*I keep the names of all those willing to aid us,*" *the priest said as he began to shuffle through the papers.*

*Sofia noted that the paper was made in her own paper mills and felt a surge of longing for her father, who had run the mills until the day he died.*

"*Here,*" *Father Tim interrupted her thoughts,* "*I received this information only six months ago. There is a family, a brother and sister, who live in Aquapendente. Umberto and his sister, Lucia. Umberto was tortured. He was suspected of concealing information about known heretics. He refused to cooperate, so his tongue was removed. Lucia's husband feared for his own life after that and abandoned her.*"

"*The coward,*" *Gio fumed.*

*Father Tim smiled at Gio.* "*Given enough time on this earth, Gio, we each find our own unique form of cowardice. It is different for everyone.*" *Gio reddened slightly.*

"*Does the woman, Lucia, have children?*" *Sofia asked.*

"*I do not know. But here is how you can find them.*" *Father Tim told Gio where the brother and sister lived.*

"*Now,*" *Father Tim continued,* "*you should rest a bit, but I think you had best leave before daybreak.*"

## JULY 2, 1585

We slept a few hours at Father Tim's that night but left well before dawn with his blessing and a sack of additional supplies and food. By the time the sun was up we were far from Montalcino. Despite our dress, we did not wish to take chances by travelling the main routes. I had been all over Montalcino. Regardless of my attire, someone might recognize me, so we stayed near the roads but not on them. That made travel slow.

My pregnancy burdened our travel, as well. I was forced to stop often for the pressure on my bladder. Gio, or rather, Roberto, was patient and accommodating. He insisted we dismount every few hours for a rest. I was surprised at how easily I nodded off leaning against a tree or a rock.

We camped at night but built no fires. Our meals consisted of dried meats, fruits, and nuts. It was two more long days before we reached Aquapendente. On the outskirts of the town, we found a small cave. Gio settled me inside, pulling large tree branches to conceal the opening. He hid my horse nearby and went to Aquapendente to find Umberto and Lucia.

When the couple heard that Father Tim had sent us, they embraced Gio. He told them that we had narrowly escaped arrest on false charges of heresy. Umberto and Lucia were told that we were siblings, as well. It served no purpose to tell them the truth and would only put them at more risk.

Although the couple had no idea where the little cabin might be found, they were able to direct Gio to the estate of the former earl, Bella's father. Gio planned to go back to Aquapendente once he had me settled. Lucia agreed to come to help deliver the baby when the time came.

Lucia, it turned out, did have two children. One of them was young enough to be nursed, born after her husband abandoned her. So, a problem I had worried about was solved. Lucia would be able to nurse you until you were delivered to your new home.

While in town, Gio went into the local tavern. He knew that if any word of the queen's disappearance had made it this far south, the tavern would be the place he would find out. He heard nothing, but that did not necessarily mean that word had not reached Aquapendente.

Just in case he was noticed, Gio left town the opposite way that he had entered, then circled back around once he reached the woods. When he returned to fetch me from the little cave, I was sleeping soundly, so soundly, in fact, that I never heard him. He did not wake me but let me sleep until I was rested.

We spotted the estate, Bella's childhood home, easily enough. It was well cared for. I could not help but wonder who had taken it over. The rogue group that had attacked Bella's family farther north, on her husband's lands, were not officially sent by the Church. That was why my mother could not discover the identity of the murderers. If they had been Church affiliated, the Church would have laid claim to the lands of the family. The estate had remained empty for many years. Bella could never bear to return. Seeing Bella's home, knowing that someone was benefiting from the murder of her family, made my blood boil. It was all I could do to stay mounted and not ride onto the estate and confront the people who lived there.

As we rode around the fields surrounding the estate we kept ourselves well into the trees. However, we needed to keep the estate visible to attempt to stay on course to find the hidden cottage. We did not even know if the cottage was still there. Was it inhabited? After all these years who knew what might have happened to the little structure?

When Gio determined that we had travelled as far north as we needed, we began a switchback fashion of riding, in hopes that the cottage would be easier to spot. After an hour, we crossed a tiny trickle of stream and moved out into a small meadow. We dismounted, allowing the horses to graze. It felt good to walk some, although my backside was aching from so many days of riding.

Gio skirted the meadow to the north, I to the south, both of us exploring to try to find any sign of a structure. As I wandered in and out of the trees at the end of the meadow, I spotted it. It seemed abandoned and was overgrown with brush and ivy, but it stood solidly, hidden well within a grove of tall trees. I went back to the meadow and called out to Gio.

With the reins of our horses in our hands, we made our way back to the little stone cottage. There was no sign of life. Surprisingly, the small windows were intact. The front door was unlocked. Gio opened it and entered, then beckoned me in.

How many years had the place sat empty? It had never been used but was built as a refuge for the earl and his family to hide in, if they ever need to escape. The inside was a simple, open rectangle. There was a table surrounded by three chairs. Opposite the table were two beds, wooden platforms with grass-stuffed mattresses. I suspected the mattresses would be filled with insects, possibly even rodents. There was evidence of field mice everywhere. Everything was covered in a thick layer of dirt. Cobwebs and spiders seemed to be the main inhabitants.

I looked back at the door. We had left a trail of footprints in the dirt. A broom lay on the floor near the entry. I tried to bend to pick it up to start sweeping but could not get down far enough. Gio squatted, lifted the handle, but the twine that may once have held the twigs and slender branches had disintegrated long ago.

"I will fashion a new one," he declared.

It was tiny, filthy, and infested, but this was my new home. Before I could rest, I needed to begin to clean. A bucket sat near the fireplace. I asked Gio to fetch water from the stream. By the time he returned, I had torn an undergarment into strips to use for rags and started in on the desperately needed task. Gio dragged the mattresses outdoors and emptied the contents. One of the coverlets was salvageable, and he began the task of filling it with dried grass. By the time it was dark, we had the little place cleaner. We lit a fire in the fireplace, but put it out quickly, having clearly upset the birds nesting in the chimney.

So, the first meal in my new home was much the same as those we ate on the road. Gio promised to clean the fireplace. Perhaps he might even catch something worth cooking in the large pot that hung from the arm in the fireplace.

We fell asleep that first night without trouble, because we were exhausted. Gio's creation of a softer mattress for me was better than the ground I had tried to sleep on for several nights. He slept on the hard platform adjacent to mine. Night sounds of the creatures in the forest lulled us to sleep If I dreamed at all that first night, I have no memory of it.

Gio spent two days scouting the perimeter of the cabin and hunting small game. Even as a child he loved to hunt with his father. His bow and arrow were as much a part of him as his sword. I remember how he and James would hold shooting contests in the open fields near Montalcino castle. Gio always won. He was an exceptional marksman with an arrow.

He taught me how to clean and prepare rabbit. We were hungry enough for fresh food that we ate it clean of its bones, but without herbs and spices it lacked flavor.

I cleaned what I could and tried to make the place as much a home as possible. Gio had made plans to meet Umberto outside of town. Umberto and Lucia had purchased supplies and Umberto was bringing them so that Gio could show him the way to the cottage. He was concerned that my time was growing close, and he wanted Umberto to know how to get here with Lucia in adequate time to help me deliver.

I know that Gio was desperate to know if word of my disappearance had reached Aquapendente, but he did not ask, for fear that he might rouse Umberto's suspicions of who we were. We were determined that the two of them only ever know us as the siblings, Roberto and Maria.

The two men returned to the cottage late afternoon. 'Roberto' questioned the young man about his ability to find the place again, and Umberto reassured him that he could. The sack that held the new supplies was emptied, and 'Roberto' instructed Umberto to return the next day with more of the supplies. Then he gave Umberto a rabbit, to make it appear that he had just been out hunting.

When night fell, Gio expressed concern over waiting until my labor started to call for Lucia. He was adamant about having Umberto bring his sister to stay with us until the baby was born. Too exhausted to fight him, I agreed.

When Umberto arrived the next day, we told him to bring his sister and her children. The plan was that they would load a wagon and tell townspeople they were off to visit family in a northern village. To be perfectly honest, I was glad that Lucia was coming. I was weary and frightened. The thought of children in the little place cheered me. And knowing Lucia was near for your birth comforted me.

*Sofia heard the wagon's approach before she saw it. It was not the wagon, so much as the crying of the baby. She went out to meet the family. Gio was already outside, chopping wood, and buried his ax in a log to greet them.*

"*Thank you for coming, Lucia,*" *Sofia welcomed her with kisses on both cheeks.*

"*It is my pleasure, Maria,*" *she said to Sofia as she reached up to lift her oldest down from the wagon. "How are you feeling?"*

"*Hungry and tired.*"

"*Ah,*" *laughed Lucia, "then all is normal."*

*When everything was brought inside, 'Maria' expressed her appreciation for the material purchased for her. "What a lovely color, Lucia. It is perfect."*

"*I thought it might work for curtains and baby clothes alike,*" *she said. "I hope you do not mind; I brought a bunting for the baby. It is an extra one I made, but I never use it anymore."*

"*Thank you. That was very thoughtful of you.*"

*When the sun set, Umberto built a fire in the fireplace, now free of birds. Lucia insisted on preparing the meal. While she might not know that this was her queen upon whom she waited, it was evident enough that 'Maria' was a noble woman and, therefore, accustomed to being served.*

"*Lucia, I would be appreciative of any instruction you might give me on simple food preparation,*" *Maria ventured.*

"*You look tired now,*" *Lucia said as she expertly took over the cooking. "Sit and rest with the children, tomorrow is soon enough for some basic instruction."*

*Gratefully, Sofia sat. The infant, Michelena, started to fuss. Sofia picked her up from the little cradle she arrived in and held her. The baby cooed and gurgled at her and soon fell asleep in Sofia's arms.*

*As they sat to eat a very flavorful rabbit stew, Lucia told of hearing rumors when she was in town making purchases.*

"*I overheard the merchant while I was buying the cloth,*" *she said as she mashed carrots and potatoes for her children. "He* said that the entire country is looking for Queen Sofia!" The look on her face reflected no suspicion that it was, in fact, Queen Sofia in whose presence she sat. "I am willing to wager that she has come to some foul play."

"What makes you think that?" Roberto asked, his spoon halted in mid-air.

"We heard rumors that the queen was with child," she said. "A pregnant queen without a husband would be targeted for heresy by any number of her enemies. I imagine that queens must be especially vigilant when it comes to . . . "

Lucia stopped and gaped at Sofia. Her spoon fell from her hand, and she paled, visibly.

Sofia knew in an instant that the poor woman realized who she was. While she had no intention of revealing her identity to Lucia and Umberto, she was faced with having to make an instant decision, whether to deny the woman's instincts, or confirm them.

Gio attempted to maintain the guise. "Lucia, whatever you are thinking, do not worry yourself. My sister is no queen, although she does seem quite fond of ordering me around," he laughed nervously.

Lucia's eyes never left Sofia's. The two women stared at each other long and hard. The crackle of the logs was the only sound. Finally, Sofia reached her hand across the table and placed it on Lucia's arm. The poor woman was shaking.

"Lucia," Sofia offered quietly, "whether I am the queen or not, my unborn child and I are at your mercy. Are you up to this task?"

Lucia tore her gaze from the queen and looked at her brother, who returned her gaze and nodded, almost imperceptibly. When Lucia looked back at Sofia her eyes were brimming with tears. "Whether you are the queen or not, you are in danger from men who kill, defile and torture for their own greed and sick pleasure. I will do all I can to help you."

"Thank you," Sofia said as she grasped Lucia's hands in her

*own and kissed them.*

It was never discussed again. I saw in Lucia's face her understanding of my identity. To her enormous credit, she continued to refer to me as 'Maria'. The little cottage was cramped, but only Lucia, her children, and I slept indoors. 'Roberto' and Umberto slept outdoors.

Over the next few days, Lucia did her best to teach me how to bake bread and create simple stews. I was used to issuing orders and mediating disputes between my subjects. When I was not leading the kingdom from Montalcino castle, I was traveling, intervening and fighting on behalf of my subjects against the Church. It baffled me that I found the task of being queen so much easier than baking a decent loaf of bread.

As the time for your birth grew ever nearer, I slept less and less. I knew I would be giving you up. That fact tore at me. Quite honestly, I did not know how I was going to manage to separate myself from you. I longed to hold you in my arms, to kiss your sweet face, to sing you to sleep. I did not know yet if you were a boy or a girl, but it did not matter. What mattered was that I loved you. Your life inside of me gave my life meaning and hope. I was alive again in ways I had not felt for many, many years.

On Lucia's third night with us, I had finally slipped into a restless sleep in the early hours of morning. I was dreaming that the archbishop found me, and that he was beating me with his fists. I felt the blows and turned to flee, but he chased me. I fell. He stood on top of me, on my lower back, jumping. The pain was excruciating. I woke up.

The pain did not leave me when I woke.

"Lucia," I called in the dark. "Lucia!"

She roused herself and went to the fireplace to catch a twig on a dying ember and used it to light a candle. She was at my side quickly.

"Is it your waters?"

"No," I cried, "my back. I think my back is breaking."

"Stand up," she ordered and helped me out of bed.

We walked around and around the little cottage. The pain in my back did decrease a little, but then the labor pains took over. Lucia led me back to bed. By the time light began to fill the sky, the pains were more regular but too far apart to indicate a quick birth. Lucia left me to fix breakfast for everyone. I found myself desperately wishing for my mother and Bella. Lucia was wonderful, but like all children, I wanted the love of my family close.

Gio did come and sit with me. He held my hand and uttered reassurances, but I could see the fear in his eyes, and I did not have the strength to comfort him. I sent him to eat with the family.

I dozed on and off between the pains. By evening the pains were close together. My waters broke just after the evening meal. Lucia announced that it would not be long. I could not conceive how women endure such travails over and over. It made no sense to me.

Lucia ordered the men outside. The children were already asleep.

I will spare you the details of your actual birth. Lucia told me it proceeded normally without complications. She said I was blessed with an easy birth. What I will tell you is that when she laid you in my arms all the pain disappeared. Even the memory of the pain vanished. When I looked at your sleeping face, I knew why women endured such torment over and over. Love. I was overcome with the purest, most overwhelming love I had ever known.

## JULY 3, 1585

Lucia was to nurse you. She was concerned that it would only make things more difficult for me later if I chose to nurse you at all. She was also worried that you might have difficulty transitioning to her. She advised me to allow myself to dry up as soon as possible after your birth.

So, I agreed to allow Lucia to nurse you throughout the three days you remained with me once you were born. The human body is a fascinating thing. Every time I heard you cry, and watched as Lucia gave you her breast, my own breasts throbbed, my nipples oozed, and my heart broke for want of holding and feeding you.

That first night, however, I felt you stir next to me. The moon was bright, offering light to the inside of the little cabin and I watched you sleep, wishing you to feel my love. When you opened your eyes, you seemed to know that I was your mother. Your tiny hand wriggled out of the bunting, and I stroked and kissed the little fingers. Your grasp on my index finger was strong. When you started to fuss a little, I could not resist. I ached to nourish you with my own milk. Lifting you to my breast, I felt such a surge of emotion at your first suck. How would I give you up? How could I let you go? It would not be possible.

We fell asleep, you at my breast, in my arms. When morning came, I opened my eyes and saw Lucia standing over us shaking her head. Sheepishly, I said, "I could not resist."

"You may as well continue until we leave, then," she said.

But she was right, nursing you was going to make losing you all the more difficult for me.

The morning you were to leave, I was certain I would die. A mother cannot give up her child, her infant, without losing herself, her soul, her reason for living. As I watched the wagon with you, Gio, Lucia and her two children disappear into the woods, my legs gave way, my heart shattered. It felt as if my very spirit left me. I crumbled to the ground, and everything went dark.

I woke from my death sleep that night. Umberto sat next to me, watching like a mother hen, his fear-filled face relaxed into relief when I opened my eyes. He poured me a cup of wine and handed it to me. I drank the entire thing in a few large swallows.

Umberto stayed with me. He was to stay until Gio and Lucia returned, when he and Lucia would go home to Aquapendente. Then Umberto was to steal away once a week after that to bring me supplies.

The pain in my breasts as the milk dried up was nothing compared to the pain in my heart. I got up every morning. I went through the motions of the day. I walked to the meadow and sat. I had no energy to do anything I did not have to do.

Several days after your departure I lay curled up on the blanket in the field. Under the warmth of the sun, I thought about my life. It is amazing what we human beings endure. I do not understand how it is we go on in light of the atrocities we heap on each other, in light of the pain we bring to ourselves.

As I thought about the pain I had handed out to those I loved, I wished, selfishly, for my own end to come. I could not find a reason to continue my life, but I had made promises, and I would keep them. I have caused enough misery already.

I dozed, thinking of Bella—her strength, her courage, her spirit in the years after the death of James and my mother. When I woke, I spotted a doe moving cautiously out from the woods. She looked around for signs of danger. When she determined the meadow was safe, she moved into it. I did not see the fawn until she turned, grazing and nuzzled her offspring. I did not move. Slowly, they made their way closer to me. At one point, the doe started when she saw me. Her ears pricked up and she watched me for some time. She must have decided that I was no threat, for after a while, she resumed her grazing.

When the deer left, I went back to the cottage.

## JULY 13, 1585

I have not written for many days. I barely have enough energy to get up. This is more than the need to heal and rest after your birth, although I am certain that my body still needs to recover from the ordeal. That women of lower classes can resume their work within a day after they deliver astounds me. Perhaps their bodies are used to hard physical labors and heal more quickly and easily. It does cause one to wonder about the easy life of noble women and our inability to endure such travails.

It has been ten days since you were born, five since Lucia and Gio left with you. The pain I feel is no less than the loss of a limb. No, it is much worse. I would readily give up an arm or a leg to have you here, lying upon my breast, breathing your sweet, soft breath in and out.

I do not know when they will be back. Gio had calculated that they would be gone no longer than twenty days if there was no trouble. Hopefully, all has proceeded according to our plan. I am beginning to fret about things. There was no guarantee that Gio's sister and brother-in-law would take you in.

Umberto is sweet, but I do wish he might be someone with whom I could converse. He nods and gestures when I do address him, but I can tell he is uncomfortable with his inability to communicate. He hunts some in the day, chops wood for the fire and makes minor repairs to the cottage. It must be difficult for him to be here with me, but he smiles whenever he catches me looking at him.

Not surprisingly, my thoughts often turn to Bella. Memories of her strengthen me. I vow, here and now, to try to hold onto her spirit as my guidance and lamp when all around me is darkness.

### JULY 25, 1585

Gio and Lucia returned sooner than anticipated. As soon as Umberto and I greeted them, Gio and I walked to the meadow. I could not wait to hear the details of how things went on the journey.

It is July, and while I am certain that the flowers bloomed, and butterflies flitted about us, I was aware of nothing but the sound of Gio's voice. I clung to his arm as we walked, feeling weaker than I had when he left. He spread the blanket out on the grass, and we sat.

*"How did she fare on the trip?"* Sofia asked anxiously. *"She was so tiny; I was certain we should have waited until she was a little stronger."*

*He took her hand and waited for her to look him in the face. His smile was soft and full of tenderness. "You know that would have made it so much more difficult to say goodbye. As it was, you had trouble letting her go."*

*Sofia's eyes dropped. Her shoulders slumped. "It would not have mattered if I had never even seen her face. She was my life before she was born."*

*He watched as a few tears dripped from her eyes onto the blanket.*

*"Sofe," he whispered softly, "you did the only thing you could do. In your heart, you know that. She will be loved. She is safe."*

*Sofia swallowed hard, inhaled deeply and looked up at him. "Tell me everything."*

He offered her a smile, crossed his legs in front of him and began. "She is most assuredly your daughter. And, even at only a few days old, Catherine Isabella showed all signs of living up to her namesake's courage and determination," he laughed. "Not that I have much experience with babies, but I certainly expected more crying during the long ride to Voghera." He plucked a long, slender blade of grass and twirled it between his fingers as he continued. "We had no trouble on the road. We were simply travelling as husband and wife with three children. No one stopped us or questioned us. It was quite surprising." His face held a look of question as he made the last statement.

"What is it, Gio?"

"You will think me mad," he shook his head.

"I will not, I promise."

"There were times when I sensed your mother near." He coughed and blushed as soon as the words left his mouth.

Sofia smiled and reached for his hand. "Do not be embarrassed," she said. "I have felt that same presence many times since I conceived the baby."

"Well, then," he continued, "I believe that her grandmother may be watching over little Catherine Isabella still."

"How did your sister and brother-in-law receive her?"

"With open arms and hearts full of love," he smiled. "Francesca has longed for a child since she was a child herself. Her inability to conceive was starting to change her in ways that broke my heart." He tossed the grass back into the meadow. "When I handed the babe to her, her face was brighter than I have seen it since her wedding day."

Sofia forced a smile but felt the wrenching agony of giving up her only child even as she understood the joy her sacrifice gave to Gio's sister. "She deserves happiness," Sofia said softly, "after all, I took her father from her, too." Robert died not knowing that his wife was pregnant with his daughter.

"I wish," Gio said, ignoring her statement, "that you could have seen my grandfather's face when I told him the child's name. He looked at me as if I had just given him a treasure beyond compare."

Sofia's hand covered her heart. "How is he?"

"It is clear that the worry about your disappearance and our safety has taken its toll on him," Gio said. "But when he saw me and the baby and then heard the baby's name, there was only relief and joy in his tears."

"Just knowing that your grandfather will be part of Catherine's life consoles me," Sofia said.

"He gave me a message for you." Gio uncrossed his legs, bent them to his side and leaned on his hand.

Sofia waited, realizing that she had longed for some word from Lord Giovanni and found herself eager for any word from him.

"He wanted to write to you, but knew that it would be too risky, so he made me repeat his words to make certain I told you exactly. He said, 'Tell Queen Sofia that her courage and her sacrifice do her great honor.' He wanted you to know that our family will not rest until all Montalcino knows the truth. And," he shifted again to face her and looked directly into her eyes, "he said that it is Montalcino's greatest loss that you do not serve as her Queen."

Sofia's tears flowed as she listened, with gratitude, to the words of Lord Giovanni. Gio moved closer to her and held her as she cried. When her crying stopped, he said, "My grandfather also said to tell you that your mother would be very proud of you."

Sniffing, she reached for Gio's hands. "Gio, I want you to promise me something."

He watched her eyes, almost fearful of what she would ask.

"I want you to promise me that protecting and serving Catherine Isabella will be your utmost priority."

He looked at her, his pain written in every crease on his face. "Sofe, please, why would you ask such a thing? You are the queen.

It is you I have sworn to protect."

"My life as queen," she said so softly that he had to work to hear the words, "is over. I will never return to the throne. Likely, I will never see Montalcino castle again."

"You do not know that for certain," he interrupted. "We, my family and I, will fight for your return. We will try to clear your . . . "

"Gio," she put her fingers over his lips. "It will not happen. I do not even want it to." She let go of his hands and raised herself to her knees, then sat back on her heels in front of him. "Do you not understand? I am finished. The best thing I can do for Montalcino is done. I have given her a new queen."

Gio stared at her, wondering if there was anything he could say to change her mind, but knowing there was nothing. Her mind was made up. Nothing would change it. He dropped his head into his hands.

She reached out and placed her hand on his head. "You were born to serve the queen, just not this one."

Slowly, his head moved back and forth. "It is not right. It is not fair."

"Fair is not something I have learned to expect from life," she smiled. "I have taken so much from Montalcino. My daughter is the one good thing I can give in return. With you by her side, I know Catherine will be the kind of queen that Montalcino needs—and deserves." Her hand dropped back down into her lap. "If it is a life she chooses."

Gio did not respond. In the silence, she could feel him struggling with the promise. As she waited, the doe and fawn wandered out of the woods. She indicated, with a nod of her head, for Gio to look to his right. He smiled slightly, watching the deer as they grazed peacefully.

"Whether I am left here to grow old," she continued in a whisper, "or discovered and tried for heresy no longer matters to me. The only thing that matters is protecting Catherine and seeing her take her rightful *place on the throne.  Will you promise me to see that through, no matter what happens?"*

*A long, slow sigh, from deep within him escaped. "I promise."*

*Sofia raised her hand and placed it on Gio's face.  His beard was soft under her fingers.  Her gratitude was in her eyes and the sadness of her smile. "Thank you."*

### JULY 26, 1585

Lucia, Umberto, and the children spent the night upon Gio and Lucia's return from Voghera.  Lucia raved about what a good baby you were.  She found that she enjoyed the travel. She had never been far from Aquapendente.  After dinner that evening, she and I made a list of some of the things that might make my life a little easier and more pleasant in the cottage.  She promised to send things with regular supplies every week.

When they left the next morning Gio talked of staying a few more days.  I insisted that he must start back to you that very day and reminded him of his promise.  He agreed, but only on condition that I accept his visits once a month.  He had estimated that alone on horseback he could reach the cottage in two days. He would not allow me to deny him.

When he was home, his grandfather told him that the council, led by the archbishop, were governing Montalcino.  Apparently, the archbishop had the support of Rome to lead in the absence of a king or queen.  No one had the courage to argue with the Holy See. The archbishop publicly vowed to find the "cowardly queen who stole away under cover of darkness in shame and sin."

At least I could rest in the knowledge that even if they found me, no one would find you.

My days are long and lonely.  The time I spend with you,

writing to you, is bittersweet. I cherish the thought of you some-day reading these words but would so much prefer telling you stories of your grandmother's bravery and courage from across the room rather than across the kingdom. Your mother has lived a life full of regret, and while I do not regret sending you off to live a safe and, hopefully, happy childhood, I long for news of you. I wonder if your hair is growing in and changing colors. Who will you look like? My list of questions about you grows daily. Sometimes my mind fills me with fear, and I think I must leave this place and come to you, but then I go to the meadow to calm myself. Ultimately, my heart knows I have made the right decision for you.

I do go to the meadow every day. It is such a peaceful place. The doe and her fawn come regularly, and always around the same times of the morning and evening. They have become my family now, and I find myself looking forward to their visits. The doe seems to have accepted me. She moves out into the open field and seems to be looking for me. Perhaps that is just my imagination, but the thought does give me some sense of being, of belonging.

Once the mother and I acknowledge one another, the fawn appears. I love that the doe risks herself for the safety of her offspring. Somehow, it connects us, the doe and me, and vali-dates that I have, at long last, done something well and right by protecting you. I feel myself beginning to heal. Slowly, my spirit is returning to me. I am nourished by this place, the soli-tude and quiet beauty. God is here and sometimes I feel the gift of His presence so powerfully that I swear every blade of grass is alive with love.

I wonder if you will read these words someday and think your mother quite mad. Perhaps you will. Perhaps I am. But if it is mad-ness that creates the kind of fierce protective instincts of a mother for her child, then we are all mad. And it is a necessary madness.

## JULY 27, 1585

I awoke this morning with thoughts of trying to explain the governing structure of Montalcino to you. There is much that you will need to know, should you choose to sit upon the throne of your ancestors. But, after much deliberation about how to approach the topic, I decided that there will be others to whom that task may fall. Gio's family has a better understanding of government than most. That knowledge, combined with their inherent sense of fairness and astute political insights will serve you well. I would rather the time I spend here with you be more personal in nature. Oh, that I could know you and share in your thoughts as you grow!

I know that Lord Giovanni's family, including those you will know as your parents, will instill in you a loathing for the way our Church has twisted and knotted itself into a hideous creature of greed and power. Perhaps you will choose to fight the Inquisition in the same way that your great grandfather, your grandmother and your mother (finally) fought. My prayer is that by the time you are old enough to understand, it will be finished. But that is a prayer I do not, any longer, expect to be answered. Is it possible that a strong, decent religious leader will come along, become pope and abolish the rule that brought hundreds of years of punishment, greed, thievery, and torture? It is unlikely that he would be able to do so without a great fight. For now, the Inquisition thrives because those who support it thrive. For now, the benefits to those in power are too great. I fear it will take another Messiah, a warrior Messiah, to come to earth and wipe out the men of depravity who claim that their brutality is the will of God.

Your grandmother fought the horrors and injustices of the Inquisition more courageously than you can imagine. As I began to travel the kingdom, I was showered with stories of her bravery and compassion. She boldly confronted men in power, using her authority to abolish their greedy reigns, while comforting and caring for the victims like a great mother. Few women could do what she did. For that matter—few men could accomplish what your grandmother accomplished. I wish with all my heart that you and I both could sit in the glow of her love and soak up her knowledge, her wisdom and her love. I have wondered if, like me, your grandmother felt hope during periods, brief periods, when it appeared as if the Inquisition might be waning. Sadly, those periods were short lived and men whose lives are ruled by fear insured revival of the depravity.

You may choose to ignore your heritage and live your life as a citizen of Montalcino instead of its queen.

That, my love, is my gift to you. Choose well. Choose wisely. Choose love and life and happiness in whatever form it presents itself to you.


Umberto has just left. In addition to the supplies that sustain my life, today his sister included a tin for baking pies. I discovered a small patch of wild strawberries near the stream that runs close by. I thought to try to bake myself a strawberry pie. How hard can it be?

Much dearer to my heart is something else that Lucia sent, some powders for painting. Your grandfather was a gifted and talented artist. Hopefully, one day you will wander the halls of Montalcino castle and gaze upon his works of art. He would often invite me to his quarters. There he would teach me the art of mixing colors, stretching canvases and applying simple paints to create images of beauty and love. I learned the basics of the brush stroke from him. Sadly, I did not inherit his gift. Nevertheless, I plan to paint something for you, not on canvas, but on a wooden board that I found outside the cottage.

The weather-worn board is large, around three feet long on one side and two feet across. I think that, perhaps, it might be left over from the construction of the cottage. Perhaps it was the beginning of some table or bench that was never completed. It is two boards connected on the back by two narrow pieces of wood. The elements have rounded the edges, but it is the perfect size for what I intend to try to create. Several layers of paint should help to create a surface that will work for my intent.

My plan is to paint a family tree for you. Funny, I remember complaining to my mother about how I did not care to learn my family history. She was insistent that, as the youngest of a royal line, it was expected that I know from whom I was descended. Now, I am glad to have that knowledge at my fingertips . . . quite literally.

JULY 30, 1585

It has taken me several days, but I have made my own brushes. The rabbit skins left by both Gio and Umberto have provided me with a means to do so. The rabbit fur is fine and soft. It is perfect for fashioning brushes for the kind of detail I will need for the family tree. I have affixed rabbit hair to the end of some sturdy twigs using thread that Lucia sent. The most difficult part of the procedure was to trim the hairs to a point. My knife dulls quickly, and I must sharpen it often.

Working to prepare my materials has given me time to think about how to approach my project. I have decided to begin at the bottom of the board, with you, and work my way up to the top as far as I can go. The tree shall be just that, a tree, with leaves of the family hanging from its branches.

The creation of the tree forces me, finally, to accept that I really know nothing about your father's history. I am afraid that your family tree will be quite unbalanced in that regard. I am sorry for that, my love, as I am sorry for so many things. But I will tell you what I can about your father.

Your father, my darling, will likely never acknowledge you. You were conceived in a single moment of weakness, an unplanned and unexpected passion. I did not love your father, but your father loved me. His love for me was forbidden by his vows. Your father is Archbishop Pietro Biondi. It is he who is behind the plan to have me arrested and tried for heresy.

Lest you think that I hate him for this, know that I do not. Your father is a good man, whose sin torments him. I could see that I was a constant reminder of his vulnerability and his human failings. He will likely never acknowledge you as his because to do so means that he has failed his God. Also, if our plan succeeds, he will never know that you exist unless you choose to assume the throne. The archbishop's sin, I believe, is intolerable to him. Forgive him for that. He needs our forgiveness. I saw in his eyes that he will struggle the rest of his life for feeling that he failed God. Too well do I know how regret becomes a part of us. It seeps into our skin slowly but is finally absorbed fully through and through and into the soul until it becomes as much a part of us as the color of our eyes. His eyes. That is where the regret resides in your father. I saw it in the way his look of compassion altered from kindness to lovesickness to confusion, then, ultimately, pained regret. From there it was only a short time before the look hardened as it transformed into denial. For some, perhaps, cutting ourselves off from our regret is the only way to survive.

Oh, dear, I must try to remember not to abuse strawberries again and leave baking to the experts. The burnt pan of mush that emerged from the fire was not even recognizable. Fortunately, I do not depend on my cooking or baking to sustain me. An apple tree near the cottage looks as though it will supply me with much luscious fruit, but cooking does not seem to be in my best interests.

### AUGUST 4, 1585

G io arrived a few days ago. My anxiety over his being away from you vanished as soon as I saw him. The isolation has gotten the better of me, I fear.

I had realized, and have given considerable thought to, the dangers to my humors without the company of anyone to share my thoughts, my feelings, my voice. What took me by surprise was the sudden awareness of how much Gio's embrace emphasized the lack of touch in my life.

I suppose one never really thinks about such things until they disappear from us. It is only in our want, or our need, that absence is magnified.

Gio's hug was so like his grandfather's: warm, full, and big.

*"How is your grandfather?" Sofia asked when Gio was inside and settled with a cup of wine.*

*Gio did not answer but bent forward, leaning his elbows onto his knees. He stared down into his wine. When he looked up Sofia could see that he was crying.*

*"Oh, no, Gio," she got up and went to him. She knelt before him and wrapped her arms around his neck. "No, no. Not him." She cried as she, too, began to weep.*

*Together, the cousins cried. Their tears of grief blended, weaving a hymn of love and sadness for the man they both loved so dearly. When at last Sofia sat back on her heels, sniffing and wiping her face, she said, "Tell me."*

*Gio put his cup on the floor beside him and told her that in his last weeks, his grandfather was happier than he had been for some time.*

*"I wish," he said, "you could have seen him with your daughter. That child brought him more joy than you can imagine." Gio smiled at the memory of his grandfather's delight. "He loved to hold her. I often found him talking softly to her, smiling, and cooing. Once when I asked him what he was saying to her, he said, 'Secrets, my boy, for her ears only!" He would laugh and turn his full attention to her again. Later, when I would return, they would both be sleeping soundly. He would be in his favorite chair, his head tipped back and snoring softly. She was always on his chest. His arm held her securely under her bottom and her fist," he chuckled, "held tightly onto his beard."*

*Sofia smiled at the picture that Gio painted. "I am glad they had each other, if only for a short time."*

*Gio got up and wandered over to the open door of the cottage. He leaned against the frame and stared out for some time. Sofia came up behind him and slipped her arms around his waist. She held onto him tightly, resting her head against his back.*

*"They had their little routine," Gio finally said. "Every afternoon after my sister fed Catherine, my grandfather insisted that it was 'their time.' So, Francesca settled the baby with him and used the time to bake."*

*Gio cleared his throat. "That is how we found him. Catherine was sleeping soundly on his chest, but he was gone. He just died while they napped. I wish you could have seen him, Sofe. He had the sweetest smile on his face."*

*"I am glad he died peacefully," she said, "and with his arms around Catherine."*

Gio stayed only four days. I could not allow more time than

that.  But we filled those days with our memories of Gio's grandfather.  Our first evening together was a celebration of Lord Giovanni. I managed to make a decent dough, from which I made spaghetti and drizzled it with olive oil heated with sage.  Gio produced two bottles of wine he had brought with him.  They were the remaining bottles that I had given to Lord Giovanni before we all left Montalcino castle.  The scent and taste of the wine filled me with longing for my home.  I wonder why it is that smells can evoke such emotion.  Several times, as I wander through the wood before I reach the meadow, I stop to inhale deeply.  A small stand of chestnut trees reminds me of the chestnut festivals in Montalcino.  The nuts are not yet ripe, but when I break one open, the smell transports me to the little bridge leading to the castle.  For a moment, I am there, surrounded by proud sentinels, trees as tall as the castle, home so close I expect it to be steps away when I open my eyes.

Time with Gio is difficult to grasp.  Time, in general, has become a mystery to me.  Long days alone seem endless as I hunger for human contact.  When Gio does arrive, his presence is always bittersweet.  I fret so that he is away from you and find myself tense and anxious about his being away from you. But the days and hours he is with me fly much too quickly.  As I watch him ride away, I feel the relief of knowing he will be watching over you again in a few days, but my own days seem to grind down to a slow-moving existence punctuated by my sadness and occasional hunger.

I do not know what I would do if not for the now daily visits from my deer friends.  We meet mornings and evenings in the meadow where I sit with this journal. Last week, before Gio's visit, I sat on my blanket writing and eating some carrots that Umberto had brought.  The doe made her way over to me and stood at the edge of the blanket.  It was the closest she had ever come.  She stood, almost expectantly, until I held out a carrot on my palm. I was delighted when her soft doe lips tickled my palm as she took the carrots. When the carrots were gone, she meandered back to her fawn and continued grazing. Such a pure and simple act but one that highlights a day otherwise filled with loneliness.

Gio's visit also brought me news of you, which comforts me while simultaneously creating the ache in my heart that I always work to keep at bay. He tells me you are growing, smiling and cooing with great enthusiasm. Your adoptive parents are loving and attentive. You bring them much joy.

I had hoped that my disappearance might be enough to dissuade the archbishop and others from searching for me. It was a foolish and naïve thought but one that I nurtured hopelessly. News from Montalcino, through Gio, has crushed that folly.

The archbishop, with the support of Rome and financial backing from my own Privy Council, has apparently hired a trio of mercenaries to ferret me out of my "cowardly" hiding place. I confess to occasional thoughts of walking into Aquapendente and turning myself over to the authorities. Fortunately, my anger at all the injustice surfaces, and for a while, I seethe with righteous indignation. I will not turn myself over to anyone. Let them earn their wages. Hopefully, I can deplete the funds enough to be a concern. Montalcino has never been a wealthy kingdom. Perhaps the best revenge is to stay hidden long enough to use up what little funds are in the reserves!

I have continued to work on the family tree. Umberto brought more oils to mix painting powders.

I used the majority to cover the large plank of wood. Spots of it were a little too rough, so I created a way to smooth out the battered wood. Using crushed seeds, I rubbed them across the splintering parts of wood with the pestle from the mortar. My technique works quite well in smoothing surfaces. I have used it on the table and chairs to avoid splinters from cracked sections. Perhaps if I had not been queen, I might have been an inventor!

The family tree is blossoming. I have, in fact, covered the entire wood in a dark green. A heavy, thick trunk runs up the middle with thinner branches painted off the main on either side. I intend to create leaves of lighter green, reds of varying colors and possibly yellows, on which I will detail the actual family members and the dates I can remember. First, however, I need to determine where and how many leaves need to be on each branch. It is a time-consuming project, but one that keeps my mind occupied and my hands busy.

### AUGUST 10, 1585

Although the days are still warm, I can already feel the coolness in the early morning. The season will be changing soon. I am afraid of the shortening days. I am afraid of the bareness of trees that will make my hideaway more visible. I am afraid of the encroaching fingers of fall that will be followed too quickly by the icy hands of winter. I am afraid of the loneliness that will blanket me like the snow on the mountaintops. I am afraid.

### AUGUST 20, 1585

My darling, forgive my not writing much in these past weeks. Know that it was not because my thoughts strayed from you, rather, my mind turned on you almost constantly as I worked on the family tree. Painting your history has kept me sane, and kept my mind from spiraling down into my fears about a long, lonely winter.

Umberto did not come last week.  I will not starve, I have enough dried meats and flour to last for some time, but my alarm is increasing.  Where is he?  What has happened?  Have the arch-bishop's minions come to Aquapendente?  Is it too dangerous to come to me?

I worry that Umberto, Lucia and the children are in danger. They have endured enough hardship for a lifetime.  If Umberto does not arrive this week, I plan to go to Aquapendente to check in on them.  I pray they are safe.

All my senses are on alert.  I find myself jumping at the small-est sounds.  My sleep is restless.

### AUGUST 25, 1585

Still no sign of Umberto.  I almost went into town to see if I could find him but decided to give it one more day.  I am nearly finished with the family tree.  I do hope you will have it someday.

The day is warm, and I can tell that there will be few more of them.  I will spend what time I can outdoors giving myself to the sun and being with my doe and fawn.  The fawn is growing quickly, as I am certain you are.  Oh, that I could see you and know you!

### AUGUST 26, 1585

The moon was half full and directly overhead when I heard a horse in the middle of the night.  It is interesting to me that even though I thought my life was to be quickly ended, my prayers were for you, my child, my innocent daughter.

Even as I prayed, I slipped off my cot and grabbed your

grandmother's sword.  I would die fighting.

The knock was Umberto.  I nearly fainted with relief.  That relief was short-lived.

*"Umberto," Sofia cried, "thank God you are well! I have been so worried."*

*The young man held up his hand and listened just outside the door before finally coming in.  Hearing nothing but the sounds of night in the forest, he came in and closed the door behind him.  Sofia lit a candle. "What has happened? Is Lucia alright? The babies?" Sofia could not stop her questions from flying off her tongue.*

*Umberto nodded.  They were fine.  Everyone was safe.*

*"Something has happened, though," Sofia pressed.  "You did not come at all last week, and now, here you are in the middle of the night."*

*Umberto nodded again, his face a solemn mask of concern. Worry lines creased the ridge between his brows.  There were dark circles under his eyes.*

*"Sit," Sofia ordered.  She poured him some wine and sat at the table across from him.*

*Trying to ascertain all that had occurred was difficult.  Umberto used nods and grunts to convey information.  He was unable to read or write, rendering his ability to communicate frustrating.  Sofia could only ask questions.  Umberto answered as best as he could, but details were nearly impossible to gather.*

*"There is danger," Sofia began.  He nodded.*

*"Have the authorities come to Aquapendente?"*

*Yes, then a frustrated look.  No.*

*"Not authorities, but someone."  Emphatically, yes.*

*"Are they still there?"*

*No.*

*"Were they looking for me?"*

*Umberto's head dropped. When he lifted it back up his eyes were filled with concern. Yes, he nodded.*

*"Were you and Lucia questioned?"*

*At this Umberto nodded and waved his arms in a wide circle.*

*"Many were questioned." Yes.*

*"Did they seem satisfied that I was not in Aquapendente?"*

*Umberto shrugged.*

*"Have they gone?"*

*Umberto's look and gesture indicated that while the men had gone, he was not certain that they were gone for good.*

*"That is why you are here at night," Sofia said. "That was wise." She got up and paced around the little cottage. When she sat down across from him again, she said, "I do not want you to come again, not even in the middle of the night."*

*Umberto grunted and looked horrified at her suggestion.*

*She tried to reassure him. "Umberto, my friend, you have risked your life to care for me. I am deeply indebted to you and Lucia. But I will not put you and your sister in further danger." She got up and went to the cabinet where she kept her food supplies.*

*"I have," she showed him, "enough flour, dried foodstuffs and oil to manage for several weeks." She came back to the table. "Until the weather turns cooler there are wild roots, chestnuts and a few berries throughout the wood."*

*He stood and rushed out the door, returning a moment later with a sack full of food.*

*"And now I can live for over a month with what I have." She smiled and sat down. "I want your promise that you will stay away unless you are absolutely certain that there is no danger."*

*Umberto sat quietly. He dropped his head into his hands and shook it back and forth. She could tell that he did not like the idea of leaving her here indefinitely.*

*She needed to convince him to stay away.*

"Umberto," she said quietly, "what they did to you last time is nothing. They will do much worse to you and Lucia if they find you have been hiding me," she said. "And they will not spare the children," she added with emphasis.

He looked up at her sharply. Her point hit its mark. He stared at her in horror, and then she watched as his entire body gave in to her instruction to stay away. She felt an outpouring of gratitude and affection for Umberto as she reached across the table and placed her hand on his.

She watched his face crumble as he nodded.

"You are a courageous man," she smiled at him. "You would have been a remarkable soldier." It was not much, but the gift was given. He received it with gratitude. His back straightened ever so slightly as he allowed the generosity of her words to fill him. "Your duty is to your sister and her children."

He nodded and stood to leave. She walked him the few steps to the door. Before he left, he turned to Sofia. His eyes glistened with moisture as he knelt before her. Sofia placed her hand on his head. "Be safe, my friend, and give my love to your sister and her family. I will always remember you."

He stood, turned, and was gone.

### SEPTEMBER 8, 1585

It has been nearly two weeks since Umberto was here. How is that that I miss conversations with a man who could not speak? The thought amuses me. But miss him, I do. He had been my only regular contact.

I wonder if Gio will come this month and worry that he, like Umberto, is required to be more cautious.

The likelihood that the archbishop's thugs would head to

Voghera was never in doubt. But Gio's absence tells me that they may be keeping an eye on him. Perhaps his long absences from home have ignited questions.

Oh, my sweet one, perhaps I am alone too long. Perhaps I am losing what sanity was left to me. I hope it is not careless of me to begin to tell you about how you came to be where you are. It feels as if I have been here forever. I crave human contact. I want so desperately to hold you—to tell you everything. But I must be careful. I have written little these past days. The urge to complete work on the painting of the family tree drives me. Gio created a perfect hiding place for it. Underneath the frame of my sleeping cot, he attached four strips of wood. The painting slips between the wood and the bottom of the cot so that only that back of the old wood on which I paint, shows. If anyone were to turn the cot over, they would see only an addition of wood that appears to be a reinforcement of the cot itself. Very clever, I think.

Gio also knows where this journal remains hidden when I am not writing in it. I am, after all, determined that you should have it someday.

The weather changes daily. Days continue to shrink. Frost is on the meadow in the morning. My little fawn came to the meadow alone today. She has grown tremendously these past two weeks. I looked, in vain, for her mother. She was nowhere to be found. I fear hunters may have killed her.

*Sofia waited until the fawn left the meadow. Her thoughts swirled in her head as she thought about the disappearance of the doe. By the time she got back to the cottage, her fear about the doe had created a near panic in her. If there were hunters nearby, she was certain to be discovered.*

*She paced around the little cottage for the remainder of the morning. By noon she had calmed some and fixed herself a small meal,*

*wishing she had some wine. She had finished the last of the wine days*
*ago. Water had been her only source of liquid for three days.*

*As she sat and chewed slowly, she thought about Gio and her*
*daughter. Not knowing what was happening was intolerable. "I am*
*hiding," she thought, "to keep my daughter safe. If she is in danger,*
*what good is my hiding?"*

*She did not finish her meager meal but began to pace again.*
*The more she moved, the more her thoughts clarified. The clearer*
*her thoughts, the less ambiguous she felt. A plan developed in*
*her head.*

## SEPTEMBER 11, 1585

Catherine Isabella, I have found it intolerable to remain where
I am. You may or may not still be safe. Without a visit from
Gio I have no way of knowing. I suspect there is danger, and if
that danger is the result of the search for me, then I know what
I must do.

I will leave my hiding place at dawn. I am sorry, my love, but
the family tree will remain unfinished unless some miracle occurs.
With any luck, I will return to complete it soon.

I am not afraid to travel alone. Perhaps living alone these
past months has trained me for this next task. In my peasant disguise, I am coming to Voghera. I will not reveal myself there but
plan only to try to discover whether you and Gio's family are safe.
If you are safe, as is my most fervent prayer, I will continue to
hide, perhaps in another kingdom. At the very least, I will disappear without endangering anyone else with knowledge of my
whereabouts.

If you are not safe . . . if the fact of my hiding has caused
harm or danger in any way, I will turn myself in. I will be tried

and executed.  So be it.  I am no longer afraid.  But, before I die, I must know that you live, and live safely and happily.

I will attempt a good night's sleep.  Tomorrow I come.

PART TWO

_____SINS AND SACRIFICES

Sleep did not come easily for Sofia that night. Her body tingled in anticipation, her mind raced with fear for her daughter and Gio's family. Her nerves buzzed in anxiety as she envisioned leaving her hiding place. Part of her was eager to leave her life of solitude and loneliness, but even in disguise she knew that she was easily recognizable. Anything, she thought, even if I am discovered and put to death, is better than this life I have been forced to live.

As she struggled to sleep, she wondered whether she should just leave in the night. She even got up and dressed for travel. But when she opened the door of the cabin, there was no moon. The pitch black of the forest made it nearly impossible to see. "I will walk off a cliff in this blackness," she said out loud. And she returned to her bed still fully clothed.

It was not until the early morning hours that she finally fell into a deep, exhausted slumber, content with her new plan. She intended to be certain that Catherine Isabella was safe, then quietly slip out of the country into anonymity.

She dreamt of both Catherines, mother and child. In her dream both lived, her mother caring for her baby. She watched from a distance, unable to connect to the scene, as if she were blocked from it by a thick, heavy glass. Calling them elicited no reaction. Her voice bounced back at her, as if she were in a large, cavernous room. They could not hear her, they could not see her, so she had to be content with watching them together. And she was.

As the dream continued, her mother and her baby played together. The baby laughed in delight as she was tossed into the air and caught by her grandmother. The child's laughter grew louder as she shrieked with happiness . . .

The shriek is what woke her. It was not from her dream. It was the creaky hinge of the cottage door. She was awake, instantly, but as she attempted to sit up, she met the tip of a sword in the middle of her chest.

The predawn light had just begun to filter through the trees, but there was enough to see that three men had entered. The one holding the sword against her smiled, but there was a cruelty in his eyes.

"Going somewhere, Queen Sofia?" he jeered.

She pushed herself up slowly, backing away from the point of his sword, cursing herself for not leaving in the night when she struggled with sleep.

When she did not answer, he added, "Actually, you are. Get up, you are coming with us."

Sofia got up slowly, trying to determine if she could maneuver close enough to grab her sword. He saw her eyes dart to it and stepped between her and the sword laughing, "I do not think you will need this," he said as he picked it up and tossed it to one of his compatriots.

The other two had been ransacking the cottage. When Sofia was guided away from her bed, one of the men pulled her bedding off the wooden frame and slashed the coverlet with his sword, spilling the grass and filling everywhere. "Nothing," he said. Then in a single move he reached down, tipping the bed frame up against the wall. The painting remained in place, the backside of the old wood visible. For a moment, Sofia thought he would rip it from its hiding place, but all he did was stab the point of his sword at it. She could see a touch of the dark green peeking out from one of the corners of the painting, but in the dim light, to the unknowing eye, it was just a dark spot of old wood.

"The place is clean," he said, "apart from this little sack of gold." He smiled.

"A little reward for our trouble in finding you." The man holding her at sword point smiled at her again. "How thoughtful."

Until then, the third fellow had said nothing.

"Let us go," he finally spoke. "The archbishop is waiting."

They had a horse waiting for her along with their own.
Ropes from her horse to two of theirs ensured that she would
not be able to escape. Her hands were tied together, then tied
to the ropes around her horse's neck. Once mounted, they
began the ride toward Aquapendente.

So, Sofia thought as the horses' hooves padded on the soft,
dewy ground, the archbishop has found me. Now he can try to
erase me from his memory. I hope it will give him some peace.

The men said little as they rode but commented periodically on
the success of their task. "Did you really think you could hide forever?" one of them asked her. She said nothing but rode the entire
way in silence. The colors of the clouds before the sun peeked over
the horizon sang to her soul. She both ached and was relieved that
she would not see another sunrise. As her eyes drank in the beauty
of the sky they blurred with her tears. Her prayers were silent. Her
conversation and gratitude were for God alone.

As they neared the edge of town, the sun breached the horizon. On the outskirts of Aquapendente, a small rise provided the
perfect spot for alerting visitors to the dangers of heresy. It was
where some of those tried, convicted and executed were often put
on display in gruesome manners. The spikes were tall and deeply
embedded in the ground, their pointed tips reached toward the
sky like thick knitting needles. Sofia saw that a body dangled hid-
eously from one of the spikes, and even from a distance she could
see the silhouettes of scavenging birds pecking at the head of the
body hanging there. As they neared the spikes, she forced her eyes
closed, not wanting to look upon the spectacle of some poor soul
dying a torturous death. She prayed.

When the party drew closer to the spikes, her horse stopped. Every hair on her body was raised in fear. "Am I to join this soul?" she thought. "Is this my end?" Her stomach lurched at the thought of being thrust upon one of the spikes to wait for death while birds pecked at her eyes. Even as she thought this last, a turkey vulture sitting on top of one of the spikes screeched at her.

She looked up. Umberto's empty eye sockets gaped at her. She nearly fainted, and would have, but for the pain that shot through her heart. How she managed to stay on her horse was impossible to say, for when the pain in her chest subsided, the blood drained from her face, rendering it numb in the process. She heaved, but her stomach was empty. Only spittle dripped from her mouth.

It was his voice, the one who had held the sword to her breast, that brought her back to her strength, her resolve. "Your friend, I believe." The way he made the statement made it clear that Umberto was how he found her. She wondered how and hoped that Lucia and the children were spared.

They continued their slow journey toward Aquapendente. There were no people in sight. As they entered the outskirts of the town, the streets were ominously empty. As they neared the square, Sofia heard the cacophony of the crowd. When the town center appeared, the noise sounded like a celebration, but as her horse was led into the crush of people an eerie silence settled over the square.

Sofia looked around, scanning the crowd for any sign of Lucia. If Lucia were present, Sofia could not find her. If Lucia were not there, then perhaps she and the babies were safe. It was not until she had satisfied herself that Lucia was not among the town folk, that she noticed the pillar. To the side of the pillar sat an abundance of firewood and kindling.

This is how I will die, she thought. She closed her eyes

and prayed that Lucia did not already suffer the same fate.

"Bring the prisoner forward!"

The familiar voice felt oddly comforting to Sofia. And, though she knew it would not remain so, she allowed herself a moment of relief in knowing that she would soon leave her life of sorrow behind. She looked up. There, high on a makeshift dais, sat Archbishop Pietro Biondi. A small writing desk was next to the archbishop. A young man she recognized from Montalcino sat there, nervously fidgeting with pen and paper, ready to record every word of her trial.

Her horse was led forward to the edge of the platform and stopped. One of her captors came to assist her off her horse. She ignored him, brought her leg over in front of her and slid down the horse landing on her feet. Her hands remained tied in front of her. Two of her former guards had descended the platform and pulled at the rope connected to her wrists. At each elbow two more guards appeared and propelled her forward and up the steps. When she stood directly in front of the archbishop, she held his gaze.

"Queen Sofia?" he began with so much sarcasm in his voice that the crowd chuckled. She looked anything but a queen. She was in peasant dress, and her hair was disheveled.

"You," he continued in a more serious tone, "have been brought here on charges of heresy." He opened and unrolled a scroll. "You are charged with lustful and wanton behavior, lascivious conduct, and adultery."

The adultery charge surprised her. She wondered who had the audacity to accuse her of sexual relations with a married man. Not that it mattered. None of it mattered.

"What do you have to say to these charges?" The archbishop interrupted her thoughts.

Sofia stood silently. She had no intention of responding to

any of the charges. Almost as if she were sitting alone in her little cottage hideaway, her thoughts were her own. How ironic, her mind mused, I am guilty of so much . . . yet I will be tried and executed for lies. My sins stand tall as boulders, marking milestones on the path of destruction created by me, yet it is my innocence that drives me to the gates of hell. As she thought this last, the corners of her mouth flickered a small, sad smile.

The archbishop saw the smile. "I fail to see what amuses you, Queen Sofia." The anger in his tone was punctuated by the slither of words as they hissed out of his mouth through teeth clamped tightly by his clenched jaw.

He stood and made a show of walking around her thin frame.

"You have lost a considerable amount of weight," he said looking her up and down. "Or," he paused for effect, "the child of your sinful ways, the child you carried in your lascivious womb when you sneaked away from Montalcino, has been delivered."

He stopped in front of her, his eyes narrowed and bore into hers. He waited for her to respond. She remained silent, matching his stare.

"It is of no concern to me whether you attempt to speak," he said loudly as he sat back down, "or not. Your wordless friend gave us enough information during his interrogation. We know the male child died during childbirth."

He stood again and moved next to her to address the crowd. "Your Queen not only abandoned her throne to hide her sin, but in doing so she risked the dangers of childbirth without benefit of assistance. In doing so, she caused the death of the child who could have been your King! She," he shouted to the crowd, "has left Montalcino without an heir!" He turned slowly to her again and added, "All to hide her sin and shame."

Sofia listened to him as he continued to berate her. She had always expected to be afraid when this moment came, and she had been when she saw Umberto's lifeless body spiked on the road. The archbishop was the father of her beloved child, but he would never know. He did not deserve to know. He did not want to know. The thought occurred to her that she might expose him, might say the one thing to the hypocrite standing in judgment of her that would make him pause, stumble and reconsider his intent to have her killed, but she was suddenly flooded with the understanding that Umberto died protecting her child. A peaceful calm filled her. The knowledge that Catherine remained a secret, that no one knew the baby existed, gave her the strength to face her fate. Catherine might remain safe. And so, the words, "the child was yours" rose up from her anger and quickly disintegrated like a child's sandcastle melted by a single wave. If she could only know that Lucia and the children were safe. If only . . .

Her thoughts were jerked back to the present reality. He was asking her, again, if she had anything to say in her defense. Her refusal to answer his questions was frustrating him. She could tell from the way he moved from his seat to standing and speaking to the crowd.

"Good," she thought. "Let him struggle. I will give him nothing. He deserves nothing."

"Confess your sins!" he urged Sofia.

As he nearly shouted this last, she thought she saw the beginnings of fear in his eyes. If she confessed, she realized, he could acquit her.

"Confess," he said more softly, the slightest hint of pleading in his voice, "and spare your life." Still, she stood, stoically mute.

"You leave me no choice, Queen Sofia," he announced loudly, but his voice had lost its potency. "Your silence condemns you." He sat, nearly fell, with a look of confusion and defeat on his face. "Your punishment will be carried out at once." He did not look at her again.

"Such hypocrisy," she thought. "I will never understand how priests, nuns, and even cloistered monks, justify their mistresses and lovers and condemn others for the same sins."

Lord Navona from her Privy Council stood. "Queen Sofia of the Kingdom of Montalcino," he addressed her. "You have been found guilty of promiscuity, wanton lustfulness, and adultery. Further, you attempted to hide your sins by abandoning your subjects to give birth to a child conceived without benefit of the Sacrament of Holy Matrimony." He looked out over the crowd, clearly enjoying the rapt attention of so many. "Your penance is death by fire." He paused. "At once."

The crowd shouted approval, but Sofia noted that many eyes met hers, holding sorrow in what appeared to be expressions of sympathy. From her position on the dais, there were many to the sides she could see. Those whose eyes met hers did not join in the exuberant shouts. She returned their looks with grateful eyes, accepting the last gifts of kindness she would know on this earth.

Four guards from her own court, mounted the stairs to the dais where she stood. Surrounding her, they marched her down the stairs, through the crowd and toward the beam in the middle of the square. Her hands were untied from in front of her and tied behind the beam. Even as the kindling piled high around her, her thoughts were of her daughter. If they think my child is dead, where has Gio been? Dear Lord, she prayed, let me die knowing my child lives. I beg of You, give me that knowledge and I will suffer this death secure in the knowledge that You are the only judge whose sentence I will accept.

She hoped to be able to die without a whimper, without a cry, but she did not know if that was possible. Would the pain be so great that she screamed in agony against her own will? Would the flames fuel and lick at her resolve, finally forcing her to cry out for mercy? She did not know.

There would be no mercy. That much she did know. As the wood pile surrounding her grew higher, her heart started to pound. She felt her knees weaken. If she had not been so tightly tied to the pillar, her legs would give out underneath her. Her body trembled violently; her chest rose and fell in quick bursts of tiny breaths. She wanted to scream before the wood was even alight, but she did not. Even in her panic, she knew that there would be no rescue.

She closed her eyes to keep the fear from escaping. She clamped her teeth down on her tongue to keep the screams of terror in. She prayed for God to bring her home. Silently, she begged forgiveness for her sins, for courage, for peace.

She bowed her head as her mouth murmured softly, "Help me, help me, help me." She choked back the sobs desperately beating for release in her breast and at the back of her throat. "Let death come quickly, Lord. I am so afraid."

The sounds of the sticks and wood being piled around her stopped; as did her heart, her breath and her hope. She remained perfectly still, her ears acutely aware of every sound. Perhaps, she thought, I can hold my breath when the flames overtake me. If I can pass out, I will not die suffering in agony.

Whatever last vestige of mercy she might have hoped for was dashed when she heard the whoosh of flame from the torches. There was no ring of gunpowder around her neck to explode and kill her the instant the fire reached that high. That would have been in place already. But she had hoped for the wood to be soaked with the flammable liquid to speed the fire. It was not to be.

She heard the crackle of the fire as the kindling ignited. When she opened her eyes, she saw only two of the three men who were holding torches to the pile. One was behind her, she could not see him, but she heard the snap and sound as the flames grew at her back.  For some reason the flames she could not see frightened her the most.  Perhaps it was because she preferred to face her killer.

Her killer.  She looked up to the dais.  The archbishop sat leaning on the arm of his chair, his eyes covered by his hand.  She willed him to look at her, willed him to look her in the eyes to share this terror . . . to share his sin.  He did not look up.

The flames caught and grew.  A wall of smoke wafted up before her, momentarily blocking the crowd from her vision.  The heat built all around her as the fire crept closer and closer, like a prowler sneaking up to steal her soul.  The closer and more intense the blaze grew, the more her cry threatened to escape.  It was as one wall of smoke parted, making way for the shifting waves of heat, that she saw him.

At the edge of the crowd, between two small houses, on a horse, Gio appeared.  His horse was lathered with foam and breathing hard.  Gio's face held a look of pain she recognized too well.  It was the same face she knew her own held when she discovered she was too late to save her mother.

The heat from the fire was intense.  It crept toward her dress and began to singe her hair.  But when she saw Gio, she was able to give voice to the cries that needed to escape.

"Catherine?" she screamed.  "Catherine!"

The archbishop looked up at her, but she did not notice.  Her eyes were on Gio.  The murmuring crowd voiced their surprise, "She calls for her mother!"

"Sin upon sin," someone shouted, "you should call for God!"

She heard none of it.  Her eyes locked with Gio's as his tears spilled out.  He nodded and forced the smile that told her Catherine was alive and well.

Her clothing caught fire, and breathing became an act of excruciating pain as the heat seared her lungs.  Thank you, Lord.  Catherine is well, your mercy is great, she thought as she raised her eyes to the heavens. She closed her mouth to the heat and unbelievable pain that had begun to engulf her.

The suffering was unbelievable. The skin began to melt from her body. Her head arched back. There was no containing her screams of agony. She opened her mouth to let them escape.

She never saw the arrow that put her out of her misery. It flew through the flames, pierced her heart and caught fire with the rest of the wood.

So engrossed in the delirious delight at watching the queen burn, the crowd was oblivious to the arrow. They waited for screams of pain that never came. Even the archbishop, whose eyes were riveted upon her from the moment she screamed the name "Catherine," did not see the arrow.

If any had been aware enough to know that an arrow had taken the life of the queen burning within the raging fire, they would not have been able to say who shot it. Gio was gone.

Gio knew his arrow would end Sofia's suffering before it reached her. Even though his hands shook with rage and overwhelming grief, his aim was true. He turned his horse as soon as the arrow left his bow and returned to the little cottage.

Once inside, he removed the painting from the underside of the bed frame and set it near the door. Next, he went to the fireplace. As they had seen Father Tim do, he knelt and removed a small brick from the side, near the floor. He reached in. His hand emerged with the journal.

Gio remained kneeling on the ground for some time. If the crowd, robbed of the screams of Queen Sofia by an unseen arrow, had been near the cottage where she hid all summer, their hunger would have been satisfied. Gio clutched the journal to his chest as his cry wailed loud and long, carrying itself beyond the treetops, through the clouds and to the very heavens.

In the meadow, a young fawn startled at the scream as she

grazed near the place where the carrots were sometimes found. When the sound stopped, she moved to where the grass was flattened, and curled herself up to rest.

Gio did not linger at the cottage. He got what he came for, mounted his horse and made his way to Castiglione d' Orcia. There, he found Father Tim in his little chapel, on his knees, alone.

When Gio entered, Father Tim did not get up, he did not turn around. He heard the horse arrive, heard the fall of steps as Gio entered.

"Is she dead?" Father Tim's voice echoed in the silent, empty space.

"Yes." Gio walked up the aisle of the little church. His pace was slow. His eyes bore into the crucifix hanging over the altar. Falling onto one of the pews, he sat, waiting for the priest to finish his prayers. When Father Tim crossed himself and got up a few moments later, Gio said, "Why do you even bother? What good has it ever done?"

Father Tim walked over to Gio and sat next to him on the pew.

"Do you really want to know?"

Gio snorted. "No."

"Tell me what happened," the priest urged softly.

"I arrived at the cabin and found it empty, ransacked. She was gone." His eyes clouded over, remembering the desperation he felt when he found the cabin in disarray and Sofia nowhere. "I rode as fast as I could to Aquapendente. She was not hard to find." He leaned over and placed his head in his hands, elbows resting on his knees. "The whole town was in the square and . . . "

Gio crumbled, sliding off the pew onto his knees on the floor. A huge sob rose up from deep within him.

He wept briefly. Father Tim placed a hand on his back. Gio pulled himself back up to the pew. "The flames were already surrounding her by the time I reached the edge of the square.

Her clothing was starting to burn."

He got up and walked away toward the altar a little. When he turned back to Father Tim, he said, "She saw me and called out her daughter's name. It was the only thing that mattered to her, knowing that Catherine was safe."

"Were you able to reassure her without revealing yourself?" Father Tim asked.

"Yes," Gio answered. "Then I killed her."

Father Tim waited for Gio to explain, wondering how he could have managed to kill someone who was already being killed.

"I shot an arrow through her heart," he said softly. "I could not bear to watch her writhe in such agony." Gio's face reflected everything . . . his sorrow, his guilt, his loss, his unbelievable pain. "I do not care that killing her means I suffer for eternity . . . I already live in hell."

"Gio," Father Tim said as he got up and walked over to him. "I do not believe that you committed any sin by speeding Sofia's death. It was an act of compassion. I am glad you could help her die by eliminating the kind of torture she would have endured." The priest reached out a hand and placed it on Gio's shoulder. "Even a minute less of the kind of pain she would have suffered in the flames was an act of mercy."

Father Tim wanted to comfort Gio further, but at that moment someone entered the chapel. They both turned to see Lucia framed in the doorway.

Lucia's expectant face revealed itself slowly as she walked up the aisle away from the purple glow of sunset pouring in through the door. When she was close enough to the two men, she saw the look on Gio's face. It stopped her dead.

She stared at him for the longest time before, finally, asking, "Both of them?"

Gio walked over to her. When he stood directly in front of her, he said simply, "I am sorry."

She collapsed into his arms. He lifted her motionless body. Father Tim said, "Follow me."

Once inside his home, Father Tim wet a cloth and laid it on Lucia's forehead. She came out of her faint. Gio sat nearby as Father Tim held her hand.

She sat up. "Do you know what happened?" she asked.

"Not any details, and I did not stay to find them out. They burned Sofia. I found Umberto's body outside of town," he hesitated, not knowing if she could take hearing how he had been tortured.

"On the spikes?" she asked, her horror clearly reflected in her face. The look quickly faded, replaced with grief over the loss of her sweet, kind, gentle brother. "He was so proud to watch over her. I suppose they followed him. I am sorry for you, too, Gio. I know you and Sofia were close."

It was the first time she had ever used Sofia's real name.

"Father Timothy from the village of Castiglione d' Orcia to see you, Archbishop," his secretary announced. The archbishop had converted the living area of his predecessor's quarters to his office. His desk sat near the windows where previously floor to ceiling drapes used to hang. The drapery was still there but pulled back to allow in the light.

The archbishop looked up, a puzzled look on his face. "Send him in but make him wait a few moments."

Minutes passed, during which time the archbishop attempted to ascertain what might possibly bring that heretical priest within his reach. When Father Tim entered the room, the archbishop remained seated in a large, comfortable chair near the crackling fire, his face a mask of judgment and disdain.

"Archbishop Pietro," Father Tim greeted the cleric. As was proper, the priest knelt and kissed the ring on the outstretched hand of the archbishop.

Still, the archbishop said nothing. Coolly, he waited for the priest to experience the discomfort in his lack of greeting.

Father Tim felt no such discomfort, for he was beyond cowering beneath the glare and criticism of his convictions. When the archbishop did not offer him a seat, or a glass of refreshment, the priest said simply, "Archbishop, I will promptly get to the reason for my visit."

The seated superior raised his eyebrows and lifted his hand waving it nonchalantly, palm up, as if to say, "Proceed, you are wasting my valuable time."

"I have come to hear your confession," Father Tim said solemnly.

The archbishop's eyes widened, his body stiffened as he glared at the man still standing in front of him. "What nonsense is this?" he demanded, the rage instantaneous on his face. He stood, his face red with fury. "How dare you come to my quarters and insult me. I should call the guards and have you arrested at once!" He started for the door as if to make good on his promise. As he made his way he said, "You will burn like the queen for your audacity!"

"You may call the guards, if you like, Archbishop," Father Tim said calmly. "But, before you do you should know that it is because of Queen Sofia that I am here."

Archbishop Pietro Biondi stopped dead in mid-stride as if he had been hit midsection by a catapulted boulder. He closed his eyes and tried to catch his breath before he turned around. As he turned, he worked to make his face hold on to the vestiges of his outrage, but his pallor, so fiery red a moment ago, had paled. He narrowed his eyes at the priest. "What can a heretic from the grave have to say to me?"

Father Tim held the archbishop's glare. "What convinces you that she was a heretic? What was her crime?"

"Do not play games with me, Priest! You, as well as all Montalcino knows, she was a lascivious whore."

"I knew Sofia from the day of her birth," Father Tim offered quietly. "She was many things, but she was no whore. She was, in fact, a virgin."

"Well, you are wrong. God and I know better." The archbishop made his way to his desk, where he sat with a look of contempt.

"Let me clarify," the priest continued, "she was a virgin until the night of Lady Isabella's death."

Father Tim watched and waited until the enormity of his statement wove its way into the reaches of the archbishop's memory. As he watched, the face of the man behind the desk altered slightly. If he could have seen the archbishop's hands, he would have witnessed them begin to shake uncontrollably.

"What is this?" the archbishop asked suspiciously. "Are you attempting to blackmail me? What did that whore tell you?"

"Only this," the priest said as he stepped closer to the desk, "that as she grieved in the church, you consoled her. As the result of that consolation, to which she freely admitted succumbing, she became pregnant."

"Lies!" The archbishop stood and fumed. "How dare she implicate me in her life of sin!" He went to his side table and poured himself a large goblet of wine, gulping it down without pausing for a breath.

"It is no lie," Father Tim said, "and the sin was not hers alone." When his stunned and shaking superior failed to respond, or even turn around to look at him, Father Tim continued. "It is easier to paint others the villains than to admit our own weakness. Queen Sofia knew you to be a fair and righteous man of the cloth.

She did admire and appreciate your effort to place God above all things, especially considering the destructive path taken by your predecessor." Father Tim waited just a moment before adding, "And, she knew that you loved her."

Father Tim walked over to where the archbishop still stood facing the wall. "Queen Sofia was pregnant. You were correct in that accusation. But there was only one time that conception could have occurred."

The archbishop remained facing away from the priest. "You do not know that," he said, his voice hoarse and heavy.

"Think back on that night," Father Tim encouraged him. "We are not experienced in the ways of such things, but surely you noticed there was blood."

When the archbishop remained silent, Father Tim continued. "Queen Sofia kept a journal. I have read it . . . "

"There was no such document! We searched the cottage!"

"It was hidden very well, and only one person knew where to look for it. In it, she tells of the night that Lady Isabella died and what happened in the church." The archbishop struggled against his memory but was unable to block it from surfacing. How many times had he thought about that night and worked to erase it from his mind, from his body's aching need to have her again. Eventually, he did block the memory when he absolved himself by thinking that she had tempted others, not only him. She was a temptress and that was the only way to explain his falling prey to her seduction. Images from that night seeped through the wall he had constructed around them, like blood oozing through a bandage. There was blood, he remembered it confusing him, concerned that he had hurt her in his all-consuming passion.

"God," Father Tim said gently, compassionately, "made men like us and filled us with the desire to serve Him, but, after all, we are just men. And Queen Sofia was a woman, one who stirred you.

Your sin was not in loving her or wanting her. Your sin was in the lie you told yourself and made others believe."

The archbishop's shoulders slumped. His head dropped. He fell hard onto his knees. "Oh, dear God, what have I done?" he cried into his hands.

Father Tim walked the few steps over to the weeping man and placed his hand upon the archbishop's head. He spoke, in Latin, the words of absolution and forgiveness that were the sacrament of Confession. He made the sign of the cross and walked quietly to the door. With his hand resting on the handle, he turned back to the broken, weeping man. "Two last things you should know, Archbishop: you have, and always had Sofia's forgiveness, and, you have a daughter."

Father Tim closed the door quietly behind him.

Archbishop Pietro Biondi stayed kneeling on the floor for some time. His legs would not support him, that much he knew. Eventually, when he could stand, he made his way to his bedroom and walked to the foot of the bed. He sat on the edge.

A dressing table sat opposite him. Looking up, he stared into the mirror, into his tear-streaked face, now lined with pain. His head shook slowly back and forth, back and forth. When it stopped, he waited, staring at himself, as if his refection owed him an explanation. When he could look at himself no longer, he slid off the bed onto the floor, turned and knelt against his bed.

Pietro Biondi spent the remainder of the day in prayer. He never heard his secretary enter or stand silently at the bedroom door before leaving.

He remained on his knees for the entire night, dozing period-ically, then jolting awake, still on his knees. He prayed. He begged God to show him what to do. He asked for forgiveness. He tore at his clothing. He cried and prayed some more.

Before dawn he pushed himself slowly from the bed, his

legs cramping and his knees sore.  God answered his prayers in a
dream.  The archbishop removed his robes and placed his ring on
the dressing table.

Archbishop Pietro Biondi packed a few belongings and left
Montalcino castle on foot.  No one saw him leave.

## YEAR OF OUR LORD 1600

Giovanni Oddono gave his niece, Catherine Isabella—who was in reality his cousin—her true mother's journal on the event of her fifteenth birthday. Her family celebrated the day, and when dinner was finished, Gio, along with his sister Francesca and brother-in-law Pasquale, sat the girl down by the fire. Gently, lovingly, they told her the story of how she came to be their daughter and who she really was.

She was quiet for some time but appeared calm and almost accepting of her identity.

"Why have you not told me before this?" she asked without anger. The question and her demeanor held the air of curiosity and confusion. Then, as if piecing together pieces of her life, she asked her parents, "Is this why you wished for me to wait before committing to a convent?"

Gio looked at Francesca and Pasquale. It was Pasquale who answered. "Daughter, and you will always be my daughter regardless of your path, it is your life to choose the convent if you desire." Pasquale leaned forward and took Catherine's hands in his. "I can only ask your forgiveness for waiting—and asking you to wait before deciding your future." He bowed his head. When he lifted it, he added, "Yes. The answer to your question is yes."

Francesca stood and turned to face the fire that was now only embers in the fireplace. "Catherine, you are so strong, so spiritual, so . . . so determined. But you are also wise. Your father and I have watched your wisdom, compassion and courage increase these past two years. In part, we waited and watched for that." She turned toward her daughter. There were tears in her eyes.

Gio saw the tears and went to his sister. Placing his hand

on her shoulder, he turned to Catherine and said, "You do not remember your grandfather."

"You were named for him," Catherine said, smiling softly at Gio. "And I feel that I know him from the stories you have always told me about him."

Gio smiled and nodded, remembering some of the stories shared in this house about his namesake. "He was a gift to us all," Gio said. "It was he who asked us to wait until as close to your sixteenth birthday as possible to tell you the truth about your lineage."

Catherine nodded, accepting this new fact. She stood up, and the irony of her almost regal stature, struck her family for the first time. "I have only ever wanted to be a nun," she said softly. Moving over to the window, she looked out at the nearly full moon and sighed. "I have only ever wanted to serve God."

"Catherine," Gio said as he walked over to her. "You do not need to decide tonight. Take Sofia's journal…"

"She was really my mother?" Catherine interrupted him. "The queen of Montalcino was my mother?"

"And you are named after your grandmother, who was also queen. Your great grandfather, Edward, was king before her." Gio said. "Wait here, I have one more gift for you."

Gio disappeared and returned with a large package wrapped in canvas. "This is for you, as well."

Catherine sat down again and untied the ribbon that held the canvas. When it dropped to the floor she was astonished to see the family tree that held her ancestors names on leaves.

"Your mother," Gio stopped horrified that he might have offended his sister. "I am sorry, Francesca."

Francesca smiled. "Do not worry yourself, dear Gio, it is a fact. One that has always been true. Catherine is a gift Sofia bestowed on me for safe keeping. It does not offend me to share the title."

Gio nodded, turned back to Catherine and said, "Here you are." He pointed at a leaf on the very bottom of the giant tree. "Your mother painted this for you while she was in hiding after having given birth to you. She sent you here to keep you safe."

"I am not sure that this will change my desire to enter the convent," Catherine said softly. "If you do not mind, I would like to be alone."

Catherine's uncertainty was unusual. It spoke to her surprise and confusion at the news. In her fifteen years on the earth, she was always thoughtful, devout, kind, loving and most of all she seemed to know what she wanted. For as long as she could speak, she spoke of nothing but becoming a bride of Christ. That, above all, had always been her utmost desire.

Catherine kissed her parents and Gio goodnight, thanked them for a "unique" birthday celebration and turned to leave. Her eye caught the painting of the family tree—her family tree. She paused, ever so briefly, to let her eyes wander over the leaves. Her head shook back and forth, as if she were trying to dislodge the idea of her newfound identity. She left the room, but not, her family noted, without Sofia's journal.

The moon's light filtered through her window, offering the room a sweet, blue glow. Then Catherine did what she always did when she retired to her room for the night, she slid to her knees at her bedside. Her curiosity about the journal was strong, but her need to commune with God was stronger. She put the journal on her bed, crossed herself and bowed her head.

"I thought I knew what you wanted from me. Is this a way to test my devotion? My dedication?" Catherine prayed. She felt an uncertainty she had never known. "Show me what you want. I am so confused," she begged God. "I have lived my life believing that I was destined to be Your Bride. I have never wanted any more than that. Is this information supposed to change what I want?"

Her prayer vacillated throughout the night. One moment she was crying, the next, she was fascinated by her newfound knowledge, then determined that it made no difference. In the end, just before dawn, her puffy and bloodshot eyes found the journal still on the bed where she had put it.

She was suddenly compelled to read it. Perhaps it would help her to dismiss the notion, the preposterous idea, that she was heir to the throne of Montalcino. She stood, picked up the journal almost angrily and held it up to heaven. "I will not let this change my mind."

She heard her words as they echoed in her ears. "Oh," she gasped in horror of herself. "Dear God," she said as she sat on a chair near the window where the scant morning light hinted at the day. A new wave of tears, these of remorse, dripped from her eyes. "Forgive me. Not my will, but thine."

Catherine read. So completely absorbed was she in the journal, that she did not hear her mother knock softly, open her door to peek in and gently close it again. She did not feel the sun as it rose and warmed the room. She did not hear the birds as they began their morning chorus of chirping.

Several times during her journey through her mother's journal, she wept. Nevertheless, she did not stop reading until the last word. She was spent.

Still in her clothes from the day before, she rose, made her way to the bed, and lay down. She slipped the journal under her pillow, curled herself against the ache in her heart and fell into a deep slumber.

Catherine woke in the late afternoon from a dreamless sleep. There were no dreams to tell her what to do. There was no voice in her heart that made clear her path. She was still exhausted, but her hunger and thirst, not to mention the smell of baking bread from her mother's kitchen, drove her from her bed.

Francesca was working on a needlepoint with her back to her daughter. Gio and Pasquale were nowhere to be seen.

"Mama," Catherine called weakly.

Francesca whirled at the sound of her daughter's voice. "Catherine," she cried, dropping her work into a basket and running to her. "You must be hungry!"

Catherine fell into her mother's arms and sighed. Francesca simply held her daughter until Catherine pulled away. She smiled a tired smile and nodded. "I am."

Francesca wrapped an arm around Catherine, and led her to a chair at the table. "Sit," she said as she poured a cup of water, and a cup of wine, and sliced the girl some of the fresh bread. Catherine reached for the olive oil that always sat on the table and drizzled it over her bread. Francesca went to the kitchen and returned with a bowl of olives and hunk of cheese and sat down next to her daughter.

"I will not ask," Francesca said almost tentatively, "but know that I am here if you want to talk."

Catherine sipped her wine, set her cup down and reached for her mother's hands. "Thank you, Mama. I am not quite ready but will be grateful for your guidance when I am."

Francesca patted her daughter's hand as she smoothed the tablecloth. "Gio and your father went to the cemetery to visit your grandfather's grave. They should be back soon."

Catherine only knew of Lord Giovanni as her grandfather. Reading about him in the journal made her wish she was his grandchild. She felt a stab of longing for the man she did not remember and who she would never know.

"So," she said to her mother, "he really was not my grandfather?"

Her mother shook her head. "He might as well have been for the way he doted on you, but, no, he was your great uncle."

Catherine cut a piece of cheese and ate it in silence. When she had finished her bread and ate a couple of olives, she refilled her cup and said, "I think I need to spend this evening alone. Will you please make my excuse to Gio and father?"

Francesca lifted her hand and placed her palm on Catherine's cheek. "Go, my child," she said as she nodded and smiled. "Be with God."

Catherine kissed her mother and disappeared to the sanctuary of her private room. After changing into her sleeping gown and washing, she knelt again in prayer. She paced, prayed, sat, and tried to think both critically and spiritually about the decision, the choice, before her. Long after she heard her family retire, she continued to ask God for direction. Sometime after midnight, she crawled into bed, reached under her pillow, pulled out Sofia's journal, and fell asleep with it against her breast.

Catherine rose early the next morning and was already at the breakfast table when her parents and Gio entered the dining room. There were only two servants in the house. Giacomo had been with the family since before Catherine had arrived. He served the morning meal and disappeared into the kitchen.

"You look more rested," Francesca said as she kissed her daughter on the head.

Catherine got up to kiss her father and Gio. "I am, Mama," she said. "And I would like to discuss something with all three of you."

"Speak, my daughter," Pasquale said with so much concern and love in his voice that Catherine could almost hear his heart breaking for her.

"I have read the journal," she said as she stabbed a piece of apple and took a bite. When she finished chewing, she put her fork down and stood up. "Sofia, has made it clear that the decision to assume my role as queen is a choice—one that I may feel free to decline." She walked around to the back of her chair and placed her hands upon the high back.

"I wish the choice was a simple one," she continued. "It is not. I had hoped for a sign from God that I should continue my pursuit of becoming a nun. There has been no sign. The more I consider the weight of this decision, the more I feel that I do not know enough to begin to consider what to do."

Catherine walked around the table and knelt beside her Uncle Gio. "Uncle, is it possible for me to go to Montalcino? Might we go as a family for a visit? Would it be too dangerous for my parents? Is it possible for me to meet this Father Tim?"

Gio looked at his sister and brother-in-law and saw the concern in their eyes. Turning back to Catherine he said, "It could be dangerous, but it is your right to go. I will do everything in my power to protect you and your parents. As a member of the Privy Council and grandson of the former Lord Giovanni, I can request accommodation at the castle as guests. That should be no problem."

Catherine looked around the table. "The concern on all of your faces is too obvious," she said, standing to address the three of them. "Tell me what bothers you."

Gio stood. "Catherine," he said softly. "You are the spitting image of your mother, Sofia."

The family's arrival at the castle was uneventful. As guests of Gio, and Catherine's apparent status as great granddaughter of the deceased and long-serving Privy Council member, Lord Giovanni, the family was entitled to visit the castle as guests. Whether the fact that they had never done so would raise questions would be interesting. They brought only their own household servants and were situated in a suite of rooms on the second floor of the royal wing.

Gio had his own room. Following the execution of Queen Sofia, he had, long ago, assumed the role and room vacated by his grandfather. The threat of discovering the existence of an heir to the throne of Montalcino was diminished after both Sofia's death and the disappearance of the archbishop. Gio, in anticipation of Catherine's potential claim to the throne, thought that his presence on the Privy Council lent itself to determining the dangers and risks of such a decision.

Catherine spent many days wandering the castle, often with her parents, Gio accompanied them when his duties did not prevent him doing so. Catherine had not anticipated the emotional responses that were awakened in her as she learned more and more about her family. As they wandered the halls, Gio pointed out many of the paintings done by Sofia's father, King Ambrose. Many were of Queen Sofia as a child. Portraits of her as an adult had all been removed following her execution for heresy.

"Why have the childhood portraits of Sofia been left?" Catherine asked Gio.

He turned to her and smiled. "I pressed the Church to allow them by insisting that the Church was complicit in the destruction of the child, Sofia." He let his eyes wander back to the small portrait of Sofia as a girl. "I really think they just allowed the portraits because they were tired of my endless pressing about them."

"What happened to the other paintings of her?"

Gio looked at his sister and sighed. "The Church burned many of them before I could stop them. I did manage to save several from the flames."

Francesca placed her hand on Catherine's shoulder. "They are wrapped in canvas at home. They are yours whenever you want them." Catherine smiled at her mother.

Gio was again looking at the small portrait. "The Church wronged Sofia horribly. Twice."

"You must miss her very much, Uncle Gio," Catherine said as she took his hand.

Gio nodded and turned to hide his tears.

Catherine did fall in love with the castle itself. That fact surprised her. Perhaps it was connecting to the past in tangible ways that made that possible. Initially, she loved excitement and bustle within the halls and the conversation and laughter during meals in the great hall. It was all so different from the quiet and solitude of her home in Voghera. But when she wanted quiet, she found solace and sanctuary in the church. It was as if she felt the presence of her mother, grandmother and grandfather wrapping their arms around her as she sat.

Regardless of her enjoyment of the castle and castle life, Catherine was still unsure as to whether she wanted to be queen. The reality of the situation, according to Gio, was that the Church acquired all the assets of Montalcino castle and its paper making enterprise, as the result of Queen Sofia's heresy and death. The fact that there was no known heir made the task all the easier. The Church, through its most current representative, Bishop Martine, had been governing Montalcino since Sofia's execution and Pietro Biondi's disappearance.

According to Gio, Bishop Martine was very much an advocate of the Church and its interests. This was Gio's biggest concern. The entire Privy Council had become a mere symbol of government to appease the citizens of Montalcino. The council did very little real governing and seemed mostly in place to carry out the interests, laws, duties and directives of the Church.

So, the question became, what fears and furies would Catherine's claim to the throne create and was she up to the task of unleashing those demons.

She found herself, more and more, spending time in the castle church. One afternoon, after she had spent the morning in prayer, Gio came to the Church, where he knew she had been.

"We need to speak, Catherine." Gio sat the girl down in one of the pews near the altar, then proceeded to check the confessional and vesting rooms to ensure that they were alone.

When he returned, he sat down next to her, a look of concern evident upon his face.

"I have been confronted by the bishop," he began. "It has come to his attention, from several sources that the resemblance between you and Queen Sofia is . . . striking."

Catherine looked at him with worry and shook her head. "I do not suppose my name helps, either."

"Likely not," Gio responded. "Have you made a decision, yet?"

Catherine lowered her head. "I am sorry, Uncle Gio," she offered. "I do not know what God wants of me. I want to do His will, but I cannot determine what it is." Frustration filled her voice.

He sighed. "It is a big decision and not an easy one. I have no doubt," he whispered, "that the Church will feel threatened, even if you claim the throne without intent to recover the family assets."

"I wish I knew what to do," she said in exasperation.

"For now," Gio said, "perhaps we need to determine what other obstacles lay in our path should you choose to be queen. There is a Privy Council meeting this afternoon," he announced as he stood and began to pace in front of the altar. "I will post guards at your door. Please stay inside your quarters with your parents until I come to you."

She nodded and asked, "What are you going to do?"

"I am going to tell the council the truth," he responded. He reached up to comb his fingers through his hair and ended up grabbing a handful. "We already know that the bishop will be opposed to your assuming rule. What I have been unable to determine is how much support or opposition there might be from members of the council." Gio sat next to her again. "Either way, your life will be in danger. But how much danger will be clearer once I have laid our cards on the table."

She said nothing for a moment, then stood. "I may not know which path God wants for me, Uncle," she said as she looked directly into his eyes, "but I am not afraid to die."

He stood in front of her, returning her steady gaze, and smiled. "You are more like your mother and grandmother than you can know." He pulled her into a great hug.

The Privy Council meeting began as all Privy Council meetings began. A long-winded prayer from the bishop set the tone for the dull, endless meetings. There was little for the council members to address. Accommodating the Church was second nature to everyone on the council after years of Church rule. The only reason most of the men in the room stayed on the council was to protect themselves, their families and their own assets from becoming consumed by the Church.

In the years since Sofia's execution, the council had dwindled. Attrition, in one form or another, had taken its toll. Only Lord Navona, the very member who had pronounced the execution verdict upon Sofia the morning of her death, remained from her reign. The others, those who did not die from age or illness, retired in the years since, leaving the council small. There were only four other members aside from Bishop Martine d'Avelo.

When the prayer ended, the bishop sat. Except for Lord Navona, Gio watched as the rest of the council settled down with their customary vacant expressions, while they waited for the archbishop to tell them what was expected of them today.

Lord Navona, Gio noted, had the look of a conspirator about him. His eyes sparkled with anticipation as he adjusted his papers before him, then looked at the bishop and smiled.

"Gentlemen," the bishop began, "I am certain that you are all aware of the rumors circulating the castle."

Gio's stomach clenched, then relaxed. So, he thought, the Church intends to make this easier for me than I had hoped. He was ready. He had planned to bring up the issue himself. It was better that the bishop raise the alarm. This might be just the opening he needed.

The council members sat up. He had their attention. "I never met the queen who fled her people but am informed that several who knew her are astonished at the resemblance between her and Lord Giovanni's niece," he said as his eyes narrowed and bore their glare into Gio. "In fact, I understand that she is almost an exact replica of the former heretic queen, Sofia."

"Or," Lord Navona interrupted, "that her name bears witness to what we hoped was an extinct line of royal depravity." His smirk as he finished his remark gave Gio a chill.

All eyes turned to Gio. He looked around at the men at the table and forced his eyebrows up into what he hoped was a look of surprise. He chuckled, "If I did not know better," he started, "I would say that some form of womanly hysteria had taken hold of the council." He paused and looked around. "Are you suggesting that my niece is being suspected of being someone other than who she is?"

"The remains of the child carried by Sofia were never found," Lord Navona said as he leaned across the table in an accusatory manner. "I know. I led the search party myself following Sofia's execution."

"So," Gio stood and walked over to the window that overlooked one of the many courtyards of Montalcino castle, "that leads you to believe that Catherine, the only child of my sister, must be heir to the throne of Montalcino?" He turned and looked back at Lord Navona.

"Obviously," the bishop answered, "there is more to our suspicion than failure to find the body of the purported male child." The bishop stood.

"Your sister, it is known, had tried for years to conceive a child," the bishop stated smugly. He looked at Gio as he walked toward the window where the younger man still stood. "Do not look so surprised, Lord Giovanni," he smiled. "We have done our investigating into the matter."

This fact did surprise Gio, and he wondered who and how the bishop got his information.

"It seems," the bishop continued as he turned back to the council, "that suddenly, one fine day, a little over fifteen years ago, you," he directed a pointed glare at Gio, "returned from unknown places. With you was a strange woman, whom, I believe, assisted your sister to give birth to a child."

Gio's mind swirled. They had all been so careful to pretend that Francesca was pregnant for months. They even destroyed her blood rags. Francesca sewed padding into her dresses. What could possibly have gone awry? "Ah," Gio said smugly, "that explains it, then. The baby was delivered by someone unknown."

"Do not play coy with me!" the bishop turned on him. "Your sister was never pregnant. The child was smuggled in by you and presented as your sister's own child."

This was Gio's opening, the chance for which he had hoped. Without acknowledging any of it, he strode back to the table and looked at the men seated there. He looked around the gathering, rubbing his beard to appear deep in thought.

"Fine," he said as if considering the bishop's words as a mere suggestion. "Let us consider the bishop's reasoning," he said, as if he were amused by the thought of it. "Let us say that my sister . . . in fact, my entire family and all of our servants, have concealed this great secret." Here Gio smiled and shook his head creating the image of a man who was totally unbelieving of what he heard. "Let us pretend that my niece, a child raised far from Montalcino, and who has dreamt of nothing but entering a convent since she was able to speak," he added with emphasis, "is heir to the throne of Montalcino." He stopped walking and sat back down in his seat. "What," he continued, "would she, or any one of us gain, if she were who you say she is?"

Gio looked around at the faces, hoping to discern if any were hopeful that the Church may lose some of its power. But he could not read the expressions of any but the bishop and Lord Navona. After some discussion, which only served to reinforce the fact that the other council members were afraid to engage in any real talk of what Catherine's real lineage might mean for them, the meeting adjourned without any proof or acknowledgement from Gio that Catherine was, in fact, the heir.

"How can they not see that I am no threat?" Catherine cried. "Even if I choose the role of queen, it would be in title only . . . I would allow God to lead through me." The family had just seated themselves for a private dinner in their suite. Giacomo, the servant who had come with them had brought the meal to their quarters for the family. Gio had had an uneasy feeling since the council meeting and had not left Catherine's side.

Giacomo placed the food on the table and was pouring the wine. Gio noticed his hand tremble as he poured. A look at the sideboard revealed that the jug of wine from which the family had been drinking was still there. Giacomo had produced a new bottle.

Gio watched and waited, knowing that the servant would step back to wait while the family prayed over their food. As soon as the prayer was finished Gio stood.

"Before we begin, I should like to propose a toast," he said forcing a smile. He picked up Catherine's wine goblet and carried it over to the servant, Giacomo. As he held the cup to Giacomo, he watched the man's eyes carefully. The servant's pupils widened in fear, and all the color drained from his face.

There was not a sound in the room. Gio continued to hold the wine out to the servant. Slowly, with the knowledge that he was a dead man no matter what he did, Giacomo took the cup of wine. He lowered his eyes momentarily, away from Gio's penetrating glare.

When he looked up again, his eyes were full of tears. He had been with the Oddono family for years, but the promise of gold and threats from the bishop, had been difficult to resist.

Giacomo held up the goblet of wine toward Catherine, Francesca and Pasquale Oddono.

"Forgive me," he said. He downed the entire contents of the cup in four large swallows. The poison did not take long.

Catherine watched in horror as Giacomo writhed in agony, clutching his stomach as he foamed at the mouth. He was dead in a very short time.

"Catherine," Gio said firmly as he lowered his head. "You must dress," he said gently as he looked back up at his niece. "We leave at once."

Catherine looked at her mother, who in turn looked at her husband who had paled. He nodded. Francesca Oddono understood.

"Leave us," she said. "I will dress my daughter."

Despite Catherine's questions, her mother, the only mother she had ever known, the mother who loved her, who cherished and doted on her, dressed her in silence.

Francesca's face was unreadable to Catherine, and that alone frightened her. She had learned to read her mother's moods in her face. She knew her mother's sadness and joy, her pain and her fears. This was a new look, one that frightened Catherine simply because it was new. She gave up asking questions, obediently allowing her mother to dress her.

When she was dressed in traveling clothes, and her hair was brushed and pulled back with a tie, her mother indicated that she should go to her father and uncle who waited for her in the outer room.

Catherine paused at the door, an overwhelming sense of foreboding filling her. She turned and could not help but fly into her mother's arms. Francesca embraced her, covering her face with kisses, but said nothing. Finally, pulling herself from the crush of her daughter's arms, Francesca held her daughter's face between her hands and kissed her on both cheeks.

"Go now. Your father and uncle wait." She pulled every ounce of strength from within her to smile at her beloved daughter. "And know that I love you with all of my heart."

When Catherine had left the room and closed the door, her mother fell to the bed, burying her face in her daughter's pillow. The howl that escaped her was consumed by feathers and heard by only herself and God.

Catherine wanted to ask where they were headed but chose to remain in prayer, trusting God and her father and uncle. The trio rode wordlessly on horses, the men on either side of her. They managed to sneak unobtrusively from the castle under the guise of riding to the flower fields.

It was late afternoon on the second day's ride from the castle when they turned off the main road, onto a small path through the woods. Before long the path opened to a small clearing. At the far end of the clearing was a small hermitage.

As they neared the cluster of simple buildings, Catherine realized that monks worked in the garden outside the bigger of the houses. The monks worked in silence and were all draped in brown tunics. Some of them had their hoods pushed back off their heads, some worked with them on. Thick ropes were tied around their waists. Rosaries hung from the ropes. One of the monk's looked up as they approached. It appeared as if he had been expecting them. Gio and Pasquale dismounted and nodded to the monk. Catherine saw her father hand a small bag to him.

"God bless you, my son," the monk said quietly. Catherine heard the clink of coins in the small bag.

Pasquale turned to his daughter and helped her to dismount. When she stood in front of him, he, like his wife, took her face in both of his hands and kissed her gently on both cheeks. "It is fine, my sweet child."

Gio appeared at her side. "It is time."

Another monk appeared at Gio's side. He indicated, wordlessly, that they should follow him.

Pasquale nodded to his daughter and watched her walk arm in arm with her uncle, following one of the monks, to a small door that opened through the ring of adjoining huts and to the center of the hermitage compound. Pasquale remained to tend to the horses.

Catherine looked around the inner circle of the hermitage. It was beautifully filled with flowers that were well tended, although many of the flowers were dying due to the cooler nights. There was a simple rock path that meandered around and through the garden and another wider path that connected to each door in the circle. They walked to one of the doors nearest the entry to the outside. The monk knocked on the door. Another young monk appeared and stepped outside. Both monks disappearing after bowing to the pair.

"Behind this door" Gio said softly, "you may find the answer to your prayers. Perhaps your destiny, your God, has led you here."

She looked at him, waiting for more. Finally, he said. "The monk who lives here is dying. He has requested to speak with you."

Catherine looked at him, full of questions, all of which disappeared as he reached for the door handle. "His name is Pietro Biondi."

Catherine felt her knees nearly give way. Her heart raced and she looked up at Gio, wide-eyed.

"Take your time. Your father and I will wait for you as long as you need us to," Gio said. Then he kissed her cheeks, turned and left her there.

She took a deep breath and stepped through the doorway into the tiny room. She smelled the sickness before she could see anything. As her eyes adjusted to the dim candlelight, she saw the old monk lying on the bed near the wall. He was sleeping, his breath labored.

Slowly, she made her way to the bed. As her racing heart gradually began to slow, and her own breathing returned to normal, she felt her body begin to relax.

The body on the bed was gaunt, pale, and sad. His face was deeply creased with lines of torment. Although how she could see the sadness and torment was beyond her. Perhaps it was sadness that permeated the room. Perhaps it was just that she knew his history.

As if it were why she had come, she knelt at the side of the bed and pulled her rosary from the bag she always kept tied to her waist.  Her heart, always so generous in its ability to love, filled with compassion for the dying man.  She cried softly as she prayed.

She was so lost in the meditations of her rosary that she did not notice that the labored breathing of his sleep had stopped. It was not until she felt his hand on her head that she realized he was awake.

"Why do you weep, child?"  He had prepared himself to see the face of the woman he had both loved and despised so long ago.  Sofia's face still haunted his dreams.  And so, it was with that expectation that he braced himself to recognize her.  But he did not see Sofia's face look up at him.  The face that met him was that of his own mother, and it filled him with an ache of love and memory so powerful that his eyes filled with tears.

She reached up and took his hand in both of hers. Her rosary wrapped itself around both of their hands.

Finally, when he could, he spoke.  "You pray the rosary for me?"

"Yes, Father."  Her voice was so quiet, and his hearing had been failing him for some time, but he heard in her response the acknowledgment of who he was . . . of who she was to him. Monks were addressed as "Brother."  She would not have made that mistake.

"Thank you," he said.  Then he was taken with a fit of coughing.  When he was finished, she helped him sit up and placed additional pillows behind him.

"Something troubles you . . . daughter," he smiled wanly at her.  "Tell me."

She was kneeling again at his bedside.  A single teardrop welled and spilled down her cheek.  The back of his curled fingers reached for her face.  As they met the soft skin, the teardrop broke at his finger, melting into nothing, dissolving to spread between her skin and his hand. The last face he had reached out to touch was her mother's. It was just as soft. She was just as beautiful.

"You are dying," she said simply. "Please do not trouble yourself with my problems. God will guide me."

He smiled weakly. "I asked for you," he said as he struggled for a breath, "because I wished to beg your forgiveness before I die."

"My forgiveness is not necessary," she shook her head. "Only God has the power to forgive."

"Still . . . " he pleaded.

She looked at him with such wisdom and compassion that he thought he might weep. "You have my forgiveness, as you always had my mother's."

"Then I can ask for no more." His brow was drenched in sweat. Catherine found a washrag in a bowl of cool water. She wrung it out and placed it on his forehead. "Now, please, tell me," he said when she had finished, "what troubles you."

She placed the rag back in the bowl and pulled a chair up to his bedside. "I do not know what God wants of me," she lamented as she raised her eyes to the ceiling. "I have lived my life believing that I was called to the sisterhood. Becoming a nun is the only thing I have ever wanted."

He smiled, remembering his own fervent desire as a child. Serving God as a priest drove him, pushed at him relentlessly, until, at last, he left his home for seminary.

"But . . . " he urged.

"Although my parents encouraged me, every time I brought up the subject, they told me to be patient. I did not understand, until now."

"Now," he said gently, "now that you know that your real mother was queen."

She sighed and nodded. "Either way is an opportunity to serve God. I know that. But I do not know what God wants me to do."

"You have prayed?" he asked.

"I have not stopped praying." Her frustration showed in her face. He heard it in her voice. "It is as if God has abandoned me when I need Him most!"

He pushed himself up a little and held out his hand. She took his gnarled fingers in hers. His hand was cold. She warmed it between her own.

"God," he whispered, "never abandons us, though we all have times when we feel He has left."

Catherine was so hungry for someone with whom to share her love of God that she clung to his every word. She felt his words settle into the place within her that already knew, already understood a truth she had never heard uttered before. She nodded.

"Tell me," he said, "when did you first feel the call to become a nun?"

Catherine told Pietro Biondi of that first memory. She was attending Mass with her parents, sitting between them. They were kneeling in prayer, and she was trying her best to imitate them.

Catherine's eyes closed as she recalled that morning for him. "I remember the smell as the sensor swung from the priest's arm. Smoke wafted up, blurring the candlelight on the altar. The choir was singing, and there was a pause in the music. Then, a single voice, a young boy's voice, rose and filled the church. When I looked up, I saw both my parents deep in prayer. Tears were streaming down my mother's face, but they were not tears of sadness, they were tears of joy." She paused and opened her eyes, smiling. I remember thinking, "I want that."

Catherine sighed and smiled, "After that I felt the pull to be in church whenever I could. I preferred to pray in my room rather than play with friends. By the time I started receiving Holy Communion, I already knew that devoting my life to the service of God was all I wanted."

"But now you are unsure how God wants you to serve Him?"

"Whatever life I choose" she shrugged her shoulders, the fact of my lineage makes it likely that I will not survive very long . . . even if I try to disappear into a convent. So perhaps I make too much of the decision." She looked at him and smiled. "I am tiring you. I should leave."

"Do not go," he squeezed her hand. "Your visit refreshes me."

She smiled at him and nodded. They sat in silence for a few minutes, and then she asked, "Have you ever felt abandoned by God?"

"More times than I care to remember, daughter." His rheumy eyes drifted past her as he remembered the agony and suffering he felt in the aftermath of her mother's execution at his hands.

"You disappeared soon after my mother's death," Catherine said as if she had read his mind. "Is this where you came?'

"Eventually," he said. "I wandered alone for many weeks in the forest. I ate only what I could find. It was my self- inflicted punishment for what I did to her." Another coughing fit overtook him.

She found a cup of water and brought it to him, lifting it to his lips. He took a few sips and sat back against the pillow.

"I thought never to hear from God again," he whispered. "The weather was getting colder, and I feared dying in the cold. I told myself that even that was too good a death given what I forced her to endure." Pietro Biondi shook his head slowly and sadly with the memory. "Still, my cowardice made me a desperate man. I fell to my knees and cried out to God for the first time since I had run from Montalcino. I begged God's forgiveness for my life of sin. That first coldest of nights, I prayed for God's mercy and help and promised Him that if I lived through the night, I would find a way to serve Him without my interference."

Catherine was absorbed in every word Pietro Biondi said. She did not take her eyes off him.

When he regained his breath, Pietro smiled wanly at her. "I truly did not expect to live through the night."

"But you did," Catherine said reaching for his hand again.

"Indeed," he said. "I woke up to a heavy frost and found myself covered with a thick animal hide that was not mine. A small fire was burning not far from me. Two monks were traveling in search of a new home.

The one they had lived in for many years was torched by the Church." He stopped, his breathing coming in short, raspy breaths. It was clear that talking took huge effort. When his breathing was better, he continued, "I stayed with them. They had been searching for this enclave. I was blessed to be accepted here."

"And you kept your promise to God?" Catherine asked with a knowing smile.

He smiled at her, nodded, and closed his eyes.

"I am happy for you then," Catherine said with so much love and understanding that the dying monk opened his eyes to gaze upon her face. Again, his eyes filled with tears. He felt God's grace infuse him with love for this child, his child.

"Daughter," he said weakly, "my daughter." His eyes tried to drink in every feature of her face. The intimacy of the moment filled him with an energy he had not anticipated. He pushed himself a bit higher on his pillow, taking her hand in his. "We may never know what God has in mind for our life's work. We can certainly not even begin to comprehend His whys or ways. For all I know, my entire life, all my ambitions and failures, my sins and regrets," he paused and looked down at their clasped hands before looking up at her again, "all of it may have been to lead me to this precious moment with you."

Catherine remained silent as he spoke, her heart quickening a bit with each word.

"Whatever decision you make, whatever tempests you endure, whatever joys or heartaches accompany you, remember this—all of our life here in this mortal skin, is designed to bring us closer to Him. Never doubt that."

She smiled at him, but her smile was full of sadness and doubt.

Pietro saw that she needed to find an answer to her dilemma. "You must know the priest, Timothy, from Castiglione d' Orcia."

"I know of him," she replied. "I know he was instrumental in work with my grandmother, Queen Catherine, and my own mother. As I have been raised in secrecy, it has only been in the past weeks that I have ever been away from the small village where I grew up."

"Timothy is as fine a servant of God as I have ever known. We have kept in touch since I came to be here. It was he that shook my eyes free from the blindness that had overtaken them. But for the good Father Timothy, I might still be persecuting and working for the Inquisition." He leaned back on his pillow and was again struggling for breath.

"Father Timothy must be getting on in years," he said. "I would guess him to be near sixty or more by now."

"Why do you mention him?" Catherine asked.

"Because child," he said, "should you be led to follow in your mother's and grandmother's footsteps, I have no doubt you would do so with an eye on your subjects and your heart on God. Father Tim is someone in whom I believe you might have an ally and friend."

She looked at him with a wry smile. "And do you, good father, have someone in mind should I decide to pursue a life as a bride of Christ?"

"I believe I do," he managed a small chuckle that quickly turned into a coughing fit. She helped him lean forward and rubbed his back until it subsided.

After a sip of water, he said, "I know of a convent in Spain. They are devoted to helping the poor. They may even be preparing to send a contingent to the new world."

"America?" she said, her eyebrows raised and the tiniest bit of both interest and panic crept into her voice.

He nodded. "At least there," he said, "you would not have to be constantly on alert for assassins wishing to destroy any knowledge of your existence," he said with a mild shrug. "And I would happily send you to Spain with a letter of introduction from this order. We are both discalced."

"There is much to consider," she said.

A light knock came on the door and the young monk entered with hot tea and wine. "Brother Pietro," he said, bowing, "you are looking refreshed."

"I am feeling quite invigorated, Brother Mark."

The young monk turned to Catherine. He did not meet her eyes but said, with head bowed, "You have generated a healthy effect on our brother. Thank you. I will return shortly with an evening meal."

As Brother Mark left, Catherine was surprised to see the sun very low on the horizon. Without windows, it was difficult to distinguish day from night in the little hut.

"Father," Catherine said as she returned to his side, "may I stay with you through the evening?"

"You may stay as long as you want to or need to," he said.

A gust of cooler evening air had blown into the hut when Brother Mark left. Catherine looked around and saw that the small fireplace against the back wall was out. She went to the little woodpile and found a tool to hack off some kindling, set a log on the kindling and got a fire going with a candle. When she returned to his side, Pietro was shivering. Catherine found another blanket at the foot of his bed and put it on him.

"Catherine," he said, suddenly weaker, "will you allow me to pray for you?"

She knelt at his bedside. "I can think of nothing I would like more." With her hands folded and head bowed, she waited.

Pietro Biondi put his knobby hand on her head. She could feel the coldness of it and worried that he was not yet warmed, but when he began his prayer, all else left her thoughts.

"Heavenly Father, God of Mercy and Love, I come before you with my meek stirring of love to beseech you on behalf of this child, our child, your precious daughter. Help her to discern Your desire for her as she contemplates a future that she so clearly wants to devote to you. Whether that future be as a bride of Christ, in service to you as a sister of a convent, or as a God-loving Christian Queen to the people of Montalcino, help her to know Your will for her life. Guide her to a future that will best serve You. She is a willing servant with a loving heart full of grace and beauty. Use her as you see fit. Lead and she will follow. Bless her days and nights, her inhalations and exhalations, her dreams, her coming in and her going out. Fill her with the presence of Your Holy Spirit and hold her in the safety and comfort of Your arms for You alone are the reason for our living and being. You alone can guide us in the ways of Your mercy, Your compassion, Your truth. Be with us this night and bless Catherine with Your presence that she might discern her life's path. In the name of Christ Jesus, we pray. Amen."

The prayer took all his energy. How he managed it without a coughing fit she could not say. He collapsed back onto his bed drenched in a heavy sweat. His breath came in short, shallow breaths, and he seemed weaker than when she had first entered the room.

Catherine brought the washcloth to his brow and dabbed the perspiration. She continued to press the cloth over his face, his head and neck. "How," she wondered, "is it possible to love someone I have never met before with such a full love?"

He opened his eyes. "Please," he whispered, "the small writing table." His eyes pointed to the corner.

She brought the small lap table and helped him to right himself for writing, though she feared he had little enough strength to breathe, let alone write. The ink well was nearly full, and paper and quill were inside.

"I must take care of these last items of my life's business." It was an effort for him to speak. "I beg you, stay. Sit in silence. Empty yourself of thoughts. Open your heart to God's presence only."

"I will stay," she said. "And pray for you."

"No." he said with some urgency. "No prayers now. No thoughts. Just be still and know . . . know . . . "

His eyes closed. The last of his life seemed to be ebbing away. He appeared to fall asleep, the writing implements still in his lap.

Brother Mark knocked gently and entered with a tray of meager nourishment. He saw the old monk sleeping and quietly put the tray on the table. Whispering softly, he said to Catherine, "I can stay with him now. Your people are in the dining hall. You may join them there."

She shook her head. "You have a place where they may stay the night?"

He nodded.

"I will stay here with your ill brother," she said softly. "I will tend to him through the night."

Brother Mark looked over at the sleeping monk. As if he understood what was about to happen, he went to the monk, knelt and kissed his hand. "Goodbye, Brother," he whispered. "May God carry you gently home."

He stood and started to leave, then turned toward Catherine. "He taught me more in my short time here than I have learned my whole life. He is a true man of God." For the first time, Brother Mark looked up and directly into Catherine's eyes. "You are very special to him. I am glad you have finally come."

"Why do you say that?" Catherine asked.

"I have been with the order for only eight years, but there has not a day gone by that he has not wept in prayer for a child named Catherine." He turned and reached for the door handle. "Prayers for you have been a daily part of this order since before my arrival." His head bowed ever so slightly. "Your arrival here, for all of us, is the answer to a very long held prayer."

The young monk slipped out the door without another word. As he did so, Catherine heard the hoot of an owl from the woods surrounding the small, impoverished monastery. She stood staring at the closed door after Brother Mark left. How could it be that an entire cell of monks had been praying for her for so long? She experienced an overwhelming sense of both astonishment and humility.

If her wonder at the events of this day were surprising, they were nothing compared to the confusion they created in her about her future. She turned back to the man who was her father and, again, sat down beside him. He seemed to be sleeping rather more peacefully than he had earlier. His breathing was less raspy, but more rhythmic. More than anything, she longed to get down on her knees and pray—for the dying man, for her parents and Uncle Gio, for the people of Montalcino, and for herself. Her need to lay her soul bare to God and beg his direction sought to overwhelm her. She tried, as he had suggested, to empty herself of thought, but the emphatic directive seemed an impossible task. Her thoughts plagued her one after another after another. Every time she found her attention focused on yet another thought, she dropped it and freed her mind. It was an endless dance, one that frustrated her at first. It was like trying to wipe an outdoor table clean of raindrops during a storm. Finally, though, the rain eased, and the drops became few and far between as she settled into an awareness of nothing. Her doubt, confusion, and anguish about her path disappeared. At some point, she fell asleep in the chair.

When, finally, Catherine opened her eyes, the candles had burned down to almost nothing. The fire was out. She might have sat there for hours or days. She had no concept of how much time had passed, so fully and lovingly held in God's presence. The silence surrounding her was so complete that, at first, she was confused. It was then that she realized that the monk was not breathing. She looked down at him. His face looked peaceful, the creases of pain and struggle gone from around his eyes. She was able to see that he must have been a handsome man in his youth. Their hands were still clasped, but as she looked at his lap, she realized that he must have let go of her hand at some point during the night, for there were four separate letters written in his very shaky hand. She looked back into his face, and for the first time realized, as she closed them, that she had his eyes. She smiled. "Be at peace, Father." Then, ignoring the letters, she fell to her knees. Holding his cold hand in hers, she began to pray for his soul.

Brother Mark knocked gently just before dawn. He entered softly and immediately took in the situation. The dinner tray from the previous night was untouched. He placed the breakfast tray next to it and knelt next to Catherine to join her in prayer. After a short time, he said to her, "I need to inform the other brothers. They will come in to prepare his body. Shall I send in your family?"

Catherine had all but forgotten about her father and uncle. Her concern since her arrival was the dying monk.

Brother Mark, waiting for her reply, noticed the handwritten letters resting on the lap desk of Brother Pietro. He picked them up and looked at them. "These are all for you," he said, "I do not know where he got the strength to write them. He has been able to do nothing for the last week." He handed the letters to Catherine.

Catherine looked down at the dead man who was her father one last time. "Thank you for the gifts of this night," she whispered. She looked up at Brother Mark. "He must have been a remarkable person," she said. "I know you will miss him, and I hope I did not deprive you of spending this last night with him."

"All happens as it should," the monk said with a smile. "You have deprived me of nothing. Come, I will take you to your people."

Catherine ate a meager breakfast in the dining hall with her father, her uncle and seventeen monks. Breakfast was eaten in silence, and when finished, Catherine felt a heavy exhaustion fall upon her. As some of the monks proceeded to clear the tables, the one who greeted them on their arrival came over to their table.

"Brother Antoni," Gio said as he stood to greet the older monk. "We are grateful for your hospitality."

Brother Antoni nodded his acknowledgement and turned to Catherine. "We have prepared a place for you to rest. You have had a long journey, followed by a long night. You must rest now."

The monk spoke as a man used to being obeyed. Catherine

had no qualms about following his orders. She was, admittedly, exhausted. But more interesting to her was the fact that she also felt an incredible peace. She looked at her father, whose face conveyed his concern over her night with Pietro Biondi.

She reached for her father and hugged him. "I will tell you and Uncle Gio everything, but I must rest first." Catherine kissed her father on both cheeks and turned to do the same to her uncle, then hurried to catch up to Brother Antoni, who was already outside the door of the dining hall.

The small room to which Brother Antoni led her was identical to Pietro's room. It had a hardwood kneeler, a table with one chair, a cross on the wall, and a bed.

"There is a towel and fresh water for cleansing," he said as he pointed to the bowl on the table. "The carafe holds some of the ale we produce here." There was no pride in his voice, just fact, Catherine noticed. "The bed linens are fresh. Please enjoy your rest."

As the monk turned for the door Catherine said, "Please, Brother Antoni, may I ask you a question?"

He turned, slid his hands inside his sleeves, and nodded.

"Brother Mark indicated that this order has prayed for me for many years. May I ask why?"

"I have been here," Brother Antoni said, "since before Brother Pietro arrived. "He was the most tormented man I had ever met. For months he stayed to himself. I would often hear him sobbing in his room which was next to mine." Brother Antoni stopped and seemed to weigh whether or not to continue. "One night I went to him. I could not bear to listen to him continue agonizing alone. I offered to hear his confession." Here, Brother Antoni looked up into Catherine's eyes and said, "So, my child, I know who you are and who you are to him."

Catherine's hands had moved up to her heart as she listened to the old monk. "Please, tell me that he has not tortured himself for all these years in such agony."

At this, Brother Antoni smiled. "Your concern for him speaks to your generous heart," he said. "He was a broken man when he arrived, but as he repaired his relationship with God he healed. Only God and he know if he continued to torture himself over his past, but he did seem more at peace. He beseeched the order to pray for you daily. It was important to him, and we also prayed for your visit."

Catherine smiled. "Thank you, Brother Antoni, for being so candid. I would very much like to rest for a bit."

The monk bowed and let himself out.

Catherine was exhausted. She undressed and slid between the covers in the small bed. Although she closed her eyes, sleep refused to come. "How can I be this tired and not be able to sleep?" she wondered. "The letters!" she thought. She got out of bed and lit an extra candle, found the letters in the pocket of her coat and brought them back to bed.

The first letter she unfolded was written to her.

*"Dearest Catherine,*

*I am humbled and grateful for your visit. Thank you, a thousand times over for your loving care and compassion in what I know must be my last hours. I am happy your mother found a way to keep you safe from me, from the Inquisition, from so much.*

*For what it might be worth, I believe that you would make a wonderful queen for the kingdom of Montalcino. Your poise, grace and compassion are what is lacking in so much of the country. And your spiritual aspirations could be met in the service of your kingdom as much as they might be as a nun. God will use you in whatever capacity you allow Him to.*

*But you would also be a wonderful nun.*

*Since I do not know which path you might choose, I have written three letters, as you shall see. Use them however you see fit. Or do not use them at all. The choice is entirely yours. I have no doubt that you will choose wisely.*

*Whichever path you choose, be at peace. Serve others. Love always. Pray often. Sit and BE with the Divine.*

*Your loving father, Pietro Biondi*

Catherine let the letter fall to her lap and thought about the man she never knew until yesterday. How could such a thing as meeting him, loving him and losing him have happened with such speed and clarity? How, she wondered as she thought about the timing of his death, could the events of the past day be anything but a divinely assisted miracle? She shook her head and opened the second letter. It was addressed to a Sister Marie Frances, Convent of St Joseph in Avila, Spain.

*Sister Marie Frances,*

*This will be my last letter to you. I am near death and have a personal request.*

*The young woman bearing this letter has been known to me for her whole life. She has always dreamt of being a sister, and I can think of no finer sisterhood of saints than your order. As both our orders follow the directives of the Unknown Monk and your founder, Teresa, who penned our contemplative directive, I send her in full faith and trust that you will help her in her quest to serve God.*

*Quite apart from her lifelong desire to become a bride of Christ, her life has recently become endangered. I know you plan to send some of your sisters to America at some*

*time in the future and am of the belief that she would not
be in danger far across the sea.*

*Please take this special child, who is dear to my heart,
under your caring and prayerful wing.  I would be very
grateful.*

*Yours in Christ, Brother Pietro Biondi, Italy*

Catherine's eyes were filled with tears before she had finished
reading the letter to the convent in Spain. She set the letter with
the one addressed to her and continued to marvel at the events
spilling around her like mountain snowmelt during a sudden
spring.

"Lord," she prayed, "help me be worthy of all this love you
are bestowing upon me."

After sitting another few minutes, just staring at the candle
flame, Catherine reached for the third letter. Her hands shook as
she unfolded it.  She was anxious and excited about how it might
guide her life.  It read:

*To All of the Peoples in the Kingdom of Montalcino, to
the Privy Council of Montalcino and especially to Bishop
Martine d'Avalo,*

*I write to you this last confession before I die and beseech
you to right a wrong for which I am wholly responsible.*

*Sixteen years ago, in a singular weak moment of the
flesh, I committed an act for which I have begged God's
forgiveness.  Now I must beg yours, as I have also begged
forgiveness from the others who have suffered for my
weakness.*

*Catherine Isabella Oddono is the daughter of Queen
Sofia of Montalcino.  I know this because, in fact, I
fathered her when I took advantage of Queen Sofia as*

*she mourned the loss of someone she held dear. I, Pietro Biondi, Former Archbishop of Montalcino, am guilty of much. Queen Sofia was a virgin at the time of my crime. Because I could not suffer the humiliation of what I did, it was all too easy for me to cover my own eyes and imagine her a temptress. She was no temptress. She could have exposed me but did not. She took my secret sin to her fiery death—the death to which I assigned her. She was innocent. Our daughter is innocent. I beg you do not punish the daughter for the sin of her father.*

*Sofia's child—my child—Catherine, has every right to assume the throne of Montalcino. Should she decide to do so, I wish to assure you that she will do so with a heart full of compassion for her people. Like her mother and grandmother before her, she will work tirelessly for justice and righteousness. She does not expect any inheritance from the Church as a child of an archbishop. She expects no recompense from the Church for monies already collected for and used by the Church. She wishes only to govern her people and return to Montalcino as a God-loving servant. I beg you let her do so. She has committed no sin by being born and only recently has she become aware of her true identity.*

*I left Montalcino in shame and secrecy when God, in His mercy, helped me to know all of which I was guilty. As I am about to leave this earthly plane, I do so with eyes wide open. I ask that you and the Church peacefully return Montalcino to its rightful heir. Give her the respect and support she deserves. And, if possible, forgive me as she has and as God has.*

*Yours, Pietro Biondi, former Archbishop of Montalcino*

The fourth letter was nearly identical to the one to the people of Montalcino. It, however, was written to the pope. Catherine read it and realized that it should only be sent if, and when, she decided to become queen.

She looked at the four letters spread out on the bed. And then Catherine wept. When she had no tears left, she rose and poured herself a cup of the ale Brother Antoni left for her. While she was deeply moved by the letters he had written, she felt no closer to a decision. If anything, she was empty—bereft of any ability to even consider which path to take. So, she lay back down onto the bed and fell instantly into a deep slumber.

When she woke in mid-afternoon she was disoriented. After her brief confusion, she left the small room and went in search of her father and uncle.

Greeting them with kisses, she asked if women were allowed into the chapel.

"Let us find Brother Antoni," her father said. "I think he is in the outer garden."

The monk smiled at the question and nodded. "Follow me," he said. A path led around the circle of adjoining rooms to the back of the campus.

Catherine was aware of the crunching of the stones under her feet as they followed the monk. The scent of the trees reminded her of home in Voghera, and she felt a stab of pain in her heart that felt like an acute loss. When they arrived at the chapel door, Brother Antoni stopped and turned to her.

"You are welcome to use the chapel whenever you like, but I must ask you to avoid the hours of our prayers. The monks pray at five in the morning, at noon and at seven in the evening," he said.

"I will be aware, Brother Antoni," Catherine said as she nodded. The monk bowed and left.

Catherine looked around and saw a pair of wooden benches

nearby. "Will you both sit with me?"

Gio swept his hand toward the benches and waited for father and daughter to sit, then joined them.

A great silence enveloped them for a moment. Even the birds in the trees halted their chatter, as if expecting something important.

Catherine's head was bowed, but now she raised it and looked into her father's eyes. "You," she said, "are the only father I have ever known." Pasquale smiled and waited.

"That," Catherine said, "has not changed."

Pasquale closed his eyes and lowered his head. Catherine saw a tear drip onto his forearm. She took a breath and continued. "I still do not know what my future holds. I would like to spend some time in the chapel in prayer. If I still feel, afterward, that I must wait longer to decide, then I will accept yours and Gio's counsel in terms of what to do next." Catherine heard the cry of a hawk overhead and looked up. "Oh, that this decision was as easy as taking flight," she said. She kissed her father's hand, still in hers, and released it. She stood and reached into her the pocket in her underdress, pulling out the letters from Pietro Biondi. "I will leave these with you," she said, picking out the letters that were addressed to the convent, the pope and the people of Montalcino. "He wrote four letters during his last hours. Reading these will give you the information that will allow me to pursue whichever path I feel led to by God."

Pasquale took the letters. "There are only three letters," he said as he looked questioningly at her.

"The last is for me, personally," she said. "I am not ready to share that one yet. Of those three, the one to the people of Montalcino is nearly a duplicate to the pope and the Holy See."

"I understand," Pasquale said. "You pray, we will wait." He kissed her forehead.

"I will be here for some time I suspect, Father," Catherine said. "You are both welcome to join me."

Pasquale raised a hand to his daughter's cheek and shook his head. "You go in and pray, child."

Gio grinned and said, "I cannot remember the last time I entered a holy place. I fear it will collapse if I enter."

Catherine smiled and shook her head at her uncle. "It would do no such thing," she reached for him and kissed his cheeks. "I will come find you when I am finished."

The men nodded and watched her enter the chapel.

"I will stand guard, Pasquale," Gio said. "Go wander or sit if you like. I know you enjoy the library here. Please feel free."

Pasquale sighed heavily, thanked Gio, and handed him the letters. "I am not quite up to these just yet," he said. Then he turned and went off to be with the books.

Catherine felt instantly at home inside the chapel. She felt God in the very air. At the center away from the door was a wooden kneeler. A book of prayers was open, and she went to it. Kneeling, she looked up at the cross in front of her. "Here I am, Lord," she whispered. And, again, "Here I am."

Gio sat on the ground just outside the chapel. He leaned up against the wall under a small window and watched a squirrel spiral up a tree. He opened one of the letters that sat in his lap. It was the one to the convent in France. When he finished reading it, he put his head against the wall behind him and closed his eyes imagining what his life would be like if he left this place that had always been home. He contemplated the losses in his life—his father, Robert, whose lifelong duty was to protect the Queen of Montalcino, Catherine. He could not help but think of that day so long ago when Sofia rode into Montalcino with the bodies of his father, the queen and James, his best friend in all the world. He thought he would never forgive Sofia. He still wondered at the mystery of how he did. His grandfather, he supposed, was instrumental in that forgiveness.

"I miss you, Papa Gio," he whispered to no one.

When his grandfather had told him what had happened to Sofia and the danger to which her life had been exposed, his anger at her circumstance and his instant forgiveness of her mobilized him in ways he thought were lost to him forever. There was no question but that he would protect her in any way he could. But she was dead now, too.

Without warning, Gio found himself talking to the God he had refused to talk to for all these years since his father's murder. "I do not understand You," he said. "I could not protect Sofia—something I thought you created me for. How am I supposed to protect Catherine?" He pulled up his knees and buried his head in his hands. "If she enters a convent and goes off to America, where is my duty, my life's purpose? Am I supposed to shadow a nun to a new world? How does that serve anyone?"

Gio sat and let his thoughts wander to what a life in another country would look like. An overwhelming sense of loneliness and grief swept through him. To combat it, he dropped the first letter on the ground next to him and picked up the second one to the people and Privy Council of Montalcino.

His feelings shifted almost instantly as he realized that he had hoped this was the path that Catherine might choose. He knew it was unlikely, but it was so easy to picture his own role in the life in which she chose to be queen. That, he knew, was a life that pulled him.

The longer he sat there pondering her choice, the closer he came to understanding that he had a choice, as well. "If she chooses the path that I think she will," he thought, "I will accompany her safely to the convent in Spain. I will stay and watch over her until she sets sail for America." He stood up and began to pace. "If she seems fully out of danger, I will let her go and return home."

He did not let his thoughts wander beyond his own homecoming. That would only lead him to an emptiness that, for now, he could not face. He had just picked up the letters and folded them when Pasquale appeared.

"My concentration is on the letters," he said to Gio. "Have you read them?"

Gio nodded and handed them over to his brother-in-law. Pasquale walked slowly to the bench where he and Catherine sat less than an hour prior. He read the letters in silence and looked over at Gio who continued to pace slowly in front of the chapel door.

"What do you think she will do?" Pasquale asked.

Gio started over to Pasquale shaking his head. "I know what I want her to do, but I believe she will choose to be a nun. It is what she has always wanted, no?"

A sad smile washed over Pasquale's face. "It is not that I wish her to choose the kingdom. The danger would be enormous, but she would be near. It is my selfishness that wants her to stay."

"Mine, as well," Gio said as he sat down beside Pasquale.

They sat in silence until, at last, Catherine emerged from the chapel. The look on her face was confused rather than decisive.

"You will both think me mad," she said.

Neither said a word in response as they stood at her approach.

"I cannot explain it, but I feel I am supposed to go to the Voghera waterfall." She shrugged her shoulders and looked hopefully at the men. "It sounds like lunacy, I know. Father, Uncle Gio, please take me there. Somehow, God wants me there and I must go."

Most men would have been angered at this new delay. Most men would never have indulged the girl as far as they had already. Most men might have turned her over to the authorities and allowed her execution for heresy. Pasquale and Gio were not most men.

Her father nodded, grateful for more time with his daughter. Gio instinctively fisted his hand over his heart, bowed his head and immediately left to prepare their departure.

The waterfall just outside of Voghera was a beautiful, private place. Well hidden in the forest in the foot of the mountains, it was the place that Lord Giovanni had introduced to Queen Catherine and her great love, Isabella. When one climbed up the rocky embankment adjacent to the falling water, there was a hidden ledge behind the falls. It was a sanctuary of healing and restoration, so full of spiritual wonder that there was a sense of heaven present to those seekers of such things.

Catherine, Pasquale and Gio arrived there after several days.

Eight monks had left the hermitage compound where Pietro Biondi died. Had anyone followed and been waiting for Catherine, her father, and her uncle to leave the cluster of buildings, they would have been unable to discern the identity of the three from the monks with whom they travelled for all were clothed in the hooded robes of the order.

When the group reached the main road, the eight "monks" parted ways in groups. Two appeared to head for Montalcino, three set on a course northward, toward France, and three took a southern route appearing to head for any number of places unknown. Additionally, when Catherine and her father and uncle arrived at the hermitage they were on horseback. The eight monks leaving the compound were mixed on horses and donkeys. Catherine had just mounted one of the horses when Brother Antoni walked over to her and handed her a small, wrapped package. "A gift," he said, "from the brothers who will continue to pray for you." His face had always been unreadable, but Catherine saw something in it as she thanked him for the gift. Her impression was that he knew something that he was about to share, but he bowed and quickly walked away and disappeared into the compound. The party was leaving, so she tucked the package into her bag, having decided to open it when they made camp for the night.

"Uncle Gio," Catherine said softly as their horses carried them away from the hermitage, "are you terribly disappointed?"

"No," he said as he smiled at her from beneath his hood. "I think you make a fine brother."

She laughed. It was the first time he had heard her laughter in so long that he could not help but join her. Even Pasquale, usually more serious in nature, laughed as well.

"My mother has returned to Voghera, has she not?" Catherine asked as the horses clip-clopped along the road.

Pasquale said, "Your mother assumed that you would be journeying on to a convent. It was not safe for her in Montalcino, so we sent her to live with your aunt until our return."

Catherine's aunt, Francesca's sister, lived not far from Voghera, on a farm in the country.

"Do you think she is safe?" Catherine asked.

"Your uncle provided trustworthy protection for her. We would have heard if anything had happened," Pasquale reassured her.

On the second day of travel Gio was convinced that they were not being followed. Although he remained tense, alert and cautious, he turned their course westward to begin the long journey toward Voghera. He kept them near the roads but within trees whenever he could. By the time they reached the waterfall, he was exhausted.

Now, as Catherine looked up at the place where the waterfall hid the covered ledge, her anticipation increased. Since the overwhelming feeling in the monk's chapel that she was to come here, her need to get here had only become stronger.

"Uncle Gio," she said tenderly as she reached for his cheek. "Rest. We are safe here. I know it in my heart."

Gio smiled. "Once you are safely behind the falls I will rest, Catherine."

"Father," she said as she turned to Pasquale, "I cannot explain it, since I do not know what lies in store for me yet, but . . . ." She hesitated and looked baffled by her own thoughts.

"What is it, daughter?"

"I—I want my mother to be here." Catherine looked at her father as if she were hoping he had some answer for her about why she made the request.

Pasquale looked into his daughter's eyes and smiled with an understanding she did not feel she deserved in the moment.

"You could not know, because we never told you, but your arrival into our lives saved your mother and me in more ways than I can count. I have learned more from being your father than life could ever have taught me without you." He paused and reached for her hand. "I know that I may lose you to a convent and another country. Your mother knew that when she said goodbye to you in Montalcino."

Catherine's eyes dripped tears down her cheeks as she thought of her mother's last farewell. Her father pulled her into his arms and said, "It matters not the reason you need your mother here. I would travel to the ends of the world to bring her to you if necessary. Your desire is all that is needed." He hugged her hard. "Now," he said, "I will depart to retrieve your mother. Climb your waterfall so your poor uncle might rest."

He held her shoulders while he gently pushed her to his arms lengths. "Your destiny awaits."

Catherine kissed him goodbye and admonished her uncle to sleep, then began her ascent to the place that pulled her like a magnet. When she reached the ledge, she slipped behind the falling water then poked her head and arm out to wave to Gio to let him know that all was well, and no one was lying in wait for her. He waved back and settled himself on the ground so that his eyes, when opened, were watching at the point where Catherine disappeared. He was soon snoring softly lulled into sleep by the sounds of the rushing, splashing water.

Catherine was glad of the monk's robe over her traveling outfit. The air was turning chillier and the mist from the waterfall made the temperature on the ledge even cooler. She had also carried a blanket up with her and wrapped it around her. The ledge was quite large with an overhang that gave some protection—almost like a cave. Catherine moved to the back wall and sat down with her back against the cold stone. She drew her knees up to her chest and wrapped her arms around her legs. She inhaled the moist, cool air and gave herself over to the sounds of the cascading waterfall. "Home," she thought to herself. "This is home."

She felt at peace here and settled into her surroundings, relaxing her body and mind into a tranquil state of just being with the rocks and water. Then, out loud, she said, "Here I am, Lord." She intended to begin praying but was immediately struck by the memory of Pietro Biondi admonishing her to sit silently without prayer, without thought, without any judgement. She remembered the instruction to be still and wait for God. And so, she did.

It was only when the sun had moved off the falls that Catherine came back to herself with a shiver. She realized she must have sat behind the waterfall for some hours for the sun to be so low in the sky. Her legs were numb, and the chill was brisk. Nevertheless, Catherine laughed and said, "Thank you, God. Thank you for this time."

When the feeling returned to her legs, she got up, stretched and peeked out from behind the waterfall. A small fire was blazing. Around it were her uncle, her father and her mother.

"Mama!" she called.

Her mother's face burst into a smile of such happiness as she stood and walked over to where Catherine would soon climb down.

When Catherine reached the bottom boulder, she turned and jumped off to fall into her mother's arms. Both women shed tears of joy in their reunion embrace.

Her mother had brought fresh bread, Voghera wine, olives and cheese. They family feasted on the delicious tastes of home, then settled in for the night.

Catherine was grateful that her family did not press her for a decision, although she hoped that one was forthcoming. As she waited for sleep to come, listening to the sounds of night in the forest, she reflected on her experience behind the water. She could not explain it. She did not sleep, but neither was she awake for all that time. She had conscious thoughts. In fact, she was plagued by her thoughts. At times it felt as if she were fighting with the thoughts to leave her. At other times it felt like she had no thoughts at all, and she was jolted back to herself by that very thought. How odd it was, but not at all frightening. It was as if a great peace and love filled and surrounded her—and she felt both present and totally elsewhere as if she were in a womb of love. With her heart full of the memory, she finally drifted off to sleep.

Catherine was dreaming an intense dream that in many ways did not feel like a dream, but more like reality, but she was shaken from the dream by the sounds of her family whispering nearby. The fire was out. Gio would not allow a fire during the day for fear that the smoke would attract attention. Catherine got up still pondering the dream and went to join her family.

"Your father told me that you met Pietro Biondi," her mother said. "I am sorry for his death."

"I was glad to be with him when he died," Catherine said and she reached for a piece of apple her mother had sliced. Her expression was one of mild puzzlement without a trace of sadness.

"It was not long that you were able to be with him," Francesca said. "I am sure you were a comfort to him."

"I have shared," Pasquale said, "with your mother, the letters with which he provided you."

"It was very kind of him to do so," Francesca said. "I was surprised to hear that he had been with the hermitage all this time," she continued as she passed Catherine a plate with some bread. "He disappeared so quickly, and no one ever heard from him or of him again."

"Actually," Catherine said as she dipped her bread in a bit of olive oil, "he had remained in touch with the priest from Castiglione d' Orcia."

"Father Tim," Gio said with his mouth full of bread. "That is how Biondi was able to get word to us that he wanted to see you."

Catherine nodded. "Apparently they communicated regularly."

The air was filled with unasked questions, and for a few moments the quiet was awkward.

Suddenly Catherine remembered the package given her by the monk before they departed the hermitage. She had always been too tired, or it was too dark to see, when they had camped each night of their journey.

She got up, found her bag, and pulled the package from it and returned to the group. "I had forgotten that Brother Antoni gave this to me as we were getting ready to leave the hermitage," she said as she sat down near her mother.

"Do you know what it is?" her mother asked.

"It has the feel of a book," Catherine answered as she began to unwrap the gift.

It was, indeed, a book. There was a note on top of it.

"Brother Pietro left this in the care of the Brothers. It has special meaning to many of us and has been copied by our own scribes several times, so we have others for our monastery. The writings are letters of an Unknown Monk and are said to have been written to one of his students. It is said that he lived sometime in the 1300s. The original letters were in the safekeeping of a Benedictine ascetic, Augustine Baker, who stayed with us for a winter several years ago. Brother Pietro painstakingly copied the letters. We had them bound.

"The book is yours now and I believe it to be in good hands. Peace be unto you,
Brother Antoni"

After reading the note aloud, Catherine turned the book over in her hands. It was beautifully bound in soft leather. She opened it to find exquisite handwritten pages on a very high-quality parchment.

"It is beautiful," her mother said. "And the note about the history is intriguing."

Catherine nodded. "I am more than intrigued," she said as she turned to the first page and read silently:

"Here beginneth a book of contemplation, which is called the CLOUD of UNKNOWING, in the which a soul is oned with GOD."

Catherine looked up and into the faces of her family. She stood up. "I know you are anxious for my decision," she said. Her face was a mix of concern for them and anguish for herself. "I have none yet, but perhaps there is something in this book that might help me."

"Read," her father said. "We will abide."

Catherine sighed. Her smile was full of gratitude as she turned and walked downriver where the water was calmer than at the base of the waterfall. She found a place in the sun and sat to read. She was so engrossed in the book that when her mother came to bring her a plate of food and a cup of wine, she shook her head.

"We just ate the morning meal," Catherine said.

Francesca smiled at her daughter and shook her head. "Look up, daughter. The sun is overhead. You have been reading for hours."

Catherine looked up in disbelief and only then realized she was hungry. "Sorry, Mama," she said as she smiled sheepishly. "I will come and join you for the meal."

As the two walked back up the river to join Catherine's father and uncle, she said, "It was more than just reading, Mama. There is profound spiritual knowledge in the writings of this monk—whomever he was. I feel as if I am being let in on a secret way to commune with God."

Francesca said nothing, knowing her daughter needed to hear her own words to integrate what was happening to her.

"Pietro Biondi tried to teach me some of this in his weakened state. It is very different from what we have been taught, but it somehow feels right. It is not against what we have learned. I feel as if it goes deeper in some way."

The women reached the place where the fire had blazed the night before. The smell from the ashes and burned wood hung in the air mixing with the scent of pine.

Catherine took the plate of food from her mother and sat. After giving thanks for the meal, they ate silently for a few minutes.

"I hesitate to ask this," Catherine said sheepishly, "but is it possible for us to go to Castiglione d' Orcia?"

"What do you expect to find there?" Pasquale asked.

"My future."

PART THREE

_____REDEMPTION

The trees surrounding the little church and home of Father Tim were ablaze in reds and golds in the late afternoon sun several days later when Catherine and her family rode into the courtyard. A smallish woman emerged from the house sweeping as she came through the door.

"Bon giorno!" Gio called from his horse.

The woman turned, startled. She was looking into the sun and could not see who had called.

Gio dismounted and walked over to the step on which she stood.

"You have not changed one bit, Lucia," he said grinning.

"Gio!" she exclaimed dropping her broom and stepping into his open arms. She kissed him on both cheeks then stepped back to look at him shaking her head. "It is good to see you, again."

"I am happy to find you still here," Gio said. "How are you? How are the children?"

Lucia had taken a handkerchief from her apron pocket to dry her eyes. She laughed, "No longer children, I am afraid."

"I want to hear everything about them," Gio said. "Is Father Tim here?"

"Ah, no," she said, still wiping her leaking eyes. "He and young Tim should be back soon. They went into town to minister to sick and hear confessions of those unable to come to church."

"Young Tim?" Gio started, but the sound of a throat clearing caused him to turn. "Lucia," he said, "you remember my sister, Francesca and her husband, Pasquale?"

Lucia's hand flew to her mouth as she shouted her surprise. "My, God! Of course, I remember!" She jumped from the porch and wrapped her arms around both of them. She was now openly crying. Francesca was crying as well, and even Pasquale could not hold back a few tears at this heartfelt reunion.

Lucia could not yet see Catherine, who had been standing behind her parents watching the people closest to her embrace a woman she had never known. The tenderness and affection they obviously felt for each other made her smile.

"The bambina!" Lucia pushed herself away from the couple and searched their eyes. "What happened to the bambina?"

Francesca and Pasquale both smiled and turned behind them.

Lucia stared in wonder and disbelief as the identity of the young woman settled sweetly into her understanding.

"You," Lucia started amid a fresh welling of tears. "You look so like her it is almost like seeing a ghost."

Catherine held out her hands to Lucia. "And you," she said pulling the woman toward her, "must be the very Lucia who risked so much to save my life." Lucia pulled her hands from Catherine's and covered her face with her hands, catching a sob in her now drenched handkerchief. She knew that this was the true queen of Montalcino. She knew that she should not do what she did next, but she could not help herself.

"Forgive me," she cried as she threw her arms around Catherine and wept.

Catherine embraced Lucia and let her cry.

When Lucia found her voice again, she stepped back and looked around her at all of them and exclaimed, "Oh, Father Tim will be so delighted to see all of you. I cannot wait until he arrives. Such a celebration we must have!"

Gio and Pasquale went back to attend to the horses.

Father Tim lived on the outskirts of Castiglione d' Orcia. The property had a small church, a rectory, a stable and a small hermitage. Lucia had lived with Father Tim, caring for him and helping with the parishioners since she had fled Aquapendente when, all those years ago, her brother insisted that she escape with her

children when he set out to warn Queen Sofia about the impend-
ing danger of being found.  The rectory had only one bedroom
for Father Tim.  Lucia slept on a cot in the kitchen no matter
that Father Tim insisted that she take a room in the hermitage
for herself.

"I am more comfortable here, Father," she had told him time
and again.  "Easier for me to be close to the kitchen."

The hermitage was a small one but had three separate rooms
each with its own door to the compound.  Lucia got the guests
settled in the hermitage and set off to create a feast.

The evening sun was splashing playfully through the autumn
leaves by the time Father Tim rode into his courtyard.  The young
man with him dismounted and took both horses and started
toward the stable.  He could see there were horses in the fenced
yard connected to the stable and wondered briefly about them,
but people often used the hermitage on their way from one place
to another.

Gio was on the porch and watched the priest dismount slowly
and with care.  It startled him how much the priest had aged.
There was little dark left in his hair.  It still held a splash of pepper in its salt, but his beard was all white now.  His face was lined
with age.

Tim placed his hands on his backside and stretched, arching
his back.  His face turned toward the sky and Gio saw a small
smile grace his face.

"Only you," Gio called out, "could ride in after a day of ministering to others, be bone tired, and still find a reason to smile."

Tim turned toward the porch and saw Gio.  The smile grew
instantly wider, and the priest took several energetic long strides
toward the porch.  Gio bounded down the step and threw his
arms around Tim, patting him ferociously on the back.

"What a great surprise to see you, my friend!" Father Tim

exclaimed as he held Gio at arm's length to have a good look at him. "Is everything well? Are we able to visit? Have you been to the monastery? Did Catherine meet—"

Gio's laughter cut him off. "Everything is fine, my dear priest. And you may ask Catherine yourself. She is the reason we are here."

Father Tim's eyebrows rose in disbelief.

Gio said, "Come inside and meet her."

The bustle of Lucia, Francesca and Catherine creating a meal filled the little rectory with such marvelous smells and sounds. Pasquale was bent over the fireplace getting a fire started. No one heard the door open, but Catherine saw the last of the sun stream in through the door and looked up.

"You must be the renowned Father Tim," Catherine said as she walked over to him. "It is an honor to meet you."

"The honor is mine," the priest said with tears in his eyes. He spoke with such love that Catherine reached for his hands and kissed them, for she at once was touched and moved by his humility and demeanor.

"How is it," Tim said as he reached up to place his right hand on Catherine's cheek, "that you seem to carry your grandmother's presence with you? It is as if she is in the room."

Catherine smiled. "I was hoping you might be able to tell me. I have felt her spirit with me for several days now. If I am not mistaken, she has brought me here."

The room was reverently still. Even the fire ceased crackling as the exchange between Catherine and Father Tim took place.

Catherine and Tim were locked in a gaze that no one dared disturb. No one wanted to, for it was almost a holy gaze that held the entire room transfixed.

Then, almost imperceptibly, Father Tim's head nodded, as if he acknowledged that something sacred had transpired. He sighed deeply and smiled. "We will talk," he said and looked around to see Francesca and Pasquale for the first time.

"My friends," he said. "It has been too long." He walked over to both, kissed them one at a time on both cheeks and hugged them.

"You know my parents?" Catherine asked.

"We met just once," Tim said. "At your grandmother's and Gio's father's funeral."

"You are kind to remember," Francesca said. "It was a difficult time."

Gio walked over to his sister and put his arm around her. "Better days ahead, I think."

She smiled and they all turned as the young man who had been with Father Tim walked in the open door.

Father Tim walked over to him and drew him into the room.

"This," he said with a note of pride, "is my nephew, Tim."

"Nephew!" said Gio. "I did not know you had any other family than your brother!" Gio strode over the young man and greeted him. Pasquale and Francesca did the same. Only Catherine hung back.

Tim laughed and shook his head. "Nor did I," he said, "until this fellow showed up on my doorstep about a year ago. Apparently, my brother, Thomas, had married, but even he did not know he had a son. Tim knew about me, but I never knew about him until he arrived."

"Everyone sit!" demanded Lucia. "It is time to eat."

"Timothy," said Father Tim, "would you do the honors?"

The young man bowed his head and everyone else followed suit with hands folded as he said grace.

The meal done and the dishes cleaned, Catherine asked if she might go into the church.

"Of course," Father Tim said. "Tim, would you escort

Catherine and light the candles for her? I am afraid it will be too dark inside without even a moon yet," he said to Catherine.

Tim grabbed a stick from the pile near the fireplace and held it to the flame until it caught, then headed for the door. Catherine followed.

The air was chilly outside, but there were still a few crickets chirping. An owl hooted somewhere to their left and then came an answer from a tree close to them. Tim walked resolutely to the door of the church. The door was unlocked, and Tim stepped through to light the way. Catherine stayed at the door while he went around the perimeter of the church lighting the candles along the wall. When he finished, he turned to find Catherine on her knees at the altar, her head bowed in prayer. He left her alone and went back to the rectory but did not enter. He sat on the porch in case Catherine came out and could not see her way. He lit a lantern and sat down to do his own praying.

It was the young novitiate's habit to go to the church each evening alone to pray. He was a tad put out that this strange woman had managed to invade what he considered his own private house of worship. He tried to pray on the porch, but he found himself stewing about the unexpected situation and visitors. He had never met his father, Thomas, who worked for the resistance to the Inquisition. His father did not know about his birth—or even his mother's pregnancy—because he was rarely in one place long enough for messages to reach him. Thomas died before Tim was born but neither he nor his mother knew that until much later. It had been Thomas's intention to tell his brother, Tim, about his secret marriage to Emilia when he next got to Castiglione d' Orcia with information on the resistance. He was murdered enroute to visit Tim. Thomas did not yet know he was to be a father when he died. Father Tim knew nothing of Emilia or the child.

Emilia had been a secret. The secret was to protect her. Thomas always knew that he took his life in his hands because of his work. He had no intention of endangering Emilia. She did not find out about her husband's death until more than a year after the occurrence. A man she recognized as having spoken to Thomas once privately appeared at her church for mass. It was never advisable to miss a Sunday mass unless you wanted to be interrogated for heresy, so everyone showed up on Sundays.

Emilia waited outside the door of the church for the man—whose name she did not know.

She approached him trembling and holding her baby in her arms, not knowing who or what his role in the Inquisition might be. Gathering her courage, she asked if he had heard from the man, Thomas, with whom he had met in the village more than a year previous.

He looked at her with an expression of horror, placed his hand at her back and steered her away from the parishioners exiting the church.

"Why do you want to know?" he demanded.

Without saying a word, for she could barely bring herself to speak she was so frightened, she looked pleadingly into his eyes then indicated the baby in her arms. "I am his wife," she said, her voice trembling.

His shoulders slumped as he took in the situation. He took a deep breath, let it out very slowly and told her that Thomas was dead. The man genuinely ached for her and could do nothing but offer her some money to help her get by. She never saw the man again, nor did she ever know his name.

Emilia also never told her son anything about his father, except that he had died while she was pregnant. However, two years ago, she became quite ill. Tim was fourteen. He adored his mother and took good care of her as she was dying. When it became clear that the end was near, Emilia told him all she knew.

"You are a good boy," she said, her voice barely audible. "You will be a good man."

"Mama," he said, kneeling by her bedside, "do not, please."

She reached for his hand and held it with trembling, bony fingers. "You need to know about your father."

"I know, Mama," he said, "he was a good Catholic, and he died before I was born."

She shook her head. "Listen, my son. Your father was part of a group fighting the Inquisition. He was the bravest man I ever met. I wish you could have known him. He would be so proud of you."

Tim was confused. "Why have you never told me this before?"

Emilia was struck with a violent coughing fit. When it subsided, she was drenched in sweat and asked for a cup of water.

"Forgive me," she said, her eyes filling with tears that ran down her cheeks. "I was afraid if I told you everything that it would put you in danger. You were too young for such a perilous secret."

The pain on his face conveyed his confusion over his own feelings. She could tell that part of him understood yet another part felt betrayed. He said nothing.

She needed him to speak to her, to share what he felt. Knowing he must be angry, but wanting to hear his voice, she asked him what he wanted to do with his life. "What is your dream?"

"To be a priest," Tim answered without hesitation and with a note of defensiveness. "You know that," he said, "and you know that I am speaking to Father Ignacio about becoming a novitiate next year."

"I know," she nodded. "I know."

Tim had been an altar boy since he had been a child. In their little town there was surprisingly little intrusion by the enforcers of the faith. Mostly folks went about their business and practiced their religion as the Church instructed. The terrors inflicted by the Church on other communities seemed to have passed over their town. However, Emilia did tell him about the things happening around their country as he became old enough to understand. Emilia supported his faith with her own beliefs about the basis of Christianity, but she always helped him to balance his faith with actions and taught him to be careful about what he said and did in public.

Her eyes closed, and it was clear that the conversation was tiring her. Tim held her hand and let her rest, wondering what he would do without her.

"You are named for your uncle," Emilia said after a short time. "I know little about him other than that he is a priest somewhere in the region of Montalcino. I do not know if he is dead or alive. I only know that your father looked up to him and that they worked together fighting the ugliest parts of our Church's beliefs."

Tim sat back on his heels, stunned by this new bit of information about his family. He was speechless.

"When I am gone," Emilia said so softly that Tim had to strain to hear her, "find him."

Emilia died that very night. She was buried in a small cemetery behind the church. A few people she knew were on hand, but her own father did not come. Tim walked the few miles to his house to tell him, but the man did not care. He cared for nothing and no one since his wife died. Tim did not like the man, anyway, and saw him on rare occasions when his mother tried to involve him in their lives. She finally gave up when Tim was about ten.

With no reason to stay in the town where he grew up, and newfound knowledge that his uncle was a priest, Tim went in search of the only person he knew who could tell him about his father. It did not take long for him to track down Father Tim once he got himself to Montalcino.

The air was getting cooler, and the longer Tim sat on the porch waiting for Catherine to leave the church, the more unsettled he became. Who did she think she was? He had just as much of a right to pray in the church as she did. When, finally, he reached the end of his tolerance he nearly stormed off the porch and marched to the church.

Catherine was no longer on her knees at the altar. He saw her sitting in the front pew. He closed the door without regard for the clatter it made and strode down the aisle. She did not move but continued to sit in silence. Tim moved into a pew on the opposite side of the aisle a row back and knelt. From his spot he could watch her. He wanted to make her as uncomfortable as possible so that she might get the message and leave him in peace.

Catherine continued to sit. Her head was erect, and her eyes were closed. She seemed to have a small smile on her face. She did not move. Her lips did not move. Her breath was slow and steady.

Tim could not pray. He was agitated. He realized he was angry, and that fact made him more agitated. He did not like change, and this upset his evening routine. Finally, he pulled out his rosary and began to work the beads. He was more than halfway through the cycle of prayers when he looked up and realized Catherine was gone. He never heard her leave. The door never made a sound. She never made a sound. He turned to be certain she was not just behind him somewhere. She had left him alone and what happened to him next he could not explain. A pain gripped his chest. He tried not to cry out, but he lacked the ability to control the wave of emotion that exploded from him. The sob that escaped him was full of pure grief.

Tim stayed in the little church, weeping on and off. He wept for his mother and the loss of her. He wept for the loss of his grandfather, whom he had always hoped would want to be part of his life, but who wanted nothing to do with anyone. He wept for his father who never knew he had a son. Finally, he wept for himself.

Tim's uncle found him in the church the next morning before the sun was up. The candles had long since burned down, but even in the scant predawn light Father Tim could see the dirty tear lined streaks on the boy's face. The old priest sat down on the pew next to his nephew, careful not to wake him and prayed silently as the day began.

"Uncle?" Tim whispered as he opened his eyes and sat up.

Father Tim opened his eyes and smiled at Tim. "I cannot tell you how many times I awoke to find myself here over the years," he said. "Was it a good rest?"

The young man rubbed his eyes and ran his fingers through his hair. As his memory of the evening before came back to him he felt nothing but confusion. He shrugged.

"Is there anything you want to talk about?" Father Tim asked.

The boy shook his head.

"You might," Father Tim offered as the boy turned to leave, "want to wash your face before you do anything else."

Father Tim went about replacing the candles that had burned down to nothing during the night. When he was done, it had always been his custom to kneel at the altar to pray before beginning his day. However, his knees were now achy, and it was not so easy to get into or out of a kneeling position on the stone floor. He sat in the first pew and asked for God's help for Catherine.

The door to the church opened, and Catherine entered. "Father Tim," she said, "I can come back later if you are in prayer."

"I am in prayer about you, dear child," he said as he stood to greet her. "Come sit with me."

Catherine walked up the short aisle, genuflected, crossed herself and sat next to the priest. She looked up at the cross over the altar and then down at her hands in her lap. "I am not certain where to begin," she said.

"You are troubled," he said, "may I ask the source of your concern?"

Catherine told him about learning of her true lineage. She told him about her lifelong desire to be become a nun. Then she told him about her time with Pietro Biondi.

"I am glad you met with him," Tim said. "I believe he had truly suffered for the part he played in your mother's death. It tormented him, you know."

Catherine smiled one of those very sad smiles of understanding. Then realizing that he might not know, she said, "He suffers no longer."

"For that," he said, "I am glad. May he rest in peace."

Catherine stood up and walked over to where a shaft of sunlight streamed in through one of the windows. "I was with him when he died," she said. "It was a peaceful death."

"Was he able to offer you any advice?" Father Tim asked.

She walked back over to where Tim sat and joined him again on the pew. "I thought so, but now I seem more conflicted than ever." She paused and closed her eyes almost as if she were in pain. "Father Tim," she finally said, "do you believe that God leads us to what He wants us to do? I have always felt God's presence and direction in my life. I thought God wanted me to become a nun. Now I do not know what God wants." She looked up at him with a look of frustration that he knew so well.

He smiled. "What do you want, Catherine?"

"I do not know!" she said a bit more loudly than she intended.

He laughed softly. "It would be so easy if God just told us, would it not?"

"Well," she said, and smiled at the thought, "would it really be such a bad thing?"

"Poor God," he said. He looked up at the cross and gazed at it for some time. "Sometimes I imagine God must feel like the parent to a world full of children." He stood and walked over to the altar then turned back to her. "Growing children want to prove they can do things they are not ready to do. They dig in their heels and rebel to assert their independence and fight against the very things they are told to do." He chuckled and looked back at her. "Can you imagine the resistance and opposition God would have had if He had ordered someone to die on the cross for the likes of us?" He came back and sat down next to her again. "Catherine," he said gently, "God wants you to know what you want. It does not matter to Him if you want to be a nun or a queen. He will be with you no matter your decision. God is giving you the right and the ability to make your own life decision. He will not abandon you if you want to be queen, just as He will not abandon you if you decide to cross the sea and become a nun. And, make no mistake, either choice will be fraught with suffering. And God will be in the suffering, as well."

He stopped and saw the look of pain in her eyes. "You are named," he continued, "for two of the most remarkable people I have ever known. I watched those two women struggle and fight and stand up for the people of this land during some of the greatest injustices and horrors ever known. In fact, your grandmother and I had many long talks during her reign as queen. I considered her and Lady Isabella peers and confidantes. Both your grandmother and your mother were born into their roles and into the expectations that they would assume them. You have a choice. You may choose not to be queen. You may choose not to be a nun. You need not be either of those things. Perhaps, in time, you might decide to marry and become a mother. Do you not see, Catherine, your mother made certain that you could decide for yourself?"

Catherine took a great breath and smiled. "You mean like God gave Christ the ability to decide that He would die on the cross?"

Father Tim laughed out loud. It was a joyous sound and his eyes filled with the tears of his own laughter. He shook his head. "You are definitely your grandmother's granddaughter," he said as he wiped his eyes with the back of his hand.

She stood again. "Wanting to be a nun was easy when I was Francesca and Pasquale's daughter. I could stay and serve the people of my own country. Knowing now that my life is in danger if I stay makes things more difficult."

"Understandably," Tim said. "And being a nun in a far-away land complicated that decision?" "I love my family and Montalcino," she said.

"How can I help, Catherine?"

Catherine seemed to be in thought for a minute.

She reached into her pocket and pulled out the book that Biondi had written from the Unknown Monk. "Help me understand this better and be able to get to this place in my prayer life. I think that the answer is here for me, but I am not sure how just yet."

Father Tim opened the book and read the beginning. "I have heard of this," he said, his eyes opening wide, "but only through talk of it." He turned the pages reverently.

Catherine was surprised at his response to the book and watched as he immediately began to absorb the content. "I have," she said, "already begun to practice some of what I understand. I would consider it a great help if you were to read it and offer your insight."

Tim closed the small, bound book in his hands and held it to his chest. "Perhaps," he said, "we can help each other to understand its meaning."

The shaft of light through the window had moved a short distance from where it began. "I believe," said Catherine, "that my mother and Lucia are waiting for us to return for breakfast. Shall we?"

Together they left the church and went back to the rectory where the group was already eating heartily.

Much to Catherine's delight, she learned many things about the lives of Queen Catherine, Lady Isabella, Gio's father, Robert, and grandfather, Giovanni, and how they and Father Tim fought the oppression and injustice of the Church. The stories were both horrifying and inspirational. She said as much to her mother as they walked in the woods the next day.

"I feel as if my eyes have been opened to a world I have never known," she said as she walked arm in arm with Francesca.

A bright, red bird flitted among the trees, seeming to follow them as they walked. Catherine pointed to it whenever it appeared near them.

Francesca smiled and nodded. "We tried to help you understand the differences between what the Church had become through the greed of men and still hold true to the Christ message," she said. "It is a difficult balance to protect your child from the sickness in the world and illuminate it, too."

"Made," said Catherine as she helped her mother step over a large fallen log, "more difficult by your knowledge of the possibility that I might choose to be queen some day?"

Francesca sighed, and her step slowed. Catherine slowed with her.

"Queen or nun, either way I knew we would eventually give

you up to a world in need."

Catherine stopped and turned her face up to the treetops. "Queen or nun," she said, "that seems to be the dilemma."

They stood for several minutes with the sun nearly overhead and sparkling through the thick umbrella of the forest, and neither said a word.

"So," Francesca finally said, "what do you think of Father Tim?"

They turned and began the walk back to the rectory.

Catherine smiled, raised her eyebrows in wonder and said, "He is a treasure. I do love hearing the stories you are all sharing about the past. They make me proud to be part of such a noble and brave family."

Francesca gave her daughter's hand a squeeze, but said nothing, for she heard in her child's voice something she had never heard before. It frightened her.


When they returned to the rectory, Catherine asked her mother to excuse her as she wished to go to the church to pray. She entered, found it empty and wanted again to try to follow the instructions laid out in the *Cloud of Unknowing*. And so, she knelt in the last pew, closed her eyes, and thought about a word that would be meaningful to her, that would remind her of her intention to be still—to just sit with God when her mind wandered. She had given days of thought to what that one word should be. On their journey to Father Tim's, she found herself thinking much about the lives of the saints about whom she had studied all her life. She thought about the martyrs, the apostles, Mary the mother of Jesus and Mary the Magdalene. Now, her thoughts went to the conversation at breakfast this morning, about the courage of her ancestors. In a soft but resounding heartbeat, she heard the word in her heart. It was the word she realized they all had said to God.

The word was, "Yes."

Later that day Catherine wandered the perimeter of the compound. Sometimes she found that walking helped her to think better. Her mother was inside helping Lucia prepare the evening meal and she knew she should offer her assistance, but her need to be outdoors in the autumn sun was insistent.

"Catherine!" Father Tim called as he and Tim entered the compound from their day in town.

Catherine looked up and smiled at the dusty pair. "It is a gorgeous afternoon, no?" asked the priest.

Catherine took a deep breath and replied, "Not only gorgeous, but glorious. How was your day in town?" she asked.

"Filled with people in need of prayer, confessions, forgiveness and love," he said. "There seems to be a never-ending need for such things."

"It must be exhausting," Catherine said with concern.

"Not for Tim, here," he said placing his hand on his nephew's shoulder. "I remember that when I first became priest here, I found the work exhilarating. But," he added, "I was a much younger man, then."

"I confess," Tim said, "that I do love bringing the love of Christ to people."

Catherine looked at him and saw not only that he meant what he said, but she saw a softness in his eyes that had not been there upon their first encounters. Initially, she had felt a distance. She had felt like an intruder. Those feelings were gone now, and she felt drawn to the young man in ways she could not explain.

Father Tim looked down at himself and his dusty robes. "I will excuse myself. It is my habit to tidy a bit and spend some time in prayer before Lucia feeds us!"

Tim laughed. "You are heading off with that little book

again, Uncle. You cannot fool me."

"Just so," the priest said. "I am caught—but leaving just the same." He turned, and with a little more bounce in his step, headed off to the church.

"It seems," Tim said to Catherine when they were alone, "that you have given my uncle quite a gift in sharing your book."

"It makes my heart glad, then, to be able to share it with him," she said.

They walked together into the center of the compound. "Catherine," he said with a hesitation in his voice, "I would like to ask your forgiveness."

"Whatever for?" she said, stopping and turning to look at him.

"I was less than hospitable when you first arrived. I," he paused, seeming to struggle a bit for the right words. "I did not understand that I was possessed of an anger that perhaps I did not admit."

Catherine listened and said not a word.

"That first night, when you went into the church," he said softly, "I found myself fuming at you for, of all things, sitting in my church when it was my time to do so."

They came to a rock bench as they walked, and Tim indicated that he wanted to sit.

"It was not," he continued once they were seated, "until I barged into the church like a recalcitrant child that something began to happen to me. I was confused when I saw that you were sitting so quietly and seemed so content and so oblivious to me and my anger that I tried to calm myself with the rosary."

Tim took a deep breath, bent over and rested his elbows on his knees. "You left," he said. "You left so quietly that I did not hear the sound of you leaving."

Catherine could see that he was struggling to tell her something that was important to him. She reached over and quietly put her hand on his arm.

"When I realized I was alone—that you left without allowing me to confront you—I was overcome with enormous feelings of loss." Tim's eyes filled with tears, and he stopped speaking.

"You have lost so much," Catherine offered.

Tim wiped his eyes with the sleeve of his robe. "It comes in waves still," he said. "My uncle has been so understanding in helping me to talk about these things. But I did feel that I owed you an apology for my behavior that night. I was rude and you did not deserve the treatment I doled out."

Catherine squeezed his arm. "I will not deny that I felt your anger that night, but I do know that the hardness has left your face. Your eyes are softer now and I understand."

He looked at her with gratitude. "Thank you."

"You," she said with admiration, "are going to make a very good priest."

The next day was Sunday. Lucia was up early preparing a midday feast. On Sundays many from the town came to the little parish church to hear Mass and the sermons of Father Tim. For Lucia, it was especially sweet because her youngest child, Michelena, came with the family for whom she worked. Michelena was housekeeper and nanny to the children of the Novali family in Castiglione d' Orcia. Lucia's son, Angelo, came on occasion but worked in a town farther out and it was not always possible for him to come.

Father Tim and Tim had been up early and at the church preparing for the Mass. Catherine had entered the church at sunrise to find them lighting candles and preparing the altar.

"Is there anything I might be allowed to do to help?" she

asked when she realized what they were doing.

Father Tim asked if she would light the candles around the sanctuary. He gave her a twig lit from another candle.

"I have," he said, "been quite engrossed in your little book. You might find some of what I have come to understand in the sermon today."

Catherine stopped in her task and looked at him with a wry smile. "I look forward to hearing it."

"I hope you do not mind, but I have been sharing much of it with Tim," he said, indicating his nephew.

Catherine moved to the next candle on the wall. "What do you think of the work, Tim?"

"I find it," he paused and thought for a moment as he prepared the wine for communion, "to feel like a truth I have always know but seem to have forgotten. I wish I could explain better what I mean."

Catherine turned and looked at him with surprise. "I know," she said, "exactly what you mean. It is validating in ways that just feel like, well, like truth."

Tim reacted with as much animation as she had seen from him since she arrived. "Yes," he exclaimed. "That is exactly so! It is truth that we already know but has been hidden from our own hearts!"

They both turned to the sound of Father Tim's laughter.

"Well," he finally said, "there goes my sermon!"

Catherine found herself excited to hear more of what the men found in the book. Since her resounding "yes" of yesterday, she had been practicing sitting and returning to the "yes" and trying to keep her heart open to God. Interestingly, she found herself remembering words and phrases from Sofia's journal. They seemed continuously to pop into her head many times since her alone time of yesterday. Most particularly, the phrase from the journal that encouraged her to choose the future that held "love and life" for herself. She had given much thought to whether serving God as queen or nun would meet that requirement.

Preparations complete, young Tim went to the door of the church and opened it. A few people had been waiting and Catherine left to find her parents. She spotted them leaving the rectory. They were headed toward her.

As she waited for them, her attention was drawn to the cry of a baby. She looked to see a young woman emerging from the path through the trees. She was holding an infant and had the hand of a young boy. Catherine was struck by the beauty of the young mother and wondered what it would be like to be so young and to have two babies already to care for. Again, the phrase "choose love and life" echoed in her head.

"Shall we?" Pasquale said, focusing Catherine's attention on heading back into the church.

"Yes, Papa," Catherine said, turning and taking the arm of her father on one side and her mother on the other.

"Your sermon was inspired, Father Tim," Catherine said as the priest came to the rectory after visiting with parishioners in the courtyard after mass.

Father Tim smiled at her. "Inspired by your little book, Catherine. Thank you for sharing it with me."

Young Tim had come in behind his uncle, heard the exchange and said, "It may have been inspired by the words of the Unknown Monk, Uncle, but you brought them to life in a way that gave them meaning to everyone."

"You are," Pasquale offered, "a remarkably gifted man of God."

"Nonsense," Tim said, obviously uncomfortable with the praise he was receiving.   "What is remarkable is that this unknown monk—who lived hundreds of years ago—seems to have been able to access the very things that have hovered at the edge of my soul for much of my life." Tim shook his head and looked around the room at this small group of people who felt like family. "It is as if being a parish priest thwarted my ability to connect to God in the way my heart desired."

Lucia, who had been listening intently, but busy putting the finishing touches on the midday meal, stopped what she was doing and offered her insight with the truth of her observations. "You barely have time for yourself, Father.  You are either in town ministering, or people come here for your ministry, or you are preparing to minister." She shook her head, again. "Priests have no time for anything!"

The group looked at her with more than a touch of surprise.

"Well," she said, "it is true.  I have watched this man give more of himself than a hundred men have energy for.  When do you get to rest and be with God?"

"She is not wrong, Uncle." Tim said.  "I have watched you and tried to keep up with you for a year now.  It is exhausting."

"Enough talk," Lucia said.  "Where is Michelena?"

"I am here, Mama!"

Everyone turned to see the young woman walk through the door.

"I apologize," Michelena said.  "The children took longer to say goodbye this morning."

Catherine was surprised to see the striking young woman with the two children she had observed earlier and remembered that Lucia's daughter served as nanny to a family in town.

Young Tim greeted Lucia with kisses on both cheeks and a hug.  Father Tim kissed her cheeks and introduced her to his guests.

"You," Michelena said almost reverently, "are the family to whom we travelled so long ago?"

Francesca's eyes opened wide. "You cannot possibly remember that trip. You were a baby yourself!"

Michelena chuckled. "No, I do not remember the trip. What I remember is the infant in my mother's arms. Just a vague memory of my mother holding another baby."

"I was that baby," Catherine said stepping forward to greet Michelena.

The women kissed on both cheeks and before anyone could say anything else, Lucia said, "Sit! Eat!"

The meal was delicious, simple peasant fare, but so well prepared that it all disappeared.   For Catherine, however, the meal was really second to the lively conversation and laughter around the table. At home the food was always good, too, but the conversation was generally more academic, more—was the word she was looking for, "controlled"?  Whatever it was, Catherine was totally enraptured with the constant flow of laughter, chatter, and conversation. Again, love and life, floated through her mind.

When the meal was complete, and all was cleaned up, Michelena and Tim started for the door. "Catherine," Tim said, turning back to her, "Michelena and I usually go walking after meals on Sunday. Would you care to join us?"

"Are you certain it would not be an imposition?" she asked.

"Not at all," Michelena responded. "We would love for you to join us."

Without hesitation, Catherine accepted. She realized that she was closest in age to Tim and Michelena and found herself coveting time with them.

"So," Michelena started as they followed the path into the woods, "what do you think of our little hamlet, Catherine?"

Catherine pulled her wrap around her as they moved into the shade of the trees. "I must admit," she answered, "I did not expect to like it so much. Especially today."

"Why today?" asked Tim.

"Well, between your uncle's sermon and the joy and interactions at the meal, I do not think I have ever quite felt so at home or so content. I suppose that does not make much sense."

Tim was the first to respond. "It makes perfect sense. I grew up without much of a family. It was just my mother and myself. I loved my mother very much, but it was a lonely existence. Sundays here are my favorite day of the week."

"Mine, too!" Michelena joined in. "The family I work for is very nice and they treat me well, but I miss my mother and I almost feel like Father Tim is my father. My brother and I grew up here after . . . well, after . . . "

Catherine heard and felt where Michelena's hesitation came from. She reacted quickly to ease the woman's discomfort. "It is fine, Michelena. You grew up here after your uncle and my mother were murdered."

"It was a long time ago," Michelena said. "But sometimes I still hear the grief in my mother's voice, and I know she misses him. We were very lucky to be taken in by Father Tim. How long will you be staying?" she asked, changing the subject.

"I do not think we can intrude on Father Tim's hospitality too much longer. We came so that I might find some help in determining whether I want to be a nun or a queen." Catherine was tired of hearing herself say the words, let alone still not have an answer. She sighed.

"So which way are you leaning?" Tim asked.

They had come to a small clearing in the woods. Michelena had been carrying a quilt and lay it out in the sunlight. Tim grabbed two corners and helped straighten it out. The three of them sat down, soaking up the sunlight.

Catherine was surprised at how comfortable she was with these two people whom she had only recently met—Michelena just today.

Michelena looked at Catherine. "So, which shall it be, queen or nun?" she asked.

Until this very moment, Catherine would have said she still had no idea. But she heard herself saying, "I believe I want to stay. I really do not want to be far from my family. I do not want to travel across the sea. I love it here."

Tim and Michelena gaped at her.

Catherine looked at them with as much surprise in her face as there was on theirs.

"I do not know where that came from!" she said. "I cannot believe that I just—"

Quiet exploded on the quilt. It was full of understanding of what Catherine's words meant. The silence was loud and overwhelming. It was Michelena who finally broke it.

"So, you will be staying, Your Majesty?"

Catherine's heart stopped. She looked into Michelena's eyes and saw not only the truth, but the playfulness there.

"I guess I am," she said. "Oh, my goodness. I guess I am!"

Catherine started to chuckle. Michelena smiled and then Tim started to laugh. Before long all three of them were caught up in gales of laughter.

Catherine felt free. Perhaps for the first time in her life she felt her heart and soul breaking free in ways that were indescribably delicious, comforting, exciting, joyous, intimate and more spiritual than she ever could have imagined. Catherine felt herself flooded with a kind of happiness that was new and exciting.

Francesca saw the relief in her daughter's eyes as soon as she returned to the compound.

"She has made a decision," Francesca thought, and she felt her stomach clench. "I gave her up to you once already, God, and you brought her back to me. I do not think I could go through giving her up again."

Catherine said nothing to her mother but went directly to the church and did not come back. When it was nearing dinner time Father Tim went to the church. He found Catherine sitting silently. She heard him come in and smiled when she saw him.

"There is a peace about you that is new," he said looking at her face.

She nodded.

"You have made a decision, then?"

"I have." Catherine stood and walked over to him. "But it cannot be my decision alone." Tim cocked his head in question.

"I have been sitting here for some time," she said. "I have made the decision to stay, to be queen, but am not foolish enough to believe that I can do the thing alone. I know that my Uncle Gio will stay by my side and protect me, but that will not be enough. It will mean that my family must come with me to Montalcino, as well, and give up the life they have known. It also means something else."

"What is that?" he asked.

"I do not want, ever, to be without spiritual guidance. That would be more than I could bear."

Father Tim waited for her to say what was on her mind.

"Father," she said, "will you come with me?"

Tim looked into her eyes and saw her seriousness. He looked deeper and saw her fear. And when he looked inside himself, he saw the answer to his own prayers.

"Yes," he said ever so softly. "Yes."

Francesca closed her eyes and thanked God silently for Catherine's decision, then instantly worried about what the decision would mean for her daughter's safety but said nothing as the group around the dinner table erupted into chatter and questions.

Catherine smiled at the response and held up her hand to silence the group. When they quieted, she said, "I know you all must have a thousand question and concerns." She looked at her mother as she added the last word. "There is much to consider and to do to prepare for this, and I will not pretend that I know what all is involved."

Catherine looked at Father Tim, sitting next to her at the table, and reached to place her hand on top of his. "First things first," she said. "Father?"

The priest cleared his throat and said simply, "Catherine has requested that I be with her in Montalcino as she assumes her place as queen. I have agreed. Montalcino is not that far from Castiglione d' Orcia and I believe," he paused and looked at his nephew, "that you, Tim, are ready to care for the people here. They have taken to you well and I believe your dedication to them and to God will continue to serve the people of this community."

Tim looked at his uncle, then scanned the faces around the table. When he finally spoke it was to say, "Uncle, I am honored that you think I am ready, but I assure you I am not!" There was a tremble of fear in his voice.

"And that, dear nephew, is exactly what makes you ready. Always hold that humility in your heart. God will guide you."

"And," Michelena spoke up, "you will have my mother to help you here."

"Actually, Lucia," Catherine said, "I was hoping you might join Father Tim and me in Montalcino. You are a master at cooking, baking and organizing. I am hoping you will be willing to take charge of everything in the castle kitchens."

The look on Lucia's face was one of surprise and trepidation.

"Lucia," Catherine said, "I will need someone I can trust to oversee the kitchen and whatever staff might be left or need to be hired. I can think of no one better. Will you do it?"

Lucia's bottom lip began to quiver. She could not answer for the lump that formed in her throat but could only nod.

"Thank you," Catherine said.

"Mother, Father," Catherine said turning to her parents. "None of this will happen if you are not able to be with me in Montalcino." She stopped and said nothing more.

Pasquale looked at Francesca. What passed between them was seen only by them. Everyone else at the table only saw the pair look at one another. Whether they had years or minutes of discussion about the possibility of this moment no one could say. But, when Pasquale broke eye contact with his wife, he turned to Catherine and said softly, "We would be nowhere but at your side."

Catherine let out a sigh of relief, then turned to Gio. "Yours will be the most difficult task. I know this. I wish to give you the same choice that Queen Sofia gave me," she said. Do you desire to be the Captain of the Guard?"

Gio said nothing, but stood up from the table, walked around to where Catherine stood, bent on one knee and placed his fist over his heart. "With honor and pleasure, my Queen."

When Gio stood, Catherine turned to the group. Her eyes were misted with tears. "There is much to do. Let us give thanks for this food and begin preparations for what, I anticipate, will be no small task in taking back the throne for all the people from whom it has been stolen."

After the meal, as everyone but Lucia and Michelena sat near the fire to begin to discuss the difficulties that lay ahead,

Catherine observed Lucia hug a tearful Michelena goodbye before the young woman left to return to the family she served in town. She made a note to check with Lucia later.

"We need allies," said Gio, "that is the most pressing concern. If we do not march into Montalcino prepared to overthrow the existing leadership, we may as well abandon our plan right now."

Pasquale agreed. "I will ride back to Voghera first thing tomorrow," he said. "I know I can count on at least a few families that will do whatever they can to help."

Gio shook his head. "There is no time, Pasquale. We must move quickly. Father," he said to Tim, "we need to keep the operation as small as possible. I have an idea that may help us if you are willing."

Tim listened to the idea and nodded. "I agree."

Francesca sat quietly throughout the discussion, but when it appeared that the next steps were set, and the conversation was over for the evening, she said, "And what will my role be in all this strategy?"

"Mother," Catherine said, "I need you by my side for every part of this. Starting with hiring staff outside of this immediate group. Where do we begin?"

"We start small," Gio said. "No offense, sister, but we need to know that everyone we bring can be trusted."

"Of course," Francesca said. "And there may be some few in Montalcino who might be glad to have Catherine as monarch. How will we assess their potential loyalty?"

"That is one of the reasons that I am grateful to you, Lucia," Catherine said to the woman who had stayed on the outskirts of the group after Michelena left. "As the person in charge of everything that happens in the bowels of the castle, you will be privy to much of what goes on."

"Catherine," Francesca interrupted, "you will eventually

require at least one lady to assist you in your everyday affairs. That will be the one of the first people that will need to be as trustworthy as those here."

"Michelena!" Lucia cried out.

They all turned to look at her. She instantly covered her mouth with her hands, regretting her outburst.

"My apologies," Lucia said. "I am so overcome with so many feelings. This is happening so quickly. I do want to serve you, Cathe-," she hesitated and altered her address, "Queen Catherine, but it will be difficult for me to be so far from my own daughter. I did not mean to suggest that you would be interested in her. She and I will be fine."

Catherine stared at Lucia with a questioning look on her face. "But," she finally said to Lucia, "she has a position already. What makes you think she would even be interested in serving a queen who is not even certain that she will be able to assume the throne?"

"It is just a mother's intuition," Lucia responded. "She does love the children she serves, but has, on occasion, complained about the parents."

"Lucia, I have only known your daughter for one day, but feel I have known her for a lifetime," Catherine said. "I did not have many friends growing up but feel an affinity with Michelena. Perhaps, we might see her in town tomorrow and see how she feels about such a change in her life."

Young Tim said, "Michelena is a good woman. She has been a friend to me since I arrived. You would find none better to serve you with loyalty and honesty. Although I would be sorry to see her go. Her honesty has helped me in more ways than I can count."

Catherine nodded. "Tomorrow, then."

Early the next morning, following the meal, Father Tim suggested that they all move to the church to pray about the path they had all chosen to take.

"Heavenly Father," Tim said when all had gotten down on their knees, "we lift ourselves and the kingdom of Montalcino into your Holy Presence. We ask for your guidance, your mercy and your grace for each of us as we embark on this dangerous but necessary path. Help us to rely on You and to know that You will be present with us in love as we strive to right the injustice and destruction that has ruled for too long. In the name of all that is holy we pray. Amen."

"Amen," the group echoed as one.

Lucia, Father Tim and Tim, Pasquale, Francesca and Catherine walked the mile through the woods to the town of Castiglione 'd Orcia. There was no conversation. Each person was absorbed in their own thoughts or prayers as they walked. When they reached the outskirts of the town square, Catherine smiled, taking in the bustle of people going about their day.

"It has been so long since I have been in the center of a town that I did not realize how much I missed it," she said to her mother.

"There is something about a town center and all of its people greeting one another, sharing life and laughter, that is important," Francesca said. "Perhaps that is what life is all about."

Catherine slipped her arm through her mother's and squeezed.

Father Tim spotted a man near the center of the square. The man had been sitting on one of the benches and rose when he saw the priest.

"Gio," Father Tim said turning to him. "There he is."

Gio turned to Catherine and nodded. Then, he, Pasquale and young Tim followed the priest. They disappeared into a small café.

Catherine, Francesca and Lucia did not have to wait long.

As they walked around the square, looking at wares, Catherine turned and caught a glimpse of Michelena with the two children she watched. She waved.

Michelena was obviously surprised to see them but walked excitedly over with the children in tow. "What a wonderful surprise!" she said, kissing all three of them.

Catherine could not explain the feeling that gripped her when she first spotted Michelena. It was a slight feeling of fear mixed with a joy that she felt in her very center. Again, she wondered what it would be like to have children. It was a thought she would have never in her life entertained. She had never given thought to falling in love or being intimate or bearing children. Her life had centered around her love of God and her marriage to Christ and never to the physical nature of human love with another.

She wondered silently, as Michelena greeted her, if that might now be a thought she could, or even should, entertain.

Michelena's happiness at seeing them gave Catherine her own happiness. Quickly, however, she said, "Michelena, you must introduce us to anyone we meet, or anyone who might, ask as relatives."

Francesca said, "I am now your mother's cousin, and this is my daughter, Catherine."

"Ah," Michelena said, clearing understanding the reasons. "I understand, Cousin Francesca." She introduced the children. "Franco, these are cousins of mine who have come to visit my mother. Can you say hello?"

Little Franco, who was about two, hid behind Michelena's skirts. "He is very shy," Michelena said. She was holding the baby, who could not have been more than six months old. She was a beautiful baby, with dark brown, wavy locks and large brown eyes. "This," she said, "is my little angel, Angela."

Catherine looked at the baby. "Hello, Angela."

The baby smiled and gurgled. Catherine was instantly enchanted.

Michelena saw the look on Catherine's face. "Would you like to hold her?"

Catherine reached for the baby, already smiling and anticipating the closeness of the child. She smiled at the baby in her arms and had difficulty taking her eyes off that face.

Lucia laughed. "You look like a natural mother, Catherine!"

Catherine looked up and blushed. "Please do not give my mother ideas, Lucia. I think I will be quite busy for some time," she said. "Michelena, is there a place we might talk in private?"

"Follow me," she said.

They walked to the opposite side of the square. The stalls thinned out and there were not as many people. A little bit down from the square was a blacksmith shop. A young man was holding something with a pair of tongs and pounding away at it on his anvil. The sound grew louder as they approached.

"Vito!" Michelena shouted. "Vito!" she called louder.

The young man looked up and smiled. "Michelena, marry me!"

Michelena shook her head and laughed. "I would consider it if you did not say the same thing to every woman who passes your shop!"

Vito's laugh was hearty and honest. "Lucia," he called, "marry me!"

Lucia shook her head and smiled at the young man. "Someday, Vito, you will mean it, and no one will believe you."

Vito smiled. He was good-natured, and he loved to make people smile. "And who," he asked, "are these beauties you have brought?"

Lucia spoke. "Vito, these are cousins visiting. This is my cousin, Francesca and her daughter, Catherine."

Vito bowed deeply and with good humor. "And what might I do for such a brood of beauties?"

"Might we sit in your mother's garden a bit?" Michelena asked. "I would like a bit of time to chat before they head back with my mother to Father Tim's. I will not have another opportunity to visit, and your mother's garden has such a peace about it."

Vito's mother and father were both dead, but Vito kept up his mother's garden as best he could in her memory. He picked up the item he had been hammering on with the tongs and laid it back into the red, hot fire. "Please," he said as he walked from the open air of the smith shop and around to the back of it. There, he opened a gate and ushered them in. "You honor my mother with your presence." He closed the gate and left them alone in the garden. It was not long before they heard his hammer clanging again.

The garden was a breathtaking vision of fall colors. The flowers of fall were in bloom and the trees were resplendent in their autumn hues.

"How lovely!" exclaimed Catherine.

"Vito cares for it himself." Michelena bent down and instructed Franco not to pick any flowers. There was a stone bench and chairs under a metal arbor covered with rose vines. "Vito built this for his mother."

"Impressive," said Francesca. "What happened to his parents?"

"His father was apparently murdered for trying to stop an execution of a family he knew to be good people. They were, like so many I fear, targeted as heretics. Who knows why? Vito was young at the time but had been watching from his window with his mother as his father tried to intervene. The men tied him up and dragged him off with the family to execute."

"How awful," Catherine said, and she held the baby closer.

"It did not happen here," Michelena said. "But he and his mother did not feel they could stay safely in the place where it happened. They moved here after that. His mother found work at the bakery to support them. When Vito was old enough, he learned his father's trade and set up his shop to take care of his mother. She died two years ago of pneumonia."

"I keep telling her that Vito would be a good husband," Lucia said. "My words fall on deaf ears."

"Mama," Michelena said, "please?"

"Oh, never mind," Lucia said.

"Michelena," Catherine said, "I wonder if I might ask something of you. And, please, feel free to say no if the offer does not appeal to you."

Michelena looked at her mother and then back at Catherine and said, "Ask what you will."

The baby started to fuss, and Lucia reached for her. Catherine handed the baby over and took Michelena's arm to walk her away from their mothers.

"I can see the worry in your face," Michelena said as they walked arm in arm. "What you plan to do must be terrifying."

"I struggle with whether or not it is fair for me to put my family and . . . and so many others in harm's way," Catherine said.

Michelena stopped and took Catherine's hand in hers. "What you are doing is so brave," she said as she looked into Catherine's eyes. "When you told us last night about your plan, I heard the concern and fear in your voice. I also heard the courage. Something inside of me was awakened when you made your announcement. I cannot explain what it is, but I awoke this morning so full of hope. I have not felt such hope in a long time. In fact, you already have my answer. I will do whatever I can to serve you."

"But you do not even know what I want!"

"It does not matter," Michelena said without hesitation. "I am yours for whatever you need."

Catherine was speechless. She could only look at Michelena and shake her head. "But," she finally uttered, "I could be a horrible queen and your life could be threatened because of me."

"When do I assume this new life of danger and horror?" Michelena said with a laugh.

Catherine shook her head and chuckled. "How did I live this long without a friend like you at my side?"

Michelena shrugged.

"I want you to be by my side. The official title will be Lady-in-Waiting, but what I need is a friend that I can trust. You must promise me that you will be honest with me."

"Are you certain you know what you are asking?" Michelena questioned. "You should talk with Tim. He will tell you I can be very brutal when it comes to sharing my thoughts."

"I have been forewarned," Catherine said. "And I count on that honesty."

Angela let out a wail that caused them to turn. "I need to tend to the baby," Michelena said. "It is time for her to eat."

Catherine nodded and they turned to walk back to their mothers and the children.

Michelena took the crying baby from her mother, then turned to Catherine. "I will give my notice to their parents and come to the rectory as soon as they have found someone to replace me. It will not be hard, there are many young women who would jump at the opportunity. That will also give me time to learn what a lady-in-waiting does!"

"What will you tell your employers?" Francesca asked.

With a sly grin, Michelena turned to her mother and said, "That my mother can no longer handle the work at the rectory alone."

"Ungrateful child!" Lucia exclaimed and started laughing.

It was late afternoon before the men returned from Castiglione d' Orcia. Catherine had been sitting in Father Tim's little church since after the noon meal. He found her there, sitting so peacefully that he was not even certain she was breathing. He walked quietly up the far side aisle so as not to disturb her.

"Father Tim," she said softly.

He stopped and turned. "I did not wish to disturb you, Catherine. I only wanted to retrieve the monk's book to continue my study."

Catherine smiled. "I hope you do not mind, but I was wishing I had it earlier. I thought it was in your private room, but as I walked around the church and up to the altar, I spotted your place for it. I have it here, but you may certainly have it back. I found what I was looking for." The priest walked over to her. "Anything you would like to share?" He sat down beside her.

"I thought," she said with a wry chuckle, "that once my decision was made that I would feel better. I do, but now there are new concerns." She looked up at the cross and the look on her face changed to one of such utter sadness that he did not move.

Finally, with a wry chuckle of his own, Father Tim said, "I cannot tell you how many times your grandmother sat here with that very same look on her face. As difficult as it was, your decision, I fear, was the easy part."

Catherine was still and silent for some time, but eventually squeezed the priest's hands. "I am afraid."

"If you were not, I would be," he said. "Is it a general fear of ruling a kingdom or something specific that causes your fear?"

Catherine turned, finally looking at him. "I am not so much worried about the ruling in general, as I feel that I will be surrounded by people who will be honest with me and helpful. I trust

God to guide me in the day-to-day affairs of governance. But this overthrowing of the current government puts lives at stake before I can even assume the throne. And there is no guarantee that we will succeed, is there?"

"There are never any guarantees," he said sadly. "Did anything you read or contemplated today help?"

"Here," she said, suddenly animated, "Chapter twelve where he talks about not weeping so much for the sorrow of our sins, or the Passion, or thinking too much on the joys of heaven—no matter how much grace it will get us, but rather *this blind stirring of love* which he calls the best part of Mary. I think he is talking of Mary of Magdalene."

"A chapter I have contemplated much, as a matter of fact," Tim said. "In particular, I find the first and the last passages of the chapter relevant to your decision and how you have approached it." He took the book from her and said, "I believe you have, as the chapter begins, 'beat on the cloud of unknowing between you and God with a sharp longing of love,' much like Mary—and, yes, I do believe he is referring to Magdalene—but here, at the end of the chapter he says that the blind stirring of love is the best part and that without it, no matter how many other virtues we have, without that love we all have crooked intentions."

"I have been sitting here all afternoon trying to determine if my own intentions have secrets of which I am not even aware," Catherine said with more than a little frustration.

Tim laughed. "And what have you come to?"

"It is possible," she said shrugging her shoulders.

Tim stood and paced slowly up to the altar and back to where she sat. "Do you believe that being a queen will bring you glory or riches?"

"I suppose that is a possibility, but those are not things I seek. If I am honest, those things are the exact opposite of what I built my life's dream upon."

"What about power?" he continued. "You will have power to wield and be able to decide on life and death issues for the people of Montalcino. Is it power you seek?"

"I do not even wish my enemies death," she said. "And until recently, I did not even know I had any."

"What kind of queen do you imagine yourself to be?" Tim asked.

"One who rules with fairness, who protects the people and serves them, one who can be a model of God's love."

"And what," he said sitting back down next to her, "ulterior motives can you discern from the depths of your soul as you contemplate these questions?"

"Apart from the realization that I love being surrounded by the community I have found here?" she asked in exasperation. "There is something so strong, and that feels so right about all of you, that I worry I am being distracted by my own desire to stay connected to all of you."

"Do you believe that God wants you to sacrifice your joy?"

"Is that not what part of devoting oneself to a life of religious service entails?" she asked.

Tim smiled and scratched his beard. "I believe," he said softly, "that God wants us to find and cherish the joys, be happy for the beauty and love that is here for us to relish. Gratitude is the first stop, not refusal."

Catherine looked at him. His perspective startled her and understanding settled over her in a new way.

Tim smiled again as he stood and took a few steps. "You came to me for guidance," he said turning to her. "I knew for some time that you were coming to see me. I did not know when you would come, but I knew that you would be here, and I knew that you struggled with this decision."

He waited for his words to hit their mark. It did not take long.

"How?" she asked. The look on her face was one of concern and confusion.

"Your grandmother came to me in a dream," he said. "I rarely have dreams. Every once in a great while I do have them. The ones I have are generally powerful, profound and prophetic. I have had only a handful of such dreams in my life."

Catherine looked at him with a combination of relief and wonder. The relief was that there was no spy who had warned him of her coming. The wonder came from somewhere else.

"When we were in Voghera," Catherine said, "where we waited for my mother at the waterfall, I also had a dream." She stood and walked past Tim to the foot of the altar and looked at the cross. "My grandmother came to me," she said as she turned to the priest. "It felt as real to me as your standing right here in front of me."

Tim smiled and breathed deeply. "She told you to come here?"

Catherine nodded, turned and smiled back at him.

"God truly works in mysterious ways," Tim said.

At dinner that night Gio expressed his relief at having found eighteen men willing to march to Montalcino castle.

"I am concerned that we not wait too long before we march on Montalcino. The longer we wait, the more the danger that word of our plan will get to the castle."

"Uncle Gio," Catherine said. "I have been giving much thought to our approach to taking back the throne and castle."

Gio stopped talking. "What are your thoughts?"

"I know and understand your concerns," she said. "You want to protect me, and I love you so much for that, but I do not want unnecessary bloodshed if there is a way prevent such a thing."

"I want no bloodshed, either," Gio said with a touch of defensiveness in his voice. "All I am proposing is that you stay hidden in Montalcino until such time as we remove the current Privy Council and their staff."

"And how do you expect that to happen if you march into the castle with armed men?"

Gio stood up. "Do you think you are just going to walk into the castle and ask for them to vacate? Do you think you can just thank them for holding things together for you?"

"Gio!" Francesca said firmly. "Catherine may be new to this sort of thing, but at least hear her out before you intimate that she is being foolish."

Gio took a deep breath and sighed. "My apologies to every-one," he said. "Catherine, I am sorry. It is my fear for your safety that makes me so agitated."

"I know, Uncle Gio," she said softly to him. "But I do think I have a plan that might work for both of us."

Gio sat down and listened, as did the rest of the group. There was much discussion. By the time the meal was finished, a plan was set.

Gio and Pasquale went off to town again the next morning. Only young Tim accompanied them, and he went to begin to minister on his own to the people who needed him. When they returned late in the afternoon Michelena was with them.

"So soon?" Lucia said hugging her daughter.

"So many young women were vying for the job that it was filled by noon,"-Michelena said. "I spent the afternoon packing my few belongings and playing with the children."

"Was it hard to say goodbye?" Catherine asked. She had come through the door as Michelena was telling her mother.

The two greeted each other.

"It was hard," Michelena confessed. "But I have no regrets. I told them I would come back to visit them as often as I could."

"But they think you will be here," Lucia said with some worry.

"Mama," she said, "by the time they realize I am not here, we can, hopefully, tell them the truth."

"The truth will be known at any rate," Catherine said, "regardless of the outcome."

Michelena went to her and took her hands. "You are worried."

"Of course," Catherine replied. "How can one not be worried?"

Michelena took Catherine's hands and kissed them. "It will be fine. I know it will."

Catherine could only smile at Michelena's confidence. "I will be glad when this is over."

In the short time that had passed since Gio spirited Catherine away from Montalcino Castle, he had missed at least four scheduled Privy Council meetings. Likely, there had been more. Of his absence, he heard nothing. He did not even know if he were still a council member, or worse, if there was a price on his head. And so, the decision was made to have Father Tim request to appear before the council.  His nephew volunteered to ride to the castle with the written request and wait for the answer.

"No one there knows me," he said. "When I was searching for you, uncle, I did not even see the castle.  I only spoke to a merchant in town who directed me to you."

"Are you certain, Tim?" Catherine asked.

"Not only am I certain, but I can likely ascertain how well the castle is guarded."

Father Tim added, "Tim, you will also wear a collar.  An unknown priest is likely not going to be a threat to anyone at the castle.  And you will be wearing one soon enough."


Young Tim rode back into the compound just after the evening meal.  His horse was lathered, and he was covered in dust.

"You are a mess!" Lucia shouted when she saw him.

"We have an answer!" Tim shouted as he entered, holding up

the letter.

Gio took the letter from him. "It is the Church's seal," he said, tearing it open and shaking his head in disgust.

He read the response. "Father Timothy, it is unlikely, given your history with former monarchs of this kingdom, that any request you might make of this council will be greeted with approval. Nevertheless, be advised that you are granted a short audience at the next Privy Council meeting to be held day after tomorrow at ten. You will be allowed no more than ten minutes of council time. Yours in Christ, Bishop Martine d' Avelo."

Gio put the letter on the table. No one said a word until Catherine spoke.

"You are the only one who knows this bishop, Gio. What can we expect?"

Gio scratched his beard and shrugged. "The Church did not keep any bishop or clergy at Montalcino for longer than a year after Biondi disappeared. It is my belief that they thought a shorter period would not allow for any one person to be comfortable skimming off the Church's profits."

"And," Pasquale added, "knowing that someone new was coming in to continue meant that your books had better be clean?"

"Probably," Gio added. "Again, that is only a guess on my part."

"A rather logical guess," Father Tim said, "given that the tendencies of this papacy appear to follow suit with everything else."

Young Tim left to tidy up and take care of his horse, but before he left, he said, "Lucia, is there any food left? I am starving."

"Go," she said. "I will fix you a plate."

"It looks," Catherine said, "as if our plan is working, so far, anyway.

Gio nodded. "Tomorrow, then, you and Michelena will head

into Montalcino and find Father Tim's friend. Stay in the room as much as possible."

"I will make food for you to take so that you do not have to be seen more than necessary," Lucia said as she finished a plate for Tim.

"There will be a three-quarter moon tomorrow night. The men from town will travel to the outskirts of Montalcino on horses late tomorrow and set up camp in the dark. Then, the morning of our meeting with the council, Catherine will meet us at the bridge to the castle and the three of us will be escorted to the meeting room."

"It sounds dangerous," Michelena said. "Catherine, are you certain this is how you wish to proceed?"

"It is the only way I am comfortable trying," Catherine said with as much reassurance as she could muster. "If anything goes wrong, we have our backup in place, but I am hoping to appeal to their sense of reason first. I must try, at least."

"Michelena," Gio said, also trying to assuage her fears, "we are prepared, should anything go wrong."

"Let us hope it goes well," Francesca said, slipping her arm around her daughter.

Catherine and Michelena left Castiglione d' Orcia rectory together on one horse. They left early so that they did not have to push the horse too much.

Michelena knew the way to Montalcino, as she had visited with her brother and mother a few times during their years with Father Tim. She sat in front on the horse and led it along a well-worn road.

"It is actually a beautiful ride to Montalcino," Michelena said when the rectory disappeared from view through the trees. "I know a nice place to stop where we can have our midday meal, but we should stop often to give the horse a rest."

"That sounds wonderful," Catherine said.

"Is everything alright, Catherine?"

"I am a little nervous, I guess, but, yes, I am fine," Catherine said.

There was no disguising the worry in Catherine's voice. Michelena heard it.

"Tell me about growing up in Voghera," Michelena said. "Besides always wanting to be a nun, what was your life like?"

Although Michelena could not see it, Catherine smiled, sensing that the other was trying to distract her from her worries.

"You are sweet," Catherine responded. "I know what you are doing, and I appreciate the gesture."

"Well," Michelena said with a laugh, "you are not going to make this easy, are you?"

Catherine laughed, too, just as the horse jolted climbing up a rock. They were ascending a foothill where the road wound around the side of a mountain. Catherine grabbed Michelena to avoid falling backward off the horse.

When Catherine felt balanced again, she loosened her grip on Michelena's waist.

Michelena reached down with her left hand and placed it over Catherine's. "Best to hang on while we are on this rocky stretch of road."

"I am not trying to make things difficult," Catherine finally resumed. "I have never been very comfortable talking about myself. What if you told me about life growing up with your mother, brother and Father Tim. I am a better listener and that would take my mind off what is about to happen."

Michelena's voice was low and soft. She told of life in the

rectory. She talked of her mother's sadness and how she remembered her uncle who had no tongue. There were many stories of
those who came to the rectory seeking Father Tim and his help
to hide from the harsh enforcers of the C hurch.

"I often lay pretending to sleep during nightly visits from people who lost whole families, or whose families had turned against
them to save themselves. Good people," she whispered. "So many
good people whose lives were destroyed . . . " her voice drifted off.

Catherine's head dropped against Michelena's shoulder as she
sniffed. Listening to the stories filled her with a desperation to
make things better. But she dared not voice such a thought. For
all she knew, she might be dead this time tomorrow.

They rode in silence for some time, until Michelena reached
down, squeezed Catherine's hands, which were still around her
waist, turn her face to Catherine's head, still resting on her shoulder and said softly, "Are you awake?"

Catherine turned her head. Their faces were so close together
they almost touched. "I am," she said, but did not move.

Michelena was still for just a breath then whispered, "We can
rest here for a while. It will be a good place to let the horse graze."

Catherine looked up and saw that they had reached a sunlit
meadow whose grasses were already turning golden from the chillier nights. "How beautiful."

Michelena swung her right leg over the horse's neck and
dropped down. She reached up to assist Catherine down.
There was an awkwardness to the dismount. Catherine was
used to horses and able to mount and dismount with ease,
but perhaps it was Michelena trying to help her that threw
off her balance. Michelena caught and righted her.

Catherine felt a definite tremble but was unsure as to whether
it was Michelena or herself that mildly quaked. She broke the
silence, "I am usually much more adept on a horse."

Michelena stepped back, found her voice again and said, "Of that, I have no doubt."

Together they spread a quilt on which to eat a meager lunch. The horse stayed near, grazing on the yellow grass.

Michelena stretched out on the quilt and looked up at the clouds as they passed across the sun. She closed her eyes after a bit.

Catherine got up and wandered in the meadow. A deep blue sky dotted with clouds spread out over her and down to the line of golden grasses that swayed gently in a soft breeze. On her return to Michelena it was the grandeur of the mountains, already topped with snow, that cut into that same blue sky. "What an artist you are," she said to God.

The short walk felt good after being on the horse all morning. She saw a lake on the other side of the field and wondered if this could be the flower field that her mother talked about in her journal.

As Catherine ambled back, she could not help but smile for the beauty of the earth. As she neared Michelena, however, she noticed tears slipping from Michelena's eyes.

"Michelena," she said, sitting down on the quilt next to her, "what is it?"

Michelena, who had been lying supine on the blanket, opened her eyes and looked at Catherine. "It is nothing, dear queen, it is nothing."

"Do not," Catherine said. "Do not look at me with tears in your eyes and tell me it is nothing. I do not want our relationship to be based on secrets."

Michelena pushed herself to a sitting position, and looked at the horse in the meadow. "I guess I might be a little worried, too." She said, but they both knew she was lying.

They passed only a couple of other travelers on the road.

Greetings were cordial, but not extended. Catherine was grateful, for she did not wish to be social.

A family in a wagon had just passed them. All nodded and said hello, but no one stopped or inquired about two women alone on horseback. When the family was well past them, Catherine broke the silence that felt like a wedge had been driven between them.

"Tell me about Vito," she said. "Is he someone who is really interested in marrying you?"

Michelena snorted. "Hardly. Vito is just Vito. He is very sweet, but everyone knows he is in love with the daughter of the butcher. Honestly, everyone knows that except the daughter of the butcher."

Catherine laughed lightly. "Why has he not told her?"

"Because he is afraid she will reject him."

Catherine had been sitting with her hands resting behind her on the horse's rear. She leaned forward and tried to bring them forward now, but they had fallen asleep, and her shoulders ached from holding the position so long. She grimaced but said nothing. She had been trying to keep her distance from Michelena. Why, she could not say, but she struggled to understand what had happened in the meadow and could make no sense of it.

"Would the butcher's daughter reject him?" Catherine asked.

"That is hard to tell," Michelena answered. "She tends to act as if she is superior because her family has a little more money than most people in town."

"Well," Catherine said, "that is her loss, then. Vito does genuinely seem like a delightful young man."

"He is, and I am happy to count him as one of my dearest friends," Michelena added. "He is one who has joined your uncle's small army, you know?"

"I did not know. But I am not surprised, given his history."

Michelena pulled the horse to a stop and announced that the horse needed another break. "I can feel that she is walking slower."

Michelena swung her leg forward over the horse's neck and lowered herself. She immediately went to the head of the horse, "Are you ready for a little rest?" She stroked the horse's neck and then reached into her pocket and pulled out a carrot. The carrot disappeared into its mouth, and she began to chew.

Catherine let herself down and stretched her arms, then shook her hands back into life. "How much farther?" she asked.

Michelena looked around, got her bearings and said, "About another hour, I would guess."

"Are you really so anxious, Michelena?" Catherine asked pointedly. "You know you do not have to stay with me, once we are in town. I can manage on my own if you have changed your mind."

"I have no intention of changing my mind," she said. "Just because I have concerns is not reason to turn back. This is right, and I am with you." Her voice sounded a little defensive.

"My apologies," Catherine demurred. "I did not mean to upset you. I am just trying to understand what is happening. It feels as if we were close one moment and far away the next. I apologize if I have offended you."

Michelena's head dropped, and she sighed heavily. "I am the one who should be sorry. Things are changing so fast, and I fear my feelings are slower at catching up with me. Please forgive me, Catherine."

Catherine took her hand in response and pulled her back to the road. "Let us walk for a while. We will be in Montalcino in plenty of time. I do not think Father Tim's friend expects us much before the evening meal."

Michelena let herself be pulled back to the road. The horse

finished chewing the carrot. Michelena held her reins in one hand and Catherine's hand in the other. Whatever storm there was had passed.

On the outskirts of Montalcino, Catherine pulled her hood up, afraid that someone might recognize her from the castle two weeks ago.

"It seems like so much longer ago that I was here," she said.

"You have been through quite a bit since then," Michelena said. "And not even in one place."

They were dressed in the simplest of peasant clothes so as not to attract attention. Walking through Montalcino with a horse was quite a usual activity. When they reached the section of town where most of the storefronts were, they slowed their pace.

"I think I see Father Tim's friend up ahead on the right," Michelena said.

Catherine looked up. "Let us take our time to get there and feign that we are actually shopping."

Michelena nodded and allowed Catherine to set the pace.

No one gave them a glance and when they arrived at the little vegetable stand, they nodded to the woman.

"Hello," Catherine said politely. "Do you have any cured olives?"

The older woman looked up at them and replied. "Olives are inside. You may go in and look. I will be happy to tie your horse around back."

Michelena and Catherine nodded and entered the small shop. There they passed bins of nuts, different varieties of tomato, and bunches of herbs hanging to dry from the ceiling. Toward the back of the little, dark shop they found olives marinating in a giant barrel.

A bell rang on the front door. They turned to see the woman closing the door and moving toward them. "Are these the kind of olives you are looking for?"

Catherine responded, "Are you Antonita?"

The woman gave a quick nod.

"Father Tim sent us," Catherine said.

The woman's face instantly lost its lines of worry. She broke into a warm, welcoming smile.

After turning to check the front of the shop to make sure no one was in the vicinity, she quickly ushered the girls up a narrow staircase.

She lived in a small set of rooms above the vegetable store that she owned.

"I will take care of your horse. There is wine, fruit, cheese, and olives on the table. Please make yourselves comfortable. The shop must remain open until the usual time so that no attention is drawn to my absence. The neighbors will be concerned and come to check on me otherwise."

Antonita returned later and apologized for being so abrupt. "I did not want to take chances that might arouse suspicion," she said. "Your horse is out back. I do not think anyone noticed you, but if anyone had, I was prepared to tell them that you were the daughters of an aunt passing through."

Catherine stood and went to hold her hands out to the woman. She kissed her on both cheeks. "We are so grateful for your help, dear woman. We do not wish to cause you any trouble."

"What kind of trouble?" she asked. "After all Father Tim has done for me I would do anything for anyone trying to hide from the enforcers. They are a cruel and hateful group who have given us nothing but hell!" she said.

Catherine shared a look with Michelena. It was obvious the woman had no idea who Catherine was and that was what they had hoped for.

They had a meal with Antonita, and she showed them where they could clean up and sleep. There were two small rooms off the main room. One was Antonita's bedroom; the other was a spare. Each room had one wooden frame with a mattress, a table with a lantern and a wash basin. Antonita brought them a towel.

"I am sorry," Antonita said, "but I rise quite early to prepare and purchase the produce to get the store open for customers. I retire quite early."

Michelena reassured her that they were quite exhausted from their travels and would also retire early. "Thank you so much for sharing your home and food with us," she said. "Will we see you in the morning before we leave?"

"You must leave through the store, and I will have to show you to your horse. I will be downstairs before dawn. Sleep well."

"Good night," Catherine said. "And thank you, again."

Antonita nodded and disappeared into her room. The rooms had no doors, but soon a soft snoring could be heard rolling out from Antonita's room.

Catherine lit the lantern and sat on the side of the bed. "It is clear she does not know who we are or why we are here."

"That is a good thing," Michelena said. "In small towns everyone usually knows everything about everyone."

Catherine nodded. "I am tired."

"As am I," Michelena said. She went to the washbasin and picked up the washrag next to it, wrung it out and brought it over to where Catherine sat staring into the flame of the lantern. "Let me wipe some of the day's dust from your face," she said.

The water was cool, but the gentle washing was refreshing.

"That was nice," Catherine said. "Thank you."

When she had washed her own face and removed her overdress and undergarments down to her chemise and drawers, Michelena looked at the smallness of the mattress and shook her head.

"I am happy to sleep on the floor, Catherine," she whispered. "It would not bother me at all."

"Do not be silly," Catherine whispered back. "We can manage this for one night."

Michelena pulled a brush from their small bag of belongings. "Let me brush out your hair."

"It is not necessary, Michelena."

"Please sit, Catherine. Necessary or not, I would like to do it for you."

Catherine sat on the edge of the small mattress and allowed the gift.

"My mother has always enjoyed brushing my hair at night," Catherine said dreamily. "I missed the ministration more than I expected when we left Montalcino castle in such a hurry and went in opposite directions."

"Then let us be certain that it is part of your nightly routine," Michelena said. "Your hair is beautiful."

"You have a nice touch," Catherine whispered almost sleepily.

Michelena laughed softly. "It is remarkable how quickly one learns a gentle technique when brushing a young child's head of hair. The baby was too young, of course, but little Franco's hair was always a mass of knots. If I were not gentle, his screams would drown out Vito's hammer and anvil!"

The lamp sputtered. "Let us get that lamp out so we do not use all of Antonita's oil," Michelena said.

When they were both ready, they climbed under the blanket. The blackness was absolute.

"That was quite thoughtful of you to think about the oil," Catherine whispered.

Catherine prayed, which was her normal routine before retiring. Not wanting to make Michelena uncomfortable, or appear to make a show, she dispensed with her usual prayers on her knees at the bedside. When she and Michelena seemed to settle into comfortable sleeping positions, she closed her eyes and prayed about the next day.

"Please, dear God, I beseech you to allow this event to be free of bloodshed. It is not my desire to see anyone hurt as the result of my choice. If possible, help calm heads and hearts rule the day and the people involved. Search my heart and help me to hear Your guiding voice. I cannot do this without You and would not even consider it if it meant that assuming this role would take me farther from you. Be with us tomorrow, keep all involved safe and help us to grow closer to You."

"Are you praying?"

"I am."

"Me, too," Michelena whispered. "Are you afraid?"

"Yes."

Michelena turned to her side toward Catherine and wrapped her arm around her. "It will be fine," she whispered into Catherine's ear. "It will be fine."

Catherine slipped an arm under Michelena's head and wrapped her arm around the other woman's waist.

They fell asleep clinging to one another.

Michelena awoke to the sounds of muffled weeping. She opened her eyes to see Catherine kneeling at the side of the bed, hands folded, and face pressed into the mattress. Instinctively, she reached over and placed her hand on Catherine's head. No sooner did the kneeling woman feel the touch than a sob escaped her. Michelena scooted over toward her and wrapped both arms around Catherine's head.

"Please, do not cry, my friend, my almost queen!" Michelena cried.

Catherine looked up. The fear in her eyes startled Michelena.

"Catherine!" she said firmly, placing a hand on each side of her face and forcing her to look in her eyes.

"What is it?"

"I cannot feel God! Catherine cried. "I have been awake most of the night praying and searching for God's presence and found not so much as a whisper!"

Michelena waited for the next wave of weeping to subside before she asked in disbelief, "Have you always felt the presence of God whenever you have desired it, just by asking?"

Catherine wiped her eyes with the back of her hand and sniffed. "Until I learned that I was really the heir to the throne, yes!" she almost shouted.

Michelena let go of Catherine's face and maneuvered herself to the side of the bed, shaking her head.

Catherine stopped crying. "What?" Catherine asked as she pushed herself up and turned to sit on the bed next to Michelena.

Michelena turned to Catherine and said, "You have always felt God's presence, whenever you have wanted or desired to feel that presence until you discovered your true identity." Her words were spoken in a manner that hinted at a question but held a touch of accusation. Catherine heard the accusation.

"You do not believe me?" Catherine asked.

Michelena pursed her lips in thought and said, "It is not that I do not believe you. It is that," she paused and considered her words before speaking again. "Perhaps," she continued, "my childhood with Father Tim created different expectations of God in me." She got up from the bed and walked the two short steps to the window.

The sun's rays were just peaking over the horizon and the town was awash in a pink glow. As she turned back to Catherine, she realized just how small and barren the room was. She stayed where she was and said, "Father Tim always taught us that no life was exempt from suffering. He even taught us to expect it." She looked at Catherine who was staring at her and listening intently.

Michelena kept her distance, as she was unsure what to expect when she said what intended to say next. "Your life must have been very blessed until now, if you always felt God with you. I cannot imagine what such a gift must feel like." She looked at Catherine and her face softened, filling itself with a look Catherine had never before seen. "Much of what I learned from Father Tim has formed my life in ways that, perhaps, give me a vastly different perspective," she continued. "Catherine, we do not need to plead with God to bless us with His presence. We live in that presence. It is in each breath we take. God's presence is not with us only when we feel it, it is even with us when we do not feel it. It is especially with us in our darkest times." She paused again and took a few steps toward Catherine and knelt in front of her.

"My favorite saying of Father Tim's is that God's presence is in every breath we take."

Catherine did not move. She sat silently, barely breathing.

"Perhaps," Michelena said softly, "breathing might be a good place to start."

Catherine blinked. She felt the truth in everything Michelena said. She hung her head and covered her face with her hands. When she dropped her hands, she looked deep into Michelena's eyes.

"I am so sorry, Michelena. I am a fool and perhaps even a coward. I do not know what came over me." She closed her eyes, lowered her head and shook her head back and forth.

Michelena reached for her hands. "You are scared. It is understandable." She kissed Catherine's hands and said, "God's grace often comes in ways or at times you might not expect, but His presence is constant. If you pay attention, you can look at these past few weeks and see how God was present in different ways, perhaps through different people. For all you know the small army that is waiting for you is God's presence."

Catherine returned the hand kisses to Michelena and smiled. "My Uncle Gio saved my family from a poisonous death at

Montalcino. I met the man who gave me life and he gave me so much more than I could have ever thought possible through his words and his writings. I met your mother, who saved my life when I was born." Catherine looked into Michelena's eyes and said, "And now I have you, who sees things that are truths I need to hear, and who is my friend. I am blessed. I will not forget again."

Michelena smiled and said, "Good. Then let us dress. You have a throne to recover and a small army waiting for you and your instruction!"

Antonita was setting up bins of fruits and vegetables in front of her little shop when Catherine and Michelena came down from the apartment. They made their way to the front of the store just as Antonita was shouting a greeting to another merchant on the opposite side of the street. After a brief exchange, Antonita turned and entered her shop.

"Oh, girls, good morning. I hope you slept well!" she exclaimed.

"Like babies," Michelena lied. "Thank you."

"And now, dear woman," Catherine added, "we will be on our way."

"Wait a moment," Antonita said. She reached behind a bin of nuts. "Here is a small sack of food for your journey. Nothing much, but you must eat." Michelena reached for the sack and thanked her.

"You are too kind," Catherine responded as she kissed the woman on both cheeks. "May God be with you always."

Michelena carried the sack of food and together she and Catherine walked their horse to the road.

"She has so little," Michelena said. "Yet her heart is large."

Catherine nodded, glad she had left a gold coin on the woman's table. She took a deep breath. "Quite large," she responded.

Michelena heard both the acknowledgement and the apprehension in Catherine's voice and reached for her hand. They walked in silence to the end of the town and slipped into the woods surrounding the town and separating it from the castle. The bridge where they were to meet Father Tim and Gio was a short walk through a wooded area filled with chestnut, oak, and pine trees. The bridge crossed a small creek that ran down through the town. Father Tim and Gio were waiting. A small group of soldiers were standing amid the trees.

Catherine, Father Tim, and Gio walked across the small bridge to Montalcino castle. Michelena waited at the bridge. There were no guards posted at the outer of two walls of the castle. Gio turned and signaled a wide circle in the air to Vito, who had come to join Michelena at the bridge. The signal indicated that the plan was now being initiated.

"It seems the Church has become quite lax in guarding the outer perimeter," Gio said as they approached the opening to the outer wall.

"No one dares to challenge the Church unless they desire to be tortured," Tim said sadly. "Perhaps that will make our visit here easier."

Father Tim had led the small army in prayer just outside the town where they had camped overnight. His prayer was for a peaceful transition and safety for all involved.

"I pray you are correct, Father Tim," Catherine said. She was shaking so badly she was afraid she might have difficulty standing.

There was one guard at the opening to the interior wall. He leaned on the wall with one foot against the stone. When he heard the crunch of gravel he straightened up and looked frightened.

"Oh, Lord Gio," he said, visibly relieved. "Welcome back." He looked at Catherine. "I was not told to expect anyone."

"Rest easy, Angelo," Gio said to the young man. "Father Timothy is expected, and my niece, Catherine is traveling with me. I have invited them to join me and to meet the council."

"I am not certain I should allow anyone in without checking,"

Angelo said with uncertainty in his voice.

Catherine said, as planned for this contingency, "Uncle, I thought you told the council that we would be joining you."

"I did," Gio said to her. "Someone must have forgotten to tell Angelo."

Catherine looked at Angelo and smiled sweetly. "I do not want to cause this young man any trouble," she said. "Perhaps we should wait here."

"Angelo," Gio said, shaking his head. "I will take full responsibility should these people cause any trouble. Father Tim, here, is expected," Gio said as he produced the official letter from the bishop for Angelo to see. And if I keep the council waiting, they will not be happy. I have already missed several council meetings as it is, so either way the problems caused will all be mine."

Angelo stood straighter and said, "I guess it is fine. It is only a priest and a young woman. It is not as if you are trying to enter with an army."

Gio smiled and thanked the young guard who turned and waved to the soldier at the door to the castle. The trio was waved through to the council room.

When they arrived at the Privy Council chamber, there were two guards at the door. The guards recognized Gio, who simply said, "We are expected."

The guards opened the double doors to the chamber.

"Bishop, gentlemen," Gio said as he entered, "Allow me to introduce Father Timothy from Castiglione d'Orcia and my niece, Catherine Isabella from Voghera."

The doors to the chamber closed behind them with a clank. Bishop Martine stood up and glared at Gio, then his eyes bore into the priest's and Catherine's and back to Gio.

"What is the meaning of this?" the bishop demanded. He looked wary, afraid and angry all at the same time.

"Forgive my uncle," Catherine said. Her voice was calm as she strode toward the bishop, knelt in front of him, took his hand and kissed his ring.

When she stood, he looked more relaxed.

Catherine hoped her gesture of respect might give her the opportunity to present her claim in a more civil manner. She felt a calm settle over her that was not present a few short moments ago and turned to the few meager council members, who had no trouble remembering her from her recent visit.

"My lords," she said with a curtsy.

"My niece," Gio started, "has something to discuss with the council. She has requested Father Timothy to be with her as her spiritual advisor. As you know, my niece is a woman of great faith."

Lord Navona, ancient, angry and one of the stingiest and meanest of men Gio had ever known, replied, "My niece is a woman of great faith, as well, Lord Gio, but I do not invite her, unapproved, to council meetings."

"I am aware," Catherine said, holding up her hands, "that this is most unusual. Please forgive my uncle for such a breach in protocol, but there is a good reason for our visit today."

The room was silent.

"You see," she said softly, "Lord Gio is not really my uncle."

Catherine glided to the end of the long table, opposite to where Bishop Martine still stood at the head of the table.

"From the events that surrounded my first and last visit to Montalcino castle, you had already guessed that my mother was Queen Sofia. The attempt on my life was proof of that."

"There was an attempt on your life?" Lord Puglia asked, clearly shocked at this bit of information.

"Yes, my lord," Catherine said, nodding to him. "I am afraid there was. And, if not for Lord Gio, I believe my entire family would have been murdered.

Lord Puglia looked directly at Bishop Martine who continued to glare at Catherine.

Catherine raised her eyes to meet the bishop's and continued, "And, I have brought proof as to the identity of my father."

Lord Navona stood up. His hands were gnarled and his voice gravelly. He looked at Catherine and spat, "What do we care who that whore slept with. If you think you can walk in here and simply claim to be the heir to the throne, you must think we are fools."

Catherine kept her voice steady. She ignored Navona and turned, again, to the bishop. "Bishop Martine, I believe the council will find this document illuminating," she said as she took the letter written to him from Pietro Biondi from Gio. She handed the letter to Lord Puglia, who was closest to her, and in whom she already felt a sense of potential fealty.

"Lord Puglia," Catherine asked, "would you kindly read the letter for the benefit of the council?"

Puglia took the letter and cleared his throat.

" 'To All of the Peoples in the Kingdom of Montalcino; to the Privy Council of Montalcino and especially to Bishop Martine d'Avelo,

*I write to you this last confession before I die and beseech you to right a wrong for which I am wholly responsible.*

*Sixteen years ago, in a singular weak moment of the flesh, I committed an act for which I have begged God's forgiveness. Now I must beg yours, as I have also begged forgiveness from the others who have suffered for my weakness.*

*Catherine Isabella Oddono is the daughter of Queen Sofia of Montalcino. I know this because, in fact, I*

*fathered her when I took advantage of Queen Sofia as she mourned the loss of someone she held dear. I, Pietro Biondi, Archbishop of Montalcino, am guilty of much. Queen Sofia was a virgin at the time of my crime. Because I could not suffer the humiliation of what I did, it was all too easy for me to cover my own eyes and imagine her a temptress. She was no temptress. She could have exposed me but did not. She took my secret sin to her fiery death—the death to which I assigned her. She was innocent. Our daughter is innocent. I beg you do not punish the daughter for the sin of her father.*

*Sofia's child—my child—Catherine, has every right to assume the throne of Montalcino. Should she decide to do so, I wish to assure you that she will do so with a heart full of compassion for her people. Like her mother and grandmother before her she will work tirelessly for justice and righteousness. She does not expect any inheritance from the Church as a child of an archbishop. She expects no recompense from the Church for monies already collected for and used by the Church. She wishes only to govern her people and return to Montalcino as a God-loving servant. I beg you let her do so. She has committed no sin by being born and only recently has she become aware of her true identity.*

*I left Montalcino in shame and secrecy when God, in His mercy, helped me to know all of which I was guilty. As I am about to leave this earthly plane, I do so with eyes wide open. I ask that you and the Church peacefully return Montalcino to its rightful heir. Give her the respect and support she deserves. And, if possible, forgive me as she has and as God has.*

*Yours,*
*Pietro Biondi, former Archbishop of Montalcino' "*

"Outrageous!" screamed Lord Navona. "You have no right to the throne. The Church will have your head! Guards!" he called. His voice so hoarse it was barely audible.

The doors did not open. Catherine said gently, "Gentlemen, I know this is a shock to you, but I assure you that I am the rightful heir to the throne of Montalcino. I intend to assume my place as queen immediately. I would very much like to do so without violence or bloodshed. The only question that remains is whether this council will agree to return the throne peacefully?"

Bishop Martine had said nothing thus far, but now he walked around the table as if starting for Catherine. Gio stepped in front of him and said, "You may address the queen from here."

"Very well," the bishop said, nodding curtly. "Before this can be allowed, I need to inform the Holy See. No transition can take place until they are informed. The Church continues to rule in Montalcino until such time as the Pope is informed."

"Understandable," Catherine said almost sweetly. "That is why Pietro Biondi also left a nearly identical letter for the Pope and the Holy See. It was delivered early this morning."

Bishop Martine stood speechless. His fury could be seen in the visible tremble as he raised his hand to point his finger at her. "I will not leave this castle until I hear from Rome."

Navona was ready to explode. "Guards!" he screamed again.

This time the doors opened. The armed guards that had let Catherine, Gio and Father Tim enter just a short time ago were gone. In their place were five armed men the council did not recognize.

Gio turned to them and spoke. "Please escort Lord Navona to his quarters and see that he packs and leaves Montalcino by dusk."

Two of them marched over to Lord Navona who began to yell obscenities at them. He tried to fight them off as they easily each grabbed one of his arms and led him out of the council chambers.

That left Bishop Martine, Lord Puglia and Lord Murano. Catherine and Gio looked at them. Their eyes shifted back and forth from the bishop to Catherine. Finally, Lord Puglia smiled and looked at Catherine.

"I am yours to command, my queen," he said and walked around the table to kneel at her feet.

"As am I," Lord Murano said, doing the same.

"You will regret this, gentlemen," Bishop d'Avelo said with a sneer.

The two lords stood, faced the bishop. "Perhaps," Puglia said, "but not today."

Catherine turned to Father Tim and two of the remaining armed men and said, "Father, would you kindly accompany the bishop in gathering his belongings. Feel free to send men with him to Rome if he wishes."

"I do not need babysitters!" the bishop shouted.

"Nevertheless," Gio countered, "my men will help you pack."

As they left the room Gio asked Vito, the remaining soldier in the room, if he would check the state of the guards they had overtaken and be sure all was in order. "Please have them all brought to the throne room to await further instruction."

Vito nodded.

"Does he know where the throne room is?" Catherine asked.

Gio laughed. "Likely not. But he has proved himself competent and able to handle any task I have given him. He will find it."

Catherine and Gio were quickly satisfied that Lords Puglia and Murano were, indeed, happy about her rule. They told her stories of how, over the years, the Church had taken more and more of the taxes that were meant to care for the kingdom.

"We were but puppets," Lord Murano said. "They had no use for us, but we stayed to keep our own heads and the heads of our families safe."

"What of the other families, the other lords from around the kingdom?" Catherine asked.

"Many stayed for a time, Your Majesty," Lord Puglia said, "but they grew tired of the game."

Gio spoke for the first time. "I did not wish to burden you until you had made your decision, my queen, but when the others left, their families were harassed by enforcers of the church. When those lords requested to return to the council, they were denied by the bishop."

"Let us send word that we would like them back, shall we?" Catherine asked them.

Gio smiled and nodded. The two lords replied in unison, "Yes, Your Majesty."

"We need to move now to address the most immediate concerns regarding the needs of Montalcino—first and foremost that of preparing for any retaliation from Rome," Lord Puglia stated.

"Agreed," Catherine replied.

"Perhaps," Gio said, "we might give ourselves a few days to get out word of the transition here, see what kind of support and military force we have and then meet to discuss how to get Montalcino back to an enterprise that serves its people."

"Speaking of military force," Catherine said, "we should not keep whatever soldiers we may have waiting much longer."

The Lords Puglia, Murano and Gio escorted Catherine to the throne room.

"You are falling into the role as if you were born to it," Gio commented as the lords walked behind them excitedly talking about the events of the morning.

Catherine stopped, looked at him, smiled and, for a moment, looked confused. She instinctively placed her hand over her heart, realizing at once that her fear of the night and morning had instantly dissipated at the perfect time. "Thank you for your grace, dear Lord," she prayed silently.

They walked down the corridor to the throne room and could hear the chatter of voices long before they arrived.

Catherine and Gio looked at each other in surprise. They had been expecting shouting and arguing. There was none. Only the sound of conversations and some laughter reached their ears.

"We cannot be this lucky," Gio said.

"It would be the answer to a night-long prayer," Catherine said.

Together, they entered the throne room from the back and walked up the two steps to where the throne sat. All the voices instantly quieted. Catherine stood, with Gio beside her. She spotted her father talking to one of the guards who had been at the entrance when she arrived. He turned and saw her. His smile told her everything. And then another miracle.

One by one every man in the room knelt before her.

Catherine could not move. She had not expected this display of respect and was unsure how to react. She turned to Gio, who indicated that she should take the throne. She was not even certain she could walk to it, but somehow managed. She looked at the throne, felt a twinge of intimidation and opted to stand.

"Please rise," she said turning to the room now filled with fifty to sixty men.

When the soldiers were on their feet again, and the rustling of swords and clothing and armor ceased, Catherine said, "I am the daughter of Queen Sofia, granddaughter of Queen Catherine and great granddaughter of King Edward. I am the rightful heir to this throne and have taken it back from the Church this day. The Church has held rule believing that there was no heir. I thank the Church for keeping the kingdom of Montalcino operating during these many years. However, the Church is now released from this responsibility and we, together, will restore a government to serve our people."

"All hail Queen Catherine!" shouted someone from the back of the room.

"Queen Catherine!" came the resounding reply.

Catherine looked briefly at Gio and smiled. When she turned back to the men she said, "I know many of you have been here serving under Bishop Martine and the Church. I thank you for your service. Lord Giovanni," here she stopped and held her arm out to indicate him, "will meet with each of you to discuss whether you wish to continue to serve under me. Should you decide in favor of staying, I must warn you that his training will be rigorous!"

"Captain?" she said, turning to Gio, "Do you wish to address these men?"

Gio walked closer to Catherine. He turned to the group of about fifty men present. "As Captain of the Queen's Guard, my primary responsibility will be to protect and serve Queen Catherine," he said. "We will have much work to do should you decide to stay. It was," he smiled, "far too easy for us to enter the castle today."

A small wave of laughter rolled around the room.

Catherine spoke again. "You need not stay if you do not wish. If you stay you will be expected to work hard and take an oath. Lords Puglia and Murano have already indicated that they will send men from their own homes for training. We expect other lords to return to the council and make the same offer."

"For now," Gio said, "I will begin meeting with all guards in the courtyard. Any of the men who came with us today from Castiglione d' Orcia, you are welcome to speak with me about a role here, as well. We thank you for your part in this day. You will not be forgotten as we set about reestablishing Montalcino under a monarchy."

Another cheer went up. As it died Gio turned to Catherine.

"My queen, may we take our leave?"

"You may," Catherine said.

When the men all cleared the room and Catherine was alone, she turned to look at the throne. Her thoughts went to her ancestors who sat on this throne before her. She took a step toward it and reached out her hand, as if to connect with the past. "Help me be worthy of this task," she whispered to the shadows of the dead.

"Have you sat in it yet?" her father's voice said softly from behind her.

Catherine turned to find him smiling at her. She shook her head.

"What are you waiting for?" he asked.

"I am not sure," she answered.

"As you have done your entire life, daughter, you will sit when it is the right time to sit."

She smiled at him and walked down the steps. "You know me too well, Papa," she said as she slipped her arm through his.

"Come," he said, "your mother has arrived." Together, they walked out of the throne room.

The rest of the day was a whirlwind of activities. Catherine found herself exhilarated by all there was to learn. Her first task was to visit the castle church. It was deserted and cold. It had a dank odor to it, almost as if it had not been used in some time. The thought made her sad. Her anger flared when she saw that the eternal flame had been allowed to burn out. She opened the great double doors to air the place out and then began to explore the church. She found frankincense in the vesting room but no flint. Remembering a steel fire barrel roaring near the hermitage, she took a candle from the altar and walked the short path down to the fire and lit a candle. When she returned to the church, she lit and set a new candle into the red sconce.

"Be present here again, and never leave, my Lord," she said out loud as she crossed herself. She set the lit candle in a candlestick on the altar and went back to the vesting room where she had left the incense. When she returned to the altar, she lit the incense and let its smoke flow up and begin to fill the room. Kneeling at the communion rail, Catherine, finally, felt the stress and anxiety of the morning lift from her to mingle with the smoke. She stayed on her knees in prayer for some time before leaving through the back rooms with the candle.

Catherine knew, from her mother's journal, that there was a secret passage from the church through to the kitchens. She had to open several doors before she found one from which a cool draft moved her hair. Stepping into the closet, she pushed at the back panel. It opened and the whoosh of musty air nearly blew out the candle. She felt a sudden chill, remembering how this passage had been used to manipulate her mother when she was so young. "I must ask Father Tim to exorcise this place," she told herself. From the position of the church in relation to the castle, she knew that she would be underground for several hundred meters. She braced herself, glad she had absconded with a new candle. There were supports throughout the tunnel, but the only light came from her small flame. Catherine was quite unnerved by the silence, but she persevered, whispering prayers aloud and trying to ignore that her words were quickly absorbed by the dirt walls surrounding her.

Her steps were slower than her normal walking pace and she knew that she must account for her halting pace. She gave herself more than the time she would have normally allotted for the anticipated distance. Finally, she saw a flicker of light through a crack ahead of her. Approaching the light with caution, she paused at what she discovered was another door. She listened.

"Why in heaven's name does anyone need this much food stored? It is enough to satisfy several armies for a month!"

Catherine recognized Lucia's voice and smiled, blew out her candle, set it down and pushed against the door with both hands.

Lucia screamed as the shelves beside her began to move. "Dear Christ in heaven," she said, dropping to her knees, "save me from this unknown—"

"Lucia!" Catherine said, stepping from the other side of the opening, "It is me, Catherine."

"Thank you, Jesus," Lucia said, crossing herself.

Catherine helped the older woman to her feet but could feel that she was trembling.

"I am so sorry, Lucia," she said wrapping her arms around the woman. "I did not mean to frighten you. I was so anxious to get out of that tunnel. I heard your voice and felt flooded with relief. Forgive me, dear lady."

Lucia shook her head and laughed off her fear. "I am just glad it is you," she said, reaching to brush some dirt off Catherine's face. "Where have you come from?"

"The church."

Lucia's eyes opened wide. "Holy Mother of God," Lucia said as tears sprung to her eyes. "Sophia and the bishop." She took a square of cloth from her sleeve to blow her nose. "I had forgotten."

Lucia peeked into the black of the tunnel and crossed herself again. "Poor child," she lamented. "Poor, innocent child."

Catherine nodded, then pushed the wall closed and looked around at the sacks of flour, rye, and sugar. There were barrels of oil, meats and fish preserved in salt. "You are right, Lucia, this is more foodstuffs than several armies need." She shook her head. "When you have determined what we should keep on hand, please send soldiers into Montalcino to hand out supplies to neediest of families.

Lucia nodded. "I will consult with some of the staff," she said. "I have never been required to serve so many people. But even I know this is more than we need."

Catherine looked around a bit more. "Lucia," she asked, "have you seen a stairway going up anywhere nearby?"

"Yes," Lucia said, "and a door to a cellar down to where the wines are kept."

"Show me," Catherine said.

Lucia led her around shelves of preserved jams and pickled items to the base of a narrow, iron spiral staircase.

"I think I have explored enough for today," Catherine said.

Catherine found her way out of the kitchen and back to the Privy Council room. From there, she wandered to the queen's office. She remembered where it was from the tour with her uncle when they first visited. She opened the outer door, where the secretary usually sat. It was obvious that it had been in use, and she wondered who had used the office. The bishop had his own office near his quarters. She continued through to the main office of the queen.

The medium-sizedroom had windows to an interior courtyard. She was drawn to the windows behind the desk, where she stared out at a tranquil setting. Although most of the flowering plants and shrubs were losing their leaves, she knew that in full bloom the gardens must be splendid.

Turning, she was glad to see a fireplace with two chairs and a small table between them and bookshelves lined with books. There was wine in a jug, she poured a cup for herself and went to sit at the desk. It did not take her long to understand that Lord Navona had used this office as his own.

"He probably had his own secretary, as well," she thought. "I suppose that is something else I will need."

Catherine knew nothing about the running of a kingdom, but she began to rifle through the papers on the desk and found several interesting letters. She put them aside to discuss with Gio and her father. After she had tidied up the desk and arranged things in piles that seemed to make sense, she got up to peruse the books on the shelves.

By late afternoon, Catherine had discovered many things about Montalcino and had more questions than answers. She found Gio still talking with soldiers and potential soldiers in the courtyard and left him to his task.

It was nearing dusk when Catherine finally found her quarters. She got a bit lost in the search but knew she had found the right hallway from Gio's directions of earlier. She was exploring her rooms with a reverence she usually felt when she was in church. Her thoughts were not so much of her mother, Sofia, but of her grandmother and Lady Isabella, who had lived and loved in these rooms for so long. Her mother's journal spoke of the women so lovingly, and she tried to imagine how difficult it must have been for them to keep their love a secret.

Catherine ran her hand along the long wall of bookcase to the secret door at the back. She opened it and looked down the long staircase that disappeared into the darkness. She was latching the secret door when a knock came from the main door of the room.

"Come," Catherine called.

Father Tim and Gio entered. Catherine went to hug them. "I am so grateful to you both for all you have done today."

"There is still much to do, Catherine," Gio said. "Tomorrow will be another busy day."

Catherine nodded.

"There will be," Gio continued, "no bishop to preside over your ceremony."

"Ceremony?" Catherine asked.

Gio laughed a low, short laugh. "You must officially assume the role of queen, you know. There must be a certain regal transfer of power and blessing."

"Oh," Catherine said, clearly not anticipating such a thing.

Father Tim said, "If it meets with your approval, until we establish the response from Rome, Gio and I thought that I might perform a blessing."

"We will attempt to smooth things over with Rome," Gio said, "and invite an emissary to perform an official ceremony, but I do not think we should count on their eager involvement."

Catherine sighed and smiled. "I can think of no one I would like more to do this, Father. Thank you."

"One more thing," Gio said. "Lord Navono made himself quite at home here in these very quarters." "Oh?" Catherine said.

"I have blessed the rooms, Catherine," Father Tim said. "Holy water has been sprinkled everywhere."

"Thank you," Catherine said. "I have been wandering around these rooms and feel no presence of the Lord Navono, only my grandmother and Lady Isabella."

Father Tim looked around, and his face was suddenly full of sadness. "No matter how long they have been gone," he said, "and no matter how often I visited with Queen Sofia in these very rooms, it is always Catherine and Bella whose presence I sense here, as well."

"You miss them very much," Catherine offered.

The old priest's eyes misted. He nodded but said nothing else.

Gio filled the silence. "I came to see how the packing was going, as the soldiers were told to allow him to pack his clothes only. I had no intention of allowing him to take anything of which he might deem himself worthy," Gio said. "He had his back to the door when I arrived and was picking up something from that corner."

Catherine turned to look at the corner to which Gio pointed. There was nothing there.

"What was it?"

Gio left the room and returned a moment later. "My father had this specially made for your grandmother when they were young. Your grandmother always hated that women were not allowed to train in the military arts. He taught your grandmother in secret how to fight with swords. He once told me that he had the blacksmith create this especially so that she could wield it easily. It is lighter than most swords and made to protect her hand."

Gio held out Queen Catherine's sword to Catherine.

"She wrote about this in her journal," Catherine mused, reaching for the sword. "My mother, Sofia, wrote about her mother's sword. It was one of the few things she took when you came to help her flee." Catherine's eyes filled with tears.

Gio handed her the sword. "It is yours now. I thought it gone forever. I am happy it is returned to its rightful place, to its rightful heir."

"How did Lord Navona end up with it?" Catherine asked.

Father Tim shook his head. "He claimed it was a gift. The men who found Sofia in the hidden cabin must have had some connection to him as well as to Biondi. That is something we will probably never know, I fear."

"With your permission," Gio said, "I thought this would be a perfect symbol if you were to wear it tomorrow during your ceremony."

Catherine hefted the blade. "It is so light," she said, astonished at the weight and intricacy of the hilt. "I will wear it, uncle, but I will never use it. Might we have it mounted in honor of your father and my grandmother?" Gio nodded. Now his were the eyes reddening.

Catherine saved him. "Let us ask Vito to mount the sword and engrave the plaque? I would also like to ask him if he might be interested in being blacksmith for the queen."

Father Tim laughed out loud. "That might give him the courage to finally ask the butcher's daughter for her hand!"

Catherine smiled. "I am caught playing matchmaker, I see." She laughed as well.

"Until tomorrow, then." Gio said, hugging his niece, for he would always think of her that way. "Sleep well, my queen."

"You both, as well," Catherine said, seeing them out.

When they had both gone, Catherine lay the sword on the table, sat down and imagined Gio's father, Robert, and her grandmother sneaking off to practice fighting. "You must have been some force to be reckoned with, grandmother," she said softly, smiling at the blade.

Another knock interrupted her thoughts. She did not move, for her exhaustion was catching up with her.

"Come," she called without looking up.

"I thought you might be hungry," Michelena said, setting a tray with cheese, bread, olives, and wine on the table.

Catherine looked up. "Michelena!" she cried. "I have looked for you all day! Where have you been?"

"Mostly helping my mother get things organized and under control in your kitchens, my queen," Michelena said with a laugh. "I looked for you, too. When you did not appear for dinner, I thought to bring you something. You must eat, you know."

"You," Catherine said, standing up to greet her, "are a blessing to me."

A wave of sadness suddenly swept over Michelena's face. Catherine saw it. "What is it, Michelena? Tell me what saddens you."

The strain and worry of the morning, the separation and exhaustion of the day caught up with Michelena. She burst into tears and between her sobs she said, "I was so worried this morning after you left. I feared that things might turn violent, and I might never see you again. You might have been killed!" Michelena wept harder.

Catherine pulled the woman into her arms to console her. "I am here. It is fine," she said. "We are fine, and all is well."

Catherine continued to hold Michelena, gently stroking her head, her hair, until the weeping began to subside. "I did not," Catherine said, "realize how much I missed you today." Catherine placed both hands on either side of Michelena's face and pulled it away from her breast so that she might look into the woman's reddened eyes. "Until you walked into the room."

Michelena's eyes held Catherine's and Catherine saw her own desire reflected in them. She felt the pull of her heart and a tingle in her loins that she had never in her life felt before. Her exhaustion was replaced with undeniable desire. Her hands continued to hold Michelena's head. Her eyes continued to hold Michelena's eyes. Her entire body began trembling uncontrollably. She was filled simultaneously with a fear and longing that had been buried deep within her very essence. She did not plan it, but she could do only one thing.

Catherine bent her head slightly and pressed her lips against Michelena's.

"I believe I have wanted to do that since the first time I saw you in the courtyard in Castiglione d' Orcia," Catherine whispered.

Michelena suddenly felt a wave of shyness, but responded, "I must confess that I was drawn to you from the moment I met you on Sunday. I never dared to hope that you might feel the same."

"In spite of your trying to hide it," Catherine responded, "I knew." Catherine smiled, but her smile conveyed a touch of sadness and concern. She reached for Michelena's hand and drew her to the table where they sat. Catherine reached for the jug of wine and poured them each a cup.

"Michelena," she said as she raised her cup and then took a sip. She placed her cup back on the table and looked directly into Michelena's eyes. "My feelings for you descended on me like a sudden wind and they have grown so quickly this week." She paused. In the silence that hung between them like a quivering pendulum suddenly confused by direction, Michelena reached for Catherine's hand.

"These past days—and weeks," Michelena said gently, "you have endured what can be a lifetime of questioning, searching, decision and action for most people."

Catherine's eyes had dropped to her lap. Now she looked up at Michelena again.

"Catherine," Michelena continued, "my queen," she stopped, smiled and got on her knees in front of the queen. "Your tasks as monarch are your priority. That must be so." She took Catherine's hands again and kissed them. "You and I need do nothing. I am happier than I can express to know how you feel. That kiss will carry me for some time. I have already waited a lifetime for it."

Catherine's look shifted from worry to one of gratitude. She pulled her right hand from Michelena's and rested her palm against the kneeling woman's cheek. "Oh, Michelena," she said, her voice as soft as a sigh, "these feelings I have for you are—are—sacred. I do not know how else to describe them. It is as if my heart found home when I found you. How can this be anything except—except—"

"A miracle?" Michelena asked. "At the very least, you are a God-given gift to me. And," she continued, "I am content to live my life in close proximity to you, if that is what God has planned."

❧

Following the initial days of organizing, hiring, firing and getting to know the inner workings of the castle, things began to settle into a routine of sorts. Catherine and Father Tim met early every morning in the church to begin their day with prayer and quiet contemplation. When she returned to her quarters, Catherine was greeted by Michelena with a light breakfast. They ate together, then went to Catherine's office to begin to decipher the documents left behind by Navona. Gio often joined them.

"Uncle," Catherine said during one of the first mornings, "to what does this document refer?"

Gio took the paper from her hands and looked it over. "Montalcino castle used to produce paper," he said. "It was really a profitable concern for many years. There used to be a paper making facility down a bit from where the hermitage is."

"Why did we stop producing paper?" Catherine asked.

Gio dropped the paper on her desk and sighed. "Like everything else since the Church started running Montalcino, it was decided that paper making was not as profitable as increasing taxes and enforcing the collection of those taxes." Gio walked over to the bookcase and ran his finger across several spines. "Here," he said, pulling a book from the shelf. "This tells the story of how Montalcino was one of the first to begin producing paper. The book itself is written on Montalcino stock."

Catherine took the book from him and opened it. "My mother's journal was made here," she said.

Gio, back looking through the books turned and said, "That is right, Sofia's journal was made here. In fact, your grandfather, Ambrose, made it especially for her."

"It is a truly beautiful book," Catherine said.

Michelena had been reading the journal in the evenings as she and Catherine rested at the fireplace in Catherine's quarters. "It is an incredibly high quality," she added. "Is there a reason we cannot put the paper making back into operation?"

"I have seen some of the large stone vats leaning aside the wall on the east side of the hermitage," Gio said. "Let me see if any of the old families that used to run the operation are still here in Montalcino. Although it would not surprise me if they took their talents elsewhere."

The thought of bringing paper making back to the town excited Catherine in a way that she had never felt. It was as if a new part of her was opening.

"Montalcino is surrounded by vineyards," Michelena said. "I trust the church left us to our winemaking?"

Gio laughed. "Perhaps not as profitable as the church would like, but a necessary endeavor for all!"


As the weeks passed, one lord after another returned to the Privy Council. Their relief at the return of a monarch was palpable.

Lord Santori was the nephew of the old Lord Bagglioni from Roccalbegna. Lord d'Anza was from Arcidosso. At the first meeting where they were all present, Lord Santori remarked, "It amazes me that the entire air surrounding the castle feels lighter."

Lord Murano nodded. "It is true, my friend. There is an energy that begins in the town and carries into these very walls."

Catherine listened with interest to the men at the table.

"I believe," Lord Puglia said with a smile, "that our Queen has brought hope and compassion back to our little kingdom."

Catherine, still not quite comfortable in her role as ruling monarch, blushed at the compliment.

Later that night, Catherine and Michelena sat on the heavy rug in front of the fireplace. It was the time of day that

Catherine loved most. She and Michelena were getting to know one another. And they were allowing themselves to grow into their affections. Michelena sat leaning against the heavy chair. Catherine sat leaning against Michelena and drew one of the woman's arms around her.

"Do you know what I find interesting?" Catherine asked.

"Hmmm?" Michelena asked dreamily.

"My father has been quite astounded at the differences between my reign and my grandmother's."

Michelena was rubbing Catherine's earlobe, but stopped to ask, "In what ways?"

"Apparently," Catherine said, "there was nothing but enmity between my grandmother and her council. Papa was greatly concerned about that when I made my choice."

Michelena stopped rubbing Catherine's ear and reached for her wine goblet. "Well, if you think about it, your grandmother ascended the throne after the death of her father. That council was all men and probably not happy with suddenly having a woman in charge. Then there was all that horror when she was killed, and Sofia was suddenly the new monarch. It must have been a very chaotic turn of events."

Michelena pulled Catherine into her arms. "You, on the other hand, my queen," she said as she set her goblet down, "have given these lords back the kingdom the Church pulled out from under them. You have given them back their purpose, their dignity and their ability to help their own towns in ways that were stolen from them. It is different because you saved them."

"And you," Catherine said, pulling Michelena's face toward her own, "are becoming my salvation."

Michelena's breath quickened. Catherine kissed her eyes, her cheeks, her neck, then raised her mouth to her lips and ran her tongue along them as Michelena moaned softly. Catherine stopped. Her breathing was heavy, but she smiled and pushed herself up and walked closer to the fire to warm herself. "This great stone fireplace has stood witness to so much," she thought, wishing it could share the memories of the family she never knew.

Michelena waited a bit, staring at the back of the woman she was falling more in love with every day. Finally, she went to Catherine and slipped her arms around her waist from behind.

Catherine turned, reached up, and pushed a strand of her long black hair from Michelena's face and sighed. "When I first saw you in the courtyard with those two babies, my first thought was that you were a stunningly beautiful woman. I instantly pushed the thought away and told myself that I was wondering what it was like to be a mother—to consider the thought of having children."

"Do you want children?" Michelena asked. A crease of worry crossed her brow.

Catherine kissed Michelena's forehead, took hold of her hand and pulled her over to the window, where the moon shone brightly.

"What is it, Catherine?" Michelena asked in a nearly hoarse whisper.

"I can never remember not wanting to be a nun," she said. "That part is true."

"But," Michelena encouraged.

"But," Catherine continued, "I knew I was different. I never felt about boys the way that other girls did. I never understood what they felt that made them giggle so and titter endlessly." She looked up into the sky full of moonlight. "Perhaps deciding to be a nun was a way for me to hide from myself."

Michelena lifted Catherine's hand and kissed it gently and nodded with understanding.

"Perhaps," Catherine went on, "perhaps I might one day want children, but it is not a subject to which I ever gave consideration. I have no need of them, I suppose. That is another way in which I differed from the girls I knew growing up. They all could not wait to marry and have babies."

The window was opened just a crack and Catherine shivered as a small breeze blew in. Michelena closed the window and pulled Catherine back to the fire.

Sitting back in front of the fire—close, warm, and content, Catherine said, "When I first saw you, I understood."

"Understood what?" Michelena asked.

"I understood how girls felt about boys," she said. "In an instant it became crystal clear. And I fought those feelings until we were here."

"And now?" Michelena asked.

"Now," Catherine said, reaching for Michelena's face, sliding her hands down to her tender neck, Catherine pulled at the tie at the front of Michelena's dress. "Now I can wait no longer."

Catherine's hand slid into Michelena's bodice to cup a breast. Michelena groaned, pulling Catherine to her "My queen, my queen," she said. "I am yours."

Those first days and nights were remarkably full of a vibrant energy that exuded to everyone around Catherine.

Gio and Pasquale were the first to comment on the excitement and energy they saw in Catherine.

"You are taking to the role of monarch with an almost fierce determination," Gio said at dinner a few evenings later. "It is as if you are on fire."

Pasquale lifted a glass of wine to toast his daughter. "I agree," he said. "To my daughter, who appears to be returning the soul to Montalcino!"

Catherine blushed at the praise and simply bowed her head,

her eyes downcast so as not to reveal anything they might say. Michelena squeezed her hand beneath the table.

When dinner was finished, Catherine excused herself from the main dining hall to retire to her quarters.

Michelena whispered, "I shall join you very shortly, love."

Catherine nodded.

Soon after, Michelena entered the queen's suite.

"You have been crying!" Catherine said as she rushed to Michelena. "Whatever has happened?"

Michelena smiled. "Nothing so awful," she said. "I caught my mother's eye during the meal, and she gave me an odd look. I followed her to the kitchen to make her explain."

Catherine waited, tensing during the pause.

"My mother sends her love," Michelena said softly. "She sends her love and . . . "

"And what?" Catherine asked.

Michelena sat in one of the big soft chairs near the fireplace. She slumped, burying her face in her hands. When she uncovered her face, she looked at Catherine with a touch of fear. "And her blessing."

Catherine felt the beginnings of a fear she had not yet had to face. "Her blessing for what?" she asked with trepidation.

"For us," Michelena sighed.

It was Catherine now who fell into the chair opposite Michelena's, with a groan. "How?" was all she could utter.

Michelena stood and went to Catherine, kneeling before her. She lay her arm and head on Catherine's knee. "She said she knew it that first morning we came down after breakfast. She saw the tension between us had disappeared and was replaced by the kind of glow that only love could bring. She claims to have always known that I would never have been happy as the wife of anyone, but she worried that I might never find true love. She could see that her worries were over."

"You mean," Catherine asked with disbelief, "she is happy for you? For us?"

"Apparently," Michelena responded. "There is more, Catherine."

"I do not think I want to hear more!"

Michelena pushed herself up to her knees and took Catherine's face into her hands. "Both of our mothers are aware of the turn in our relationship."

"They have discussed it?" Catherine said with horror.

"Apparently," Michelena continued, "with some happiness."

"Unbelievable," Catherine said tossing her head back onto the chair.

Michelena rose and went to pour them each a glass of wine. "If it helps, the men are oblivious. Well, your father and uncle. I do not know about Father Tim."

Catherine was suddenly tired and wanted nothing more than to climb into bed and fall asleep. She said as much and Michelena nodded. Together, they made their way to the bedroom where Michelena began to undo the fastenings of Catherine's dress. Although exhausted from the events of the night, Michelena could not help but begin to trace her fingertips along Catherine's back. Soon, they were followed by her lips. Lightly, her hands crept around to Catherine's breasts as she slid the dress down to the floor.

Catherine, so tired just a moment before, found herself responding despite her emotional state. She leaned back against Michelena and gave herself over to the sensuality of disrobing. When she turned around to Michelena, she could not help but smile. "You make me forget everything," she whispered as she pulled Michelena to the bed.

Nothing was said by Lucia again. Francesca continued to love and adore her daughter without ever mentioning her knowledge of the relationship between the women. The men remained in the dark as far as Catherine could tell.

Catherine and Father Tim continued their time each morning to meet in the castle's church—the same church where her grandmother had once spent a night in supplication on the cold stone floor where she begged God for help when she realized how hopelessly in love she was with the Lady Isabella; the same church where her mother, Sofia, had been secretly brought to clandestine meetings with a cruel and inhumane bishop. It was, in fact, the same church where yet another bishop impregnated Sofia with her. Now, she met there each morning with Father Tim, the priest who had befriended and loved them all so unconditionally.

Catherine entered the church and found the good priest kneeling in prayer. When he heard her enter, he blessed himself and stood to greet her. He was a bit slow in getting up.

"My knees are more rebellious these days," he said as he greeted her with kisses on both cheeks. "It makes me grateful that our unnamed monk recommends sitting."

Catherine laughed. "Let us sit, then, Father."

They moved to the front of the church and Tim pulled the *Cloud of Unknowing* from his robe pocket. As he began to turn the pages, looking for the place they had left off previously, Catherine stopped him.

"Might we talk for a moment before we begin?" she asked.

"Of course," he said. "What is on your mind?"

Catherine thought she knew what she wanted to say, but words eluded her. She sat without speaking for some minutes, struggling with how to begin. Finally, she said, "I am uncertain how to approach the subject."

"Is it a royal matter or something of a more personal nature?" he asked.

Catherine flushed and could not look him in the eyes.

"I see," Father Tim said. He stood and walked up to the altar, then turned and went back to where Catherine sat. "My dear queen," he said, his voice full of love, "none of us can know the mind of God. Anyone who tells you they do is an arrogant fool." At this last, he knelt in front of Catherine. He looked up at her and smiled. "This is important, Catherine, so much so that I am back down on my knees and may require your assistance to stand again."

She smiled at him and reached for his hands. "I hope I will always be here to help you in that way."

He sighed deeply, then began. "I have known Michelena since she was a baby and like to think that I even helped to raise her," he said softly. "She is as loving and faithful a person as I have ever had the good fortune to have in my life. She brought joy and life to my life in ways that priests rarely get to experience. Watching her grow has been a great gift." He stopped speaking and tried to stand, Catherine helped him, and he sat down next to her. "You, too, have been given the gift of Michelena. I hope you receive that gift without qualms or doubts about what others may think about your love for her. That, in my opinion, would be a great sin."

Catherine's eyes filled with tears as he spoke. "I am more blessed than any one person has the right to be," she said. "Sometimes I feel as if my life is an endless waterfall of pure love." She raised his hand to her cheek. "I am most especially grateful for you and what you continue to teach me every day by just being here and sharing all that you know."

"And I know so little," he said. "Shall we see what God has to show us today?"

Catherine had been sharing much from the *Cloud* with Michelena, who was very interested in the process that Catherine and Father Tim had been exploring. It was only after the conversation about their relationship, that Catherine felt compelled to ask Michelena to join them.

Michelena kissed Catherine and thanked her for the invitation. "Oh, my love," she said, "I am so honored to be asked to join you both."

"There is a 'no thank you' coming," Catherine said, laughing.

"But," Michelena ventured, "over the course of many years I have come to my own morning practice. I do hope you are not offended, sweet. I find that when I can walk in nature, or watch the sun rise over the mountaintops or trees or listen to the sounds of the forest and birds, well, that is my special time with God. I would not like to sit in the church, study and sit more. I am sorry, but I know that my whole body would rail against such a ritual. Please do not be angry."

"I am not angry," Catherine responded. "I admit to being a little surprised. It never occurred to me that you would not want to be included in such a marvelous spiritual endeavor."

Michelena sat at the table where they had just finished a private breakfast. She took a moment to consider what she was going to say next, then held her hands out to Catherine. Catherine walked over and gave Michelena her hands.

"It does sound like a marvelous spiritual endeavor," Michelena began. "And I love hearing you talk about it and love hearing what you and Tim discover along the way. Please do not stop sharing with me. When you have had some insight or some gift during your time, you come back so relaxed, so refreshed, and exuberant. You have no idea how much I love listening to you at those times." She paused and kissed Catherine's hands. "But that is your spiritual time. Those are your spiritual gifts from God. You need those times with God and Father Tim. Your role as queen is taxing and weighs on you in ways you do not even realize. Your time in that church each morning is something I hold sacred for you.  Do you understand?  I feel as if I am not making much sense."

Catherine fell to her knees in front of Michelena.  "How am I to respond to such a loving gift?" she asked.  She buried her head in Michelena's lap and did not hold back her tears.

"Please tell me," Michelena said, "that these are tears of joy."

Catherine looked up at her.  "Most assuredly they are, my darling."

"I love you more every day," Michelena said.  "If we have a lifetime together, how will we contain such a love?"

Catherine pulled Michelena to her knees and kissed her long and passionately.  Then she stood up, ran her hands down her own dress—playfully dismissive—and said, "I must get to the throne room.  It is the day for me to hear requests from the people."

Catherine walked toward the door and looked back at Michelena, still on her knees on the floor and in quite an aroused state.

"You are developing," Michelena said as she shook her head and smiled, "quite the mischievous streak since you came into power."

Catherine blew her a kiss and closed the door while still laughing.

It was Gio, who had grown up at Montalcino castle when his father, Robert, had been captain of the guard under the first Catherine, and who then returned to Montalcino at his grandfather's request to help Sofia, who had noticed the dramatic change in things.

Then at the evening meal in the great hall one night, he said, "You know, Catherine, I remember many times of great joy here. One was during a long, snowy winter.  Lady Isabella convinced your grandmother to have a grand celebration to relieve the boredom of captivity.  It was a happy, joyous event.  But it was short-lived."

Catherine looked around. Castle staff and guards were enjoying their meal. Conversation was robust and full of laughter. She had become accustomed to the general sounds of the dining hall and had not given it a second thought. But now she tried to imagine how different things must have been in the past. The Inquisition still held power over much of the land, but the castle and her people seemed untouched by it.

"Are you concerned, Uncle?" she asked.

"No," he said. "More admiring of the change."

Michelena looked around as well, and said, "When I was down in the kitchen visiting with my mother today, the kitchen staff were reminiscing about how each October there would be a Chestnut Festival."

"I remember those!" Gio exclaimed. "The men would roast the chestnuts in huge batches over a white-hot fire and turn them with hoes. Someone was always in charge of pouring wine on them as they roasted."

Michelena grabbed a piece of sausage from the platter as it passed and said, "One of the older women said that the children used to run around under the chestnut trees trying not to get hit by the falling chestnuts."

Francesca sipped her wine. "Our grandfather always spoke of the Chestnut Festivals. He said all the townspeople of Montalcino would bring a dish to share. It did sound like a lovely time."

"When was the last time there was a Festival?" Catherine asked.

"It sounded like it has been quite a long while," Michelena said. "One woman said that they tried to have them once Queen Sofia came into power, but she did not attend and eventually the festival became a thing of the past."

"Sofia had little to celebrate," Gio said sadly. "I am not

surprised at that bit of information."

"It is just the beginning of October," Catherine said. "It looks to me as if the chestnuts are ready. Why do we not renew the festival again? It sounds like a marvelous way to get the townspeople together. I have met so few of them as yet."

Catherine stood up and tapped on her wine glass with her spoon to get the attention of all the staff and servants supping in the great hall. When the chatter died down, she said, "All in favor of reinstituting the Annual Chestnut Festival, please raise your hands."

The hall went deadly silent for a moment. Not a single hand went up, but suddenly the hall exploded in excited cheers. Everyone stood and applauded.

Catherine sat back down, very pleased with the response and enthusiasm.

Michelena leaned over to her and said, "It does not appear that they like the idea!"

It took all of Catherine's willpower not to kiss Michelena right there in the great hall in front of everyone.

The day of the festival was perfectly beautiful. There was only a clear, blue sky full of sun. Leaves of red and golds filled the valley and the courtyard. Vines climbed up the castle walls in brilliant red. Catherine enjoyed just walking around and watching all the interactions and activities. Michelena and Father Tim were walking beside of her when Antonita rushed up to them.

"Girls," she said with much concern, "I thought you were long gone by now."

Father Tim smiled. "Antonita, I would like to introduce Queen Catherine and her lady-in-waiting, Michelena."

Antonita blinked; in her confusion it took a moment to register.

"Queen?" Understanding bloomed in her face. "Queen! Queen Catherine!" she exclaimed in horror. Instantly she dropped to her knees and apologized. "I did not realize you were the Catherine who became our queen!"

Catherine laughed and reached down to the woman's outstretched hands. She pulled her to her feet. "Antonita, how could you have known? Please know that Michelena and I are so grateful to you for hiding us that night. You are a very brave woman, and I am grateful to know that women like you live in our little Montalcino."

"To think that I made such a meager meal and gave you such a tiny place to sleep," Antonita said, still apologetic.

"Antonita," Catherine said. "Do not give it another thought. We were grateful. And if things had gone differently, it was best you did not know who we were."

"Come, Antonita," Father Tim said. "We have not spoken in so long. I would like to know what you hear from our friends." He slipped his arm through Antonita's and steered her away from Catherine and Michelena so that they might meet more of the townspeople waiting to greet her. Gio hovered nearby, keeping an eye on everyone who approached his queen.

When the long line of people who waited to greet the queen had dissipated, Catherine and Michelena wandered to a long table with food and wine.

"Your Majesty," Lucia said with a grin.

"Daughter," she added. "Please sit and I will bring you a platter of food."

"Thank you, Lucia." Catherine said. Turning, she and Michelena found a table at which sat a young girl of no more than ten years of age.

"May we sit with you?" Catherine asked.

The girl nodded without looking up. She was engrossed in a

little book she was reading.

"What do you read that has you so captivated?" Catherine asked the girl.

"It is a book written by the nun of Avila in—" The girl happened to look up as she responded and realized that it was the queen who addressed her. She jumped from her seat and dropped her book. Her face turned several shades of red as she dropped to her knees and began to apologize profusely.

"Up, up, dear child," Catherine said with a very broad smile.

The girl picked up her book. Slowly, the look of panic that had overtaken her began to fade.

"So," the queen continued, "tell me about this nun in Avila. Spain?"

"Yes, Your Majesty," the young woman said. "I have been studying her work. This is her book called *The Interior Castle*. She was a mystic."

"How so?" Catherine asked.

Catherine and Michelena sat down at the table with her and Catherine encouraged her to sit as well. Lucia arrived with a great platter of food and a jug of wine with cups.

"Thank you, Lucia," Catherine said and indicated that their surprised table mate should help herself.

"Thank you, Mama," Michelena said.

Gio stood at the end of the table and continued watching. It was Catherine's first real outing as queen among so many people and his nerves were on high alert.

"What is your name?" Michelena asked the girl.

The girl reached for a chestnut. "I am named Pagola, but everyone calls me Pippa."

"Well, Pippa," Catherine said, "I want to know about this mystic nun."

Pippa's face beamed. "Her name was Teresa and she

could levitate!"

Michelena stopped chewing a piece of roasted chicken. "What?"

"The other nuns say that she would go into a trance while she was in prayer and they say her body would rise off the ground,' Pippa said a tad defensively.

"It is fine, Pippa," Catherine said, "Michelena is just surprised, not disbelieving."

"More intrigued," Michelena said as she finished swallowing a gulp of wine.

"In this book," Pippa went on, "Teresa tells how to enter the castle that is your soul so that you can get closer to God."

"Pippa," Catherine asked, "where did you get your book?"

Suddenly, Pippa looked afraid again.

Catherine saw the look of terror and responded instantly, reaching out to stroke the girl's head. "Do not worry, Pippa. I only ask because I should like to read it myself."

Pippa's shoulders relaxed. "I am sorry to get afraid, Your Majesty. I have gotten myself in trouble before for always reading things and not being careful."

Catherine sighed. "I know, child. But if I have any power to change things, we will be allowed to read whatever we can get our hands on. How does that sound?"

Pippa smiled. "That sounds like heaven, Your Majesty. And my grandfather brought me this book back from his travels. Would you like to read it?"

"I would indeed, Pippa," Catherine said, smiling at the generous offer. "But it sounds as if you need to finish it. I will find a copy for myself. Might I have a look at yours?"

Pippa handed the book to the queen and reached for a piece of chicken just as Vito approached the table.

"Your Majesty," he boomed. "Michelena," he bowed, then

more softly, "marry me!"

Catherine laughed. "You are incorrigible, Vito. And how is the butcher's daughter from Castiglione d' Orcia?"

"Turned me down flat, Your Majesty!"

"Then it is her loss, Vito," Michelena offered.

"It is just as well," Vito said. "I am very busy as the queen's blacksmith. I get very little time to get to Castiglione d' Orcia. I fear my mother's garden will turn to weed next season."

If things get to be too much, Vito," Catherine said, "you must speak to Gio about an apprentice. I am willing to wager that there are many fine young men who would love to learn a trade."

Gio heard his name and turned his head. At that very moment he saw a flash come from his side and felt the push of an elbow.

A short blade was thrust in front of him toward the queen. Michelena screamed. "No!"

Gio was pushed off balance but grabbed at the arm with the blade. He missed and struggled to regain his footing. He reached, again, for the arm and violently pulled the man, crashing into the table and overturning it as he fell. Vito reacted and managed to twist the blade from the fingers with his right hand as soon as Gio pulled the would-be assailant to the ground. His training kicked in and he quickly maneuvered the assailant so that he had the advantage. When Gio was on top of the man's back, he pulled the offender's arms back. Vito held the short blade to the man's throat as Gio bound his hands. When Gio finally stood, leaving the assailant on the ground with Vito continuing to hold the blade to his neck, he turned to Catherine, who stood with Pippa, who was now peeking out from behind her.

"Catherine!" Gio exclaimed. He looked confused, as if he did not know where he was. "Catherine!"

Catherine was looking down at the rip in the bodice of her dress. At the sound of her name being called a second time she shook her head and looked at Gio as if she were utterly perplexed. "I am unharmed, Cousin," Catherine said with a calm that conveyed a peace about the seconds long ordeal that would have shaken the most hardened of men to the core.

Gio, unconvinced, looked to where her dress had been torn by the blade. His face held a look of both confusion and relief.

Other guards came running at the commotion. Gio turned to them and gave them orders to take the attacker to the dungeon.

Turning back to Catherine, he said, "We are returning to the castle. Clearly Rome has sent us a message."

Catherine knew better than to argue with Gio and when she looked at Michelena she saw the woman was visibly shaken. Lucia had come and had her arm around her daughter, who was pale and trembling. Michelena's eyes were fixed on Catherine's chest.

Catherine reached her hand down to pull the material together and turned to Pippa, who was still clinging to her.

"Pippa," Catherine said turning to embrace the child. "You are unharmed?"

"Yes, Your Majesty."

"Pippa!"

Pippa looked up at the call of her name.

"I am here, Grandfather."

Gio stepped up to prevent the man from approaching Catherine. Once he understood that the man intended no harm and was the child's grandfather, he allowed the man to approach the queen.

"Your Majesty," Pippa's grandfather bowed. "I am sorry if my granddaughter has bothered you."

"Quite the contrary, sir," Catherine reassured him. "I invited myself to her table and she graciously accepted." Then to Pippa she said, "You have had quite an exciting lunch, Pippa. I hope we might lunch again."

Pippa looked up with much concern in her eyes. "Do people

often try to kill you when you lunch, Your Majesty?"

Catherine laughed. "That was unusual, Pippa. I consider that you were here to have been my good fortune."

Catherine leaned down again to give Pippa a hug.

As she did, Pippa whispered in her ear. "Did you see it?"

Kneeling, Catherine held the girl's shoulders and looked into her eyes. Very softly she said to her, "You are speaking of the blade?"

Pippa's eyes never left Catherine's as she shook her head slowly back and forth. Catherine understood and nodded.

Catherine stood again and turned to Pippa's grandfather. "Sir?" she said.

"My apologies, Queen Catherine," he said, "I am Paulo Mattucci, Pippa's grandfather."

"Well, Signor Mattucci," Catherine said drawing Pippa to her side, "you have a very special granddaughter."

Paolo Mattucci beamed. "Thank you, Majesty. I think so."

Gio's anxiety was increasing each moment that Catherine remained in public. He coughed. "Majesty, we must leave now."

Catherine nodded and said her farewells.

Michelena grabbed her arm as several soldiers surrounded them and escorted the pair back to the castle.

"You act as if an attempt was not just made on your life!" Michelena said in a frantic whisper to Catherine. "How are you so calm?"

Catherine could feel that Michelena was still trembling. "We will talk when we are safely indoors," she said cryptically.

Francesca had been with Pasquale just coming over the bridge into town when the attempt was made on their daughter's life. A soldier came running up to them before they reached the festival and directed them back to the castle. They were waiting for

Catherine when she returned.

As soon as Catherine and Michelena were safely installed within the walls of the castle, Francesca ran to her daughter and threw her arms around her. "Thank God you are unhurt!"

Gio instructed two guards to stay with Catherine while he went to discuss something with Pasquale. When he and Pasquale were finished, Gio said, "Catherine, I would like you to remain in your quarters for the time being. I am going to interrogate your assailant, but until I have more information, I do not wish to take chances."

Catherine nodded and she, the two guards, her mother and Michelena went to the queen's quarters. The guards remained posted outside her doors.

"I am fine, Mama, truly." Catherine did her best to relieve her mother's worry. But the fact that there was a slash through Catherine's clothing did nothing to assuage her mother. When Pasquale came up to check on his daughter, he was able to calm Francesca and convince her to let Catherine rest.

When they were finally alone Michelena took Catherine in an extended embrace. Neither said a word. They simply held each other for many minutes. Finally, Catherine pulled them toward the large chairs to sit on the floor. There was already a fire in the fireplace, so the room was warm. Even so, Michelena shivered. Catherine pulled her close.

"My love," Catherine said softly into Michelena's hair, "tell me everything you saw when the attack happened."

Michelena's breathing stopped momentarily. "It was so fast. I am not even certain," she said.

"Do you remember screaming?" Catherine asked.

Michelena nodded. "But then what happened was rather a blur. I know I saw the blade strike at you, but—" She stopped and shook her head as if to clear it. She sat up and turned toward Catherine.

She closed her eyes and shook her head slowly. "Catherine, I swear that I saw the blade pierce your breast."

Catherine said nothing, but stared at Michelena for some time. The only sound was a loud pop from the fire in the hearth. They both turned to be sure that no sparks had jumped into the room.

Finally, Michelena said, "You think I have gone mad. I think so myself. Nevertheless, I thought you dead. The next thing I remember was falling backward as the table and bench on which I sat were pushed over by Gio pulling that bastardo down. When I saw you still standing there, I could not believe it. Still, I am struggling with what I believe I saw."

Catherine held Michelena. She stroked the woman's hair and periodically pressed a tender kiss onto the top of her head. As the fire began to smolder, Catherine slipped out from the embrace to lay another log and some kindling on the embers. She blew forcefully to get the kindling to catch and walked to get them wine.

"The sun is very low in the sky, my sweet," Catherine said as she handed Michelena a cup of wine. "I must tell you that I do not think you mad," she said as she sat back down on the floor. In fact, I have been struggling with my own visions of what happened."

Michelena's hand flew to her heart. She sat up and looked directly into Catherine's eyes. "What? Tell me."

Catherine took a breath. "I, too, saw the blade and I saw it coming right at me. It was as if everything was happening in a slowed motion. I saw Gio reach for the man's wrist and grab it, but I thought him too late for I felt the tip of the blade pierce my breast, but then . . . " Catherine's voice drifted off and her brow furrowed as she remembered what she had seen next.

"But then, what?" Michelena prodded.

"Michelena, in all your life with Father Tim has he ever talked about angels?"

"What? Why?" Michelena now sat bolt upright and grabbed

Catherine's hands.

Catherine shrugged. "I think one may have saved my life today," she said softly. "I watched that blade enter my chest and then a bright and quite enormous light flashed between me and the assailant. It was just a flash, mind you, but when I looked down to see where the blade had entered, there was nothing but torn clothing."

"What makes you think it was an angel?" Michelena asked.

"I felt absolutely no fear," Catherine said. "I saw a man with a blade trying to kill me and before I had time to register any fear, I was filled with such a feeling of peace and calm. I have never felt such a serenity. More, when I embraced Pipp, she rather secretly asked me if I had seen *it* and made it quite clear that she was not referring to the blade."

Again, the women sat silently. They drank their wine. A knock on the door came just as the sun was setting.

"Come," Catherine called.

Lucia entered with a tray of dinner. A young servant was with her. She curtsied and went about lighting all the candles in the room.

Lucia set the tray on the dining table and went over to where Catherine and Michelena sat. "Have you recovered from your fright?" she asked Catherine.

Catherine stood to embrace Michelena's mother. "I think so, Lucia. And you? Did you witness the attack?"

Lucia shook her head. "I looked up when I heard Michelena scream. I saw her fall to the ground when the table tipped and her bench fell back, but I did not know what had happened until I got to her. Thank God he did not harm you!"

Lucia turned to her daughter, whom she had not yet greeted. She embraced Michelena and kissed her. She then turned back to Catherine and smiled. "Your parents have been in the church most of the afternoon thanking God for your life."

Catherine nodded. "I should be there with them," she lamented. "Gio has ordered me to stay here, however, and knowing him, he is even more disturbed by the event. I do not dare go against his wishes at present."

Lucia nodded. "Your uncle has been back and forth between the prisoner, the guards and the chapel. He seems quite agitated and has not eaten since the morning meal."

The young woman who had lit all the candles was about to depart when Catherine called to her. "Maria," Catherine called.

The young girl turned around and curtsied to the queen. "Yes, Your Majesty."

"Will you please find Father Tim and request him to come to my quarters?"

"Right away, Majesty." Maria said. The girl closed the doors to the queen's quarters.

Lucia watched the young girl leave the queen's quarters. "I do not like to leave that child alone," she said a bit anxiously.

"Do you not trust her?" Catherine asked.

"I trust the girl well enough, it is men who might see an opportunity to take advantage of the poor child that I mistrust," Lucia said.

Catherine looked up in surprise and simply waited with dread for Lucia to tell her what she meant. It was evident from the flare of her nostrils and the clench in her jaw that something untoward had happened to the girl. Lucia took a breath.

"It frightens me to think of how many men of God act with the soul of the devil," Lucia said, her head lowered. "I have kept Maria as close to me as if she were my own. Slowly, she has felt safe enough to tell me how the bishop used her—for himself and for others." Lucia looked up with a fire in her eyes that startled Catherine. "He should be butchered!" she said through gritted teeth.

"Mama!" Michelena cried as she reached for her mother and hugged her tightly.

"That poor child," Catherine said with a sigh. She sat down in one of the chairs, suddenly weak and exhausted.

Lucia released herself from her daughter's embrace saying, "Forgive me, daughter. I did not mean to frighten you." Then to Catherine she said, "My apologies, Majesty."

Catherine waved her hand. "You need not apologize, sweet Lucia. And I believe you are entitled to your anger. May it keep young Maria safe." She looked up at Lucia. "I am glad she has you to be a source of kindness and compassion. Do we know anything about her?"

Lucia shook her head. "Only that she is an orphan dropped here by an uncle several years ago."

"You have been a protector of so many of us, Lucia," Catherine said, reaching for her hand. "My mother and myself when I was first born, your own daughter and now Maria. Surely, there is a place in heaven for such a soul!"

"There need be no special place for people who do the right things," Lucia said. "But those who take advantage of children? Well, there needs be a special place for them, and I pray it is not heaven."

A knock at the door put an end to the conversation. Michelena went to get the door.

Father Tim was there with Maria, who looked a tad paler since she had left.

Michelena opened the door wide and ushered them both inside, then closed the door. Maria quickly moved to Lucia's side.

Lucia put an arm around the girl. "Maria, have you ever met Father Tim before this?"

Maria shook her head.

Lucia smiled at the girl. "I have known the good Father for

a very long time," she said. "And my own daughter grew up in his home. If I am ever absent and you need help, Father Tim is someone to whom you may go."

"You may also come to me," Michelena said.

The girl looked at her with widening eyes. "But, but you are a lady to the queen."

Catherine stood up. "Maria," she said, "it is important that you find Father Tim or Michelena if you are ever in need of help and Lucia is not available. You will do that, will you not?" Catherine smiled at Maria and waited until the child could finally nod her head in assent.

"Come, Maria," Lucia said. "We have work to do." She turned and curtseyed to the queen. Maria did the same.

When the door closed, and Father Tim was alone with the two women he turned to them. "Do I want to know what that was about?"

"In good time, Father," Catherine said.

Michelena poured him a cup of wine as Catherine greeted him. "Have you eaten?" Catherine asked.

"Not yet," he said and smiled. "I have been surprisingly occupied."

"Sit with us, please."

When they sat at the table Catherine said, "I would like to say the grace, if you do not mind, Father."

Tim chuckled softly. "I happily defer to Your Majesty."

Catherine folder her hands. "Gracious God, we, your humble servants ask you to bless this food and all the good people of Montalcino. Also, we thank you for your blessings and your protections. Give us the strength to do your will and follow your ways and please, help us to understand the confusion that surrounds us regarding today's events. Amen."

Michelena lifted her wine to Tim and Catherine. They each

lifted their cups and drank. Michelena filled bowls with stew.

Catherine offered Tim the basket of bread. He tore off a piece and reached for the oil. He dipped his bread in the oil then put it down. "Tell me what confuses you, Catherine."

Catherine took a bite of her stew. When she had swallowed it, she glanced over at Michelena, then set her spoon down and took another swallow of her wine.

"I do not know," she said with a smile, "why I should be surprised that you picked up on the word confusion in an otherwise nondescript prayer, but you do still manage to surprise me, Father."

Michelena set her spoon down. "Catherine," she said as she reached for the queen's hand. "Tell him."

In as much detail as she could, Catherine described the event of the attempt on her life earlier that day. Tim listened with a respectful interest, sometimes pausing in the eating of his meal, but never interrupting her story. When she finished, he sat back in his chair, sipped his wine thoughtfully and nodded as if in great thought, or Catherine worried, in great doubt.

Michelena could not tolerate his silence. "Father," she finally blurted out, "say something!"

Tim grinned at Michelena. "Do not worry, my Michelena," he said, "I am only trying to piece together the events as I have heard them from a great many people today." He turned to Catherine. "You are not mad, if that is what concerns you, Catherine," he said as he turned his attention back to the queen.

Tim stood and walked over to the fireplace. He threw another log on the fire and stoked it. When he walked back to the table, he did not sit but rested his hands on the back of his chair and said, "Gio is in quite a state. I have never known him to be so agitated. In part, I believe that the attack on you is something for which he was prepared. In fact, he has prepared for that kind of thing all his life."

"What upsets him, then?" Catherine asked. She stood and invited the priest over to the fire, she could tell he was tired and cold.

Tim sat in the great chair opposite Catherine. Michelena sat on the floor near Catherine's feet and asked, "Did Gio see the apparition, as well?"

"Would that he had seen that rather than what he did see." Tim took a deep breath. "Gio saw the blade pierce your breast. He saw the blood gush from the wound and even though he continued to try to subdue the assailant, he was certain you had been killed in the attack and that he had failed you."

"Dear God," Michelena said as a sob escaped her. "Poor Gio!"

Tim stood and walked the few steps over to the now blazing fire. "There is more," he said.

Michelena lay her head on Catherine's knee. Catherine reached a hand down to lay on her head. "Go on," she said to Tim.

A man from the village came to see me with his granddaughter a little while ago.

"Pippa!" Catherine said.

"The same," Tim said nodding. "Her grandfather was worried about her and wanted me to bless her."

Catherine's head began to nod up and down. "He thought she had gone mad because she saw the same thing I did?"

"A natural concern," Tim said. "But when I talked to Pippa, she described the scene in the identical way you did, with one exception."

Catherine closed her eyes, worried about what might be coming. When she opened them, Tim was standing directly in front of her. "She described an angel with alarming detail."

Catherine sighed. "Tell me what she saw."

Tim nodded his head and went back to sit down. He leaned over and covered his face with his hands. "She described an enormous being full of such light that it was nearly blinding at first. She was behind you and jumped up when the commotion began but claims to have seen a winged being with armor and headgear. There was a sword hanging from his side. She saw the being from behind but somehow could see through it as well. He was, according to Pippa, at least eight feet tall and the light of him completely surrounded you with giant wings while one hand helped Gio hold down the assailant and its other hand pressed against your chest."

"Did Pippa see that the queen had been stabbed?" Michelena asked.

"She did not." Father Tim answered soberly.

"Do you believe that an angel is what we saw?" Catherine asked.

Father Tim rubbed his eyes and sat up. "I believe it is possible. Further, how else do you explain the fact that you, Michelena, and Gio saw you stabbed and here you are with no wound at all? As to your question, I am a priest, I believe in much I cannot see. So, yes, I guess I do believe that an angel may have saved you."

"How are we to deal with all this?" Michelena asked. "How do we explain this without sounding as if we have all gone mad? The queen was saved by an angel. Rome will have our heads for heresy!"

Tim stood. "I am not at all convinced that this is something that needs explaining. I think we wait for now. If you and Pippa are the only ones to have seen the angel, we should avoid an announcement of any kind. Let us bide our time to see what others may have seen or not seen. For now, I will only say this. Two lives may have been saved today." He began to walk toward the door. "If you had been killed in the attack, I can only imagine what your death would have done to Gio. Just thinking he had been too slow to keep the blade from you is making him question his ability to protect you."

Catherine and Michelena walked Tim to the door. He turned to kiss them both and said, "I am thankful for the angel. I would miss our daily time together. Goodnight."

"Goodnight, Father," Catherine said. "I will see you in the morning."

When Tim was gone Catherine walked over to the fire. "Gio," she said. "I hope he will not be too hard on himself."

Michelena walked over to Catherine. "You look exhausted, my darling." She took Catherine's hand and led her toward the bedroom. "Tomorrow we will spend time with Gio. I imagine this must be especially hard since he was too late in saving your mother."

"Knowing my uncle," Catherine said with sadness, "this could destroy him anyway. He lost his faith when his father was killed. Everything about today must open old wounds."

Before Michelena began to undo the fastenings on the back of Catherine's dress she stood before her and placed her fingers on the tear the blade had made. When she had undone the back, she came back around to stand in front of Catherine and ran her fingers along the same place the blade would have penetrated. Her fingers began to tremble. Catherine grabbed her hand.

"How is there no blood?" Michelena asked.

"Michelena, do not think about it. I am alive. I am here. Let us get ready for bed, get down on our knees and thank God for the miracles of this day."

Catherine spent a sleepless night, drifting in and out of a light sleep. In the early hours, much before her usual time, she rose, dressed in simple clothing, and left a softly snoring Michelena to make her way to the church. She took the outside path, still uncomfortable with the tunnel from the kitchen, and was surprised to see the glow of candlelight flickering through the stained-glass window.

"Father Tim," she thought, "I swear if I spent the night in the church he would still be there before me!"

She opened the creaky door and saw a figure sitting in one of the pews, but it was not Father Tim. As she drew closer her heartbeat slowed as she recognized him.

"Uncle Gio?"

Gio stood. When he turned to her, she could see that he had been crying. She went to him, threw her arms around him and a shuddering sob shook loose sounding as if it came from his very soul.

He pushed himself from her arms, wiped his face with his sleeve turned from her.

"My apologies," he said, his voice thick from crying.

When he said nothing further, Catherine went to him and placed her hand on his shoulder. "Uncle," she said, "my dearest, most beloved uncle. You have done nothing but protect me since the day I was born—before that even, when I was still in my mother's womb."

He turned on her and she heard the pain, the fear and the anguish in his voice as he cried out, "You were killed! I saw it with my own eyes. I did not protect you! I do not know how you are even standing here before me!"

Very tenderly, softly, she said to him, "Please sit with me, Uncle."

He hesitated and remained standing while she sat. She reached for his hand and pulled him to the pew. "Tell me," she said, "exactly what you saw."

He shuddered with the memory of it. "I was distracted by your mention of my name when you spoke with Vito. I had been watching him, the man always seemed to be within a few feet of us, and I had a bad feeling about him. He was just waiting for an opportunity—for me to let my guard down and he took full advantage of the situation when I turned." He stopped, ran his fingers through his hair and grabbed it as if he wished to pull it out of his head.

Catherine reached a hand up to lay on his hand. He released his hair and bent over, resting his elbows on his knees. "I saw the blade enter your chest!" he cried. "I saw it, or I am a mad man."

A nightingale sang somewhere nearby. Catherine waited for Gio to continue, sensing that he was still trying to piece the attack together—to understand what he saw.

"I did not save you, Catherine," Gio lamented. "I did nothing but pull that blade out of your breast and pull that bastard to the ground. You need to dismiss me and find someone who has their faculties intact to protect you. I am certain I am seeing things that are not real. It must be the beginning of a madness." He stopped speaking and looked up at her. "It is vital to the kingdom and to your well-being that I must resign."

Catherine felt his pain in her chest. She wanted desperately to hug him and comfort him, but she knew he would find that to be an additional humiliation. She reached for his hand. "Uncle, you need to hear my own version of the event."

He looked away again, so she said, "I saw him make a dash toward me. I saw the blade appear from his left sleeve. I had a moment of panic thinking I was about to die."

Gio pulled his hand from hers and bent over as if in pain.

"Uncle," she said somewhat forcefully, "I saw and felt the blade pierce my breast." She stopped and waited for him to register what she had said.

His head jerked up and turned toward her. His eyes were full of confusion.

"I, too," she said, "may be mad. But then so is Michelena, who saw the same thing."

"What?" Gio demanded as he stood and walked away from her.

"Are you making jest of my agony?"

"I am not, uncle." Catherine stood to walk toward the altar. "I would never do such a thing to you. But you have not let me finish." Catherine got to the front of the church and genuflected, crossed herself, then turned to Gio. "I thought myself dead. But a blindingly white light was instantly between us, between you and me, as you grabbed his hand and pulled the blade from my breast."

Gio's whole demeanor changed as he turned to watch her slowly walk toward him.

She laughed softly. "Now you think me mad."

He shook his head. "I do not know what to think."

"I am not the only one to have seen this light, either." Catherine stopped in front of him. His face was swollen and red from crying.

"Michelena?" he asked.

"No," Catherine said. "Do you remember the young girl at the table? I was talking to her about her book when Vito arrived."

Gio nodded.

"She saw it, too." Catherine said moving back to the pew. "Father Tim said that her grandfather came to see him and the girl, Pippa is her name, claims it was an angel."

Gio sat, more fell into the pew. "What does it mean?"

Catherine chuckled. "I wish I knew," she said. "I do think that at the very least—"

The doors to the church opened, the loud creak announcing the arrival of Father Tim. He stopped short when he saw them, smiled softly, and went to greet them.

"Difficult night?" Father Tim said with a touch of irony. "I hope I am not interrupting. I can return later."

"Not at all, Father," Catherine said. "Gio and I were just exchanging our versions of events. I just told him about the angel."

"Do you believe it was an angel?" Gio asked the priest.

"Whether or not I believe it was an angel is not important," Tim said.

Gio stood up. "It is to me," he said.

The predawn light was beginning to filter through the window. Father Tim looked at Catherine, then back at Gio. He took a breath. "Many would say that as a priest it is my duty to believe in angels. Perhaps that is a requirement for the position. I have never seen one, but that does not preclude my believing in them. Quite honestly, Gio, I can find no other explanation for what happened yesterday. Can you?"

"There must be one," Gio said. He began to pace the aisle on the far side of the church.

"There may be," Father Tim said. "But the explanation is clearly not that you are mad. If you are mad, then several others, including your queen are mad, as well. A mass delirium is not the best place to begin to examine the facts."

Catherine continued to sit but said, "Perhaps we need to give this a little more thought. Gio," she said standing up and turning to him. "I will not accept your resignation. I need you now more than ever. What have you determined from the attacker? Is he from Rome? Did he see anything that might shed light on the events? Has anyone else come forward to report what they might have seen?"

Gio stopped pacing. "He has not spoken yet. He was thrown into a cell without food or water, whimpering like a baby. I will give him reason to speak with me today."

Catherine heard the authority returning to Gio's voice and felt a rush of relief. "Thank you, uncle. Now, if you do not mind, Father Tim and I reserved this time for us."

Gio nodded, fisted his hand over his heart and left the church.

❧

Catherine finally had a secretary, Enrico. Her family had known Enrico's family in Voghera. Enrico's mother and Francesca grew up together. Francesca wrote Enrico's mother to inquire if the young man might be interested. He'd been a very intelligent and bookish young-ster. He was thrilled to be asked and made his way to Montalcino immediately.

Catherine paced her office anxiously awaiting the arrival of Pippa and her grandfather.

Enrico knocked and entered. "Your Majesty, Paolo Matucci and Pippa are here."

Catherine nodded. "Show them in, please."

Catherine walked to the door to greet the pair. When inside her office, she invited them to sit at the small sitting area near the fireplace. Once it held just two chairs and a small table. Catherine had a sofa brought from one of the upper rooms. It sat across from the two chairs. Paolo and Pippa sat on the sofa.

"Something to drink?" Catherine asked.

"Thank you, Majesty. We are fine." Paolo Matucci looked uncomfortable. He squirmed in his seat. Pippa moved closer to him and slipped her hand through his arm.

"Well, how are you, Pippa?" Catherine asked. "It has been a few days since we met, but I have not forgotten our conversation about your book."

Pippa looked confused for a moment, then said, "I thought you would want to talk about the other thing. You know, the thing we saw?"

Catherine smiled, suddenly full of understanding for Paolo's discomfort. "Indeed, I do, Pippa," she said. "I understand from Father Tim that you got quite a good look at our—" Catherine was not sure she wanted to say angel, but before she could finish her sentence Pippa blurted out.

"Angel! It was an angel!"

"Pippa," her grandfather admonished. "What did we discuss?"

"Your Majesty," Pippa added. "It was an angel, Your Majesty. You saw it, too, did you not?"

Catherine sat back, needing to feel the solid support of her chair. She took a breath. "I am not certain about what I saw, Pippa. I was hoping you might describe what you saw for me to help me make some sense of things."

Pippa told Catherine exactly what she saw, and her description had not altered from what she had told Father Tim. Catherine nodded.

"I think you were at a better position to see more clearly than I," Catherine said. "I saw only the brightest of lights suddenly appear between me and the man."

"That man tried to kill you," Pippa said unhappily. "Why would anyone want to kill someone as nice as you?"

Catherine leaned forward. "I will be certain to ask him when I speak with him."

"Majesty," Paolo interrupted. "My granddaughter tells me you expressed much interest in the book I brought to her."

The door opened, and Maria brought in a plate of sweets. She put it on the table that sat between the sofa and the chair.

"Thank you, Maria." Catherine said.

Pippa was eyeing the sweets with such hope in her eyes that Catherine could not help but laugh.

"You may help yourself, Pippa." Catherine then turned to the child's grandfather and said, "Pippa told me that you brought the book from your travels in Spain."

"Indeed, that is correct, Majesty," Paolo said. "I travel much in my efforts to acquire knowledge.

Catherine indicated that Paolo should help himself to the

treats. "What is your background, Signor Mattucci, if you do not mind my asking?"

"I do not mind at all, Majesty," he said as he dabbed the corner of his mouth with a napkin. "I am the son of a stableman and cook who worked for a very fine house on the outskirts of Rome. My father and mother had been with the family since they were quite young. When I was but seven years of age, my father was thrown by a massive horse that he was attempting to train for his master. The beast killed him when it accidentally stepped back and crushed his chest."

"I am so sorry," Catherine said.

"It was a very long time ago, Majesty, but I thank you. My mother continued her work for the family, and the lord of the house took me under his wing. He gave me full access to his library and treated me as one of his own children. I learned the ways of business, war strategy and politics, but I was not of noble birth and that fact was not lost on those who knew the family. I fell in love with a young maiden who my own mother was training in the kitchens. When we married, the family with whom I had lived my entire life gifted me with a small house in Rome and paid for my tuition so that I might continue my education there. My wife and I were very happy, and I found that my love for learning only increased at university."

"Pippa," Catherine said, "your grandfather is very well educated. I think you must take after him."

Pippa beamed. "Someday I want to work in his bookstore, Queen Catherine!"

"A bookstore!" Catherine marveled. "How difficult has that been during these prohibitive ages?"

"I admit it has not been easy, Majesty. One cannot be too careful." Paolo said.

"How did you end up with a book shop?" Catherine asked.

A sudden flash of sadness swept over the man's face and then disappeared. "My wife died during the birth of our only child. My daughter, Emilia, was named for her mother. When my wife died, I gave up studies at university to care for my daughter but had to find a way to earn a living. Just down the street from where we lived was an old building that used to be an apothecary until the owner was hanged for some made-up crime for which he did not deserve to be hanged."

"Inquisitor accusations?" Catherine asked.

Paolo nodded. "I was able to make an arrangement to rent the shop and thus began my life as a bookseller."

"How wonderful," Catherine offered. "And you were able to keep your daughter with you?"

"It was a very nice arrangement." Paola said. "My daughter grew up and fell in love with a young butcher who had come to Rome from Montalcino! His family has deep roots here and when Emilia was with child, they returned to Montalcino to build their family."

"And now," Pippa said happily, "there is another baby coming!"

"You are going to be a wonderful big sister," Catherine said to Pippa.

"Signor Mattucci, I wonder if you might tell me about the book that Pippa was reading," Catherine said, "the one about the nun from Spain."

"Ah, Teresa of Avila," Paolo Mattucci said with a smile. "What has Pippa told you?"

"Only that she has written several books and that she levitates," Catherine offered. "I am interested for many reasons, but primarily for my own learning. You see," Catherine paused and smiled before continuing, "I was on the verge of traveling to a cloister in Avila to become a nun when God turned my life upside down. It was only recently that I learned who I really was and found my calling in a different direction."

Paolo smiled and nodded knowingly. "God does have his ways of changing our plans, does he not?"

Catherine laughed.

Paolo Mattucci reached inside his large coat and removed a bundle wrapped in paper and tied with a bow. "For you, Your Majesty. From Pippa and me."

Catherine reached for the package and unwrapped it. In in were two books, both recently published. One was *The Interior Castle* that Pippa had been reading. The other was *The Book of My Life*. Both were written by Teresa of Avila.

It was during the first frost of winter that Gio determined that he had all the information he was going to get from the prisoner who had attacked Catherine.

"He was definitely sent by Rome," Gio said to Catherine as they sat in her office in front of a blazing fire.

"The pope himself," Catherine asked, "or his minions?"

Gio leaned forward, his most common pose when he was concerned or struggling with an issue. "The plot appears to be approved all the way to the pope." Gio sat back and looked out the windows behind Catherine's desk. The bitter winds had stopped and now a gentle snowfall sifted from the heavens. "It is so peaceful just outside your window," he said sadly.

Catherine saw the exhaustion in his face. More, she saw his desire for a different kind of world. He had changed much since the attack on her. The knowledge that she had, in fact, been stabbed and the miracle that there was never a wound to behold, created an earthquake in his soul that could not be ignored. From her bedroom window high in the castle, she was able to have a clear view of the church. She often saw him slip into the church when he thought no one was looking. His anger over his past had softened. She sensed that his faith had returned. When she was growing up Gio always left the room when talk of God or faith came up. Now as she looked at him, she was suddenly struck by the thought that his belief might conflict with his duties. She wondered how soldiers of faith justified such things as war.

"What is the prisoner like?" Catherine asked Gio.

He had been almost in a reverie. "What?" he asked.

"The prisoner," Catherine said. "What is he like?"

Gio was instantly back and in charge of himself. "Broken," he said, "but hopeful that Rome will send someone to rescue him. I feel sorry for the fellow. He believes that Rome cares about him."

"Do you plan to execute him?"

"I have no choice," Gio said adamantly. "He tried to murder my queen. He must be executed!"

Catherine nodded. The fire crackled and she poured him a bit more wine. "I wish to meet him," she said.

Gio looked at her as if she had lost her mind. "Why?"

She stood and walked behind her desk to watch the snow begin to cover a bench in the rose garden. "I am curious," she said. "And if I am to order an execution, I feel I have a responsibility to look into the eyes of those I order to die."

Gio shrugged as she turned back to face him. "I will have him cleaned up and brought to you, but I—"

She cut him off. "No. I do not want you to have him brought to me. I will visit him in his cell."

Gio jumped up. "Are you mad? It is disgusting in the dungeons! There is no need for you to subject yourself to such horrors!"

"In order for me to continue to rule as an instrument of God, I need to know, Uncle. You will be with me. I need to know what conditions I force to others to endure."

Catherine called for Father Tim and spoke with him at great length about the dungeon and fate of the prisoner there. She asked if he would accompany her and Gio to visit to the depths of the castle later that morning. He agreed. Their talk turned to the nun from Avila as they waited for Gio.

"Her writings about the soul as a castle are clearly divinely inspired," Catherine said. "I have begun to incorporate some of her instruction into our daily contemplations. The work is not easy, but I feel it is important. It seems to complement our unknown monk quite well, I think."

"I look forward to reading it when you are finished," Father Tim said.

"There does not appear to be an end to any of this spiritual work," she said. "As with the *Cloud*, I believe I will need to read and reread the work. Hopefully, it will lead me to understand better the life of the soul and our relationship with the divine." She got up and was drawn again to the window. Marie was tossing breadcrumbs to the juncos, the tiny rust and grey colored birds that wintered in Montalcino. When Maria disappeared, a flock of about thirty juncos swooped down to peck at the crumbs. Catherine smiled and thought, *"His eye is even on the sparrow."*

When Gio arrived he seemed troubled, as if he did not look forward to his task. Catherine sensed it and asked Father Tim to lead them in prayer before they made their way to the darkness.

The way to the dungeons could only be made by passing through a long series of hallways and doorways that led to the east wing of the castle. Catherine rarely had cause to even enter this wing as it was the sleeping quarters for many of the staff and servants. When, finally, they came to a thick, rusted iron door bolted with chains, Catherine took a deep breath. A guard stood in front of the door and came to attention as they approached.

Gio nodded to him, and the guard took a huge key from a hiding place in the wall. He unlocked the padlock that held the chain through the bars. He then pulled the chain from the door and opened it. It scraped loudly on the rock floor and the hinges screamed their resistance. Gio passed through first and lit a torch. Father Tim and Catherine followed.

Catherine was instantly overwhelmed by the stench. It was not hard to imagine the things that created such a powerful odor. It was a smell of pure evil, she thought. She placed her hand-kerchief over her nose and mouth and followed Gio down the worn rock stairs. The deeper they went the more she became accustomed to the smell. Some of it was mold. The rock walls were gleaming in the torchlight. Moisture seeped through and grew algae, mildew and mold. The walls closed in on them as they reached the bottom of the stairs. Then they stepped into a larger room, a kind of alcove where there were already torches burning in wall sconces. In this room were two guards and from this open space, if one could call it open, were three doors.

"This is the guard area for the dungeons, Majesty," Gio said. "This door to the left leads to cells for lesser prisoners."

"Lesser?" Catherine asked.

"Those accused of lesser crimes such as petty theft, drunken brawls and such. This middle door leads to the torture rooms." Quickly, Gio moved on hoping she would not wish to enter there. He had never used devices of torture, but he remembered his father, Robert, talking of torture during his tenure as Captain of the Queen's guard. "Here," he said, moving quickly toward the door on the right, "is where our assailant is held. These cells are for those who commit the greater crimes."

One of the guards unlocked the padlock on the door and allowed the three of them to pass through.

"Those," Catherine ventured, "who will most likely be executed?"

Gio stopped in his tracks and turned back toward the queen. She watched him steel his face and nod perfunctorily. He said nothing, turned and led the way down the entire length of the narrow, dank hall to the end.

The walk seemed an eternity to Catherine, who followed her uncle silently. She saw the change in him from behind. The closer they got to the last cell she could see him gird himself, his head lifted and straightened on his neck. His shoulders squared and broadened. When, at last, he turned and lit the torch on the wall outside the last cell, she saw his chest puff out and his face harden. She saw all this and understood the cost of this place to the men charged with its duty.

There was a small, barred window at the top of the door. Gio peered in. He had instructed the guards to replace the straw in the cell earlier. Despite her need to speak to this man, he did not wish to force her to deal with his excrement. He pulled a large metal pin on a small chain from the bracket on the outside of the door. The removal of the pin allowed him to slide the timber from brackets on both sides of the door. There were no knobs or locks in this part of the prison. The cell door could only be opened from the outside. Gio went in first, followed by Catherine and then Father Tim.

The prisoner was chained to the far wall. The only light was from the torch Gio held. He placed it in the sconce near the door.

The prisoner opened his eyes but did not move.

"Catherine, Queen of Montalcino, has arrived. You will kneel or I will help you to kneel."

The man continued to lay on the ground. His clothes were torn and filthy. His body bruised and bloody. From his mouth came a weak and raspy sound. "I kneel before no one but God."

Gio started toward him, but Catherine grabbed his arm and

held him.

She took a step toward the man. His hatred for her glistened in his eyes behind the swollen lids. "Your response is a fair and good one," she said to him. "Are you able to sit up?"

He eyed her suspiciously and slowly pushed himself upright to sit against the wall behind him.

"I have great respect for godly men," Catherine said. "But little for men who claim godliness and disobey God's commandments."

"And I," he said so softly she had to work to hear him, "have little respect for godless queens."

She sensed Gio's need to physically put the prisoner in his place. She sensed him wanting to take charge. He stayed behind her as she held up her hand.

"What makes you think I am godless?" she asked him.

"You are born of sin, from a godless queen who was born of sin from a godless queen before her."

"What is your name?" Catherine asked almost gently.

"Vincenzo," he replied, then succumbed to a bout of coughing.

"Father," she said, turning to Tim, "would you please get Vincenzo a cup of water?"

Father Tim nodded and left the cell, returning a minute later with a cup of water and a chair for the queen. She smiled, wondering how he knew she would like to be closer to the prisoner as she spoke with him.

Gio held the cup as the man drank and then stood up, not leaving the cup as a weapon for him to aim at his queen.

"Vincenzo," she said once she had seated herself on the chair and could look better into his face, "were your parents sinless?"

"No one is without sin except the Christ," he said.

"I believe that to be true," she said. "And do you believe that God holds you responsible for the sins of your parents and your grandparents?"

He did not answer but stared at her warily.

"Why was Christ crucified?" she asked him. She gave him a moment to answer.

When he spoke, there was anger in his voice. "I will not debate the gifts of my Lord and Savior with a heathen."

"I do not expect to change your mind about me, about the terrible things I am certain you have been told about me," Catherine said. "I will say this, however, those who filled your head with stories of me did so only to use you to hide their own sins. They fill people's heads with lies to frighten them and get them to act out their own sin. I believe you to be a decent man who was convinced he was serving God by believing the lies of those he thought were men of God. Do you really believe that God would send you on a mission to break one of his own commandments?"

"You," he said, "may try to trick me with your words, but it will not work."

"Search your memory, sir," she said. "You remember how the blade pierced my breast when you struck at me, do you not?"

He closed his eyes, shutting them tight, and said nothing. She waited for him to answer.

When he opened his eyes he finally said, "I only thought I pierced you. My desire and duty to kill you overcame me in the moment. Clearly, I missed my mark." He lowered his head and did not look at her.

"You did not miss, sir," Catherine said somberly. "Several witnesses, myself among them, saw the blade pierce me and the blood begin to flow. More than that, before you made your initial move, I saw the doubt and fear in your eyes."

"I missed," he said clearly. "When I was dragged to my feet, I saw that I only tore your garments."

"Sometimes," she offered, "we tell ourselves things when the truth is too difficult, too impossible to believe. You are free to believe what you will. You may cling to your belief that you did not stab me, but if you ask God to reveal the truth, you will know it in your heart. For me, I believe that a miracle occurred in that moment. You may call me a heathen, but I know that Christ lives in the world through each of us. I believe he came to sacrifice himself for our sins—mine and yours—and I am grateful for his love in the world every moment of every day." Catherine stood up and Gio took the chair to a spot by the door.

"Vincenzo, you are scheduled to be executed. I plan to stay that execution. Despite what you have been told, I am not a god-less queen. I wish I were a sinless woman, but I am far from it. There is much I regret in this life, but I will not knowingly take the life of another human being. God commands me otherwise and Christ commands me to love my enemies."

Vincenzo raised his eyes to look at her as if he could not believe what he was hearing. His confusion wrinkled his brow. His head tilted as if he thought he might be hearing things.

"I will leave you now," Catherine said. "This is Father Timothy. I have asked him to stay with you in case you might want him to hear your confession. Whether or not you do is up to you." Catherine turned and indicated to Gio that they were to leave Father Tim in the cell alone with Vincenzo. Gio grabbed the chair and walked out behind Catherine.

As they made their way back down the dark hallway Gio started to question her declaration of the prisoner's com-muted sentence.

She stopped, turned back to him, and said, "Might we talk about this later this afternoon in my office, Uncle? There is much I feel we need to consider and for now I am inclined to a bath and a good scrubbing to remove the morning from me."

"Of course," Gio said. "I am impressed that you endured

this place as well as you have, but then, your mother and grandmother both insisted on doing the same. I should not be surprised." They had reached the large area where the three hallways met. Gio instructed one of the guards to make his way to the prisoner's cell where Father Tim was hearing confession. "Give them privacy but ensure that the priest is safe and escort him back up to the east tower."

"Yes, Captain," the guard replied.

Once Catherine and Gio were back in the upper part of the castle and making their way out of the servant wing, Catherine asked, "Have the dungeons always been such hell holes?"

"They are not usually so quiet," he said. "During the height of the Inquisition one could rarely hear oneself think for the screaming of the prisoners. Once they were taken back to their cells the moaning and begging for death could be even more unbearable."

They had reached the stairway that led to the upper levels of the queen's quarters. "Thank you, Uncle Gio. I will make my way on my own from here. Can we meet in my office at three?"

"I will be there, Majesty." Gio said.

On the way up to her quarters Catherine stopped at her parents' rooms.

Her father opened the door when she knocked. "Catherine!" he exclaimed. "What a lovely surprise." As he opened the door to let her in, the smell from the dungeon entered with her. "You have come from the bowels of the castle," he said as tactfully as he could.

"Father," she turned and faced him with a look of embarrassment. "Forgive me. I shall leave immediately."

He laughed. "What is it you want, my daughter? I did not mean to chase you out."

"Is mother here?" she asked.

"She went to the kitchen to talk with Lucia. She will be back soon," Pasquale answered.

"I am headed up to take a bath to wash this stink off me. Though I fear it may never leave my nose entirely!" Catherine said. "Will you both join me for a light lunch in my quarters? I have something I would like to discuss."

"We would not miss the opportunity to spend a little extra time with you," he said. "We will be there."

It was only mid-morning, an unusual time for a bath, but Catherine requested that one be drawn for her.

By the time the water was heated and poured into the tub, Catherine had removed her clothes and asked that they be laundered and aired out before they were returned to her. Michelena dropped the offensive clothing outside the door of their quarters.

The bath drawn and the door locked, Catherine stepped behind the screen and slipped into the great, brass tub and sunk down below the water— face, hair, and all.

Michelena came to sit with her as she bathed. "Do you want to talk about it?"

"Suffice it to say that I felt sorry even for the rats," Catherine said as she reached for the soap and began to lather.

"Let me," Michelena said as she reached for the washrag and soaped it into a good lather. She started with Catherine's back. When she had scrubbed and rinsed her back, she undid Catherine's hair, letting it fall. The long tresses dropped into the water and Catherine allowed Michelena to lather her hair and pour cups of water over her head to rinse it.

"Lean back now, my love," Michelena coaxed. She took an arm and gently lathered, rinsed and kissed her way from fingertips to shoulder. After doing the same to the other arm she wiped Catherine's face and neck and kissed those, as well.

Catherine leaned back and allowed Michelena to gently wash her legs and feet. Her eyes closed; Catherine felt her body finally beginning to relax. She sank deeply into a place where she let go the tension and darkness of the morning, grateful for the warmth and cleansing of the water.

Michelena lathered her hands and rubbed them softly, sensuously over Catherine's breasts. Catherine moaned. Her nipples became erect, and she reached a dripping wet hand to pull Michelena's head toward her. She flicked her tongue around Michelena's mouth before pressing her lips to those lips that were so full, so soft. As she did, Michelena's hand slid down over her belly and disappeared beneath the water.

"I understand you subjected yourself to the most hideous sections of the castle," Francesca said after Pasquale offered a simple grace.

Catherine's sense of smell instantly returned to the vile stench of the morning. She shuddered and quickly lifted the cup of wine to her nose and inhaled deeply to rid herself of the memory.

Michelena told of the stench when Catherine returned from the dungeon.

"I had to go, Mama," Catherine said when she had swallowed some wine. "And we will discuss that, but first I would like to know if you have noticed changes in Uncle Gio."

"You are speaking of changes since the attack on your life, I assume?" Francesca asked.

Catherine sighed. "Yes. I am worried about him."

"You are concerned about his ability to fulfill his duties?" Pasquale asked with some concern.

Catherine replied quickly, "No. I have no doubts about his abilities or his determination to safeguard us." She hesitated before continuing. Francesca reached a hand to place on hers. Catherine looked into her mother's eyes and sighed deeply.

"I am worried about the toll his role is taking on him. He has changed since the attempt and this morning it seemed to take an extraordinary effort to face the dungeons and the prisoner."

"In what way?" Francesca asked.

"It was all very subtle," Catherine offered, squeezing her mother's hand. "I doubt anyone else would notice. It may just be my imagination, but he is your brother. You know him better than anyone. Do you notice anything?"

Francesca stood up, walked over to the window, and gazed out before speaking. Finally, she said, "All our lives we lived with knowledge of the horrors of torture, injustice, and families ripped apart—murdered—and worse. The things that have happened," she paused and pulled a handkerchief from her sleeve. She blew her nose into it and turned. Her eyes were filled with tears. "Catherine, my sweet daughter, you bring something new and holy to this kingdom. I know that, and I am so very proud of your courage. Your mother, Sofia, and your grandmother also tried to bring about change in their ways. They, like you, were strong, God-loving queens." Francesca returned to the table and sat down. "Your Uncle Gio will be fine."

"But you are correct, he has undergone a tremendous change. I agree with your father that the change will not compromise his ability to do his duty to keep you safe. Nevertheless, he is someone who has lost much in this life. Gio lost his faith when our father, Robert, was killed defending your grandmother. A true spiritual darkness overcame my sweet brother for many years. When he was too late to save your mother, I thought it might kill him." Francesca stopped and looked around the table at her husband, Michelena and then back at Catherine. "He believed, if only for a moment, that he had lost you. In that moment, only he can speak to what he might have felt."

A fresh wave of tears rolled down Francesca's cheeks. Catherine reached up to wipe them from her mother's face.

Francesca continued, "A miracle brought you back from certain death. That fact has forced Gio to examine his rejection of God and faith. I believe, I hope, it has given faith back to your uncle. But faith comes with its own struggles. A true life of faith means we will be tested and given trials that insist we examine our beliefs. I believe that is the change you see in your uncle. How does a man like Gio, who rejected God for most of his life—who was angry with God for most of his life—reposition himself in his world?" Francesca left the question hanging.

It was snowing when Gio entered Catherine's office later that afternoon. A blazing fire roared in the hearth.

Catherine kissed him on both cheeks and invited him to sit before the fire. Without asking, she poured them both cups of wine, gave him one and sat opposite him.

"I owe you an apology, uncle."

He looked at her with confusion.

"I honestly did not know that I was going to commute the sentence of the prisoner until I said it." She lowered her eyes and stared into her cup of wine. "Uncle, at times, I worry that my queenly duties and my faith run contrary to one another. This morning was one of those times."

Gio's head bobbed slowly. He drew a long swallow from his cup, then set it down in front of him. "I wondered if that might have been behind your generous commutation," he said.

"I cannot, in good conscience, in my heart of hearts," Catherine said, almost as a plea, "condone the murder—the execution—of any soul, no matter that they have only death and destruction on their minds."

"Not even your own death, it would appear," Gio said.

"Not even my own," she said. "Will my need to spare the lives of criminals compromise your authority?" Gio stood and walked over to the fire. He placed his hands on the mantle and leaned toward the grate. When he turned back to her, his face was red from the heat. He rubbed his graying beard and returned to his seat. "Ultimately, you are the queen, and I must follow your orders. So, the questions that arise will likely reflect my inability to influence you in this matter."

"I do not want this to be perceived as a slight on you in any way," Catherine said. "Is there any reason we cannot just make the decision to continue to interrogate the prisoner?"

"For how long?" he responded. "We cannot keep him alive indefinitely without raising questions. Interrogations have provided all we are going to get from him!"

"How have you interrogated him," she asked.

He looked away and shook his head. "Do not ask me that. Please do not ask me." He returned to his seat with a heaviness that spoke to what he must have done to gain what little information he had gained from the prisoner.

A lengthy silence ensued during which Catherine got up, poured more wine and went to the window. The snow had stopped falling. She looked for the juncos, but none were in sight. When she returned to her seat she said, "I have adored you my entire life. I have prayed all my life that you might find your way back to God. The answer to that prayer is known only between you and God, but I sense a weariness in you that I have never known."

He eyed her suspiciously, and she saw his need to defend himself. She held up her hand to silence him. "It is not what you may think. I have no doubt about your ability to protect me, to serve me in any way." She went to him and knelt at his feet. "Uncle, uncle," she said gently, then kissed his hands. "We, you and I, need to find a way to rule, to lead Montalcino by doing what is right—morally, ethically and spiritually—not by choosing which commandments to obey, or which words of Christ's to twist to our own needs or desires. How do we punish our enemies without breaking God's laws? How do we teach our people to be kind and loving without torturing them unimaginably? How, dear God, do we maintain law and order without dehumanizing ourselves and those we must arrest to prevent them harming others?"

Catherine saw in his eyes that he understood her dilemma. She lowered her head and rested it on her uncle's knee. He did not answer her question. No answer was needed. After several minutes, she went to her desk.

"I want the tortures stopped. These are the tools and the ways of a system that frightens people into saying anything they think we want to hear." She sat. "The conditions of the dungeons are disgusting and deplorable. I want them cleaned. Get rid of the rats and the straw. Put sleeping cots in the cells and keep the torches in the hall going so there is some light. Prisoners are already in cells, why do they need to be chained to the walls, as well? I cannot imagine that any guard forced to work down there is not horribly altered by the dark and dismal duty. After my short visit I felt like I had been to hell and back." She shuffled some papers on her desk. "We will always have to have prisoners and punishment, I understand that. But prisoners are still men and women. They are not animals, but it is easy to see how they become animals if the dungeons are the best we can do."

She looked up. He was considering all she had said. Both understanding and confusion were in his expression. "It sounds like you want to coddle them!"

"No," she said emphatically. "I do not want that. I do not expect that." She dropped her papers and sat back to look at him. "I do not expect this to be a popular decision with soldiers used to certain ways of dealing with traitors, murderers, thieves or would be assassins."

"Well," Gio said, "you are certainly right about that. You cannot ask soldiers to mollycoddle prisoners. Prisoners do not even expect that!"

She stood up, feeling it was necessary to stand her ground. "I am not asking anyone to mollycoddle." Catherine walked back over to the fireplace. "I have given this much thought and prayer," she said. "This prisoner, Vincenzo, is clearly not a hardened criminal. He is a pawn in a game he does not understand. He blindly followed the directive of those he believed." She stopped and looked at Gio. "How do we convince him he is wrong? By torturing him? By executing him? By treating him like an animal? That only proves his point, does it not?

"What you are proposing is a massive change in our system of dealing with criminals," Gio said. "You open us up to the possibility that criminals will flock to Montalcino because our prison is more akin to a vacation."

"That is not at all what I am proposing." Catherine was frustrated and feeling as if she was not making her point valid. "Uncle," she said more softly, "you already have two separate wings for lesser and more hardened prisoners. I am not reversing that policy. But please think about prisoners like Vincenzo. How does torture and execution solve the basic issue?"

Gio began to pace in agitation. "The basic issue being that we are too hard on criminals?"

"No," Catherine said shaking her head. "The issue is that Rome is spreading lies and innuendo about us. The pope and his retinue want control of Montalcino back in their hands. To that end they are duping others and creating assassins like Vincenzo." Catherine's voice had raised. She stopped talking and sat down at her desk with her head in her hands. "If we," she continued and looked up at Gio, "execute everyone Rome sends to kill me there will be an endless stream of assassins. Why not show mercy to them and let them see how wrong they are—how wrong Rome is? Why not make them question themselves and those who sent them?"

Gio sat down and sighed heavily. "I do not know how I feel about this. It goes against everything I know. But I do understand what you are saying." He stood up. "May I have some time to think on it?"

Catherine nodded. "Uncle, you know my vision is to rule from a spiritual perspective," she said.

He looked at her and she saw the concern in his face. "I do hope you will not expect me and my soldiers to love our enemies."

His tone was sarcastic, but she heard in it where his fear lay.

She had to take a breath to prevent responding in kind. "I do not think either of us would be happy with an army of gentle misfits. We will make no changes yet," she said. "You and I will work together to draft a new prisoner policy and present it to our staff and soldiers. We will not present anything until we are both in agreement. Does that meet with your approval?"

Gio fisted his right hand over his heart and nodded. He turned to leave without saying anything. But she thought he walked a tad lighter in his exit.

By the time winter had blanketed the castle in several thick snowfalls, Catherine had begun to understand the needs of the kingdom and the people. Her style of reign was humble and relaxed, but stern when circumstances demanded. She was respected by the Lords on her Privy Council and the guards and staff—something her mother and grandmother were unable to experience.

Catherine and Michelena grew into their various roles as time passed. Michelena was a great support and comfort to Catherine in her role as queen—often checking and offering perspectives that Catherine had not considered. They fought, as all couples do, about the little things that were symbolic of bigger things that were, for a time, hidden from their seeing. The biggest of these issues was tied to the fears that lay buried deep within each of them regarding their love for their own sex.

It was Father Tim who often helped them to make the connection to their old fears. He would sit with them and skillfully and gently guide those fears to the surface and into the light of understanding.

When they wondered at his ability to help them, he would say, "I have had some practice in that area." He would laugh. "Your grandmother and Bella, Catherine, struggled over their love for each other all their lives. And even though they spoke of it less and less, I know that it always stayed just beneath the surface."

"What stayed beneath the surface?" Michelena asked one day. "Their fear?"

Father Tim sighed. "We live in a time when any little thing someone says, or does, or might be, is grounds for execution. I wish it were not so. This is not what Christ came to teach and to die for."

They were sitting at the table in the queen's chambers. He stood and went to the window. The sun had just dipped below the horizon.

The clouds were a myriad of colors, and the sky was purpling to the west. He called them to the window to share in the beauty.

"None of us can really understand the Almighty," he said softly. "All we know is that Christ was sent to teach us that the most important thing we can do is love one another."

Catherine turned to him. "Do you really think God is accepting of our," she hesitated, then indicated Michelena, "relationship?"

Father Tim reached out to place his hand upon Michelena's cheek. "I have known you since you were a baby," he said. "You always exuded a certain delight— call it an energy—that only occurred when certain little girls came to play with you." He dropped his hand from Michelena's cheek and looked at Catherine with a smile.

"I suspect," he said to her, "that you found a similar excitement when you were growing up?" Catherine blushed and nodded.

"I," he said, "can only tell you that when I sit with God and ponder the dilemma that you both face—that Catherine and Bella faced—and that others with similar feelings face, a great peace comes over me and the words that sing in my heart are these—*male and female were made in my image.* If God is both male and female, does it not stand to reason that somehow, in us, we are all male and female if we allow ourselves the freedom to accept that image of ourselves?"

"And if we are both male and female," Catherine said, "then it may be the spirit of the other to whom we are attracted?"

"Precisely," Tim said. "There is no shame in love—however it may manifest itself—if it is shared by two people and hurts no one."

"As long," Michelena added, "as we are discreet."

"Sadly," Tim offered. "I wish it were otherwise, but until such time as your love can be honored and brought into the light, discretion is survival."

"Do you ever foresee a time when a love such as ours does not need to hide?" Catherine asked.

"We can only pray for such a time," Father Tim said. "Certainly, it will not happen in our lifetimes."

Within the first year of Catherine's reign, the dungeons were turned into prison cells that provided prisoners with a modicum of hygiene and minimal comfort. The moldy walls were scrubbed clean, and Catherine had Vito create thick metal chamber pots that were slid into openings in each cell. The pots were housed within sturdy wooden frames with holes on the top. The holes were much smaller than the chamber pots, which were emptied daily. Prisoners were given one woolen blanket and a firm cot on which to sleep. They were provided with water and given two meager meals daily. The biggest, and to Catherine, the most important change for prisoners was the ability to visit with the castle priest.

Father Tim was instrumental in advocating for the prisoners in this way, and Catherine saw it as a good way to offer prisoners a new way of thinking and being— even if behind bars.

Vincenzo could not, at first, believe his good fortune at his stay of execution. Over the months that brought changes of cleanliness and fair treatment to him, he began to question whether he had been sent on a fool's mission to kill this queen. Father Tim had visited him a couple of times after Catherine had first visited the dungeon. Once the changes took place he requested to see the priest at least once per week. Father Tim brought him communion and heard his confession.

Gio and his guards thwarted two more attempts on Catherine's life during that first year. As the prison filled, Gio reported that

Vincenzo spoke only well of Catherine in the cells.

"He appears to be a changed man," Gio said during one of the Privy Council meetings. "I would not have believed it if I had not seen it or heard it myself. In fact, Majesty, Vincenzo has made a request."

Lord Puglia blurted out, "Request! The prisoner has more than any prisoner has a right to expect, and he has a request? Impossible."

Queen Catherine smiled. "Let us hear this request, Lord Puglia, before we condemn the man again, shall we?"

Puglia apologized and grunted his assent. Catherine nodded to Gio to continue.

"The prisoner is wondering if we might allow Father Tim to say mass periodically for the prisoners," Gio said.

Father Tim periodically attended the council meetings, but only at Catherine's request. She knew he did not like them and only asked him when she knew that certain topics regarding correspondence from Rome or other religious matters were on the agenda to be discussed. He was not present this day.

"Interesting," Catherine said under her breath. "It seems to me that Father Tim would need to be informed of the request. If he is not inclined toward such an arrangement the matter is decided without further discussion. My lords," she continued, "are you in agreement?"

A general reluctant nod rolled around the table.

Following the council meeting, Catherine and Gio walked back to her office.

"I cannot imagine Father Tim denying Vincenzo's request," Catherine remarked.

"Agreed," Gio said.

"What is the current status of the old torture cell block?" she asked.

They reached her office. Gio opened the door and checked inside. Once inside he said, "The room is not used anymore. There are still some of the old torture items attached to the walls, but otherwise it is empty."

"If necessary, could we turn it into a small chapel?"

Gio gave a low, throaty laugh and shook his head. "A year ago, I would have raged up and down against the mere hint of such a thing." He went to the window behind Catherine's desk. "Today, I find myself wondering what the harm is in refusing the request."

Catherine poured him a cup of wine and brought it to him. He nodded his thanks and turned back to the view of the courtyard.

"When we were young," he said with a tinge of sadness, "Sofia, James and I would often find ourselves playing in this courtyard. I remember seeing my father and your grandmother in this room. Perhaps they were talking as we do now." He stared out the window for some time. Catherine poured herself some wine and came to join him at the window.

"I wish I could have known them," she said. "I wish I could have known every one of them." She lay her hand on Gio's shoulder momentarily, then walked over to the chair nearest the fireplace. "They would all be in awe of you. As am I."

He turned to look at her, his face a mask of puzzlement and confusion. "Nothing I am or have done is awe-worthy," he said. "I am a soldier who holds a fairly easy position."

"I disagree," Catherine said. "You are much more than a soldier. You are a confidant. You may not see the changes in you the way I have, uncle. Yours has been an almost magical transformation."

He walked over to sit opposite her. "Please tell me what you mean."

Smiling, she set her cup down and sat back in her chair, pulling a lap throw over her. "You have always been a good uncle, but when I was growing up, there was a sadness in you that seemed to hold you in a power you could not control. It was almost like you lived inside a prison of pain. It was not until I was older that I understood what you had suffered."

Gio nodded. "I was so angry for so long. I truly never thought I would forgive Sofia. I blamed her for my loss of everything."

"And yet," Catherine pointed out, "when she needed you most, you came to her rescue."

Gio snorted and shook his head. "I still cannot account for my reason in doing so. I only know that when I got my grandfather's letter about the danger she was in, I was compelled to come as quickly as I could manage. I did not want to forgive her."

Catherine sipped her wine. "And yet you did, almost in an instant."

Gio nodded. "Father Tim attributes that to a mystical experience, but I do not think it was." He reached up and scratched his beard.

"Why not?" Catherine asked.

"Holding onto my anger and blaming Sofia were ways that I kept myself in a fairly constant state of resentment. Sometimes," he said, "I would relive the sight of her coming back with the bodies just to fuel my fury at her. Anger became familiar, almost like a friend. It takes a lot of energy to stay angry. After so many years I think I was just tired of all the anger, but I needed a reason to forgive her because I was too stubborn and immature to understand how much I missed her."

"Your grandfather's letter gave you the reason?"

"It did," he said. "And you seem to have picked up where my grandfather left off."

"Now you must explain," she said.

"Your capacity for ruling, for one. More than that, however, I must say that I marvel at the creative ways in which you bring your spiritual understanding to everything you do.  Your nun, Teresa of Avila, your unknown monk, your trust in God regardless of the struggles.  Your ability to see things in ways that transform people, systems, a kingdom.  It is a gift."

Catherine laughed.  "I cannot take credit for the gift, Uncle.  I must give credit where it is due.  This is a life that requires a divine relationship in addition to the company of those who see and support that relationship.  For that I am grateful for Father Tim, my parents, Michelena, you and even young Pippa, who understand the importance of my relationship to God—and who also keep me humble by pointing out my many flaws."

"You enjoy Pippa's company," Gio said.  "How has she been since her grandfather's death?"

"I am amazed at her journey through her grief.  It has been quite the thing to bear witness to the emotion in someone with such faith.  Father Tim and I have discussed inviting her to our morning contemplations when she is a bit older.  She will be twelve this year.  We have decided to wait until her birthday."

Gio smiled.  "I am certain she would enjoy that. She seems quite advanced for someone so young," he said.  After a pause he said, "Speaking of Father Tim, I have been meeting with him, too.  I guess I have you to thank for that."

"How so?"

"Between your miracle last year and the changes instituted in the prisoner area, I found myself starting to question my resistance to the whole religion idea."

Catherine smiled.  "Turning from God—being angry at God—not wanting anything to do with religion—I believe it is all part of our spiritual journey.  Our whole lives are about figuring that out.  If we did not get angry at or question God, what kind of relationship would that be?"

Gio smiled at her and stood up to leave.  "I will see how Father

Tim feels about the idea of a chapel in the prison," he said. He turned to her as he reached the door. "You would have made a very good nun, you know."

"Perhaps," she said, laughing as she made her way to her desk. When she was alone again, she sat at her desk and thought about Gio's parting words. On some days, she found that she loved the actual business of running a small kingdom. The work, the tasks and duties, were always different. Rarely was Catherine bored. While she still occasionally wondered how different her life would have been had she chosen to live as a nun, she loved being surrounded by her family and could in no way imagine her life without Michelena.

She stood up and turned toward the window to the courtyard reflecting on that first kiss with Michelena. It was so much more than a blending of hungry mouths and lips. For Catherine it was the beginning of a profound understanding—a realization of how easy it was to hide from herself and from her own feelings and fears. That first kiss melted away the first thin but hard veneer of self-deception that she was something she was not—she was not a woman who would ever physically desire a man. That kiss planted the seeds of a love that would bring a kingdom back from near ruination. It created a reign that would continue to fight against the injustices perpetrated by the Church. Finally, it would grow—but it would not grow old. In the end, the love held within that kiss would grow stronger than either of them could have ever foreseen. It was then that Catherine realized that in the moment of that first kiss she had, as Sofia had encouraged, chosen life and love.

Catherine turned from the window and went to her desk. She opened a drawer and lifted Sofia's journal from its resting place. Her fingers traced the intricate design on the leather cover. Sofia's name, once gold, had turned brown with age and oils from being loved and read often.  Catherine clutched the journal to her breast and returned to the window, a soft smile gracing her face.

"Life and love," she mused out loud. "You offered me the very things you were denied.  Yours was a life of loss and pain.  I hope your song is happier now. Rest in peace, sweet mother, Sofia."

# Epilogue

**F**ather Tim had eagerly embraced the idea of a chapel for the prison. The old torture room was transformed. Vito melted down the old metal implements and created a beautiful crucifix that was bolted on the wall. Vincenzo became instrumental in helping to work with prisoners to change their lives. He became one of Catherine's most ardent supporters, and after ten years of exemplary behavior and based on his work with the prisoners, was granted his freedom. Vincenzo asked to stay and work within the castle. He wished to be of service to the queen in any way he could. He was allowed to join the detail of soldiers who guarded the castle.

Michelena, meanwhile worked diligently getting the old paper making facility operational again. After many starts and mistakes, Montalcino paper was being made and sold locally. She hoped that eventually the paper might be sold throughout the Italian States. Gio often commented on how Michelena's abilities and love of the paper-making process reminded him of Catherine's grandfather, Ambrose, who took to the enterprise with relish. Michelena loved experimenting by adding different herbs, flowers and grasses to the papers. Some of her attempts were dismal, others wildly successful.

Father Tim remained a faithful spiritual friend to Catherine. His insights helped her to grow in spiritual maturity in ways that heavily impacted her reign as queen and made her a beloved monarch. Her love for God grew stronger, and she passed that love down to her people—ruling with kindness and compassion.

Catherine and Father Tim met every morning in the castle church. Together they would read from the *Cloud of Unknowing* or the works of Teresa of Avila and discuss the meanings held within. They would follow the instructions from the little book by sitting silently for some time. Often, when difficult concerns for the kingdom were brought to her during her visitation time with her subjects, she and Father Tim would pray about how to help.

Father Tim would always be waiting for Catherine when she arrived at the church in the early morning before the sun rose. One morning, in the late fall of 1608, Catherine stepped into the church and thought she had finally arrived before him. It was chilly inside the church, and she pulled her wrap around her. As she strode up the aisle, planning how to tease the priest about being late, she found him. His body was already cold, and she wept over it for some time.

Lucia saw to the kitchen and servant operations with skill and more organization than the castle had ever seen. She loved the work and was happier than Michelena had ever seen her. After the death of Father Tim, however, she struggled. Father Tim had taken her in and cared for her and her children from the day Sofia and Umberto were executed. His loss was harder for her than she ever let on. She began to age quickly following Tim's death. Catherine and Michelena both noticed and tried to get Lucia to turn her duties over to her helpers. She refused. Finally, however, in 1611, she was hit hard with a bad bout of pneumonia. She recovered, but not fully, and was forced to give up her work in the bowels of the castle. It was difficult to say which event impacted her more—Father Tims's death or not being able to work anymore, but she finally gave in to death in early 1612.

Catherine's parents remained in the castle with their daughter but occasionally went home to Voghera to visit. They did miss their home and friends there. Catherine often invited their friends to the castle when weather permitted. Catherine's father,

Pasquale, died of a sudden heart attack in 1626. Her mother followed him soon after in 1627.

Gio was a stalwart and remained protective of Catherine, much as his father had been of his own Queen Catherine. Over the years he prevented several assassination attempts on Catherine's life, each one traceable back to the Church. He trained every soldier himself until he became too old to fight. He still oversaw all training and protection for the queen. He kept his promise to Sofia, to protect her child, until his death in 1629 at the age of seventy-four. Gio still loved riding and often rode to the flower fields where he, James, and Sofia spent their youth. As he thought back on those days, riding toward the lake where the three of them would swim, his horse was startled by a snake and threw him. His head hit a rock. He died instantly.

Catherine and Michelena did not travel as much as Catherine and Isabella, or even Sofia. Catherine preferred staying home and Michelena was content to stay with her. They lived together in the royal suite where Catherine and Bella lived and loved so long ago. If anyone suspected their relationship, outside of their families, they never said a word. They were good for each other, challenging each other in ways that made life fun, exciting, and passionate—and that made the sufferings bearable.

In 1631, the plague visited central Italy. It was likely brought to Italy from French and German troops during the Thirty Years' War when the election of the intolerant new Holy Roman Emperor, Ferdinand II, attempted to force Roman Catholicism on all of Europe. Pippa's mother was a victim of the plague. Pippa had long been a regular visitor and friend to Catherine at the castle. She was an integral part of the spiritual practices used by Catherine and Father Tim. After her mother's death and at Catherine's urging, Pippa moved into the castle. Catherine taught her everything she could about the kingdom and its enterprises and politics. Pippa was instrumental in creating ways to identify and assist those most in need throughout the kingdom over the years.

During the most difficult time of the plague in Montalcino, Pippa and Michelena spent much time trying to help or give comfort to its victims. It is likely that one of Montalcino's merchants had brought the plague from Florence, where some nine thousand people died from the bubonic plague. Michelena contracted the disease. Catherine never left her side. Michelena died in Catherine's arms. Catherine survived the plague, but it took a great toll on her.

There were great upheavals in political power in Europe—much of which altered the communal states of Italy. Pippa approached Catherine to ask if she might consider converting the castle into a convent. Catherine, after the loss of her parents, Gio, Father Tim and especially Michelena, found herself more inclined toward her spiritual devotions than her queenly duties. After a short period of time and prayer, she readily agreed. The castle had been built by her ancestors, and she was free to convert it to a convent. After notifying Rome of her intention, she relinquished her title of queen and dedicated the castle, now a convent, to the contemplative and impoverished life of the sisters who followed the rules and works of Teresa of Avila.

In the end, Catherine became a nun after all, fulfilling the dream of her childhood in ways that she never could have foreseen. Pippa, also a nun, was Catherine's constant companion.

In 1649, at the age of sixty-four, Catherine became quite ill. Her heart was weakened from several small heart attacks. Despite treatment with foxglove, Catherine was unable to leave her bed. Pippa stayed with her, nursing her in her illness and praying nearly continually for her friend and mentor. Early one morning, Pippa dozed in a chair next to Catherine—who had not opened her eyes in days. She was awakened by the sound of Catherine's voice.

Pippa opened her eyes to find Catherine sitting straight up in bed and engaged in animated conversation. There was no one else in the room, but Catherine's face was alive, her voice strong. Pippa felt a presence in the room and fell to her knees at Catherine's bedside.

"Pippa," Catherine said, laying her hand on Pippa's head, "do you see her?"

"See who, Catherine?" Pippa asked as she looked to where Catherine indicated at the foot of the bed.

"Teresa," she said, "our mother."

Pippa saw nothing, but believed that Catherine indeed was in conversation with the woman who established their order. She did not doubt.

"I am," Catherine said to the empty space at the foot of her bed. She smiled and whispered, "Amen."

Catherine fell back onto her pillows and breathed her last breath. She was gone, but the smile etched into her face spoke to the joy in her departure.

"I know, beloved friend," Pippa said as she closed Catherine's eyes, "that you died in the glory of your soul's castle. Be at peace."

— *Fine* —

## *A final note*


The Inquisition began in 1231. The last documented event of the Inquisition occurred in 1868. It lasted more than six hundred years.

Pope John Paul II apologized for it in 2000.

# Acknowledgments

There are many people to thank for seeing me through this sequel. Many of them are no longer here to thank, but I will thank them anyway: my mother, Lucille, whose incredibly beautiful death in 2016, was an honor to witness; my friend, Ellen Novak, also departed this life with dignity and grace—and a vision of Teresa of Avila. Both encouraged my writing in ways that surprised and sustained me. They are deeply missed.

Among the living, I am grateful for the love and support of many who share their lives with me in ways that help me to learn and grow. Thank you soul brother, The Very Reverend Douglas Travis. I learn so much from you and love you more than you know.

Stewart Warren, also a soul brother, shared so much with me. Thank you for the privilege of spending hours, days, and the last years of your life with your beautiful presence, your incredible poetry, and your courageous and remarkable death. How I miss you!

Many, many thanks to Pamela Warren Williams, Stewart's wife, who took over Mercury HeartLink with dedication and aplomb. You have transformed his work into your dream. Well done.

And to Leah Rubin, My Second Pen, whose editing and support mean so much to me.

Grace Hollen! Your final, detailed eyes are a gift. You are a wonderful new addition to my life. Thank you from the bottom of my heart.

I am blessed to have a multitude of children in my life. They are my best teachers and have enriched my life beyond my wildest dreams.

Patti and Joanie, you are my history, sisters, soulmates, and life-savers. How you have put up with me all these years totally mystifies me. I am grateful beyond words for your love and friendship.

The written works of many have contributed both directly and indirectly to this book. My thanks and appreciation to Richard Rohr, James Finley, Carolyn Myss, Cynthia Bourgeault, David Frenette, Teresa of Avila, and the Unknown Monk who penned the *Cloud of Unknowing*.

Emma, my wonderful daughter, thank you for your love and for making me laugh so very much. You have blossomed into a delightful young woman. I am so proud urney with me. It has not always been an easy one, but I cannot imagine having gone all these decades without you. Thank you for working so hard to allow me the time to create. I love that we can still take risks together, that we continue to grow and learn together, and that you can still make me laugh so hard.

*Finally, to the readers who loved* The Queen's Companion, *I hope this sequel was worth the wait.*

Happy reading.

www.maggiapetton.com

# About the Author

Maggi Petton is a poet and author of historical fiction. Her novels tell of the struggles of disenfranchised women throughout history . . . women of strength, courage and determination. Whether she is illuminating women's struggles during the Inquisition in Italy, or the American Civil War, her stories weave a tapestry of truth that resonate still. Today, more than ever, we need the depth, faith and insight of women pushed to the breaking point, who discover their strength and purpose. Maggi's characters give us that and more—they give us honesty and insight as they grow and learn about themselves and the times in which they live.

Most of Maggi's books have been finalists of the Arizona/New Mexico Book Awards. Born in Chicago, Illinois, Maggi has made her home in New Mexico since 1985, with her life partner of forty years. They have one daughter.